T0276389

Monday Rent Boy

Monday Rent Boy

Susan Doherty

Random House Canada

PUBLISHED BY RANDOM HOUSE CANADA

www.penguinrandomhouse.ca

Library and Archives Canada Cataloguing in Publication

Title: Monday rent boy / Susan Doherty.
Names: Doherty, Susan, 1957- author.
Identifiers: Canadiana (print) 20230473865 | Canadiana (ebook) 20230473881 |
ISBN 9781039006553 (hardcover) | ISBN 9781039006560 (EPUB)
Subjects: LCGFT: Novels.
Classification: LCC PS8615.A556 M66 2024 | DDC C813/.6—dc23

Jacket design: Dylan Browne
Text design: Dylan Browne
Typesetting: Daniella Zanchetta

Image credits: (pathway) George W Johnson,
(friends) Finn Hafemann / both Getty Images

Printed in Canada

2 4 6 8 9 7 5 3 1

Penguin
Random House
RANDOM HOUSE CANADA

For William Ashby-Hall

Without you, there would be no book

"Happiness is beneficial for the body,
but it is grief that develops the powers of the mind."
MARCEL PROUST

"After all, the wrong road always leads somewhere."
GEORGE BERNARD SHAW

PART ONE

Glastonbury, 1986

Chapter 1

ARTHUR

If not for an ordinary bookshop in my hometown of Glastonbury, I would have fallen through the cracks into an unsavoury life.

I was hiding behind a shelf in the Copperfield and Twist when the proprietor appeared out of nowhere and caught me cutting a page from a copy of *The Prophet*. I thought I was done for. Miss Phillips extended her palm, and I was about to give her the slim volume, when she plucked the severed page from my hand. My green Stanley knife clattered to the wooden floor. As my eyes followed the blade, Miss Phillips stood, as erect as a retired ballerina, silently reading the passage from Khalil Gibran that I had circled in black ink—one I'd planned to plagiarize for a home-work assignment. *I have learned silence from the talkative, toleration from the intolerant, and kindness from the unkind; yet strange, I am ungrateful to these teachers.*

Miss Phillips bent down for my knife, disabled the blade, and tucked it into the side-slit pocket of her green and blue tartan skirt. Despite her apparent nonchalance, I could practically hear the police sirens wail. She led me to a small bench near the wildlife section and motioned for me to sit down.

"I'm so sorry, Miss Phillips," I blurted, staring at her name tag pinned near a severe collarbone. "I'll pay for the book, even if I have to steal the money," a statement I straightaway regretted.

"Don't move," she said, and disappeared into her office. She was gone for so long I began to hope she had forgotten about me. It had been three months since I'd been ushered into the back seat of a police vehicle for stealing a box of Arm & Hammer laundry detergent from Cheap Jack's in Wells. I wasn't anxious to face the copper again, who had looked at me with open incomprehension. *Laundry detergent? What the hell?*

I was about to slink away when Miss Phillips returned and handed me a sheaf of papers stapled in one corner. Her pale blue eyes seemed tired rather than judgmental as they roamed my face looking for answers. I glanced down at the title page, and then quickly flipped through the rest. She had photocopied all twenty-six of Khalil Gibran's poetic fables— 107 pages, still warm from the Xerox machine. In that instant I felt like Jean Valjean after he stole the bishop's silver candlesticks. If only Miss Phillips knew that I had also cut a dozen pages from her *Gray's Anatomy* a week earlier in order to examine a woman's body under the covers in my bedroom. I didn't deserve her mercy, and so it hardly seemed appropriate to ask for my knife, whose handle still peeked from the pocket of her skirt.

After she took down my name and phone number, she ordered me home. I stammered my thanks and fled to the High Street. For days, the wall-mounted phone in our tiny kitchen was the only appliance I could see. If it rang, I planned to intercept the call before my mother could pick up and then stretch the beige cord all the way into the cupboard under the stairs. I wasn't certain my mother and I could survive another transgression. She'd just found a half-pound of semi-melted butter stashed under my bed, her nose somehow discerning it from all the other adolescent smells in my fusty room. She'd accused me of stealing it from Sainsbury's and I had, inspired by a screening of *Last Tango in Paris*. I'd snuck into the Revival House Theatre in Bridgwater, and after the movie, I'd taken the long bus ride home transfixed by the young Parisian girl and her clandestine relationship with a much older businessman eager for violent buttery sex. At least my mother didn't have the faintest idea about why I'd wanted the butter.

While lying on my bed waiting for the phone to ring, I made a mental list of the bits and bobs I'd recently stolen with my accomplice and best friend, Ernie Castlefrank: one Commodore calculator still in its original package, two pairs of aviator sunglasses like the ones Al Pacino wore in *Scarface*, countless Old Jamaica chocolate bars, and a Swiss Army knife with a corkscrew. My mother would have been frantic about all those thefts, but she would cry in shame to learn I'd defaced a book, her tears a far worse punishment than a tongue-lashing or a stay-at-home order.

She and I lived on our own in a cramped two-bedroom flat above Alfredo's tailor shop on Norbins Road. Alfredo owned the building, and after my father died a few years ago, my mother had done her best to pay him the rent on time, something that happened a little more often now she had earnings from selling life insurance on commission. Not only was Alfredo unfailingly kind to us both, I appreciated the cloth dummy of a shapely woman he called Lolita that he displayed next to a vintage Singer sewing machine in his shop window to attract customers. He'd recently hired a young seamstress who'd shared several copies of the Fabulous Furry Freak Brothers comic books with me and Ernie on the sly. Neither of us had the means to achieve the stoned state of blissful torpor that was the brothers' mission in life, but on bad days we both felt just as freakish and at odds with the world.

Alfredo mended for us—my mother was not good with a needle—and in exchange for the services of his lightning hands, she baked him apple pies with roasted walnuts from a family recipe that was so covered in grease it was illegible to everyone except her. It's not for nothing that Glastonbury was once called the Isle of Avalon—the isle of apples.

Mum had grown up in her parents' apple orchard in Haselbury Plucknett, a stone's throw from the town of Crewkerne, and had gone from high school straight to cookery classes at the Tante Marie school in Woking, Surrey. That's where she learned to bake with lemongrass, juniper berries and cardamom, ingredients as foreign as a ruble for anyone else in town. She came alive in the kitchen, chopping raw ginger in her Wallis Simpson apron that said, *You can never be too rich or too thin.* She has never been either, and it was doubtful she ever would be, but it didn't stop from her dreaming.

On the phone talking about premiums, she showed only a deathly boredom. Every few weeks or so, she'd lose another client, whereas the pies were fighting for space in the freezer. Her greatest wish, delivered with a punishing frequency, was that I would attend university and thereby attain the freedom to choose my own destiny. Rarely did she go so far as to explain that she wanted this for me because her own freedom had been truncated by a teenage pregnancy one year into her culinary education. Me. She hid many of the details of her chance first meeting with my dad, but I did know I was conceived after three sips of Dufftown on a train trip from Woking to Edinburgh, and that my soon-to-be father was fresh from a winning streak at the racecourse in Musselburgh. To avoid a scandal, she was confined to the family orchard for the term of her pregnancy. Likely, my grandparents were looking for a way to help her cut ties with a much older gambler. But her passion for the stranger on the train remained undimmed. Quite the opposite. He sent a marriage proposal by telegram, and she accepted. His death six years after I was born left a hole in my mother's heart that has yet to be filled.

When money was tight, which was always, she said it was a comfort to know their wedding rings and a few other unnamed valuables were housed in a safety deposit box at the Lloyds bank in Shepton Mallet. In my mother's bedroom, behind the framed reproduction of a Degas ballet dancer, hung a key with a bank routing number etched on its golden head.

"For a rainy day," she said when I was old enough to share her terrible worries about the bills, but not yet old enough to be her confidant.

When two straight weeks passed without a call from either Miss Phillips or the police, I began to think I was meant to examine my conscience on my own terms. So I went to the desk in my broom closet of a bedroom, straightened a piece of paper on its surface, entered the date in the upper left-hand corner, and dashed off a note.

> January 15, 1986
> Dear Miss Phillips,
> I extend my sincerest apologies for your awful experience with my undisciplined nature. I understand that what I did was not only wrong, but also hurtful to you and your brilliant shop on the High Street. I have been a woeful representative of all customers my age, and for that, I'm deeply sorry. As I ask for your forgiveness, please let me know how I can best rectify this situation.
> Yours respectfully,
> Arthur W. Barnes

I tucked it into an envelope and carried it to the shop the following Saturday, along with a tenner I planned to spend on purchasing the mutilated volume of *Gray's Anatomy*.

At the till, Miss Phillips scanned my letter and then me. I saw her take in my pilled turtleneck, scruffy hoodie, black plimsolls, and shaggy ginger hair that touched my shoulders. I was tall for my age, which usually meant that people had outsized expectations of me.

"Arthur, how old are you?" she asked.

"Thirteen."

She stared at me with pursed lips, as though I was pulling her leg.

To fill the dead air, I quickly confessed to cutting at least a dozen pages from the *Gray's Anatomy* and handed her the ten-pound note. I didn't admit that I'd stolen the tenner from Father Ziperto's wallet, which I'd lifted from his overcoat in the vestry of St. Nicholas, narrowly avoiding being caught by his twin brother, who kept track of the church's accounts and did other odd jobs. (Ernie and I called him the Ear Whacker, for obvi ous reasons.) Or that several petty thefts earlier, I'd overheard my mother ringing her only sister, who still lived in a house beside the family orchard, and whispering that she was worried I was becoming a kleptomaniac, a word I had needed to source in the Oxford dictionary. That was after she had caught me with a dozen Mars bars Ernie and I had lifted from a candy display tiered like stadium seating.

The dictionary defined kleptomania as a recurrent inability to resist an urge to steal items that a person does not really need. Had she asked me directly, I could have reassured my mother on that score.

Miss Phillips folded my letter of apology, and with a swivel of her neck scouted the shop for her assistant. When she spied a woman in an orange sari standing on a stool restocking high shelves, her black hair pulled up in a twist and secured with a yellow pencil, she called out, "Arfaana, will you take over the till for a few minutes?" The shop assis- tant nodded, and as she climbed down, Miss Phillips waved me into her office, shut the door, sat me down, and told me that for a hoodlum I was a half-decent writer. I hadn't known what to expect next, but it certainly wasn't the offer she made: in exchange for writing one decent review each week, I could read any book in her shop. The way her lips curled when she said the word *decent* made me think she had seen the butter under my bed. But how could I refuse? Even before I'd fallen for the Furry Freak Brothers, I'd been a reader.

Miss Phillips set me up in an alcove in the children's section into which was tucked a small desk with six drawers. A typewriter, a stack of blank paper and a bottle of correction fluid sat upon the desk. It was there, par- tially hidden by stacks of carefully chosen young adult fare, that my life as an amateur literary critic began. My first review was of *When Hitler*

Stole Pink Rabbit, by Judith Kerr. The 192-page book took me two nights to read and thirty minutes to critique. After I handed my review to her, warm from the typewriter, Miss Phillips scanned it, then read the final line out loud: "A little family who craved to live a normal life somewhere. Anywhere." From the way her eyes softened, I wondered whether she too might have been displaced at some time in her life. She pasted my words at the end of the aisle, and by week's end the book had sold out.

I next gave an enthusiastic review to Sue Townsend's *The Secret Diary of Adrian Mole Aged 13¾.* I laughed so uncontrollably when Adrian's mother locates the Falkland Islands on a map underneath a crumb of fruitcake that Miss Phillips prescribed *My Name Is Asher Lev* in order to tamp down the noise. It had the reverse effect, leaving me sniffling and blowing my nose at my small desk as my sense of social justice awakened. I decided at that moment that my larger purpose in life would be to read every book ever written, or at least the ones Miss Phillips was selling in her cozy wood-panelled store on Glastonbury's High Street. Obviously, as I began to fulfill that pledge, my marks suffered. How could anyone care about Mr. Henry's lessons about refractory angles and calculating the area under the curve when entire dynasties were in jeopardy in *England Under the Tudors?*

Soon, thanks to Miss Phillips, Rodger Mistlethorpe, editor of the *Central Somerset Gazette,* called our home and asked for Mr. Barnes. Somewhat coldly, I responded, "He died in 1979."

"I'm looking for *Arthur* Barnes. Is he still alive?"

Yes, I admitted, I was indeed alive. When he told me that my work would be featured on page eleven of the next issue, I was speechless, and finally only able to say thank you in what felt like someone else's voice. In due course, amplified by the novelty of the age of their reviewer in residence, the Copperfield and Twist became a minor destination.

My critique of Leon Uris's *The Haj* made it all the way to the *Daily Mirror,* read by three million people, which prompted my mother to bake several celebratory apple pies. She Scotch-taped my review to the fridge as a daily reminder to both of us that I was much more than a juvenile petty thief. She highlighted her favourite passage with a yellow marker: "Haj Ibrahim and Gideon Asch, an Arab and a Jew, raised from childhood to be enemies, were more alike than they had been taught."

When he saw my critique in the *Mirror*, Ernie, who liked to taunt me about everything from my big feet and masses of freckles to my bookish ways, gave me what could only be described as a respectful wide-eyed nod. One of the smartest students in our school, especially in maths, Ernie could have easily outshone me had he bothered to put in the effort, but as it later turned out, academics was not the path he chose for himself. Still, on the morning my review was published, Ernie was as chuffed as I was. Before coming to our place at teatime that day, he pilfered ten copies of the *Mirror* from Lawford & Son's newsagents on Magdalene Street. "By tomorrow, this will be old news," he said in a steady voice to justify the theft. My mother responded with three words: "Thank you, Ernie."

Two months after my debut in the *Daily Mirror*, Leon Uris came striding into the bookshop in a maroon blazer and asked for me by name. To that point Miss Phillips had mostly regarded me with probationary stern looks, but now she couldn't stop smiling. It turned out that she and her sometimes clerk and friend, Arfaana Haq, had conspired to invite him to visit Glastonbury as a surprise for me. Soon, the shop began to fill with invited guests, including Mr. Mistlethorpe from the paper and my mother in a green-and-white dress she usually reserved for Easter Sunday at St. Nicholas. She must have thought I had been miraculously resurrected. Even so, it took me a good half-hour to realize that I was being feted along with the author. As we shook hands, Mr. Uris told me he had never graduated from high school and had failed English three times, yet here he was, an internationally known writer. "Absorb raw material from all that you see, Arthur, and don't ever let failure form your character, otherwise you'll end up bitter and defeated like my father."

A voice in my head said, "At least you knew your father." I was only six when my own dad had died, and my mother's all-consuming grief had blotted his specifics from my mind. But I managed to nod in what I hoped looked like solidarity.

After he had signed books for the ecstatic customers, he had some final advice for me. Writing had been the passport from childhood to the rest of his life, he said. Everyone has a story to tell, but it takes conviction and courage to write it down. In a kind of a felted whisper, he added that buried words can become a sickness unless they are released. From then on, I carried what he said with me, although it took me a very long time to fully understand his meaning.

At the end of his visit, Miss Phillips handed Mr. Uris her treasured copy of his most famous novel, *Exodus*, and urged him to sign it for me. His inscription read: *For Arthur W. Barnes. It is extremely important to know what you don't want to find.* As he left in a hazy puff of cigarette smoke, I wanted to put on my own maroon blazer with leather patch elbows, follow him out the door and into the magical life I imagined he was leading. On that day, holding a book she'd gifted to me from her personal collection, I found consolation instead in the fact that Miss Phillips had forgiven me.

A day or so later, my mother disappeared into her bedroom and returned with two wrapped gifts, along with my copy of *Exodus*. "For you, Arthur," she said as she placed the items on the kitchen table. She sat down, folded her hands, and smiled at me. Presents were as rare as extra cash in our house.

The first gift was a tooled leather notebook with the carved image of a sycamore tree on the front cover. After I unwrapped it, she took it from my hands and ran her fingers over the indentations, again and again, as she stared down at the tree. She had a deep attachment to sycamores.

Several large ones still perched on the border of the family orchard, and she'd spent hours as a child in their embrace. The other gift was a box containing a rubber stamp, an inkpad, and a small bottle of purple ink. With the steady hands of someone adept at measuring ingredients, she poured the ink onto the spongy pad, reached for *Exodus*, and stamped its flyleaf: *This Book Belongs to Arthur W. Barnes.*

"Your turn," she said. I, too, ran my fingers over the leather indentations of the sycamore, then opened the notebook and pressed the stamp hard into the inkpad and onto the blank white page. My version was blurred, barely legible, the ink bleed immediate. I was crestfallen.

"It's perfect, Arthur," my mother said. "Only you will know this book is yours." With a smile she added, "Did I ever tell you that I came second in the *Daily Mirror* Children's Literary Competition when I was sixteen? Maybe it's true the apple doesn't fall too far from the tree." She had a faraway look in her eyes when she added, "Never stop reading and writing."

She hadn't ever told me that she'd had literary ambitions, and she left unsaid the fact that my father, dead now for roughly half my life, and I had been the ones who stopped her fulfilling them.

Chapter 2

What I didn't dare tell my mother was that as my notoriety as a successful reviewer was rising, my regular escape into books had become all the more necessary. Though Ernie Castlefrank was more or less patient when I needed to hole up on a weekend to finish my reading or go to the bookshop to use the typewriter, he and I were sinking deeper into mischief and mayhem.

The two of us had been sworn allies since we became altar boys at St. Nicholas, a poor Catholic cousin to the triumphant Wells Cathedral eight miles to the north, which was filled to the brim on Sundays with Anglicans. St. Nick's had a leaky roof, crumbling interior plasterwork, and a small, though dedicated, congregation—my mother among the most devout—all of it overseen by Father Durante Ziperto. Ernie and I called him the Zipper behind his back. He was considered a dashing figure, especially compared with his supposedly identical twin, Antonio the Ear Whacker, who seemed to slouch through life, head down, mostly oblivious to everything except his shoelaces.

Ernie and I were usually on the same rota, since we were both born in 1972 and our October birthdays were only a day apart. If not for that random bit of scheduling, we would likely never have become friends for the simple reason that the Castlefranks were semi-pariahs in Glastonbury. Ernie's older brother, Nathan, seemed to visit the police station as often as my mother attended Sunday Mass. He'd once stolen three For Sale signs and placed them around the church grounds at St. Nicholas, a joke the outraged congregants did not find as hilarious as he did.

Ernie's mum wasn't a practising Catholic, or was lapsed, or was Church of England, or nothing at all. Ernie told me the only thing his family consistently practised was alcoholism. None of them attended the Sunday services, whereas my mother's whole social life revolved around the church calendar, from Pancake Tuesday, to Ash Wednesday, to the washing of the feet on Thursday, to reliving the Crucifixion for three hours on her knees on Friday, and that was just Holy Week. There were hundreds of other saints' and feast days she marked from the pews of St. Nick's.

But soon after Father Ziperto had come into our primary school classroom to teach catechism, curly-haired, blue-eyed Ernie was baptized, confirmed and carrying the Bible up the aisle at Sunday Mass in a white surplice over a red cassock and shoes so new they squeaked. Eight at the time, Ernie was all for it, behaving as though he was an actor in a play, especially when he got to hold the thurible, spilling its smoky incense into the aisles. Being an altar boy may have been a rite of passage because Nathan had been recruited before him at about the same age.

I had to be pushed into the role of altar boy by my mother, who worried I needed a father figure in my life. When she droned on about the tragedy of my dad's death, I used to whisper, "Our Father, who art in heaven . . ." and she would smack me for being sacrilegious, then send me to my room. I spent hours lying on my bed atoning, for a time accompanied by a small Hermann's tortoise, until my mother heard that turtles harboured salmonella. She lifted it from the aquarium wearing her oven mitts and returned it to Pets Corner. I hadn't been all that sad to see it go; it wasn't as much of a companion as I had hoped.

Ernie, on the other hand, was a freak for small animals. He loved anything that could fly, scurry, scuttle or hide. He lived with his mum and stepdad in a rambling, rickety place beside the railway tracks on Dyehouse Lane. I think his mum inherited the house from her dad, long dead, but didn't have the funds to keep it up. Some of the windows were duct-taped to keep the rain out, and most of the wood trim was discoloured and spongy looking. All the trains rocketing past took me some getting used to, but Ernie found them an abiding comfort, daydreaming about where those trains might take him. He never said much about what happened when I wasn't around, but I knew from the occasional bruise revealed when he accidently pushed up a sleeve that his stepdad had an untamed temper, and when it flared, his mum kept quiet as a mouse in case the anger came her way. It got worse, I think, after his older brother left home. Until then, Nathan had taken most of the blows. Whatever savagery went on behind the Castlefranks' closed doors, Ernie welcomed any stray dog or mangy cat that wandered down Dyehouse Lane as if it were a member of the Royal Family, regarding all kinds of untamed creatures as quasi-pets—birds and mice, shrews and stick insects—and he treated them with tender affection. In turn, even crows, robins and greenfinches let him stroke, mend and feed them with bits of grapes and seeds. He was a real St. Francis.

One day after school he handed me a video camera he had cadged from somewhere, I didn't dare ask, and took me into his back garden—more weeds than garden—because he wanted me to film him interacting with some of the animals under his care. A couple of ravens had roosted in the trees by the tracks. As they cawed a chorus at a train rumbling by, Ernie spilled his usual treasure trove of details about the natural world and its creatures. As I trained the lens on him, he told me that ravens were able to fly upside down and would even turn somersaults just because they could. He said that on the ark, Noah had sent a raven out to scout for land before he sent a dove. He added that ravens are carrion birds, and that they connect the living with lost dead souls, enjoying my slit-eyed wariness over this particular nugget. Then he grabbed the camera from me and tackled me to the ground, where he tried to put ants up my nose while we laughed ourselves silly. What I can't remember is why he suddenly stopped laughing. But I know I saw something in his eyes when he pulled away, rolled onto his back, and faced the sky—something I had been trying to shut down in myself.

In large part because he lived in the dodgy shadow of Nathan, Ernie was underestimated by the other students at school, and by most of the teachers, who assumed that he'd amount to nothing, despite his maths acumen. Although young-looking for his age and tiny—the top of his head came to my shoulder—Ernie was agile. He could keep a football in the air with his knees for full-on ten minutes. I was tall, but despite my height I was never chosen for any team sports. I could trip and fall on flat ground, but maybe it was my oversized feet and scrawny chest that put me at the bottom of any roster. With no siblings and no dad, it was Ernie who rescued me from complete athletic failure. In that scraggly yard behind his house, where no one could see us, he taught me how to swing a cricket bat without looking like a tosser. While he didn't go out for anything himself, he'd picked up a lot from Nathan, who had been an exceptional sportsman with multiple trophies to prove it before he'd dropped out of school at fifteen. Ernie said it was because his classes were too boring, but I'm pretty sure Nathan decided it was more important to put some cash in his pocket. Ernie only came close to being boastful when he talked about his brother, even though, out in the world, Nathan mostly excelled at undermining everyone else's good opinion of him. It seemed like each time he turned around, he was being fired from a labouring job or caught joyriding in a stolen car.

As it turned out, just like Nathan, our own preferred extracurricular activity was stealing. Ernie and I shared a long history of petty theft, starting with Life Savers and bubble gum soon after we joined forces at St. Nick's. Then, on well-attended Sunday mornings at the High Mass, we began to pinch money from the collection plate. Mostly one-pound coins and, sometimes, if the warden was particularly distracted, the odd fiver. Soon enough we were nicking things to sustain Ernie's outdoor animal kingdom: safflower seeds for the cardinals, peaches, plums and peanuts for the squirrels, millet for the sparrows. In the early days I usually stood guard while the more angelic-looking Ernie did the stealing, but by the time we were in secondary school, I was the one lifting boxes of chocolate-covered raisins, a nylon rucksack, and small gadgets like a pocketknife or a bicycle lock, while Ernie was the lookout. Ernie taught me to "shop" the bigger stores with an umbrella on my arm, dropping items between the spokes. (An umbrella can hold an impressive number of chocolate bars.) After Ernie watched a woman in a long skirt nick a clock radio by clamping it between her thighs, we tried walking around his back garden with a radio between our legs. It's not as easy as it sounds. I was especially grateful we had no equivalent of a long skirt, or I'm sure Ernie would have convinced me to try it.

For the longest time, I thought he and I were both in it for the adrenalin rush of stealing and the shared giddy laughter after a successful heist. But then one day Ernie turned up at my place with a Cartier watch he said he'd stolen from a jewellery repair shop in the Gauntlet, the shopping walkway that linked the High Street and St. John's Square. I'd seen that watch a million times on the Zipper's wrist.

"How did you know it was at the jeweller?"

Instead of a proper answer, he insisted that a theft like this one was more of a good deed than a bad, and I nodded my agreement, deciding I didn't want to know anything else.

But Ernie had escalated, and I soon followed.

—

The day I was caught stealing a Parker fountain pen at Dearborn's department store in Bristol, Ernie told Mrs. Gregory, the store manager, that he was the one who'd done it. He was so convincing that if I hadn't committed the crime myself, I would have believed him.

While she called the police, Mrs. Gregory made us sit in her office, a shabby, windowless room with a faux wooden desk and a scratched filing cabinet, far removed from the elegance of the actual store with its chandeliers and gold-edged display cases. As we waited, Ernie leaned over and whispered, "Arthur, you are the one worth saving. Not me. No one is counting on me for anything." My eyes bugged out of my head at what Ernie was prepared to do for me, but before I could protest, he was sounding off, in a voice as saccharine as the stuff in the packets my mum used to sweeten her tea.

"Stealing is stealing, Mrs. Gregory," Ernie began. "It's illegal, sure, but it's also morally wrong, plain and simple. I'm the one who stole the pen. Arthur here isn't capable of such a serious crime. If you've read his book reviews in the paper, you'd know what kind of boy he is. He writes for the *Daily Mirror*. The *Daily Mirror*," he repeated for emphasis, while scanning the office as though he was sure to find a copy or two lying about. Even the policeman, when he arrived to haul us off to the station, couldn't budge Ernie from his fabrication.

I'm ashamed to say I went along with it, a coward who didn't want to face more of his mother's tears.

Still, someone didn't buy his story, because we both ended up in juvenile court in Taunton. There we stood, two boys of thirteen and a half, under the owl-like scrutiny of the judge. Examining us with distinct curiosity, he listened intently while Ernie, in a pressed button-down shirt and a navy necktie I'd never seen before, praised the court for providing us with a barrister. He then did his best to clear my name, insisting

I was a bystander as innocent as an Icelandic snowdrift—he was the one who wanted to gift his writer friend with the perfect pen, but he hadn't the means to afford it. After he sat down, the judge removed his round glasses and, as he polished them thoughtfully, he said to me, "You've done well to have a friend like Castlefrank. But I dare say that's not going to be enough."

I looked over at Ernie, who was a picture of serenity, staring straight ahead at the red dragon on the coat of arms over the judge's bench, his hands folded in his lap. For my part, I was badly in need of the toilets.

Our barrister furiously scribbled notes on a yellow legal pad, then stood to propose that instead of a young offenders' institution, we perform some socially beneficial labour, such as forty hours of supervised graffiti removal around town. My mother, in an uncharacteristic show of audacity, approached the bench unbidden and whispered something to the judge. He lowered his glasses to the tip of his nose and leaned forward to better hear her.

When she had finished, the judge addressed us. "It has been proposed that the service duty be changed to labour at a small orchard in Haselbury Plucknett, which is apparently on the brink of closure and unable to employ workers for the season."

The judge paused, and asked, "Haselbury Plucknett?"

"Three miles northeast of Crewkerne," my mother replied.

Her face aflame, she returned to the public benches where she sat down beside Mrs. Castlefrank. When I glanced back, my mum's red-rimmed eyes connected with my own, and I did my best to silently thank her, careful not to smile about the fact that Ernie and I would soon be working for my grandfather instead of scrubbing walls on the streets of Glastonbury.

In no time, the judge had ruled and the case was over. As Ernie and I left the courthouse, our mothers walked shakily behind us, too stricken to congratulate each other over the slap on the wrist their boys had received. To my knowledge it was the first time the two had met. Ernie's mum, a delicate husk of a woman who worked night shifts as a cashier at the canteen in the local hospital, wasn't known to make friendly overtures. And except for church, my mum mostly kept to herself, as well.

A few streets away from the courthouse, Ernie dug deep into the pocket of his jacket and palmed me a tightly rolled joint. I couldn't help but snort at his nerve.

"What if you'd been hauled off to a cell and frisked?"

"I would have said you were the one who gave it to me. You're the criminal."

Chapter 3

Our sentence to hard labour in my grandfather's apple orchard would begin after the last day of school. I couldn't wait for the final ringing of the bell to signal summer recess. As far as I knew, my mother hadn't confessed to my grandfather that Ernie and I were arriving at the direction of a youth court judge. Grandad was simply giddy to have helpers who would work for free.

For all but the last day, it was the happiest summer of my life—two idyllic months mostly spent playing in a maze of fruit trees. After we had fulfilled our forty-hour sentence, I begged my mother to let me and Ernie stay on and she agreed, happy to leave us in her father's hands—though I'm sure that was probably not what the judge had meant by supervision. Grandad still had his marbles, but not all the time. He was forever losing his picking gloves, his clippers and shears, the ladder. After a time, Ernie and I took to moving stuff around for the hilarity of it all.

The first job Grandad gave us was to make apple maggot fly traps to dangle from the lowest branches—the bait being a slop of golden syrup, warm water and yeast. The egg-laying flies begin to attack the trees in early July, so the timing of our sentence was ideal. The rest of the summer we painted fences, pulled weeds, steered clear of the bees, mowed the grass, and pruned dead branches with a handsaw. More than once, my grandfather asked if we'd snowploughed the lane, and we said, "Yup. All done," and he beamed at us.

Ernie's arms and legs turned light brown from hours in the sun. I had so many freckles Ernie thought we should finish the job by connecting them all with syrup from the slop bucket. For the first time ever, I was coordinated enough to outrun Ernie and the sloshing bucket aimed at my skinny legs.

The orchard was bordered by beech trees and the sycamores my mother loved, with their broad domed crowns. Late every afternoon we scrabbled up into the pinkish-grey arms of those trees, and swung like monkeys, amazed at the vantage point from way up high.

I was sad when my mother arrived to collect us for the new school term. Still, she looked rested for once, smiling in her long red dress and a straw sunhat with a polka-dot band. She'd borrowed Alfredo's camera and took a Polaroid of us hanging upside down from a sycamore branch—Ernie screaming with laughter, me with my hands behind my head, grinning as though I hadn't a worry in the world.

And I didn't, until I turned and caught a dangle of silver at Ernie's neck. My mother was distracted, readying the camera for her next shot while Ernie teased her about her hat that kept blowing off onto the grass, so I had just enough time to corral my shock. A sterling crucifix on a thin silver chain had swung free from under the neckline of Ernie's striped hoodie. When I was ten, the Zipper had presented me with the same kind of silver crucifix with such reverence it had felt like a prize.

"This is only for the special children," he'd said, his breath on my neck as he fastened the clasp. His own golden crucifix, nestled in his vestments, looked like it could anchor a boat. That night when I was changing for bed, my mother had asked where it came from, and I told her that Father Ziperto had awarded it to me for my dedicated service as an altar boy.

I'd been naive to think Ernie wasn't just as "special."

I couldn't work it out how I'd never noticed it before, but then it came over me. Ernie was always secretive changing for PE and games, worried that the other boys would see the marks his stepfather left on his arms and back. Then again, neither of us had stripped past our T-shirts that summer, no matter how hot we got, for unsaid reasons.

Later that afternoon, as the bus carrying us back home snaked along the single carriageway closely bordered by roadside hedges that scraped its sides, I discreetly removed my own cross and stuck it in my pocket.

That evening when my mother went downstairs to return the Polaroid camera to Alfredo, I left the flat and walked to a familiar cluster of inscribed cemetery stones on Austin Road: the Barnes family plot, clogged with flowers and climbers, and there I buried the Zipper's gift.

Before bed, I saw my mother slip the Polaroid of us in the sycamore tree into her little album, next to a picture of my smitten father holding out my mother's collection of heart-shaped lockets—each one open to reveal a tiny picture of the two of them. Mum kept that album beside her bed. That the photo of Ernie and me in the sycamore now lay so close to my dad and the lockets gave me a rare sense of belonging to both my parents, a feeling I held tight to that night as I tried to fall asleep.

Not long after my altar boy duties resumed that fall, my mother came into my bedroom one night holding up a brand-new pair of white Y-fronts. "Where did you get these, Arthur? Are you stealing again?"

Not a single acceptable excuse came to mind.

"God in heaven," she said. "Some days I don't know what kind of boy I've raised. Have you learned nothing from standing in front of a judge? Are you looking to do hard time next?"

Before I could say anything at all in my defence, my mild-mannered mother tossed the briefs at me and stomped out of my room, slamming the door behind her and yelling, "I need to be able to trust you, Arthur!"

How could I explain that I'd once tried to wash my bloodied under-pants with bleach and some detergent I'd stolen from Cheap Jack's, but that the stains proved resistant to my furtive efforts at the bathroom sink. I'd decided the only option was to throw out a pair if it got stained and steal replacements from Marks & Spencer. I'd barely managed to explain away the streaks of blood she'd spotted on my bedsheet one Tuesday morning soon after I'd resumed my Monday duties. When she'd said, "Arthur, what happened here? Are you still bleeding?" I'd scuttled past her, grabbing my school satchel, and headed for the door, insisting that it was only a scratch on my leg that had bled in the night. When she pursued me onto the landing, I'd stammered that Ernie and I had gotten into a fight and he'd pushed me into a hedgerow.

"That's not like you, Arthur," she'd said, and insisted I apologize to Ernie for my half of the argument. "There are better ways to work things out than physical violence!"

While I was at school that day, she soaked the stained sheets in a plastic pail of bleach, then pegged them on the line outside. Once they were dry, she remade my bed. That night the stiff bleached sheets made my eyes sting and my backside itch.

When Ernie came over for supper later that week, my mother wrapped an arm around his small shoulders and said, "Did you two apologize to each other? Best friends need to be able to patch up their differences, no matter who is right or wrong."

A look of surprise crossed his face, but when he caught my stricken, *please-go-along* expression, he simply nodded.

Thank God, she took him at his word and moved on. Like she always did when Ernie came up the staircase and invited himself for dinner, she simply asked, "Does your mother know you're here?" Obediently, Ernie called "home" to ask permission, giving me the flicker of a wink as he talked into dead air. When he said into the receiver, "I love you too," my mother smiled, having no idea that no one else in Ernie's life treated him with the affection she was able to show him.

Ernie ate two helpings of everything at our house at least once a week. Sometimes twice. My mother constantly worried about his weight, called him a whippet in a boy costume. That night he ate several helpings of shepherd's pie, ground lamb and carrots lathered in mashed potatoes, and said thank you about six times. When he asked my mother why the dish was called shepherd's pie, she hadn't hesitated. "The Lord is my shepherd, Ernie. A shepherd is always looking after his flock."

"What would you say about my mother's ketchup sandwiches?" he asked.

"I'd say that's what I'll order the next time I really want to treat myself."

Ernie had looked at my mother with such longing then, I was forced to punch him in the shoulder. He flicked my cheek with his middle finger, and I swear three layers of skin came off.

"No more fighting," my mother warned.

After two helpings of mint chocolate-chip ice cream, she sent us outside to ride our bikes. When I look back, I realize that it was Ernie's devotion to my mother that allowed her to get past my own never-ending faults and misdeeds, including stealing job lots of white Y-fronts from the Marks & Spencer in Bristol, and leaving blood stains on the sheets.

"Don't be late, Arthur, it's a school night. Ernie, make sure you drop back and pick up these leftovers. I'll wrap them in foil for you."

When it came to Ernie, my mother had a willingness to polish the smallest of silver linings.

A couple of days later, I went out for another night of riding around town with Ernie. I hadn't yet found a way to talk to him about the significance of the silver cross, but maybe we didn't need to talk, given that the mischief he wanted us to get up to that night was sneaking into St. Nick's to see if we could set a pew or two on fire.

We parked our bikes in the metal rack in front of the tattoo studio across the street and down from the church. I'd assumed Ernie was talking nonsense when it came to church arson, but still I trailed after him. The heavy front door was open, as always. We touched a drop of holy water to our foreheads out of habit, then crept up the aisle and lay down head-to-head between the two long pews nearest the confessional. The whole place reeked of old incense.

We heard some throat-clearing and rustling, then the sharp blast of a pitch pipe. We couldn't see them and they couldn't see us, but the choir was overhead in the loft, practising for Sunday's High Mass. For several seconds I did nothing but listen to the harmonies. My mother claimed to go to heaven each time the choir sang the psalms.

Under the cover of song, Ernie fished a box of Wilkinson matches from his pocket, along with two prayer candles he'd pinched from among the fifty flickering red glass votives at the feet of St. Nicholas near the entrance.

"We're seriously doing this?" I asked. "Hold on—did you steal these matches from my place?"

"Yup. As your mum was washing up."

Ernie ripped a match along the strike and lit the candles, then held the flames to the wood of the ancient bench, daring it to catch fire. When both candles were burned down nearly to the quick, the oak finally started to flare. Soon it was smoking so much I had to suppress a cough in my sleeve. Falling against each other and laughing like idiots, we ran outside and hid among the trees in the churchyard. We were pretty sure the fire would go out on its own, with no one the wiser except for the church warden, who soon came bolting out the door and walked twice around the grounds, his head swinging left and right like a flashlight.

And then we heard sirens.

———

In my bedroom later that night, according to my new habit, I kicked off my shoes and pulled down the duvet to examine the sheets. Perfectly white. I sat down with a sigh. I don't recall the exact words the Zipper had used to persuade me to get completely undressed in the vestry after I got back from the summer in the orchard, but I had done it. On a Monday, and every Monday since. I squeezed my eyes to stop a flood of images. I needed my own box of Wilkinson matches to burn the memories to flying bits of ash to be whisked away by a Somerset breeze.

When my mother came into my room to say goodnight, I asked her if I could look at the photo of Ernie and me in the sycamore tree. Her eyes wavered for a split second—she was somewhat reluctant to share her precious album with me, for reasons I never understood. But then she said, "Of course."

As she headed for her bedroom, I went to the kitchen, plugged in the kettle, hid the Marmite behind the toaster, opened the pantry cupboard, and pulled down a dented biscuit tin fringed with waxed paper and filled with Jaffa cakes and homemade chocolate-covered Hobnobs.

"It's not too late for a snack, Mum?" I asked, as she returned with the photo, which she'd pulled out of the album.

She turned the Polaroid over and read the date on the back. "August 31, 1986. I want to remember that day forever." She studied the image. "You both couldn't look any happier. And Ernie looks so young . . . I don't think I've ever seen bluer eyes. It must be his tan."

She handed me the photo and turned her attention to the toast and the butter and the Marmite, which she retrieved from behind the toaster.

I searched the image for the sterling cross, unsure about what I saw in our faces. Something carefree was uncontestable. I had to blink water out of my eyes before my mother turned around.

I said, "Ernie used to lie on the floor of his bedroom and imagine that St. Nick's had burned to the ground with all the church officials trapped inside. Or that they had been squashed flat by an eighteen-wheeler on the dual carriageway."

"Arthur, those are awful thoughts! Do you think Ernie is all right? Are we doing enough for his family? I know his stepfather is out of work and he once said his mum only gets two or three shifts a week at the hospital canteen. I wonder if they've applied for assistance?"

I stuffed my mouth with an entire Hobnob so I didn't have to answer. Police sirens wailed in the distance.

My mother swallowed a bite of toast, then moved to the sink, turning her back to me. "Arthur, my wooden matches have disappeared. Any idea where they've gone?"

"No," I said as soon as I got the Hobnob down.

Soon enough, she'd know that that the fire marshal had just been to St. Nick's in his bright red truck, and she wouldn't want to let herself think that Ernie and I had been watching from the trees.

Chapter 4

ERNIE

I rode in the Zipper's car for the first time the week after we set the oak pew on fire. In the vestry before morning Mass, Father Ziperto had lifted one of my arms and sniffed the cuff of my school jumper where the smell of the smoke still clung.

"Ernie," he said. "I wonder who was responsible for the fire. Don't you think whoever did such a terrible deed should be punished? It's a miracle nobody died of smoke inhalation. Though Mrs. Corbyn did faint and bashed her dentures. The repair will cost a fortune. Who do you think should pay for that?"

I stared back at him stone-faced.

He carried on. "I need you after school at four o'clock. Right here, and on the dot." After a short silence in which my eyes dropped from his face to the floor, he asked, "Was anyone with you?"

"No," I lied. Never be a snitch, Nathan had said, more than a few times.

After the morning service, I went to school and spent the whole day worrying about what else I would have to do for the Zipper. We had a timed maths test of all we'd learned that week and I handed in a blank sheet. I fully understood quadratics, but I couldn't think about anything except the four o'clock deadline.

At the end of that long day, I dragged my feet to the back door of the rectory and stood staring at the black cross that had been nailed to the wall beside it to remind us of the Crucifixion. As if we needed reminding. As I wrestled with thoughts of running anywhere but home, the Zipper came out of the door and led me, wordless, to his car. He opened the passenger door and I slid onto the beige leather seat.

As we drove away from the church, it crossed my mind to say that Arthur's mum was expecting me for tea, but in my panic, I couldn't get the words out of my mouth. The Zipper kept his hands glued to the steering wheel. He was staring at the road when he said, "I wish you were my son." I'd been looking out the window, my eyes on a streak of branches that seemed to be reaching for me, and that was the last thing I'd expected him to say. When I peeked at his face to see if he was lying, he was smiling with his whole face. My fear drained away. He wasn't going to turn me in.

We parked on a side street and walked a good ten minutes on a long and twisty road, then scrabbled down a hill to a playground with a swing set, a slide and a rusty merry-go-round. The Zipper marched past the play area to an arched opening almost fully disguised by dark green leaves. I followed him as he ducked vines and was amazed to emerge into an overgrown back garden with a house at the far end. All its lights were off.

"Shh," the Zipper said, with a sweep of an arm to indicate the proximity of the neighbours behind the hedges.

We reached the house without saying another word.

The Zipper unlocked the door, slipped off his loafers and padded ahead of me into the semi-dark.

"Have you ever seen a player piano?" he called.

"No," I said unlacing the school shoes the parish had paid for.

"It plays itself. Of course, it can be played the usual way as well. Have a look around."

Wondering why he didn't turn on the lamps, I roamed the ground floor in the dim light and took in the player-piano rolls atop the instrument, the chesterfield, the side tables covered with bowls of sweets, as the Zipper watched with arms folded. He pointed to a staircase. "Check out the upstairs." I did what I was told. A bit nervously, I made my way up one flight and tiptoed along a dark hallway to find a room with blue bunk beds. From the door, I saw an assortment of books in an open built-in drawer under the lower bunk. A pair of Spiderman pyjamas were slung on the back of a chair. I half expected to bump into another boy, but there was no one about. When I returned to the sitting room, the Zipper was at the window watching a family of squirrels scamper across the grass. "I think they breed in my garden," he said. He turned and went to sit on the chesterfield, patting the spot beside him. I sat down and scrunched my arse to the farthest end of the couch, then reached for a handful of chocolate raisins from the bowl on the coffee table. Fresh. Did the Zipper actually live here? Or the Ear Whacker? What about the rectory?

He got up to grab a roll of music from one of many lined up on top of the piano, slotted it in, and came back to me. We sat and watched the piano perform "Dizzy Fingers." The ragtime tune was jaunty, circus-like, and made me think of my father dancing in the street at the Bridgwater Carnival while pretending to play the trombone. Nathan and I had fallen down laughing at his liquored-up display of silliness, but my mother had wilted with embarrassment. It was the last straw. She kicked him out not long after, and that was it for my dad. Not even a birthday card since.

The music stopped. I was about to tell the Zipper about my father's antics at the carnival when he said, "You've been a terrible person, Ernie. People almost died. The warden is fed up to the back teeth with you. Were you smoking cigarettes in church?"

I shook my head.

"They found spent matches."

I froze.

"Were they yours?"

I was sure he already knew the answer. The grainy chocolate raisins in my mouth wouldn't go down.

"Do you want to be a better person?"

My stomach squeezed as I nodded.

"Do you kiss your mother and father each night before you go to bed?"

I nodded again, even though it was a lie. No one kissed anyone in my house. My sins were piling up.

"It's a sign of love, you know," he said, and he leaned towards me with his vestry face and kissed me on my mouth, sticky with chocolate. For all the times we'd been together, our lips had never touched. It was over so fast I didn't gag. He touched his own lips then and dragged his finger to his chin to invite me into more secrecy.

Afterwards, he drove me back to St. Nick's. We parked in the spot reserved for the priest and he pointed over his shoulder to an Atari video game console in the back seat. "I bet you like those games. *Missile Command*, is it? And *Pac-Man*? *Frogger*?" He reached back and put the lime green console on my lap. I put my thumb on the red joystick.

"How do you play *Frogger*?" He seemed genuinely curious.

"At the beginning of each wave," I said, "Frogger has to cross a highway and then hop across a river to reach the house on the other side without getting killed. There are many ways for the frog to die."

"Really? Such as?"

"Like getting squashed by a lorry or eaten by a crocodile."

"So you really need to be coordinated, I'd expect. Well, have fun with it, Ernie."

Once more he touched his finger to his lips, making the sign for silence. I walked home clutching the console trying not to think about what else the Zipper was about to ask me to do.

Chapter 5

ARTHUR

I was eight when my mother took me to St. Nick's to meet the parish priest. I was just home from a long stretch staying at the orchard. I try my best not to think about those days, even now, but after my father died, she was so grief-stricken she couldn't take care of herself, let alone a six-year-old boy with his own set of needs. So she'd sent me to live with her sister. I liked my aunt well enough and I loved spending time with my grandfather, on his own since my grandmother had died, but I missed my mother horribly. Each time she came for a visit—which wasn't nearly often enough—I'd beg her to take me back with her. All the while crushing a handful of wet tissues, she'd make excuses and more excuses. Finally, two whole years after my dad died, I rode home with her on the bus. We mostly looked out the window until she reached for my hand and squeezed. I couldn't be sure we were going home for good, so I found it hard to squeeze back.

The flat and my room were unchanged, my toys and books in their places: it was as if no time had passed since I was gone.

My mother was changed, though; she was tentative and still terribly sad, except when she was baking or at church, which had become her refuge. She spoke highly about young Father Ziperto, who had taken over the parish while I'd been living at the orchard, replacing the kindly but rickety specimen who had presided over my father's funeral.

At our first meeting, the Zipper beamed on me kindly and asked me what my favourite games were. I told the new priest I loved draughts and hide-and-seek, especially. He said that since I already knew the rules of draughts, I should learn to play chess, and he offered to teach me in the vestry after school every Monday. My mother was delighted that this man she had begun to admire was taking an interest in her fatherless son.

I can still feel in my bones the heaviness of the chess set in its carrying case, and the heft of the board with its sixty-four squares of black and white marble. The Zipper played with the white pieces, which meant he always got to make the first move. Before every game, he'd say, "It's all about protecting the queen. Never sacrifice the queen unless it's the only manoeuvre you have left."

What I remember most about those early days was how he got me to believe that his endless questions about me and my mother meant he cared about us. He said I could tell him anything and everything. I did, and maybe a bit more than that. He listened very carefully when I said that my mother still cried a lot about my dead father, and that she bought all our clothes at the Salvation Army thrift shop in Shepton Mallet. I told him that Alfredo altered her second-hand dresses in exchange for an apple pie or a glass of sherry because she didn't seem to have much money. The priest listened so intently that I added that Alfredo had seen my mother in her white slip. Even as those words tumbled out of my mouth, I felt I had betrayed her. But a few days later she got an invitation to work for a local insurance company, a job that came with a modest salary, and commissions too. As a kid I thought the job was an answer to the prayer Father Ziperto told me he would say for her. Now I figure it was a direct, not divine, intervention by a priest intent on making us both grateful.

After I had become adequately proficient in the basics of moving knights and bishops across the board, for which I was rewarded with unlimited glassfuls of Cadbury's drinking chocolate, the Zipper told me he'd be willing to play my second-favourite game with me. First, he locked the vestry door with an ancient-looking skeleton key that hung on a hook beside the coat stand. Then he told me to take off my shoes, so I could sneak about soundlessly, as well as my school uniform jacket and trousers, so they wouldn't get mussed. I hid and he found me. I loved the game, but I loved his rapt attention even more, wanting to be embraced by a man who smelled like my father—sweet pipe tobacco and Yardley soap—the man who still made my mother cry for the loss of his presence. My mother cried for me too, but only when I told lies or she caught me with butterscotch Life Savers I'd stolen from the off-licence. Once those tears were dry, she went to sleep in my father's velvet dressing gown, and despite the fact that he was long dead, I felt excluded.

Soon, each time the Zipper found me, he would take a photograph with his Canon F-1 camera. He told me that photography was a passion of his. I never did find out where he developed photographs of half-dressed children, but I only realized later it couldn't have been at a commercial photo shop. The following week, he'd show me his handiwork before he locked the photos in the bottom drawer of the cabinet where he stored the vestments for Christmas and Easter.

When the Zipper told me to take off my uniform jacket and pants, I had obeyed, just as I obeyed every other instruction the priest issued, including ringing the Sanctus bells and placing the processional cross into the brass holder on the altar. The third or fourth time we played, he climbed in beside me in my usual hiding place—the dark cupboard where the cassocks hung—and tickled me. He had to hold his hand over my mouth to mute my squeals of laughter. I remember the feeling of his warm fingers on my face, his thumb against my cheekbone. Eventually, after the tickling, he would hug me in the cupboard until my bare legs were wet and sticky. I had no idea why my legs became slippery, and I didn't ask. Nobody questioned a priest about why he locked the vestry door or why he played a secret game with a little boy in a cupboard every Monday after school. Certainly not a kid whose father was dead and whose mother wasn't sure that she could raise him on her own. Given that he was also her confessor, the Zipper must have known that I was my mother's cross to bear.

On the day of the first sticky mess, after he'd wiped my legs and helped me back into my uniform, the priest walked me home, reminding me as we went that I needed to go to Confession as usual on Tuesday. (It took me several years to realize that as I told him my sins and accepted my penance, he was doing more on the other side of the rattan screen than just listening.) He stood with me for a while in front of Alfredo's window, chatting and pulling sweets from his pockets to tuck into mine. When my mother came outside, wearing pale shimmery lipstick and smiling with her whole face, he knelt to tie my shoelaces. While he was touching one of my legs for the second time that day, he looked me in the eye with deepest affection and gave me a wink. And I knew, without being told, that I wasn't to tell my mother about our game.

Of course, she invited him in for tea. As Father Ziperto talked a chain of pleasantries, my mother flew to the kettle, charmed by his down-to-earth chumminess, his hair slicked to chocolate pudding, and his front teeth as shiny as two Chiclets. As I crouched to tie the second knot in my shoes the way my mother had taught me to do so they wouldn't come undone, she gave me a look over her shoulder, her eyebrows coming together in puzzlement. Her silent question: How had the knots I'd tied so carefully in the morning come undone?

"I'm so glad that Arthur pleaded for regular chess lessons," the priest told my mother. As young as I was, I knew he was telling a lie. He gave me a complicit little smile, and then said, "Your kitchen smells like *paradiso*"—always music to her ears.

"Thank you, Father," she said, as she served us both cinnamon-scented slices of pie. The usual creased look of strain had fallen away from her face.

"My own mother, born in Italy as you know, used to bake my favourite *chiacchiere* for *giovedi grasso*—the last Thursday before Lent. And please, call me Brother Durante," he said, in his deep, velvety baritone, putting a hand over hers.

She turned pink at the intimacy and for a brief time he looked like a man instead of a priest. I think no one other than my father had touched her like that. In that moment, I wanted my hand to be under his too.

Sitting back, he said, "Mrs. Barnes, with your permission, I would like Arthur to continue his chess lessons with me, perhaps enter a competition. He really must keep playing. Chess is infinite, and learning to recognize the patterns and many different positions requires intense concentration. Can we carry on with Mondays at four? If he does want to compete, the church will cover the entry fees. No cost to you at all, and a lot of benefit for Arthur."

"I wonder, is anything without cost these days?" my mother replied, her face still pink. "But thank you. Of course, Arthur should continue with chess, especially if you are right next to him, and you think it's a good activity for him to pursue."

She gave me a curious sideways look when she realized I was dragging the tines of my fork over the pie crust instead of eating my slice. I was still working my way through the little white lie the priest had told, surely a venial sin.

Soon after, Father Ziperto left with another couple of pieces of pie carefully wrapped in waxed paper. "I will share this with my fellow Benedictines," he said. "You're most generous, Mrs. Barnes." And after he was gone, my mother encouraged me to step up my commitment as an altar boy and serve on weekdays as well as on Sunday.

That night, after she tucked me in, she picked up my shoes and examined the cotton laces, but said not a single word about how the double knots might have come undone.

Chapter 6

After we burned the pew, Ernie became the Zipper's favoured boy. When I had been the favourite, I wore extra layers of clothing to church and to school: two jumpers and shorts as well as underpants beneath my trousers—two of everything. The extra clothing gave me a sense of security. Some days I showered two times too, with water as scalding as I could stand.

As the favoured boy, I'd also served at weddings and baptisms, earning a little pocket money, and of course I was also called upon to give the priest what he needed in the vestry on Mondays. I was given to believe I could do no wrong. The golden boy. When it was Ernie's turn, he rode in the Zipper's car and went places, sometimes overnight. If I'm honest, I didn't want to know where they went, and Ernie was tight-lipped about those trips. That is, until the weekend the Zipper took him to an alternative Christian church in Birmingham. I hadn't really missed Ernie that weekend, I am sorry to say. I'd stayed home Saturday and Sunday to read and review a fantastic 272-page novel for Miss Phillips, *Dirk Gently's Holistic Detective Agency* by Douglas Adams, which made me briefly consider becoming a detective myself.

On Monday at school, Ernie's skin was a slick larval white and he was high on something. Maybe a Valium from his mum's bathroom. His blond curls had been shaved off right down to the scalp except for a few patchy spots at the back. Several lines of dried blood made me think he had done the shaving himself. He looked as sickly as our bald neighbour Mr. Biddicombe, who lived two doors up on Norbins Road and was trying to outrun leukemia.

During first break, Ernie hustled me up to the third-floor toilets, and told me he'd been given a "holy bath" in a house owned by the Cherubim and Seraphim Church in Birmingham. When I asked what kind of church that was, he said it was some kind of superfaithful Christian evangelical order. His voice was husky, likely from lack of sleep. Or maybe from a new habit: in those few minutes we were together, he chain-smoked three cigarettes, blowing the smoke out the window. I closed my eyes for a split second and prayed that he wouldn't divulge what he'd been required to do, and I also prayed that he'd been stoned while doing it.

Then I started to laugh at the absurdity of it all—what the hell was holy about going to an alternative church in Birmingham?—or maybe it was from nerves over the state he was in. Ernie started laughing too. Soon we were howling so hard we were both bent over at the waist, which made it seem like nothing terrible had actually happened. Better that than to divulge what had been asked of us, or to worry about what was next. Ernie gave me only one more, scanty, detail: "We drove all that way for a single hour." When the bell rang, he stepped on his last cigarette butt, tossed it out the window, then used his two index fingers and thumbs to mime the taking of a photograph. One hand then became a fist and the other began to circle in the air. "Roll tape," he muttered. Like some twisted version of a thank-you note, Ernie smiled at me. I smiled back. Then we legged it down the staircase and took our places in Mr. Henry's science class, trying to concentrate on a lesson about motion, propulsion and energy.

With the teacher at the blackboard, his back turned to the class, I walked over to Ernie's desk and dropped a pile of papers on it. Over the weekend, in between breaks from reading the novel, I had done most of his written homework, looping the *g*'s and the *y*'s like he did, and hooking the sevens—we'd traced each other's writing what felt like an infinite number of times in order to become better forgers. He didn't meet my eye. I went back to my seat. As the minutes ticked by, I caught myself glancing over my shoulder to check on him. The hairless, hollow-eyed boy sitting there looked like he had left the real Ernie someplace else.

To my knowledge, nobody at St. Nick's ever questioned why a forty-year-old priest had taken a fourteen-year-old boy out of town on the weekend. Ernie's mum and stepdad certainly hadn't. I never did ask Ernie what exactly went on in Birmingham, or who else was there, and especially not why he had agreed to get in the Zipper's car in the first place. I'd learned that if you don't talk about something, it doesn't exist. On top of that, I was so flooded with gratitude that I was no longer the favoured boy, I didn't really want to know anything more.

But then I realized that Ernie had stopped bathing. A foul, inescapable stench made it hard to stand next to him when we were sent to wash the Erlenmeyer flasks in Wednesday's science class. I turned on the tap to cover my voice, and asked, "Did you step in dog cack? You smell disgusting."

He slowly tipped his head to the side, widened his eyes, and gave me the ghost of a smile, and it came over me that he'd created a kind of human repellent. The import of why he'd made himself smell so bad hit me as hard as his stench, and I hurried back to my desk to recover, abandoning him to the chore of flushing the narrow-necked flasks with hot water.

I hadn't thought to coat myself with something as repugnant as feces to put an end to a situation that felt interminable. Instead, I had become a clean freak, trying my best to wash away every thought and deed.

I forced myself not to peer at Ernie from my corner of the science lab. My right temple was pulsing like a railway signal. And Ernie? His fingernails were chewed to the nub, he had a full-on case of hives—his skin flared when he got stressed—and, judging by the redness of his eyes, he was high again. Mr. Henry droned on about the solubility of sodium chloride while I nursed my shame. I knew the source of Ernie's misery. Ernie's hives. Ernie's stink.

I still have an image of him cross-cupping his elbows in the palms of his hands standing naked in the shower stall after PE at the end of that smelly week: no way could he escape the compulsory shower the coach now insisted on after games, so no way could he retain his protective layer. When he bent forward, I had seen a glint of the silver cross, and also the bruises on his arse. I wanted it to be mud from the rugby pitch, but I knew a thumbprint when I saw it. I couldn't help checking my own for similar marks. And then I saw his shoulders begin to shake, but not with sobs. A week of despair had turned to spitting anger. Knowing I'd noticed the bruises, he hurried into his trousers. As he did up the buttons of his shirt, he hissed, "How many times does a pit bull have to bite before we decide it needs to be put down?" It was a heavy statement, given that Ernie far preferred animals to humans. For a split second I told myself his stepfather was the one to blame.

As a boy of eight, when it all began, I hadn't realized that our situation was a type of imprisonment. We were taught that the word of a priest was as sacred as the Holy Communion wafer melting on our tongues, or the peeling statue of the Virgin Mary hauled out every year to grace the Nativity scene. On my knees a few feet from the altar, I looked for signs of God in the vastness of the air caught under the domed ceiling. How were we supposed to find Him in all that nothingness? We needed the priests to wear a white collar—a visible sign of the divine. I never thought to seek God in other places, or to question how Mary's conception was immaculate, or why meat was forsaken on Friday. We were obedient.

I was ten when I started bathing every Monday night as well as on Saturday, and maybe eleven when I started to shower twice a day instead—I didn't like staring down at my naked self, floating in the bath. I was thirteen and a half when Alfredo gave me a hug to congratulate me on a review and I pushed him away so hard he fell and hurt his ankle. I stuttered that I'd been startled, but I don't know how he forgave me. I was fourteen when Ernie became the Zipper's favoured boy. In all the years leading up to the hand-off, and for a long time after, I was never exempt from the Zipper's bidding, living in a sort of paralyzed anxiety waiting to be summoned to the vestry, but I knew for sure that Ernie carried more weight than I did.

So I did my best to relieve that burden, which meant I was ready to fall in with all of Ernie's crazy plans to prove we were just boyhood friends getting up to the usual, everyday kinds of trouble. I did all I could—except share the truth of what was happening to us both.

Chapter 7

The summer in the orchard had not been the cure for our thieving. There was something so intoxicating about stealing, it was like we couldn't see that consequences were bound to catch up. Our regular haul from the collection plate paid the bus fare that, on the increasingly rare days when we were both free to hang out, took us to nearby towns, especially Bristol and Bridgwater. With what was left over, we stuffed ourselves with fish and chips from Knights on Northload, bottles of pineapple-grapefruit Lilt, King Cones, and Ready Salted Walkers Crisps.

Around Guy Fawkes day in November, Ernie used some of the cash to buy two lengths of stretchy rope. "Arthur," he said, "you and I are going to be the first boys of our age to bungee-jump off the Clifton Suspension Bridge in Bristol."

"Is it legal?" I asked. What I really meant was: Are we likely to die?

"Students from the Oxford University Dangerous Sports Club have done it," he assured me. "The distance is exactly two hundred forty feet, three inches from the rail to the water. I've made all the calculations. It's doable. I'll jump first. After a few bounces, you will lower the second rope, I'll clip it to a harness, and you'll pull me back up to the platform. And then it'll be your turn. What could possibly go wrong?"

For once, I was inflexible. "Count me out. You're going to have to do this stunt on your own."

It was a two-man job, so that was impossible. But since we were already headed to Bristol, I offered a fallback plan: more shoplifting.

That crowded Saturday at Dearborn's, still our preferred target despite the pen incident—which only heightened the thrill for Ernie— we went up and down the modern escalator banked by the giant glass windows that overlooked the Broadmead shopping quarter, scoping the opportunities. Home computers were just starting to appear for sale in the consumer electronics department and Ernie figured out pretty quickly that the salespeople were still more comfortable selling televisions. He inhaled everything he could find on computing and programming, and models like the Commodore, which had a BASIC language interpreter pre-installed, played to his strengths. While I kept a lookout, Ernie opened up BASIC on the display model and typed three lines of code beginning with *Free Today Only* and ending with *RUN*, and the screen filled with endless copies of his text. Hailing a salesperson, we insisted we wanted our free computer while he fruitlessly tried to stop the program.

"I guess they don't work," Ernie said at last, and off we walked, leaving a small crowd of curious shoppers gawping at the furious employee.

Up on the fourth floor, we roamed the various departments, keeping our eyes peeled for Mrs. Gregory and her Coke-bottle glasses. We lingered longest in the music section. Ernie hated disco, heavy metal and hardcore punk. Like his older brother, Nathan, he was into riotous punk-folk, and he stood in a long queue to actually pay for a Pogues CD called *Rum, Sodomy and the Lash*.

When he got to the cash, he beamed at the salesclerk and asked for an extra paper-handled monogrammed bag. The CD was a present for his brother, he said, and he wanted to give it to his brother in a fresh bag.

"Of course," she said.

Twenty more minutes of aimless roaming, and we finally spotted both a Sony Walkman and one of the new portable CD players sitting out on a counter instead of locked under glass. The salesperson for electronics had stepped away. Ernie handed me the extra bag and made a beeline for the Walkman as I grabbed the larger CD player. In a flash, we were riding the lift to street level and out the side door carrying our legitimate-looking bags full of stolen goods. I was practically faint that the alarms might go off, but Ernie had remembered that this door didn't yet have a sensor to detect the electronic surveillance tags on both items.

The rush of adrenalin coursing through my veins didn't stop until long after we had hopped on the bus and the puffing hydraulic doors had closed behind us. It was crowded, and we had to stand. I was sweating and remained vigilant for the store detectives, scanning every face on the pavement, peering at each car that rode alongside us as the bus looped the St. James Barton Roundabout. Ernie's serenity was impossible to fathom given that I had the strongest urge to abandon our stolen items, stowed inside the black-handled bags screaming "Dearborn," on the bus.

My slippery hands shook, my legs could hardly hold my weight, and I was suddenly awash in crashing waves of relief along with shuddering nostalgia for my innocent younger self. Ernie quickly circled my waist with a supportive arm, and he didn't take it away until the bus began to empty and we were able to sit down.

Eyes on my face, still slimed with sweat, he fished an old harmonica of Nathan's from his pocket and played a tune off the Pogues CD he had just purchased—his favourite, "Dirty Old Town." Nobody on the bus minded, and as he hit the chorus, some even hummed along. For some stupid reason, the music made my eyes sting.

A woman with chapped lips and a broken tooth, her hair tucked under a Queen Elizabeth–style kerchief, leaned towards me and Ernie. "This song reminds me of my grandfather," she said. "He was born in Ireland

but raised in the dirty old town of Salford. Seventy percent unemploy-
ment and ninety percent discouragement. My grandmother would have a
fit when he was acting the maggot, but my mother said she loved him all
the same, especially his singing. She also married a drinker." Ernie cocked
his head and nodded to show his sympathy while his fingers danced over
the tiny holes of the harmonica.

When Ernie had finished the tune, the woman in the kerchief called
"Encore," and Ernie obliged.

"Dirty old town . . . Dirty old town," she sang along.

Ernie slid his free arm around my shoulder, playing on with one hand.
His touch was so reassuring, it caught me in the throat. I didn't even think
to cringe or pull away, just sat there swaying with him, slowly letting my
acute distress melt away. The music both soothed me and made me long
for something I couldn't put a name to.

With my nerves fully recovered from our Bristol thefts, we headed to
Cheap Jack's in Wells the following Saturday to steal mousetraps. Ernie's
house was overrun: we could hear them scrabbling in the walls, in the ceil-
ings and behind the skirting boards. In my mother's *Britannica*, we read
that mice hate cinnamon, vinegar, whole cloves and clove oil, peppermint,
tea bags, toothpaste, ammonia and cayenne pepper. We couldn't buy the
supplies we'd need to create such deterrents, let alone steal them all, so
that's why we decided on traps. At first, Ernie was intent on saving every
mouse with a humane approach, but then he did some calculations based
on the number of droppings he'd noticed and realized it was impossible.
"Mice excrete up to seventy-five pellets each a day," he told me. "I figure
there are at least ten thousand poops in the house, so we have a hundred
and thirty-three mice to catch."

We spent the rest of the weekend finding ingenious places to tuck
traps loaded with runny peanut butter stolen from Sainsbury's. "Last
autumn it was rats," Ernie reminded me, as though a full-scale mouse

infestation was a gift instead of a horror that would have seen my mother hopping up on a kitchen chair.

That Sunday afternoon, we were taking in the blue sky—or rather I was standing around with my hands in my pockets while Ernie smoked in his back garden—and we noticed an injured orange and white kitten among the foxgloves by the train tracks. Its hind leg had been badly bitten by something—it was still bleeding—and the little thing could barely hobble. Ernie ran into the house for life-saving supplies and returned with his mother's best tea towel.

"Cats are the best mouse traps in the business," Ernie said, as he wrapped the damaged kitten in the soft white linen, securing it with adhesive tape from the medicine cabinet. Not this one, I thought. "We need to nurse this little guy back to health and keep him," Ernie added with complete optimism. Carefully he carried it inside and up to his room, and the exhausted mewling kitten spent the next few hours on Ernie's bed. I was still there when Ernie's stepdad—shirtless in a string vest—appeared in the doorway and went ballistic that Ernie was harbouring "such a rabid filthy thing." Then Mrs. Castlefrank, lurking behind him, spotted the soiled linen tea towel. I'm not proud that I chose that moment to head for home.

At school the next day, Ernie slid into his seat, his right eye swollen almost closed, the white streaked with blood. The teacher walked between the desks to take a closer look, then said, "Castlefrank, off to the nurse."

Head down, nostrils flaring, Ernie didn't budge from his seat. The class fell silent: we all felt his shame. The teacher put his fists on his hips, raised his voice, and insisted. "*Please* go to the infirmary. It's possible you need a stitch or two or at least a cold pack." Ernie glared up at him silently for a few long seconds, then grabbed his rucksack, stood and made for the door. "Arthur, go with him," the teacher ordered, and I scraped my chair back and followed Ernie into the corridor. His gait was off, as though his vision had been affected. I wondered what the nurse would think.

Her usual job was to comb our hair in search of nits or deal with a student who had a stomach ache.

Ernie turned his head just before he entered the nurse's office, and said, "My stepfather hit me with his belt buckle after the kitten stained my pillow. He got me in the nose, and it bled like a stuck pig. I smeared the blood on his vest. His fist came next." That he was talking about it at all was a sign that the beating had been much worse than usual.

Ernie went in and closed the door behind him, leaving me leaning against the wall outside the tiny room. His stepfather's sterling belt buckle—passed down from his own father—was inscribed "England's First Glory." After he'd hit Ernie with the belt for the first time, we nicknamed it the "first gory." I hadn't escaped out the kitchen door fast enough during one such confrontation, and I'd heard his stepdad say, "I'm not hitting you, Ernie. I'm hitting the devil inside you."

Ernie emerged from the nurse's office fifteen minutes later in an overpowering waft of witch hazel, spearmint and Mercurochrome, which took me straight back to scraped knees when I was a little kid. My mother might have given me a little slap on the backside every now and then, and bawled me out on occasion, but no one had ever raised a violent hand to me. It was something of a mystery to see triumph written across Ernie's face, or maybe it was self-satisfaction or even glee.

"Later," he said, by way of an explanation, tipping his head towards his bag, which now seemed overstuffed.

When we returned to the classroom, the teacher, reacting to whatever that look was on Ernie's face, immediately called upon him to report on his English homework. My heart sank. What with the kitten and his stepdad's blows, surely he hadn't been able to complete the homework? Ernie gave me the tiniest wink from his good eye, walked to the front of the class, and recited from memory Edgar Allan Poe's "The Raven."

He delivered the lengthy poem complete with quiet despair and darkest foreboding, made grislier by the state of his bashed-up face, and we hung on his every inflection. After he whispered *"Nevermore"*—all of us leaning forward to hear it—he returned to his seat, the only sound in the room the swish-swash of his brown corduroy trousers.

A tinge of respect in his tone, the teacher said, "Finely done, Castle-frank, finely done." Then he glanced down at his ledger and up at him. "For a passing grade, you'll still need to hand in your homework. I'll give you two more days."

The bell rang and we were dismissed. Ernie sprang from his desk, grabbed his bag and bolted from the room, me on his heels. We left the school grounds at a dead run, stopping, finally, at the cemetery on Austin Road. Winded, we threw ourselves down on the grass and then rolled over onto our backs to stare at the billowy clouds moving across the sky. From his rucksack he pulled out a satin-edged red wool blanket, and once again gave me that look of satisfaction.

"Stole this from the sick bay." At first, I couldn't fathom that Ernie would steal from the concerned nurse, the only staff member who was universally loved, but all I could think of was that each little act of defiance was a way to hold his ground.

"Don't look so fussed, I'll bring it back." And then he added, "My stepfather tried to dispose of the kitten before it was dead. In the garden waste."

"The kitten died?"

Ernie nodded. "I snuck out and brought it back to my room while it was still breathing. I don't know when it died, but it released its bodily fluids on my bed. I buried it by the tracks before I came to school this morning."

We focused our eyes on a dozen quaking aspen, trembling in the breeze, creating ripples of liquid gold. Ernie said, "Did you know, if the leaves can't move, they get eaten by insects." We listened to the quiver of a million shimmery yellow leaves, then Ernie said, "The trees look like brothers the way they stand by each other. Not one of them looks sick or in danger of falling by the wayside."

I pushed myself up on an elbow. "That kitten must have become separated from the litter. Or his mother gave up on him for being the runt. Not enough milk. We can make a marker for its grave." There were more than a dozen little sites marked by ice-lolly sticks in the grassy bank closest to the tracks—all the foster animals Ernie had been unable to save.

He said, "The runt is always ridiculously happy to be alive. If they're loved, they catch up. But I couldn't save it. I was too late."

He fell silent, and closed his eyes, likely for the first time in more than twenty-four hours. Delicate blue veins were thin streaks on his milky lids. He was impossibly small and undernourished, ungroomed wheat-blond curls growing in again after the savage scalping he'd given himself, his child-like rib cage moving up and down. In that moment he was as defenceless as the orange kitten, and I had to stop looking. I lay back down and faced the sky. There we were, far from what hurt us, being comforted by a brotherhood of trees.

Within minutes Ernie was asleep, and for a brief time he had no uncertainties. I listened to the soft whooshing sound of each exhale through his injured mouth for a while. Then I sat up and rummaged in his bag, where I found a bunch of undone essays. While Ernie slept, I'd try and finish one or two.

For English, Ernie had chosen to dissect a quote from Oscar Wilde's *The Importance of Being Ernest*: "Relations are simply a tedious pack of people, who haven't got the remotest knowledge of how to live, nor the smallest instinct about when to die."

I snorted with laughter, and Ernie opened his eyes and saw me scribbling in his notebook. He sat up and peered at what I was writing, then said, as if orating again, "From Wilde I learned that the real problems start with the dick-head people we live with." He lay back down, too tired to make more of an effort.

I said, "You don't talk about your real dad too much," but Ernie was asleep again. I got back to his assignments. An hour later he opened his eyes and answered my question. "Not much to say."

I let it go, then offering, "I saw a sign for free kittens on Norbins Road."

Ernie began to laugh, putting a hand to his cracked lips to protect them. And then I was laughing too, at the absurdity of items acquired for free.

As we were walking home, Ernie's lower lip wobbled. "Nathan's in trouble again," he said. "My stepdad took it out on me."

Chapter 8

The next day it was all over school that a twenty-one-year-old man from Glastonbury had been arrested for "possession with intent to supply"—the news passing from one student to the next like the measles. Nathan was old enough that a few of our classmates hadn't realized that Ernie even had an older brother, but soon everyone knew. Nathan had been pulled over on Magdalene Street and searched, and when the police found a dozen small baggies of marijuana inside his coat, and another larger one containing white powder, he broke free and made a run for it. He was caught, wrestled to the ground, brought to the station and booked. The story made the BBC, because the white stuff in the bag had been something called powdered mescaline. I'd never even heard of it; the BBC reported that though it had been safely used as a hallucinogen by humans through millennia, it was illegal now and carried a high risk of abuse.

After the last bell on Friday, I found Ernie sucking the life out of a cigarette in the woods behind the staff car park. "If he's convicted, it'll almost certainly mean jail time."

All I could do was commiserate.

Ernie said, "He'll also have to pay a huge fine."

"Just keep your head down around school. They'll forget about it all soon enough."

"It's down as far as it'll go. I'm licking the road."

"What's the fine?"

"Maybe as much as five thousand pounds. Nathan's lawyer told my mom that he'll be locked up in the Bristol Prison for up to seven years. Mescaline is a Class A infraction."

I whistled.

Ernie had broken out in hives as bright as new strawberries.

"Old Man Mullins from next door told my mum he's listing his house. Rang the doorbell with his cane to spit those words in her face, saying he didn't want to live next to a family whose son was part of a gang of scumbag drug dealers."

Whatever he was up to, I didn't think Nathan was part of a gang, but Mullins had become a bit of a vigilante about drugs, constantly predicting the deterioration of Glastonbury and Yeovil and Bridgwater, writing letters to the local paper calling for the police to be given the freedom to stop and search anyone at all. Long hair, serpent tattoos and motorbikes. Nathan.

Nathan had been living rough, on and off, since he'd left home. I'd walked past the launderette and seen him running his crusty sleeping bag through the washing machine, and I'd once caught him fishing food scraps out of the bin behind the co-op on Silver Street alongside the woman who stuffed her shoes with newspapers and carried everything she owned in a shopping trolley.

When he did have money, Nathan was just as likely to give it away as to hang onto it to pay for something as mundane as rent. Like the time he worked three weeks of overtime for a builder putting up a row of terraced houses in the Penhill area of Swindon and bought two bicycles with his bonus. One for Ernie. One for me. It wasn't even our birthdays. It was

Nathan who managed to teach me how to ride a bicycle. Anybody else, even Ernie, would have given up.

But I didn't really know what to think of Nathan. Nine out of ten times, his money-making schemes were illegal. Out of the blue, arriving from who knows where, he'd just appear, roaring along Dyehouse Lane on a customized motorbike with cash in his pocket for Ernie.

As we made our way over to the cemetery, Ernie was kicking rocks and flinging pebbles at the street signs. He said that only two people besides me had been able to look him in the eye since the news about Nathan broke: Mrs. Brophy, the music teacher, and Francis Culpepper, the school cleaner, who also worked part-time at St. Jerome's animal rescue in Taunton, one of Ernie's haunts.

This was a sure sign that Ernie was really in a bad way. Normally he didn't give a shit about other people's opinions. Which was good, because plenty of students at St. Columba thought the entire Castlefrank family should be shunned. In a town where even the poor were some-what houseproud, Ernie's parents didn't plant flowers or string up Christmas lights. Their front garden, littered with weeds and cigarette butts, shrouded in dead leaves, looked downright abandoned. Ernie's mum, who worked nights when she worked at all, was never seen at the school—not for concerts, not for bake sales, not for parent-teacher meetings—shunning the company of the other mothers, who were bound together by the gossip they spread like marmalade on toast. She barely even said boo to me, and I'd been in and out of their house since I was eight.

When we reached our usual spot at the cemetery, Ernie slumped to the ground and put his head in his hands. I sat down beside him and reached out a tentative hand, which he slapped away.

"Why are you hanging around with me? Leave, for God's sake," he hissed. "You're more of a loser than me. A book nerd, an idiot, a total mama's boy. I don't need anything from you. Get lost."

But I saw through all that nonsense. "It'll work out for Nathan," I said. "Somehow, it's going to work out."

And I sat with him in silence until it was time to take him back to my house for tea.

Chapter 9

ERNIE

I was lying awake on a Friday night in mid-April, a few weeks after Nathan had been busted. Well past midnight, I heard a screech of tires, followed by a jarring rumble. I went to the landing and peered out the window overlooking the street. It wasn't the police. I watched in disbelief as Nathan and three burly men off-loaded a disassembled pool table from a small lorry. It was a relief to lay eyes on him. After he pleaded not guilty at his arraignment, Mum had somehow come up with enough cash to bail him out. He'd been told not to leave town before the trial, but he'd taken off. Blinking Nathan. Still, it had been a number of years since he'd stayed here with any regularity—him sleeping under the same roof as our stepfather usually led to bloody fights.

I listened carefully, but my mother and stepfather were still asleep. I sidestepped the loose floorboards as I made my way downstairs to the kitchen, where I peered out the side window.

The green felt of the pool table looked black in the gloom, but the four corner pockets gleamed silver. The four somehow managed to manoeuvre it through the cellar door at the side of the house and down the rickety stairs. All was still quiet above me. I crossed the room to listen at the door to the basement. By the sound of it, they were screwing the legs back on, Nathan shushing some drunken laughter. Soon enough, three of them tromped back up the stairs and the red tail lights of the van disappeared down Dyehouse Lane.

I opened the door and there was Nathan at the foot of the stair.

"Hey bruv. Get down here," he whispered.

The reek of alcohol reached me where I stood. A cigarette dangled from the corner of his mouth. Closing the door behind me, I tiptoed down the steps.

"Did you steal this from the Triangle?" I passed my hand over the bright green felt and the white stencil that read "The Triangle."

"A big bet went my way." Nathan gave my cheek a light slap and picked up a pool cue and some blue chalk. "I've been missing you. Have a beer." He pointed the cue at a cooler on the floor.

"Where've you been? The judge said you weren't supposed to leave town."

"Had to. No place to sleep around here. But good news, little brother. I'm up for a job with a film company."

"Mum says you're unemployable."

"Mum doesn't know anything."

"Is the film company here in Glastonbury?"

"No, most of the filming is done on location but the studio is in Leeds and there are offices in Singapore. The Philippines. Exotic stuff. I actually have some business to take care of tonight." Nathan pulled on his beer.

How much more of the night was left?

I watched him lean over the table and pocket one pool ball after the other. Then he put the cue on the table and moved around the room in a restless fashion. He seemed particularly alert, energetic. He was on something besides alcohol.

I sat on an old folding chair and watched him circle the table. "Mullins took his house off the market," I offered at last. "He's decided not to sell."

"Mullins has gone soft in the head." Nathan stepped back from the pool table and added more chalk to his cue.

Despite all his run-ins with the police, when he was around, Nathan was the one who rushed out to fold Mrs. Mullins's wheelchair and load it into their ancient, rust-bitten car with one side-mirror taped on for dear life. Nathan had done the taping, muttering that the vehicle was more of a coffin than a method of transportation. Mrs. Mullins was the only neighbour who had paid any attention to us as kids. She'd bring us biscuits or a loaf of banana bread whenever she was doing some baking, knowing that our mum was not much in the kitchen even when she wasn't working nights. Then a diagnosis of progressive multiple sclerosis had put her in that chair.

"She'll be headed to Coldwells soon enough." Nathan pocketed another ball.

He had done community service at the nursing home for a disturbance of the peace infraction. I'd gone with him once, and marvelled at the way he could get the nearly dead, who sat drooling in the drafty social room, their knobby knees under mohair blankets, up and attempting to dance the Morris. That version of my brother made any room brighter, but then there was the one who could drink to the blackout stage, where he was no good to anyone, especially himself. And he loved his baggies, happy to ingest anything that got him out of his head. The first time Nathan snorted cocaine, he came into my bedroom at four in the morning, clear-eyed, alert and euphoric. He took both of my hands in his and told me not to worry about our stepdad or anything. Everything was going to be okay, and even if it wasn't, we'd be brothers for life.

I would have followed him anywhere, done anything, not even stopping to change out of my animal pyjamas. That night anyway. Maybe even now.

"You still in school?" Nathan set up another shot. The crack of the ball was loud enough that both of us glanced at the ceiling, listening for footsteps. "Since I didn't graduate, you know it's all on you."

"Of course, I'm still in school. I'm fourteen." I let a silence fall, and then blurted the question that was at the forefront of my mind. "Are you going to end up in jail this time?"

"I'll be fine." He laid his pool cue on the felt, positioned his cigarette on the edge of the table and pulled me into a bear hug. "C'mere, you dope. What's with all the hives? You've got no worries on my account." I could feel the hammering of his heart, counteracting his attempt to comfort me. "It won't be so bad. I promise."

When he released me, I said, "Will you be staying home for a time?" I tried to sound like I didn't care one way or the other.

"Just for the weekend. You know the old man can't stand the sight of me."

When I asked where he'd been spending his nights, he was vague. A cellar here, a couch there. In exchange for odd jobs, he'd had a room for a while at the Alma Inn on Silver Street in Taunton. Nathan was usually good at cavalier, but tonight he wasn't pulling it off. When something is stretched one too many times, it loses its elasticity.

Nathan screwed his cigarette back into the corner of his mouth, picked up the cue and lined up the next shot, one eye closed to measure the distance to the corner pocket. He banked in a ball, then turned to me again. "Ernie, want to come meet a guy I know? He's as much of a nut for computers as you are, except he actually has the equipment instead of just dreaming about it. He owns a pawnshop that's attached to that abandoned petrol station near the old Clarks shoe factory. Your kind of guy—he says that everyone is going to have their own computer at home one day. I told him you were genius at maths and had taught yourself coding out of a magazine."

"All I know is BASIC, and only in theory! But, sure, I'll come."

"Nathan, is that you?" We both looked up and there was Mum in her flowery nightie at the top of the stairs, holding a plate of sausage rolls. "Have you got a court date, love?"

She carried her plate down the short flight, and presented the sausage rolls to Nathan, who put her offering down on the workbench then gave her a quick squeeze.

"Yes, Mum. It's May seventeenth."

I did a quick calculation. Just over a month.

"It will be good to get that behind us," she said.

"Go back to bed, Mum. It's late," Nathan said. "I'll see you in the morning. Thanks for the bite."

We watched as she obediently climbed the stairs. She was used to being told what to do.

For the next two days, Nathan hung around, telling me about the film company he was going to work for. It turned out the computer guy he wanted me to meet was also an investor in the company, which was called Reel Fauna. Nathan said the company had already made two short animal documentaries that were right up my alley. My ears were tuned for Nathan's bullshit, but he knew enough to ply me with the contents. "Harp seals use their claws to scrape holes in the ice. They can stay underwater for fifteen minutes feeding on Arctic cod because their blubber keeps them warm."

On Sunday night, Nathan bought Indian takeaway, and my stepfather agreed to eat curry for the first time. He must have liked it, because after supper, he picked up his violin in his arthritic hands and, without complaint, began to play "Imagine." And he didn't curse when Nathan sang along. I hung back in the corner nursing my grudges, but our mother sat in a faded armchair in her yellow apron and smiled. For an hour or two that evening, we came close to being a real family, imagining a place where things didn't divide us.

Then after everyone else was in bed, Nathan made good on his promise to take me to meet his pawnbroker-filmmaker friend. He rolled his motorbike down the drive and along the road until we were out of earshot, then hopped on and revved it so loud I wanted to kick him in the leg. I climbed on back and we roared over to the Northload Bridge and then onto the A39. Neither of us wore helmets and the cool air rushing at my face made my lips wobble. We slowed for the stop signs but maybe we didn't, given that I kept my eyes closed and my arms tight around my brother's waist until we came to a definitive halt, a flurry of small stones spraying a hard surface. I opened my eyes to see that we were at the farthest end of the nearby village of Street, across the road from a place called Avalon Guns and Tattoos. Nathan had parked in front of a brick wall in a dark laneway that was choked with weeds and littered with bits of garbage. Two small windows high on the wall had industrial-grade steel bars.

I shivered.

Nathan asked, "You cold?"

I shook my head. I didn't want to admit that the place creeped me out or that I was finally wondering why a pawnbroker wanted to make animal documentaries. I followed my brother to a side door that didn't have a handle and watched him type some digits into a keypad.

"Eight eight one eight eight," he said, with a laugh. "But I'll have to break your neck if you tell anyone." A few seconds later there was a click and the door unlocked. Nathan pushed it open, then led me through a series of connected rooms and down a flight of stairs.

Over his shoulder, he whispered, "He calls this place the Pint Room."

I was expecting a pub set-up, but instead the large room had several couches all turned to face a wall on which hung a large screen that pulled down from the ceiling. There was an odd chemical smell. Before I could ask, Nathan told me it was fixer and developer fluids from a darkroom in a closet at the far end of the room. A refrigerator hummed in one corner, and a small lamp cast a glow that illuminated only a tiny circle of the industrial-looking space. I heard the click of a cigarette lighter and then a deep inhale. Nathan and I both turned towards the sounds.

"Is that you, Ernie Castlefrank?"

In the room's dimmest corner, a bearded man was seated in an armchair bordered with rivets that would have suited Don Corleone in *The Godfather*.

"Come closer," he said. "I don't bite."

Still, I hesitated at the foot of the stairs.

I heard the cracking of knuckles, and then the man said, "I'm happy to finally meet you. I like to know the up-and-comers. Nathan tells me you're clever."

My brother strode forward, and I trailed after him. "Ernie, this is Casper Fontaine, the computer whiz and one of the investors behind Reel Fauna." He headed for the refrigerator where he pulled out a bottle of Coca-Cola and uncapped it with an opener attached to a string hanging from the door handle. After he handed it to me, he started to pace, as usual, unable to settle. My eyes began to adjust. The man looked me up and down with his eyebrows raised. I'm not sure what Nathan might have said, but I had the feeling that I was not who Casper Fontaine was expecting to see. He sighed, or maybe it was another smoky exhale. "You look younger than your age. Nice blond hair." I wasn't sure if he meant it as a compliment.

Casper's own monkey-brown hair was coarse and cut so close to his scalp it stood up like an animal pelt. In between the moustache and beard, he had the palest of thin lips, and his large, protruding eyes made me think of a bullfrog. His wide shoulders strained the buttons and seams of his black leather jacket. He looked like a gangster but he had the smooth voice of a late-night radio host. I stepped closer.

"Have a seat," Nathan called out. "Casper wants to get to know you. I told him you'd be really helpful making our documentaries—you're brilliant at sensing an animal's distress and making them feel safe."

Fontaine was so still I thought he'd fallen asleep. But no. "Nathan says you're also batshit crazy for computers."

"That too," I said, and sat down on a leather two-seater.

Nathan went back to the fridge and uncapped three bottles of Guinness, drinking an entire bottle in one long swallow. "Cheers," he said, and tipped the neck of the second. I hoped he wasn't about to get so legless he wouldn't be able to drive us back home.

Fontaine soon launched into a monologue about mainframes, processors and microchips that was at least halfway comprehensible to me. I didn't get how all the talk about computer hardware connected with the filming of animals, but I kept my mouth shut and tried to follow.

Nathan, having downed his third beer, came to sit beside me. "Ernie, you'd learn so much from this man. Fontaine's been a techie since the seventies when nobody else in Somerset even realized a revolution was underway. He's following in the footsteps of that California geek Larry Roberts. You know, the guy who worked out ARPANET."

All I could do was sip my Coke and put my trust in my brother, who was on his way to being sozzled.

Fontaine leaned towards me, rumbling in his deep and soothing tones, "Nathan says you're self-taught. You and I might know more than just about anybody around here." He stared at me so intently I could feel sweat gathering on my neck. I edged a little closer to Nathan, who seemed to think everything out of Fontaine's mouth was wisdom from the gods.

As my eyes adjusted, I noticed a long wooden chest, maybe a toy box, along one wall. I thought I could see a small dog lying on top of it, but then I realized it was a dark brown teddy bear. I wondered if Casper Fontaine was a dad. Somehow, I doubted it.

As he continued to lecture, I tried to keep up with the jargon. At last, he asked a simple question: "Do you want to see my gear?"

I nodded. By this time, Nathan had his eyes closed, a beer bottle drooping from one hand. I poked him, and Fontaine led us through a door at the opposite end of the room from where we'd come in and up a different flight of stairs into the old garage, which he'd converted to storage. He pointed out the relays, motherboards, CPUs and other hardware that were the makings of his own home computer. I couldn't help but marvel. On a table was a huge stack of *Byte* magazines. Twenty issues, maybe thirty. I had one or two of my own, but he seemed to have every issue ever printed.

"Take a few," he said.

He didn't have to ask me twice. "Thank you."

He finished the tour by pointing out the assortment of security cameras he'd rigged around the room as a surveillance system. "Thieving is a problem," he said, and I tried not to smirk. "The only people I allow in here are those I've personally invited to the Pint Room."

I wondered why I'd made the cut. I knew my brother was proud of me, but I was a kid: surely there were adults who would have more to offer Casper Fontaine.

A little wobbly from the graveyard of beer bottles he'd emptied, Nathan dangled the key to his motorbike. "It's going on one o'clock. Ernie and I have to get a move on. He's got school tomorrow."

Fontaine pointed to me and said, "Precious cargo, Nathan. You sure you can handle all those beers and that boy?"

"Easy peasy," Nathan said, only slurring a little.

Once we were outside and standing by his bike, I asked, "Why'd you bring me here?"

"Casper told me they're shooting a doc about bird migration, and you know everything about birds, little brother. Who was the guy who told me ducks sleep with one eye open and ravens can mimic human speech? That cardinals sometimes deliberately cover themselves in ants. All that crazy-ass shite."

"But I don't know anything about making films."

"He also needs a computer guy, someone who wants to specialize in coding and software development. He's teaching me and I'm learning fast, but if it doesn't go my way in court, you can fill in for me. Nice to keep it in the family."

"Okay, as long as he knows I've got a lot to learn."

He knocked the kickstand free and climbed on.

"Who else would give you access to all those machines? You'll be on the cutting edge, Ernie." Nathan started it up, revved the engine and nodded to the back seat. I jumped on and we roared away from the pawnshop on the wrong side of the road, me praying the cold air would dilute the alcohol in my brother's bloodstream.

That night we both felt invincible. Or at least Nathan did.

Chapter 10

ARTHUR

Nine days before Nathan's trial, Ernie stole a joint from his brother's stash and came over to our flat for tea with my mother and me. After he'd had his usual second helpings and my mother had gone downstairs with the rubbish, we washed up the dishes and then retreated to my bedroom, where we lit the joint with the window open. The best part of smoking dope with Ernie was hearing him giggle, the peals rolling out of him uncontained. He didn't laugh like that much anymore, and it both pacified me and somehow lessened my fear that we'd be caught or handcuffed like Nathan, who was facing down a sentence.

Telling my mum that we needed to blow off some steam before we called it a night, we set off for a walk, still giggling. Ernie led me along Paradise Lane, then south towards Chalice Well, to an out-of-the-way children's playground with a view of the Glastonbury Tor. He ducked into an elaborate fort made of willow branches and I followed him.

"How did you ever find this place?" I asked.

"I've been coming here since last October."

"Really?" I asked. I thought I knew most everywhere Ernie went, except when he left town in the Zipper's car. "How come?"

"I don't know. Why does anyone go anywhere?"

"There should be a lamppost or something. It's ever so dark."

Ernie laughed. "Certain things should never see the light of day." As the meaning of his words melted into the night, he said, "I feel safe when I'm with you, Arthur."

His words should have warmed me, but instead I felt almost afraid. What could I keep him safe from? I hadn't saved him from anything, or even tried.

A little later, Nathan came down the drover's road, calling our names. We scrambled out of the fort so he could find us, then Ernie led us all to the swings. I was so lanky I could only sit on the seat like a lump, but Ernie could still fly, pumping his legs to swing ever higher and then leaping off at the highest arc. It made my stomach lurch, but Ernie loved it, and Nathan, drunk as he obviously was, couldn't take his eyes off his little brother, who was getting as close as he could to becoming a bird. I'm sure Nathan would have caught him if one of his jumps had gone bad.

It got so late, I prayed my mother had gone to bed and was fast asleep. The three of us walked home in the dark, our footsteps echoing in the quiet streets. Nathan took off his leather jacket with the Sticky Fingers logo and gifted it to Ernie, then pulled a harmonica from the pocket of his trousers and played "Dirty Old Town" while Ernie sang along. An upstairs light or two came on. On that walk, I briefly felt like I had two brothers, instead of a single friend.

Nathan and Ernie waited on the pavement until I waved from my upstairs window. Nathan held my eyes for a second or two longer than was necessary, and his expression told me that if he went to jail, I was the one who had to keep an eye out for his brother.

Ernie came over almost every night in the week before the trial. My mother would heap his plate like it was his last meal and send him home with leftovers for his family. Ernie was never embarrassed to leave with tinfoil pie plates loaded with my mother's spicy vindaloo, cod teriyaki and an apple pie from the freezer.

Eating my mother's cooking erased a look on Ernie's face that otherwise only went away on the days when he'd smoked enough dope to bring about a fit of laughing. Without the benefit of anaesthesia, some parts of his life had become intolerable. Mine too, but I had a few more consolations than he did.

On the night before the trial, Ernie finally told my mother that Nathan might be facing a big fine as well as jail time. As she set another piled-up plate before him, he said, "If he's found guilty, they could fine him five thousand pounds. He'll be held in contempt of court if he can't pay the whole of it and that will extend his sentence."

A look of stricken tenderness passed over my mother's face. She folded her hands and listened like she had when the BBC was broadcasting about the Chernobyl nuclear disaster in the Ukraine. She left the table and came back with a box of notepaper she'd bought at the Copperfield and Twist, along with a roll of stamps, and handed them to Ernie. She said, "Prisoners can become inspired to lead productive lives even in jail, especially if they feel supported by their family."

I thought "prisoner" was a bit harsh, but I could see that Ernie was pleased. She would have given him her favourite pen too, if I hadn't tucked it in the coupon drawer alongside the other miscellaneous junk. The Castlefranks were poor, but that would have been an insult.

Nobody was surprised that Nathan was found guilty. Not Nathan, or Ernie, or his parents, or my mother, or me, or anyone at St. Columba.

That evening, I did think Ernie was being a bit dramatic when he took me on a pilgrimage to the ridged slopes of the grassy Tor, where the last abbot of Glastonbury, Richard Whiting, was arrested and executed in 1539. A bit of wallowing was probably for the best, so I didn't protest. From the summit, we watched a particularly bloody sunset over the vast sprawl of the Somerset Levels, Wiltshire, Devon and Wales.

Later, lying on the ground inside the roofless St. Michael's Tower at dusk, Ernie pointed to the opening above us and said, "That's where the veil between this world and the next is the thinnest, and lost souls are connected—a gateway to the dead. Remember what I told you about ravens being the connectors?" Whatever pill he'd popped or joint he'd smoked to unleash his personal philosophy couldn't quite hide the resignation in his voice. Still, Ernie could always be relied on for gruesome details. "The abbot was hanged, drawn and quartered for remaining loyal to the Pope. His body was dragged by horses to the top of the Tor here. They fastened his head over the west gate for all to see."

"Nathan will come home, you know."

"A few hundred years ago people lined up to witness any public execution. Imagine applying for the job of executioner? Claiming you had those skills?"

"Weren't the butchers roped in? They wouldn't have needed training."

"I think it was mostly handed down father to son. Seventh-generation executioner. Cruelty is a human speciality, but people were more open about it back in the day." Ernie's voice cracked and tears leaked from his eyes, which he furiously wiped away. "Arthur, in the right circumstances, do you think we're capable of just about anything?"

I pulled my old transistor radio from my jacket pocket and turned it on so I wouldn't have to weigh in on what I myself was capable of. I fiddled with the stations until I found one playing psychedelic sixties music. Grace Slick was singing "White Rabbit."

Right on cue, Ernie pulled out a strip of paper covered with red and yellow dots. "Mellow Yellow or Red Star?" he offered. When I just looked at him, he said, "Nathan told me everything is fine except heroin. Some things you can't come back from."

I shivered and waved the acid away. Ernie could usually lead me wherever he chose, but not that night. Instead of picking out his own colour, though, he tucked the strip of paper into his rucksack. And carried on, morbidly.

"It won't be long before we're twenty-seven," Ernie said. "Jim Morrison was found dead in Paris at twenty-seven, Janis Joplin died at twenty-seven, with an unopened packet of cigarettes in her hand, and Brian Jones was twenty-seven when he drowned in a swimming pool."

I tried to steer us away from more talk of death. "My mother has a forty-five of Janis Joplin singing 'Me and Bobby McGee.'" I started to sing the first line, but Ernie cut me off.

"D. Boon, who just died—he was twenty-seven too. He was lying in the back of a van when the rear axle broke. He was thrown out the back door and snapped his neck. Jimi Hendrix took nine sleeping pills and choked on his vomit. His last words were, 'I need help bad, man.'"

I glanced at Ernie, amazed that he knew the specific details of the untimely deaths of so many music icons.

"Hendrix asked for help?"

"Too late. He'd written a poem about life being quicker than the wink of an eye. The story of love is hello and goodbye, until we meet again. And then he called his manager and left his last words on the guy's answering machine."

"How do you know all this? And why the bloody hell do you care?"

Clouds scooted across the darkening sky, and the Tor was bathed in shadow. In a dreamy voice, Ernie repeated Jimi Hendrix's final words. "'I need help bad, man.' How's that for an exclusive club? You have to die to join."

The thought flitted through my head—I really didn't want to belong to that club, and I didn't want to be a member of the club Ernie and I were in, either.

Sometimes Ernie could follow where my mind went without me having to say a word.

"I saw the Zipper's Renault parked in front of your flat the other day." I shot a look at him but his face was unreadable. "Your mother got in."

"You know she does volunteer work at the parish."

"I guess we all do."

We listened to the wind. And then Ernie said so softly I had to strain to hear, "What if Nathan does something really stupid in prison. The hardest part is thinking he might never come back. It's like . . ."

"A death?"

Ernie tried to sound hard. "Who gives a crap. Every step we take brings us one foot closer to the end. Doesn't matter what kind of prison you're in." But then his anger dropped away, and he looked at me instead of up at the stars. "I'm going to need to help Nathan pay his fine so his sentence doesn't get extended."

I waited for him to ask me to rob the Barclay's bank in Frome so we could rescue Nathan. He didn't.

"How will you ever find that kind of money?" I finally asked, chewing on the inside of my cheek. Our own cash tap had been turned off when the church warden finally twigged to the fact that collection plates at St. Nick's were coming up short and began to monitor them and us more closely.

"I'll think of something."

I didn't know whether to be relieved or offended that Ernie didn't intend to include me in whatever scheme he was dreaming up.

He pulled Nathan's harmonica from his pocket then and launched into a tune I didn't recognize.

"What's that?"

"A new Pogues song—'Streets of Sorrow/Birmingham Six.' About those six Irishmen who were arrested after a pub got bombed in seventy-five. The men professed innocence and insisted police had tortured them into signing false confessions, but they all got life. It's been banned on the radio."

Oh Ernie—it was a bit of a stretch to think of Nathan as an innocent man wrongly accused and convicted.

"Banned?" I said. "Play it again."

Chapter 11

ERNIE

Two weeks after Nathan started serving hard time at the prison in Bristol, I made my way over to the pawnshop with a rucksack on my back. The lights were off, so I went around the back and tapped the code Nathan had shared into the keypad. My heart was hammering in my chest as I headed down the darkened hallway in the direction of the shop, but the thought of Nathan behind bars gave me courage. Either Casper Fontaine heard my footsteps, or he had his video surveillance turned on, because before I'd made it ten feet, he popped open the back door of the pawnshop carrying a rifle. He'd shaved off his facial hair, and for a few seconds I wondered if it was the same guy.

"You buying stuff today?" I tipped my head towards my loaded rucksack.

"Well, well, well. You're dodgier than you look. Blinking Nathan—gone on us for at least a year, huh? Or is it three?"

He waved me into the shop ahead of him, returned the rifle to a glass cabinet and locked its door.

I heaved my heavy bag onto the counter and stepped back, looking around at the guns, wind instruments, a Tiffany lamp, a black leather doctor's bag, and a set of golf clubs that said Ben Hogan on the irons.

"Why'd you shave your beard and moustache?" I asked. I couldn't believe how different he looked when clean-shaven.

"Just a whim. I grow it, then shave it, whenever it strikes my fancy," he said with a smile, as though pleased I'd taken note. "Let me see what you've got."

The first item I handed over was the Cartier watch I'd nicked. Fontaine examined it, gave a low whistle.

"Vintage. Do you have the original box and documentation?"

"No. But it's real. 'Cartier' is spelled out on the seven o'clock marker. 'Swiss made' is under the six o'clock marker."

He laid the watch on the counter. "Are you in the jewellery business?"

"Today I am."

I pulled out two new calculators, five Swatch watches, a medical pager and a CB radio. Fontaine picked up each item and gave it a thorough examination. He ran his fingers over the fine engraving on the back of the pager that spelled out Dr. C.V. Cosgriff. "Let me get my ledger so I can add all this to my inventory." He tapped the CB radio. "These things are contraband. Twenty-seven megahertz is already licensed for radio control model aircraft. You got a licence for it?"

"My brother gave it to me. He used to drive a truck for work." Arthur and I had actually stolen it from a parked car—nothing Fontaine needed to know.

"Castlefrank. What's your first name again?"

He was behaving as if our first meeting in his bunker had largely slipped his mind.

"Ernest. I go by Ernie."

"I'm Casper. I go by Casper."

I couldn't help but laugh.

Then he said, "Don't worry, Ernie. I remember everything about that night, especially that your brother got himself half in the bag. I listened for a crash after you two left, but I guess you were meant to get home." He threw both hands into the air, exclaiming, "That brother of yours likes to fly close to the edge," and my heart started to hammer again. "Too close."

"That's a cool tattoo on your finger," I managed to get out. "What's it say? 'Till Death'?"

"That's right." Casper parted his fingers to better display the black letters. The Zipper had the same tattoo, mostly hidden under a signet ring that only came off if he needed to wash his hands more thoroughly than usual.

The words sprang out of my mouth. "Do you know Father Ziperto?"

"I do. It's a small town." He stared down at his tattoo like he was waiting for another question. When none came, he said, "You got any ID?"

"Nope."

"This your father's watch?" He picked it up and listened to the perfection of the mechanism.

I nodded.

"I'm required to give a list of all newly pawned items and any associated serial numbers to the police, so they can determine if any of them have been reported stolen."

"I can tell you these have not been reported."

"Well, Nathan's little brother Ernie, I guess I'm going to trust you. Let me write up a contract. Would you like a fixed-sum loan agreement and a pawn receipt? Interest rates are seventy-two percent per annum."

"I'm sales only."

"So just the cash?"

"That's right."

He studied me for a long moment, then reached forward and rubbed a lock of my hair between his fingers like it had cash value. I jerked my head away, and he smiled at me. Then he pulled a roll of notes from an inside pocket of his black leather jacket and handed me a few. I kept my hand out. I knew how much the watch was worth, and now he knew I knew. He peeled off another hundred pounds.

"You got anything else you want to hock?"

"I might."

With the cash safely stowed in a money belt under my shirt, I made to leave.

"Have you got another minute?"

Our eyes locked. His expression was innocent, fatherly.

"You're lucky to have a brother who's invested in your future, but from now on you'll need your own code to get in. You can choose the five numbers."

As unsafe as I felt, I nodded, oddly thrilled, and took a moment to picture the rotary dial on our home telephone with the letters of the alphabet under the numbers. "Seven two eight three six," I said.

"A password is only effective if you can remember it."

"Seven two eight three six," I repeated. I didn't tell him it stood for Raven. Let him figure that out, if he was so crafty.

He took a pencil and a pad from a drawer and wrote down the number. "Right, I'll enter those digits and trust you to remember them—don't be writing them down anywhere like I just did." He stared hard at my five-digit number, tore the piece from the pad, crumpled it up and swallowed it, staring at me all the time. "Do you have a driving licence?"

"No."

"You need to know how to drive."

"For what? Documentary filming?"

"Come back tomorrow and we'll see how else you can be useful."

"Nathan taught me how to drive," I found myself volunteering. I didn't add that it was in a car Nathan had hot-wired. He'd risked arrest to show me how to work a clutch in a car park in Taunton, then put the car back where he found it. "I'm a decent driver."

"I believe you. Right, if I'm to make you a licence that will withstand scrutiny, I need to take your photograph. Stand against the wall."

He pulled a camera out of the drawer of a filing cabinet. "Canon RC-701. Brand new," he said, as he aimed it at me. "Okay, look straight into the lens. Shoulders back and brush your hair away from your eyes." I did as I was told and heard a few clicks. He set the camera on the counter. "Nine p.m. tomorrow?"

"Right," I said.

I didn't know anyone who could manufacture a fake driving licence. I didn't know anyone who would ask a fourteen-year-old to come to a supposed business meeting so late on a school night. I knew two men with "Till Death" tattooed on their fingers and had no idea what to make of that coincidence. I also had no idea what I'd just signed up for, but if it would help me raise the money Nathan needed, I couldn't say no.

At 9:15 the next night, I tapped the numbers for RAVEN into Casper's lock pad. When the door clicked, I pushed it open and found him waiting in the hallway. "I'm in favour of punctuality," he said, his smooth baritone taking on an edge. "Punctual people are organized and systematic, the kind of person you can rely on."

It had been a while since anyone had counted on me to be any of those things.

I followed him down the stairs to the Pint Room. He offered me a bottle of Coca-Cola from the fridge and then settled into his leather chair. When I sat on the couch opposite him, he proceeded to make small talk, chatting with me about the Lockerbie bombing and the Clapham rail crash. I got the feeling he wanted to know if I knew stuff beyond the town limits. Was I life smart or book smart?

He asked if I'd ever been on an airplane. I hadn't. He told me he'd recently been to Bangkok on film business. I thought Nathan had mentioned Singapore. I racked my brains trying to think of animals indigenous to Thailand. When Queen Elizabeth had made a state visit to Bangkok, I'd seen an elephant in the background footage. But before I could volunteer what I knew about Asian elephants, which was almost nothing, he'd moved on to talk about coding.

I told him that, as my brother had boasted, I had taught myself BASIC. Now, thanks to the magazines he'd given me, I was learning several more languages. FORTRAN. COBOL. PASCAL. Since I didn't have my own computer, though, my grasp on them was pretty abstract.

He nodded, drumming his fingers. Then he cracked his knuckles and began to lecture. "Coding is nothing, Ernie. Coding is semantic. Keystrokes. Semicolons. An em dash. The star key. Programming is organizing that code into a concept and executing a vision. Coding is mere mathematics. A set of rules that can be understood." Still, I heard a tinge of wonder in his voice when he added, "There is the potential to write the perfect program. An impeccably executed program does not misbehave. A screen starts off as a blank canvas. It's like art. What we create is a flawless sculpture of extreme beauty and purity. Mathematics is never ugly."

This was what I thought too, although I'd never once been able to explain my ideas to Arthur, who only saw beauty in words.

At intervals, Casper spiked my soda with small splashes of vodka, or maybe it was gin—it had the piney smell of Scotch tape. Somewhat bladdered, I realized I had a better handle on marijuana and the like. My first impressions of the man had dissolved. He knew more about software than the authors of *Byte* magazine. I was fizzing with what felt like ecstasy without swallowing any actual pills.

"The first time I created a program with FORTRAN I felt like God," he said.

I longed to experience that feeling.

Eventually Casper placed a photo on the coffee table. It was of a bare-chested kid, maybe six, who wore nothing except a pair of white briefs. At first, I thought it was someone from St. Nicholas. It wasn't. Just some accidental boy with curly hair and doe eyes. He pushed it towards me. "How would you like to make some real money?"

I thought of Nathan.

Caspar poured more clear alcohol into my glass. I took a mouthful before it had a chance to sink to the bottom and winced, but I managed to swallow. I took a very long time studying the photo, weighing my options, trying to figure out where it might have been taken. My legs were loose; I felt easy in my skin for once.

"All right," I said at last. "How?"

"You bring me a couple of kids. Your friends. Younger brothers and sisters. Whatever. I take their photo. You know anybody?"

"No, I don't, and I don't have any younger siblings. But I might be able to get you some pictures like this one. You'll need to pay me for them."

"From Father Ziperto? He and I go way back."

I didn't answer, but I felt the blood pumping in both ears.

"I heard you're an altar boy at his church. You saving up for something?"

"Might be."

Casper stood up and waved me over to a large box on the floor. "This is for you. It was Nathan's idea." My eyes widened to see the logo. Commodore.

"A keyboard, a central processor, console, graphics and sound chips, and the best part? It has sixty-four kilobytes of memory. Three hundred ninety-nine pounds. Cheap. Commodore is able to manufacture their own semi-conductor chips. Drove the price down. Take it out of the box. Set it up. It's yours."

I stood there for a moment, thinking of saying no to the man who bore the same tattoo as the Zipper, but then I knelt and opened the box.

I went to the pawnshop the next day, and the day after that, bunking off school to attempt my first program. Casper had set up the Commodore on a desk beside some instruction manuals. Two weekends in a row, I rode my bike to Street in order to learn how to code. In exchange, I gave Casper three photos I stole from the Zipper's stash. Boys I didn't know. Arthur had books to read. Reviews to write. All the same, when I did see him, which was less and less, he looked peeved about not knowing what I was up to.

My first creation was Math Magician, a simple program for calculating the distance between two points in space and solving the quadratic equation. When I showed it to Casper, he called it a good start and pulled his chair a little closer.

"Are you a chess player?"

Not of my own volition, I thought, but I said, "I am."

"Thought so." He showed me how to draw a chess board using the graphics programming. "A chess microcomputer can beat a master in tournament play. You're a quick study, Ernie. I could get used to having you around."

I studied his expression, trying to figure out whether the uses he was imagining for me included the things I still did for the priest. He stared calmly back at me, giving nothing away, and I decided whatever it was he was into, I could handle it in exchange for the opportunity to learn computing and to earn more cash.

I went to Caspar's every chance I got through to the end of the school year. In the summer, I told Arthur and his mum that I'd got a job working with computers, and I went there every day, completely exhilarated by all the doors opening up in my head. Since she didn't ask, I said nothing to my own mother.

Arthur spent much of that summer working at the bookshop. I still sometimes turned up for tea with him and his mother, but smoking dope and petty thieving with Arthur had lost some of its appeal. It was typical that he never pushed me for details. I think he was relieved I wasn't luring him into trouble. And Mrs. Barnes seemed chuffed we were both working, or at least somewhat reassured we hadn't messed up our lives like Nathan had.

Then, one evening about six weeks into the new school term, as I was approaching my fifteenth birthday, Caspar walked me to his back door. "Would you help me with something next Friday," he said. It was a statement, not a request. I understood he was cashing in his chips.

"To do what?"

Casper withdrew a fifty-pound note from his billfold and pressed it into my palm, keeping his own hand over top. "Money upfront. I have this feeling that you and Nathan grew up too quickly, just like I did. I also missed out on the best parts of being young."

When he let go of my hand, he cracked his knuckles and I recoiled at the sound.

"I used to think I was given a role that didn't belong to me," he said. "I think you feel that way too. Like you're in a sort of psychological prison."

Next to Arthur, this unlikely man was now the closest friend I had. I had no idea where this was going, but I felt I had to listen.

"I studied at the seminary to become a priest," Casper said. It was not something I would ever have guessed. His leather jacket and muscled arms made him seem unfit for the priesthood, not to mention his hoarding of photos of near-naked children. But then again, there was the Zipper. Whom he knew. Who wore the same tattoo. Who'd taken the photos.

He went on. "I wanted to move to California and work in Silicon Valley, where it all began. I would have met boys like you, like I used to be.

Scientific. Mathematical. But my mother insisted I enter the seminary, and I couldn't say no to her."

I stared at him in commiseration or perhaps horror. "Why did she want you to become a priest?"

"Why? To hide me."

Before I could ask why she'd wanted to hide him, he said, "Friday. Are you in or out?" When I nodded, he zipped up his coat and retreated, calling over his shoulder, "I think I hear customers in the pawnshop."

At five o'clock in the morning on a Friday in mid-October, I set my alarm, got dressed, and rode my bicycle over to the pawnshop via the back roads and back alleys, through fog as thick as wool. I was damp through, and my hands were icicles by the time I got there. As I locked my bike to a scrubby tree, Casper came out the side door and climbed into his battered green Mercedes, which he'd parked in the narrow lane. I settled into the passenger seat and tucked my frozen hands in my armpits.

"I wasn't sure you'd show," he said, and handed me an enormous sandwich wrapped in waxed paper. He had a thermos of coffee between his thighs. He finished his cigarette, tossed the butt out the window, and off we drove, heading to Bath on the A39, the car thumping along the road well above the speed limit. A few miles out of town, Fontaine said, "I have a client who is going to meet me at a hotel."

"What is it you need me to do?"

"A boy will be there too—a kid from a care home. He's maybe eleven. Could be younger. Your job is to babysit him for a while. Give him a pop, some candy. Make him feel comfortable. Be yourself."

Keeping one hand on the wheel, Fontaine leaned into the back seat, grabbed a paper bag out of a heavy-duty nylon duffle and placed it in my lap. I peeked inside to see licorice, fizzy drinks, Twix bars, Skittles, Wispa, Lego, two ThunderCats figurines, a pint of liquor, and a couple of half-empty pill bottles.

I pulled out the two action figures and examined them. "These are for the kid?"

"We promised him a ThunderCat, so I bought two at the John Lewis toy department. You'll head back to Glastonbury mid-afternoon."

"I'm not coming home with you?"

"No, you need to take the bus."

I was okay with that. I was more than okay with earning fifty pounds for being nice to a little kid.

Chapter 12

ARTHUR

After our trip up the Tor the night Nathan was incarcerated, I didn't see Ernie much except at school, and even then, he bunked off so often I stopped craning my neck to catch his eye in the back row. Finally, one Friday night, he showed up for supper just like the old days. My mother was thrilled to see him and fed him the usual double helping. Afterward, she told us to never mind clearing up, saying it had been far too long since Ernie had come over. So he followed me into my room, flung himself down on my bed and stared up at the ceiling, wordless, as I tried to finish a review of James Herriot's *Dog Stories*—a book I chose as much for Ernie as for Miss P. and her customers, with its self-portrait of a country vet who nobly devotes his life to relieving the pains of Magnus the Difficult, Cedric the Flatulent, and every other hurting dog. Ernie, in another life. Eventually, sighing, Ernie piped up, "Nathan told me about a shop selling real cheap stereo equipment. Do you want to go?" I put down my pen, rubbed my eyes, and tore myself away from Herriot's tiny Yorkshire village.

I looked at my watch. It was after eight. "You want to buy a stereo? Now? Is the shop even open?"

"Sure. You up for it?"

In less than fifteen minutes, riding our bicycles through the moonless night, past a slew of redundant factory buildings and the Greenbank swimming pool, we were outside a storefront with heavily barred windows in the village of Street. There were no street lamps, but I could make out a small hand-painted sign: *Easy Pawn. Antiques, Curios, Jewellery*. It was long past the time when most shops had closed.

"Hockers and buyers need to be buzzed in," Ernie said.

He led me down a side alley to a door with a keypad. He entered a code and pointed to a surveillance camera above us. When the door unlocked from the inside and Ernie pushed it open, I felt like we were walking into forbidden territory—a poorly lit hallway with half a dozen unmarked doors. Silently, one opened.

A man's voice called, "Hello, Ernie. Who's your friend?"

Through the door was a claustrophobic hodgepodge of cameras, jewellery, musical instruments, power tools, coin collections and guns, presided over by a burly pawnbroker in a black leather jacket. I found it a bit nerve-racking that Ernie had used a code to enter this place. I stood there facing a glass case of firearms, waiting for some new misadventure to unfold.

The pawnbroker came over to me carrying a giant metal ring that held a scary number of keys. "Would you like to see how a handgun feels in your palm?" he asked me and unlocked the case.

"Okay," Ernie said on my behalf.

In a flash I was holding what the man told me was a Glock pistol. An automatic. It was heavier than I expected. I thought I would smell the blood-tang of metal, but it was odourless.

In a radio announcer's baritone, the pawnbroker addressed me. "If you want it, of course, I'll need to do a background check, look for felonies, any domestic violence charges, that kind of thing. I could give you a pretty good deal on a preowned Ruger."

I found myself staring at the faint traces of his moustache, which stretched from inside his nose all the way out to his sideburns on either side. I thought he was joking, but he didn't crack a smile. I handed the Glock back, feeling like I'd tripped across some new line that should never have been crossed.

"It's okay. I'm good," I said.

Ernie, meanwhile, had been scouring the shelves for a stereo. He ended up buying a second-hand four-piece Sanyo system, with not a scratch on its finish, for fifty pounds. That was a lot of money, but I found it a relief that he was about to pay for something as unwieldy as a sound system, and even more of a relief that we were going to leave the shop with an item that wouldn't need to be hidden under my bed.

Ernie told the pawnbroker, with whom he was clearly acquainted, "We rode over on bikes, so we'll come and get it later."

The man nodded and gave us a wave as we left the way we came.

There had been a prominent notice on the shop wall stating that pawn-brokers weren't allowed to sell to minors. I was so tall I could pass for older, but Ernie sometimes looked like he was twelve. I was tempted to ask him for the backstory that had facilitated the illegal sale, but I didn't. Evidently, Ernie now had a sideline that, thank Jesus, Mary and Joseph, didn't include me.

In the days and weeks that followed that trip to the pawnshop, Ernie came to first period, if he showed up to school at all, with stoner eyes and a lethargy that was unlike him. He wouldn't tell me where he was getting the dope and I didn't want to know. That he had fifty pounds to spend on a stereo was another worry altogether.

I guess I had grown tired of being his accomplice. I never said that out loud, but he got the message. I regret that now. Worse are my regrets that Ernie and I never talked about what had begun for both of us in St. Nick's vestry with the Zipper and now seemed to be pulling him towards what-ever was going on in that pawnshop.

When my grandfather called my mum that fall to ask if Ernie and I could come work for a weekend in the orchard, I wasn't sure Ernie would say yes. Grandad needed us to put grease bands around the trunks of his Red Prince trees to prevent winter moths from inching up the bark and laying eggs in the branches. But when I asked him, he agreed in a flash, showing up on his bike early the next Saturday morning with another swollen eye and cracked lip from his stepdad's belt buckle. I didn't ask what the row was about, and it seemed to me Ernie was grateful that I didn't make a fuss.

The ride, under a gleaming sun, took over two hours. As usual, Ernie was way ahead of me, his blue T-shirt the exact colour of the sky. I felt ridiculously happy to be back in his company. We were almost fifteen, but that day I felt as light-hearted as a kid.

My grandfather was waiting for us on the road by the battered For Sale sign. The orchard had been listed for as long as I could remember without any interest whatsoever from a buyer. Waving his dented straw hat, he called, "Just in time. Two strapping lads. Come and have supper."

"He means breakfast," I said under my breath.

"Grandad!" I shouted. "Remember Ernie?"

"Course I do. He's unforgettable."

We worked for seven hours straight, banding so many trees my delighted grandfather complimented us on doing a proper job and rewarded us with a quart of his homemade cider and some fat cheddar and chutney sandwiches. Sweet and delicious, the cider wasn't anything like the bitter red wine in the chalice the Zipper had us drink from, which dried out my mouth. My mother had smelled it on my breath once and gone to bed with swollen eyes. That was the same week she'd seen my stolen Y-fronts.

We settled under one of the sycamores with our feast. A little silly from cider, Ernie pulled a sterling silver keychain with a tiny red glass apple on it from his pocket. "I'm going to give this to your grandfather," he said. "Coming?"

I shook my head. "You go on. I'm happy sitting here." Mr. Holmes, our history teacher, had one just like it, and I worried my face would kink in front of my grandfather.

When Ernie came back, I asked him if he'd stolen it from inside Mr. Holmes's desk.

"No," he said. "I found another one just like it because I thought your Grandad would like it."

I was unconvinced. Some days I was certain Ernie had zero sense of right and wrong, and on others, he thought to brighten someone's week with a stupid little keychain.

He flopped down beside me. "I hope it's okay that I kind of adopt your grandfather sometimes." Maybe because I'd caught him in a white lie, he began to talk. "After Mum kicked my real dad out because he drank so much, we lost touch with him and his entire family. And my mum's parents died before I was born, I think: I don't remember them at all. She was in such bad financial shape, though, they'd left her the house in their will, and her siblings got pissed about it. They shunned her from then on, and I don't think she's ever tried to reach out to them. I think she's ashamed—of us or who she's married to now—and dreams of what she could have become without us." I waited for Ernie to say more, and for once he did. "Nathan took it quite hard—her kicking my dad out. I was so young I didn't really hang out with them, but he and Dad were besties. My father taught Nathan how to unclog a drain, fix the leaky taps, replace a light switch, although none of the repairs seemed to stick. Nathan always says he is going to try and find our dad one day. He has his Cheaneys."

"Nathan thinks your dad will recognize him because he'll be wearing his old shoes?" I scoffed. "Talk about a long shot."

He rolled his eyes. "Cheaneys last a lifetime."

"Do you miss him? Your dad, I mean?"

"I don't know. He doesn't seem to miss me. Or Nathan. Mum told us once when we were hassling her about an allowance that our dad grew up with nothing. His family didn't own a washing machine or a Hoover. They had a pit latrine. My mum said Dad's job was to make sure a bowl near the latrine was kept filled with sugar, water, white vinegar and a squish of dish soap to keep the flies down. He left home at fourteen to be a stable boy. Nathan got his shoes, but he never left me a damn thing."

"He gave you the singing gene. That's worth something. And maybe your mathematical abilities. I bet he knows a ratio from a square root."

"That's what I like about you, Arthur. You look on the bright side."

He was giving me too much credit.

"Nathan says my dad was mad for the Dubliners, and that 'Whiskey in the Jar' was the song he sang when he was out on the piss. He was handsome too—a real matinee idol. My mum fell for his looks, and tolerated his fooling around long enough for the two of us to be born. Then he gave my mother the clap and she put everything he owned in black rubbish bags and had Nathan carry them to the council bins. My dad never gave my mother anything either."

"Except the clap?" I didn't know what the clap was.

"Good one, Arthur. She made sure Mr. and Mrs. Mullins were watching as she booted him out the door carrying his one battered suitcase. Then she took the coach all the way to a chemist in London to get the medicine she needed because she was mortified Dr. Addicott would find out. For that trip, she made sure no one was watching."

I was putting two and two together, imagining Mrs. Castlefrank riddled with something like syphilis, a disease we'd been warned about in the hygiene and morality classes taught by the knowledgeable Sister Hildegarde.

"How did she pay the bills once your dad was gone?"

"After he drank his way out the door, you mean? She started cleaning houses, then worked at the pharmaceutical plant in Yeovil putting syringes in boxes. When they automated that job, she moved on to shiftwork at the hospital canteen. My mum once told me I likely had fifty siblings from

Penzance to Norwich on account of Dad's fooling around." Ernie stopped and took a breath. "I guess he was a sex maniac."

It was the most Ernie had ever said about his family in one go. The cider had definitely loosened his tongue—it might have been the most he'd ever revealed in his entire life. I was on edge that with all this talking, he might mention the Zipper. It was an actual relief when he asked me if my own dad ever drank and slept around.

"I don't think so," I said. "But what do I know? I was only six when he died, and Mum still talks about him like he walked on water. I've never told you this, but she sent me away before the funeral to live with my aunt Belinda and Grandad right here in Crewkerne. I wet the bed for going on two years so Auntie Belinda sent me back." I was trying to make Ernie laugh, but he didn't.

"Your mother gave you away for all that time?" Ernie propped himself up, wide-eyed, brow furrowed.

"She told me it was because my aunt didn't have children."

"And you believed her? She was sharing you? What mother does that?" Until that moment, Ernie had thought my mother was perfect.

My instinct was to defend her, but I found I couldn't. Instead, I rolled away so that Ernie couldn't see my hot face as I hugged my knees.

"I was a mistake," I blurted. "My mother *had* to get married. She was eighteen and my father was thirty years older. It was a disgrace. Do you know what's it like to spend your entire life thinking you weren't wanted?"

"That's all you've got to complain about? Do you think God has time to keep track of all the people who have sex before they're married? There'd be no time for anything else. Actually, what the hell am I saying? There is no God. You and I know that if anyone does, Arthur." Ernie's voice was like flint. "I'm alone. You're alone."

"I spent the first four months of my life in a dresser drawer until my father thought to buy a cot."

"Was the drawer kept open or closed?" Ernie teased, then when that didn't make me laugh, he said, "At least your father married your mother. And she must have loved him, given that she still cries about him sometimes. She could have left you at the fire station—like that Aldonna Tompkin, who left her baby in a milk crate at the front door, hopped on a bus and disappeared forever."

"That drawer, though—maybe that's why I have claustrophobia."

Ernie snorted. That was an anxiety of mine he knew all about. The first time I had a bad reaction I was with Ernie in the lift at Dearborn's department store. I couldn't catch my breath and thought I was dying. He was the one who told me it was just claustrophobia, a fear of small spaces, and that I would probably survive another day.

Still, I was glad that he didn't want to talk about any other reasons why I might have a fear of confined spaces.

"So your parents didn't have much money—you've never been as poor as us. Every week we get a box of tinned food donated by the parish," Ernie said. "And that Christly powdered milk!" He stuck his finger down his throat and made gagging noises. "And then my mother puts the empty box at the edge of the road even though 'For the Castlefranks' is written on the side in permanent ink. *Permanent* ink. It might as well say 'For the outcasts and losers of Glastonbury.'"

Ernie picked up a windfallen apple and threw it so hard I thought his arm would come off. "I'm never going to be a charity case. Did you hear me, Arthur? Never."

A silence fell between us, and then Ernie whispered, "It actually sounds like your mother went off the deep end when he died. That's love."

Suddenly, it seemed selfish of me to say that it might have been love, but that I had felt like an orphan for two whole years. Ernie had far more unplugged holes in his life than I did.

We fell silent for a while, listening to the wind drop the last of the apples onto the thick carpet of grass and leaves. "Terrible things happen for no reason," Ernie said as he lay down again. "I wish I'd had a proper father."

"Me too."

I closed my eyes and, defenceless from cider and emotion, drifted helplessly into a familiar replaying of my father's last day. He and my mother were about to go to a wedding in Weston-super-Mare and he'd opted to shower before he got dressed. My mother, fussing with her red lipstick at her dressing table, heard the familiar bang in the water pipe when he turned off the taps, and then the shower curtain being dragged along the metal rod.

He emerged several minutes later, pink and smelling of shaving soap, his dressing gown belted at the hips. In the bedroom, he dropped a quick kiss on her hair, and went to the bed where she'd laid out his black suit, his white shirt and tie. His brogues. He pulled on his trousers, then sat shirtless on the edge of the bed and reached out for her with both hands. She saw him reflected in the mirror, and she turned to see his body tremble as though an electric current had entered his foot and exited through the top of his head, carrying away his life force. He slumped sideways and she ran to him. She pushed him back against the pillow and raised his legs onto the bed, but he was already gone.

When she began to wail, I came running up the stairs from Alfredo's tailor shop, where he had been teaching me how to thread a needle. I found her gripping my father's shoulders as if she could stand him up again. His jaw hung sideways, not where it was supposed to be. No decibel will wake the dead, but my mother kept trying. When she spotted me, she sobbed harder and sent me back downstairs. Alfredo called for an ambulance, and then he blocked the door so I wouldn't see my father's body go bumping down the stairs on a stretcher.

Soon I was sent away. When my mother brought me home again, I begged to hear the particulars of my father's death far more often than was healthy. This was a story that came to me in tiny pieces. She mostly deflected my requests, but Alfredo was happy to oblige, and soon my most vivid memory of my father, Bramley W. Barnes, was a scene I hadn't witnessed, but felt like I had. My mother cherished her pictures of him, hoarded them, even. But as far as I knew, she never went to visit his grave. I went as often as I could, running my hand over the name and dates on the tiny grey tombstone, so cold to the touch and with so little prominence in the graveyard that his whole existence seemed shrunken and unimportant.

Ernie pelted me with an apple, jolting me out of my daydream.

"My father," I said.

"What about him?"

"After my father died, I was told to pack my pyjamas and some clothing. I don't remember if anyone helped me. I have a vague memory of sitting in the front seat of Alfredo's car in a swirl of cigarette smoke. My overnight case was on the back seat, but I'd forgotten my plush lamb on my bed."

"She didn't think to make sure you had your lamb?"

"I don't think she could think about anything but losing him. An hour later, I was looking into the eyes of Auntie Belinda here in Crewkerne, but the sight of my father's crooked jaw wouldn't go away. I had nightmares, but I refused to leave the spare bedroom even when I wet the bed." I didn't tell Ernie that I was afraid if I moved my mother wouldn't be able to find me.

"Are you crying?"

"No." I rolled onto my stomach and watered the cool grass with my hot tears.

"Well, at least she sent you to an apple orchard. It could have been a lot worse. I've heard of mothers who smother their unwanted babies with pillows."

"Stop it, Ernie."

"I'm just trying to look on the bright side, the way you always do. You're back on the honours list at school. You're a famous writer.

Miss Phillips at the bookshop adores you. Your mother—yeah, she couldn't handle things for a while, but she's nothing like my mother." His anger took me by surprise.

"You'd be on the mathematics roll of honour if you handed in your work. You act like you're dead from the neck up."

"And who would care?"

We heard a dog barking in the distance then, and Ernie got up and climbed the ladder propped against a nearby apple tree to see if he could spot the animal, but no luck.

I got up too, brushing bits of dried grass from my trousers, and went to stand under him. "When I lived here, I overheard my auntie talking with Grandad about my mother one time. I guess my mum went out one day and came home with three Labrador retriever puppies. She wanted to take care of something, it seemed, but couldn't. She forgot to buy dog food, or take them outside for walks, or clean up after them. They were barking and crying for days and days, and she couldn't get up. I guess Alfredo finally called someone to come and take them away." I shook the ladder. "She tried to replace me with three puppies," I shouted.

Ernie looked down at me with his mouth open.

"Why are you looking at me like that?"

"I don't think I've ever heard you shout before. Did the puppies make it?"

"I was too afraid to ask." For the first time ever, I pictured the soft brown bodies of the three exhausted, dehydrated puppies, hoarse from barking and struggling to stay alive, and realized the kind of emptiness she must have been trying to fill. Until then, all I could see was that I hadn't been enough.

From up on the ladder, Ernie looked down at me. "I couldn't keep a kitten alive." As Ernie spoke, a magpie crested across the sky, swerved, then came to rest on a branch beside him. Ernie extended his palm with a tiny chunk of apple on it. The magpie dipped its head to eat the apple, then flexed its legs and rose into the air, graceful wings outstretched.

"That dead kitten had nothing to do with you, Ernie. You'll be a famous breeder or a zookeeper by the looks of it. A real somebody."

He smiled ruefully at the bird in retreat, and imitated the sound of the magpie, then launched into a series of other expert imitations: a red-tailed hawk, a peregrine falcon, and of course, a raven. When he came back down the ladder, we both flopped on to the grass again. With my grandfather nowhere in sight, he pulled a baggie of marijuana and a pack of papers from the depths of one of his many pockets and expertly rolled a fat joint. When he dug out a pack of matches, I took it from his hands. My eyes went to the writing on the cover: *Elm Guest House Hotel, 69 Old Bond St., Bath BA1 1BP UK.*

"Keep the matches," he said.

I took great care not to look at him. Our silence when it came to certain subjects was buckled to our chests like a safety harness.

I held the flame to the joint. He took a deep drag, the end glowing red, then passed it to me, laughing as he coughed and exhaled. "I got this wicked good stuff from a friend, but I nicked the Zig-Zag papers. Almost got caught."

"Which friend?"

He didn't answer me, and I didn't push. He didn't explain what he was doing with matches from a hotel in Bath either. Instead, after two more long inhales, he winced and said, "My lips still hurt. You smoke the rest." He watched as I took a small puff, then snuffed the joint out and tucked the rest of it in my pocket. On top of the cider, it was too much.

Ernie pulled out Nathan's harmonica, placed it gingerly between his cracked lips, and played a few riffs of a lullaby.

"I thought you said your lips hurt," I told him. "And that's a new song. Where did you learn that one?"

"The Zipper."

"Seriously? The Zipper taught you a lullaby?" All of sudden, every-thing was too much.

He nodded, then shifted into one of his Pogues standards as we got ourselves up and walked back to the farmhouse.

That night, we slept over at Grandad's in the same room I'd been con-signed to when I was six. I fell asleep, still unsettled that Ernie had learned a lullaby from the Zipper.

It was a Friday night in early December. Ernie had showed up at our flat before I got home from school. I arrived to find him and my mother finishing up an Advent wreath for the altar at St. Nick's. After tea, she'd gone over to church to deliver it, along with a box of purple, pink and white candles. Ernie and I were out walking the streets, going nowhere in particular, when Ernie told me he had figured out a new way to nick as much as forty pounds from the Sunday collection. He pulled a key from his pocket, flashed it, then stuck it back where it came from.

Five or six pounds might go unnoticed. Forty seemed flagrant.

Digging a handful of shelled peanuts out of his jacket, he began to throw them into the bushes for any small animals that might be lurking unseen. I pulled a tenner out of my back pocket and waved it at him, explaining that the Zipper had been giving me money to start a university fund. Ernie fixed me with a look. In that moment silence was sufficient between us when it came to what went on in the vestry—neither of us was capable of articulating what happened behind that locked door even if we'd wanted to break the silence.

Soon Ernie was trying the handles of parked cars, another one of his errant pastimes, insisting that people who left their valuables in their cars were begging for them to be stolen. The clunk of each door was so loud I found myself nervously scanning the road for eyewitnesses. He'd bunked off school that day, and refused to say where he'd been. I tried to guess from his appearance, but he'd worn the same clothes for a few days running—a denim jacket with the arms cut off that I suspected had belonged to Nathan over a long-sleeved black jumper—so it wasn't much of a clue.

Suddenly rifling through cars wasn't enough of a rush to offset his mood. "Let's go to the pictures in Bridgwater," he proposed, blowing hot air onto his red fingers. He didn't have a hat or gloves to help stave off the shivers, and his voice had an uncomfortable edginess. I wondered if he'd taken some kind of upper.

"What's playing?" I asked.

"*The Exorcist*. We need a good scare, otherwise we might die of boredom."

And so we hopped on a bus bound for Bridgwater and got to the cinema in time to catch the late show, which was packed.

As we watched the movie, about an innocent girl possessed by the devil and a troubled priest suffering a crisis of conscience, Ernie remained unmoved. But I wasn't able to tell myself that Regan's mutilated face had been achieved with special effects and found my feelings well and truly manipulated. On the bus home, Ernie cackled at me, rotating his neck to imitate devil possession. When he saw how spooked I still was, he escalated. I changed seats. He followed, taunting me with the swivelling of his neck. That night, Ernie was the chaser instead of the chased, and he only gave it up when he realized that I was feeling truly shaken.

Maybe as a gesture of remorse, Ernie pulled a leather tri-fold wallet from the pocket of his sleeveless jean jacket and flipped it open on my lap. "All yours," he said.

In the bus-lit gloom, I could see that it was stuffed with money and pieces of ID. A clear plastic pocket held a photo of two girls in matching red velvet dresses standing in front of a tinsel-covered Christmas tree. The smaller girl had lost her front teeth, her face an explosion of gummy happiness. To this point, none of our stolen items had felt like personal property. I snapped the wallet shut and closed my fingers around the buttery leather. Stuck to the underside was a yellow bus ticket. I peeled it off and stared at the markings.

"You went to Bath today?" I asked. "Is that why you skipped school?"

Ernie grabbed the ticket from my hand, tore it in half and then in half again, and tossed the bits on the floor.

"Why did you go to Bath?"

"I had things to do."

"Like what?"

"Don't be such a Nosy Parker." He turned and faced the black road running outside the bus window.

I shoved the pickpocketed wallet into my trouser pocket, but the shiny details of the photograph were burned onto my eyeballs. The sisters were holding hands. Someone had curled their hair and tied it with red ribbon. Ernie had skipped school and gone to Bath. Anxiety tied my tongue and I stopped asking questions.

When I was with him these days, I was afraid to admit I was afraid.

Ernie got off before me, giving me half a wave from the pavement, and sloped towards home, shoulders caved, the sleeves of his jumper yanked down over his hands. When he turned down a side street, I bent to pick up the four torn pieces of the bus ticket and put them in my pocket.

I was too gutless to return the wallet to the rep cinema where I figured Ernie must have stolen it, or to contact the wallet's owner, Martin Stuart Quimby of Upper Lansdown Road in Bath. With each passing hour, I hoped I would care less about the Quimby family and their perfect little girls in front of the Christmas tree. No such luck: I became obsessed about the contents. I hid Mr. Quimby's driving licence under my bed, along with his credit card from Lloyds bank, his wad of cash, and a receipt to collect three pairs of trousers from the Regency Laundry. I couldn't hide from the uneven knee socks and hair ribbons, the delighted faces. I felt like I had walked too far into the woods and could not find the way back.

Exhausted from two nights of sleepless indecision, I discreetly set the restuffed billfold by the till at the Copperfield and Twist on Saturday afternoon when Miss Phillips stepped into her office and retreated to my desk. She seemed out of sorts for several days thereafter. I think she knew I had something to do with it, because she couldn't quite look me in the eye. She didn't question me, though she made sure to tell me when the relieved, and apparently very wealthy, Mr. Quimby had stopped in to retrieve his missing property. Magnanimously, he'd bought a dozen books from the shop and also insisted she accept a twenty-pound reward, which she made a point of telling me that she intended to put into the poor box at St. Nick's. Ernie would be delighted: he knew where the little key was kept and he pillaged it regularly.

Chapter 13

ERNIE

After I left Arthur the night we went to the cinema in Bridgwater, I changed my mind about going home. Once he'd returned from Bath, Casper had gone on to London to meet clients, and so for twenty-four hours, I lay on a couch in the Pint Room, stoned on benzos, thoughts drifting in and out like fog.

I'd arrived at the pawnshop an hour before dawn on Friday, as planned. Casper was a freak about punctuality. We had driven to Bath on the A39, as usual. After I got back to Glastonbury in the afternoon, I'd gone straight over to Arthur's flat. He wasn't home yet, so I asked Mrs. Barnes if I could wait for him and when she said yes, I helped her with her Advent wreath.

"Is there anything else I can do for you?" I'd begged when we were finished attaching the candles, and she let me unpack the decorations for their Christmas tree and test the string of lights for dead bulbs. I could tell she wanted to ask why I'd got there before Arthur, but she didn't. When he finally came up the stairs and into the flat, cradling a tall stack of books, she went into the kitchen, pulled a chicken from the fridge and began to cook us one of her delicious teas. I set the table and folded paper serviettes for each place. I needed something to be normal, but I couldn't settle. I needed Arthur to be Arthur, and he was, sorting through an enormous bundle of papers and novels in his room, oblivious to my state of mind. Everything was as it should be, but nothing felt right.

I swallowed another benzo to blot out the events of the morning.

Casper and I had arrived in Bath as the sun spread a weak web over a chilly stretch of Old Bond Street. It was my third trip in a month. We had waited in a half-empty café with a bird's-eye view of a red telephone box near the entrance. At Casper's request, the waitress had seated us in the booth closest to the door. Farther down the road, the British flag affixed to the facade of the Elm Guest House Hotel was waving its greeting. We ordered soft-boiled eggs with toast soldiers and rashers of bacon. Casper asked for coffee and I got a milkshake, which seemed like the most indulgent thing I could order with my breakfast to cover a sense of foreboding. When the phone rang outside, Casper swallowed what was in his mouth and rose from the table.

"Keep your eyes on my bag," he said and slipped outside. I saw him look left and right before he lifted the receiver, but there was no one else out on the inky street. When his back was to me, I pulled the heavy-duty zipper open and stole a quick glance inside. Video equipment, a camera, a tripod. Alcohol. I closed the bag, drained my glass, sat on my hands and watched my eggs congeal in their little white cups. From my windcheater I withdrew a book of math puzzles to calm my nerves.

When he returned, he was all smiles. Seated once again across from me, he spun his lucky penny on the melamine tabletop and held it to the light. "We have a couple of hours to kill before we head to the hotel," he said, then lowered his voice. "Once I get the envelope with the key from the front desk, you head straight up to the room. Wait for us. I'll knock three times, you open the door, and I deliver the boy. You play with him or watch some telly or both. When I return with my client, I'll knock again—the sign to leave your key on the table and make yourself scarce.

He'll use a second key. Take the fire exit to the street and catch the bus back to Glastonbury. The station is on Southgate."

I nodded to show I understood the plan, then swallowed. The milkshake sat uneasily in my stomach.

Casper checked his watch, then looked up at me and said, "Do you know how to play poker?"

When I shook my head, he brought out a deck of cards from inside his coat and called to the waitress, "Bring this lad another milkshake, and one for me too. Unless you want one of those Knickerbocker Glories with whipped cream and chocolate sprinkles?" When I shook my head, he said, a little more quietly, "Do you need me to call your school? Migraine again?" He tipped a thumb to the telephone box.

"No. It'll be fine."

He began to shuffle. "The first rule of success at poker is to size up your opponents. You check out how the other players are dressed, how old they are, how well off they seem. Haircuts. Rings. Shoes tell you a lot. You have to concentrate in order to find the fish."

"The fish?"

"The weakest player in the room. The one you target." Casper took an exaggerated look around the restaurant, as if to demonstrate his powers of observation. "The best poker players don't give anything away. They can control their emotions, are focused, intelligent and patient. Above all, they know when to fold." He tapped his lucky penny on the melamine to make sure I was paying attention to his words of wisdom.

When the phone rang a second time, there was no need to answer. Fontaine asked for the bill, tipped the waitress, and we walked towards the flag that shivered in the wind.

The crowded hotel lobby had a multitude of groupings of wingback chairs, separated by potted palms, and a decorated Christmas tree with an angel on top. The sound system was playing seasonal music. A stream of guests entered and exited the four bronze lifts, so I knew we wouldn't stand out. I was still queasy from the milkshakes. As Fontaine went to the front desk, I tried to look inconspicuous, studying the lunch menu on an easel outside of a posh bar called Fanny's Place.

After he slipped me the envelope, I took the lift to the fourth floor. The door slid open and I stepped out into a long, dark hallway. Stale air made me think of holding my breath. The wall sconces seemed to be at half-mast. I walked soundlessly on thick carpet to room 423—farthest from the lift, but closest to the fire exit to the back stairs.

I fished the key out of the envelope and opened the door to find the lights already on. A man's blazer was draped over the back of a chair and I could smell cologne—peaches and something spicy. Edible. But the bedroom and bathroom were empty. A razor, shaving cream and toothpaste were in a tan-coloured leather travel kit on the bathroom counter. A pair of pressed trousers looped over a wire hanger hung from the doorknob.

I sat on the edge of the bed for a while, then stood up and wandered the room, checking inside the drawers. I tried on the man's blazer to gauge his size, ran my hands over the smooth fine wool and felt the lump of a wallet. I pulled it from the pocket and flipped it open. *Martin Stuart Quimby. 274 Upper Lansdown Road, Bath.*

I heard the knocks, hung the blazer back on the chair, and opened the door to see a small, frightened boy. I scanned the empty hallway, then drew him inside.

Chapter 14

ARTHUR

I found Ernie in study hall flipping through a copy of *Infoworld*, his rucksack tucked between his feet underneath the table. He'd become protective of that bag, and that was fine with me. I couldn't keep up with his missed homework anymore anyway, and I told myself I really didn't want to know what was in there beyond the usual cargo of computer magazines and rolling papers. Still, when I sat down beside him, I couldn't help but peek into its opened mouth, then leaned over to tweak the red hair of the ThunderCats figure I'd glimpsed within.

"You reliving your childhood?" I asked.

He rammed the figure deeper into the rucksack, zipping it so fast he almost took off my fingers. Instead of answering me, he pulled a copy of Edgar Allan Poe's short stories from a side pocket, hunched over it and began to read. But not before I noticed the telltale Copperfield and Twist sticker on the back cover.

"Ernie, where'd you get that book?"

"Where do you think?"

"Did you pay for it?"

When he didn't answer me, I said, "You stole it from Miss Phillips, didn't you?" The theft felt as personal as a slap.

"I have better things to read than this shite," he said, and tossed the book at me, the pages, covered in his inky annotations, fluttering. I caught it mid-air, got up and put the book in the rubbish bin, depriving us both, and walked out of study hall to the dismay of Mr. Henry.

We didn't speak for the rest of the day—my preferred fighting style. I thought Ernie understood that every other shop was fair game, but not the Copperfield and Twist.

We had arranged to spend the following Saturday hanging out at his house so I could meet his new singing canary. I rode over on my bike, as planned, still pissed at Ernie. And so, when he left me alone in his room to go downstairs to find the bird a little reward of fresh fruit, I carried the cage to the window, lifted the sash and opened the cage door, and out the canary flew.

Ernie caught me at it. "You idiot! He'll freeze to death!"

We both looked down to where the bright yellow bird was hopping around the back garden in a tiny circle, cheeping in distress.

Full of regret, I trailed Ernie outside. Moving slowly and carefully, whistling a soothing tune, he was able to cup both hands around the bird. As he stood to carry it back inside, he looked at me in bewildered disgust and said, "I can't believe you would try to kill a bird."

My only defence was to attack. "I can't believe you would steal from Miss Phillips."

I jumped on my bicycle and rode home, feeling equal parts bereft and angry.

We didn't speak for a whole week and then another. Then, on Saturday night, Ernie turned up and camped just outside our front door. My mother already knew that we had fallen out, and she'd badgered me until I told her why we weren't speaking. "Maybe he stole the book as a test of your friendship," she suggested, a theory I didn't care to believe. As far as I was concerned, Ernie had been moving away from me, not the other way around: I should have been the one testing him.

To her credit, she didn't let him into the flat when he knocked. But after I'd gone to bed, she warmed up a homemade meat pie—I could smell the beef gravy from my room. Soon the front door opened and closed. Next, I heard her rummaging in the hall cupboard where she kept the extra blankets and a spare pillow. I heard the door open and close again, and then the low rumble of their conversation. I was too proud to join them, but then I heard the distinctive singsong voice of Alfredo joining in and I wrapped my duvet around my shoulders and went out to the landing in my pyjamas.

My mother, in her voluminous mint-green dressing gown with a dozen plastic curlers in her hair, was sitting on the floor beside Ernie. She patted the linoleum on the other side of her and I plunked myself down. Alfredo had settled on the floor on the opposite side of the hall and was midway through pouring glasses of Chianti for himself and my mother.

"Can you believe your mum sleeps in these things!" Ernie said to me with a wink, then reached over and squeezed one of the hard, pink barrels that decorated my mother's head. She laughed unselfconsciously, her fondness for Ernie as bright as the fluorescent lighting on the landing.

I guess we could have moved inside, but at that point Ernie pulled out a deck of cards, shuffling them like a professional. "How about I teach you all Texas Hold-'em?" he said. We stared at him, my mother's eyes already a little glassy from the wine. He began to deal, explaining the rules of poker as he went, and we each picked up our hands and tried to follow. Before we knew it, faint morning light was coming in through the tiny hallway window and we'd been playing cards for hours.

"Good heavens," my mother said. "It's nearly time to go to early Mass. I should have been in bed hours ago."

Alfredo stood, giving a mighty stretch, then wished us all good morning and headed down the stairs to his sewing machine, carrying the glasses and the empty wine bottle.

Ernie grinned at us. "Looks like I'm a terrible influence," he said. My mum bent for his plate as he gathered up the blanket and pillow and carried them to the cupboard, where he folded them away. "Sleep well, Mrs. Barnes," he called to my mother. "You, too, Arthur." And then he was out the door and down the stairs three at a time.

As we listened to him whistle his way out to the street, my mother said, "Ernie needs to know you're in his corner. And with Nathan gone, he needs that more than ever. Remember what he did for you in court over that stupid Parker pen you stole? Ernie would throw himself on a grenade for you, Arthur."

I knew she was right. But I also knew that neither she nor I understood half of what Ernie was capable of anymore. Through every hour of that absurd night, I'd wondered how Ernie had learned to play poker like a Vegas card shark.

Chapter 15

ERNIE

There were more trips to Bath after Christmas. The routine when we got there never varied. Though I sometimes caught a whiff of adult male presence, I never saw Martin Quimby in the flesh, or whoever else was meeting the boys from the care homes. In early February, waiting once again at our regular table in the café closest to the phone box, Casper confided that Quimby had recently asked for what he called "*pesce più giovane.*"

The Zipper sometimes liked to speak his native Italian to his brother, which is why I recognized one of the words. "What do you mean he wants fish?"

"Younger fish." He looked at me like I was dense. I got it.

"How young?"

Casper shrugged, then rubbed his fingers against his thumb to indicate that his prices were about to go up.

To be able to pay me as much as he did for a couple hours of my time, plus cover my breakfast and bus fare, Casper must have already been charging extortionate sums. The boys I'd been entertaining at the Elm Guest House Hotel were ten or eleven, I figured. I didn't want to know where Casper would find boys who were younger, and tried to focus instead on how good it felt to fleece a man like Quimby, so lauded and respectable, and hypocritical.

Then Fontaine startled me by asking, "Who's that older friend you hang around with? The one you brought to the pawnshop that time."

"Arthur. He's the same age as me."

Fontaine raised his eyebrows and I realized he was looking for another recruit to his team, not fodder for the Quimbys of the world.

"No," I said. "This is just you and me. Arthur is a good guy."

He held his palms up, fending off my outrage. "I'm just asking. Quimby has a number of interested friends he's directing my way, and I want to be able to keep up with demand. It's going to be very profitable because, they, like him, have a lot to lose and value how smoothly our operation runs. These are higher-ups, Castlefrank. They move in business, media and entertainment circles. Even government. They pay for the service, and the insulation, we provide. Transgression is as much of an allure as the actual encounter. That's what brings Quimby back to the table for seconds and thirds. Don't forget that. It's like any addiction." The phone rang outside, and he stepped away to field the call, patting my shoulder as he went by.

I couldn't explain my need to protect Arthur. I guess it was just because he and his mum were the only decent people I knew. Also, he'd be shit at this. A stalk of parsley. Recently, he seemed to have lost his nerve entirely. He'd had no one to teach him to be tough, the way Nathan had taught me. My brother had taken all the beatings for me when I was young, but then he tried his best to prepare me for life without him. He'd taken me to a boxing ring in Pilton to spar. Another time he'd thrown darts at me down in the cellar to train me to move quickly enough to stay out of harm's way. Fat chance when it came to my stepfather's belt buckle. The night before he left home, Nathan came into my room, saying that he and I needed to have matching homemade tattoos "in case we had to find each other one day." It didn't make any sense, really, but I lay there, tears streaming down the sides of my cheeks, as he burned a hole in the flesh of my stomach with the lit end of a cigarette, and then a matching one in his own. And after it healed, and he was gone, it was kind of a comfort. When I have a hard time getting to sleep at night, I trace that circular scar with my finger, and think of how much worse my brother has it in that cell in Bristol. Then I mentally count up the cash I'm saving to pay down his fine.

Arthur used to get as much of a thrill out of stealing as I did, but even at the height of it, he spooked like a right wimp. He thought I didn't notice the day he finally spotted my sterling cross. He looked so shocked I thought he might pass out. But I'd already seen his. And Willoughby's and Godfrey's, and a few more too. It wasn't hard to figure out who was on the Zipper's assembly line. Being awarded that cross let me capitalize even more on the Zipper's interests. I'd been on the take for years and I just assumed Arthur was too, in his own submissive way. After all, he had waved that tenner from the Zipper in my face.

But we never talked about it. Arthur's cross went missing right after he saw mine. I have no idea what he did with it. Nathan had been given one too, by the priest who'd served at St. Nick's before the Zipper took over. His might have been the first. I never talked to Arthur about that either. Nathan had lasted about a year or two in the role of altar boy. Then he did something that was hushed up—he'd defaced one of the stations of the cross with a black permanent marker—and soon after he was sent to the Heathdale School in North Somerset for children with special needs. I was only four when it happened, so it's all a bit fuzzy. And Nathan never talked about it either. The cross or the defacement.

When Casper came back, I said, "So, what about these new clients?"

"We'll need to spread out a bit. And after today, we're switching locations, adding a few more hotels, a few private residences."

He picked up the tiny black book he kept locked to his belt, invisible under his leather coat. He'd left it with me once while he was on the

phone, and I knew what it contained: names and addresses of clients, specifics of their preferences, and details about the boys, from their age, to
their eye colour, to the size of their genitals, what they preferred to eat
and drink, and what they had agreed to do in the past. Casper seemed to
draw a lot of pleasure from reading and rereading his notebook. He'd
consult it, then brief me on things I needed to know before I went up the
elevator to the hotel room. Did they like 7Up or cola. Action figures or
comics. My job was to soothe them, play with them—basically normalize
the moment—and then persuade them to stay in the hotel room until the
client arrived. Most of them looked scared the first time, but with the toys,
the treats, the alcohol mixed with fizzy drinks—the attention, basically—
they all came around.

Casper said, "Just so you know, this is a new boy today, and he's
really young. His name is Ricky."

I didn't want to know his name.

The phone rang again, and Casper handed me the Batmobile Lego kit
I was to entertain the new boy with—the most expensive toy he'd bought
so far. "He's worth it," he said, and then we walked towards the flag.

When the special knock came at the hotel door—my cue to say
goodbye to Ricky—I pretended I didn't hear it. There were still Lego
pieces to assemble, and Ricky was having such a good time, I really hated
to go. There was another knock, more insistent. Pretending I had to use
the toilet, I slipped out the door and into the gloomy hallway, then took
the fire exit to the street.

I caught the next bus home, moving to the back where I could lie
across two empty seats with my knees pulled up to my chin. In a ball,
I was unseen. I reached into the inside pocket of Nathan's leather jacket,
two sizes too big, to make sure the one letter he'd written me from prison
was still there, folded over and creased. In it, he'd confessed that he'd
stolen a chequebook from Mr. Mullins next door, forged his signature
on one of the cheques and then cashed it and used the money to buy

the drugs he went to jail for. I tried not to have too many bad thoughts about my brother creeping around our neighbour's house in the middle of the night, with Mrs. Mullins incapacitated and old Mr. Mullins already so hysterical about criminals and gutted that his wife was in a wheelchair. I knew Nathan had confessed to me because he honestly felt bad about it too. Not that any judge would care about Nathan's conscience. At the end of the letter, he asked if I would go over there from time to time to check on them, and help Mr. Mullins move his wife's wheelchair, and not to forget that the left wheel was stubborn. I wrote him back right away to say that of course I would. I didn't tell him what else I was doing for him, in case anyone was reading his letters, but since he was the one who'd introduced me to Casper, maybe he already knew. I got rid of that thought as soon as I had it.

The next Wednesday night, after swallowing a Valium, I rode over to the pawnshop to pick up my pay for playing with Ricky.

I was slouched on a couch in the Pint Room, waiting for Casper to open up his cash box, when he made a call. Holding a silencing finger to his lips, he switched it to speaker phone. I immediately recognized the voice of the man who answered: Father Ziperto. I got up to leave, but Casper motioned for me to sit down again.

"Hello, Durante," he said in his velvety baritone.

Several seconds ticked by. Then the Zipper said, "I've asked you not to contact me."

"You and I were once so close we got the same tattoo on the same hand. Didn't you say then that we could never be parted? How do you expect me to leave you alone when we have so much history together? Three long years at seminary in Birmingham, before I was kicked out. And then, just after your ordination, you were moved to Montreal. You didn't bother to say goodbye."

"That wasn't my choice. I would have preferred to let you know."

"Being shuffled around is part of the game, isn't it. Shed one's skin to begin again. We need to meet."

"Whatever is on your mind, I'm not interested."

"I'm certain you will be. How is tonight at eleven p.m.? You pick the place."

"I don't think you understand. Nothing will change my mind."

Casper let a silence stretch, then said, "I have been tracking you with video surveillance equipment."

The Zipper sighed. "All right, you win. There's a children's playground near Tiller's Row. Turn right at the Burleigh Road fork. In half a mile look for the tallest willow tree. On your left-hand side, you'll see a swing set and a few benches. It's easy to miss. If you reach a sign that says Beckery, you've gone too far."

"Goodnight, Dante. I'm assuming I can still call you Dante?"

There was a click and the phone went dead.

"Do you think he'll show?"

Casper nodded. "Thanks to you and your light fingers, we have something on him. And he knows we do."

I hadn't stopped with the first three photos I'd stolen from the Zipper. Why would I, when Casper paid me well for each and every one and the Zipper never confronted me about it, or changed the key, or found another hiding spot. There were so many, a few dozen may have gone unnoticed. Or maybe he was worried if he made it an issue, I'd say no to some of the other creepy stuff he had me doing.

Casper continued. "He'll want to know what I'm up to. Durante was careful not to show his face, but he's recognizable in some of them. I have to wonder who took those photos."

He unlocked a cupboard and retrieved a cassette recorder and stowed it in his duffle bag. "While I'm gone, there will be another delivery. Photos and videos. Brand new. Never-seen-before footage. The person bringing them has his own code. Stay out of sight. Do not leave the premises. And lay off those pills—they're dangerous. You're starting to remind me of your brother."

What could be more dangerous than what I was already doing?

I didn't hang around waiting for the guy, though. After Casper left, I gave him a few minutes, then hopped on my bike and followed. Since I knew every shortcut through town from my wanderings with Arthur, I got there first, stashed my bike, and found a place to hide so that I could watch the archway. The playground was silent except for the shooshing of the wind through the long trailing branches of the willow trees that encircled the park. Low clouds blocked the moon and turned all the shapes around me to shades of black and grey.

When I spotted the Zipper in his long flapping coat, I had the urge to run. I thought he would come through the archway from the backyard of the house he'd taken me to, but instead he came walking across the park from the road as though he'd never been here before and sat down on a bench. Soon Casper slid out of the gloom and took a seat next to him. For a few minutes they didn't speak. I was tense for the sound of a siren.

Finally, the Zipper said, "Hello, Casper."

"Dante."

Despite the darkness, I could see the shine of the priest's shoes. There was no answering gleam of white at his neck: he'd removed his Roman collar.

"You're dressed as a civilian," Casper said.

"I thought it wise in this case."

The wind picked up enough to move the swings, their chains creaking softly.

The Zipper removed a silver flask from a pocket. He unscrewed the top, took a swallow, and offered it to Casper. "Single malt."

"I remember—your favourite." Casper took a sip and handed it back.

"What do you want?" the Zipper said.

"I have some of your photographs. The duplicates are selling well. We could form a sort of partnership."

"I'm not interested."

"On the contrary, you seem highly interested. For starters, you're here."

"I don't sell or trade anything. My relationships are all consensual."

"Is that what they are? Relationships? You groom those unsuspecting little boys from when they're eight or nine, and when they hit puberty, you have their full complicity. After that, there is no turning back."

"It's not like that at all. I'm no rapist."

"No, of course you're not a rapist, per se. You're a predatory, persistent and exploitive individual, whose work I've recently been profiting from. Oh, the cunning of people like us. Remember those long conversations we used to have about how abnormal it was to remain celibate, even though we'd all signed on. And what a thrill it was to find a way to be intimate without getting caught, and even more of a thrill because it was a sin against our vows."

Casper's tone was matter-of-fact, even gentle, but disgust and hatred welled in my chest.

"You forget I know the way your mind works, Dante. I know what excites you. I was closer to you than anyone at the seminary: we once spent every spare moment together. I also know how far you'll go to protect yourself. I learned it the hard way when you turned on me, telling the bishop I was prostituting myself at the St. Pancras railway station. No one was paying me for that, as you well know. But because of you, I was denied ordination, and you weren't. I couldn't accuse you in return, as I had no credibility left. And now you try to paint a rosy picture about your 'relationships.' Come now, Dante, we're grown men. Why not be partners again? I could actually help protect you."

"Being a part of any money-making enterprise would taint it all. And I don't need your help. I can protect myself, as you well know. If it comes to that, people can be cured of certain predilections through counselling."

"Oh, that's rich. Did the bishop recommend counselling when you were transferred to Montreal? For that matter, did you think I needed counselling when we hooked up? You used to tell me that our intimacy was the only thing that saved you from crippling loneliness. On the other hand, you did turn me in. But it wasn't a good enough deflection, was it. The bishop eventually found you out. The only difference between our two situations was that you were already ordained when you were caught. You were allocated protection."

"I'm sorry if I hurt you, but I have no interest in partnering with you," the Zipper said.

When he made to rise, Casper's voice rumbled on, inexorable. "I wouldn't be so hasty or short-sighted, my friend. With what I have in my possession, I could call Scotland Yard or I could call the Bishop of Clifton. Any legal trouble that followed would bankrupt St. Nicholas. Isn't it your primary obligation to ensure the Catholic Church survives into the next century?"

The two sat in silence, the priest making no further attempt to leave.

Eventually, Casper placed a heavy hand on his shoulder. "The Bishop of Clifton meets with the Pope again next March," he said. "Someone could tip off the bishop about your recent activities and then he would be morally obliged to . . ."

The Zipper removed Casper's hand. "Rome is sympathetic to the needs of priests, as you well know. Years pass before a report is investigated in any substantive way. You should be ashamed of profiting from personal mementos stolen from me. Very personal."

"Have you reported the crime?"

"You know the answer. But those photos are mine and you need to return them."

"I believe your name has recently been put forward to be an auxiliary bishop?"

"So you're blackmailing me?"

"Don't be nasty. Too many people have no sympathy for our leanings. Isn't it a relief to make common cause with someone who does? Someone who isn't judging or calling you mentally ill? Don't people like you and me deserve to be understood? If we can't get what we want and need, we feel dead inside. And when someone like us is a priest? Both the stakes and the excitement are so much higher. But to be caught? I'm sure you know that sex offenders in prison are the lowest of the low. Vilified and preyed upon. You must try to avoid a prison sentence at all costs, Dante. What I am proposing is actually a good deal for us both."

Casper fell silent again, then nodded to the arched opening covered in wisteria vines. "Did you think I wouldn't remember this place? Is that still home sweet home?"

"It's a family asset."

"An asset indeed."

"You know I have no sentimental feelings about my childhood. My mother converted to Catholicism when she married my father, and both were prone to a literal interpretation of scripture. In the book of Matthew, Jesus gives his disciples a lot of contradictory advice. He tells them to be harmless as doves. He also says that children are the property of their fathers to be punished or even killed in accordance with the father's religious beliefs and other priorities. My father took great liberties with that interpretation when it came to my brother and me. My mother abetted him."

"With zealots for parents, you still chose the priesthood?"

"I had my reasons."

"Your parents came to your ordination, as did your twin brother. They all were so proud to see you in a Roman collar. Such a visible sign of the permanent nature of the Holy Orders. Oh yes, and chastity. Had I been ordained I doubt I would have had an audience."

There was a long silence. Then the Zipper said, "I was born this way. It chose me. Nobody puts their hand up and asks for this."

"But you chose to act, and against your vows too. Dante, how do we make sense of men who only have access to sex through force?"

"I haven't forced anyone."

"Even with your eyes closed, surely you can see the truth. We will always be pariahs, Dante." The empty swings were moving in the breeze, creaking as the wind circled around the chains.

"As I recall, your mother found you with a minor. I think you told me he was eleven. You wanted to be a software engineer. Your mother intervened, finding you a path where she thought you'd be safe."

"I saw it as an unforgivable disservice to me and my future. My mathematical mind. And then I met you. At one time that felt like divine intervention." More silence.

"I'll say it again. I don't use force. Within the limitations of my role, I am a virtuous man."

Casper turned his head to face him. "Dante, it's too late for that charade. And why bother pretending: your parents are dead, and the church protects its own."

"Yes. My parents are deceased. And you're right: they never would have understood, and neither does my brother. I do my best to hide my relationships from him." The Zipper took a sip from his flask.

"I'm detecting remorse. Most offenders detach from the deed, which allows them to transgress again. And again. The temptation wells up . . ."

"Stop."

"This house will be very useful to me, as I'm sure it already is to you."

"Impossible."

"I have photographs of you with young boys inside that house. I have video footage. I remember you telling me that some children are fundamentally second class. And look at you: You seek out those broken boys, those fatherless children, the ones who are hungry for love, for nourishment. You find them before they shut down. In your photographs, the eyes are hungry, not yet dead. That's what makes them so valuable."

"You're projecting. The boys I bring here read books and listen to music with me. We play chess. Parish children line up to become altar boys."

"I'm sure they do." Casper reached into his pocket and pulled out the watch I'd pawned. "I believe this might belong to you. I remember you as painfully punctual. Seven long years in the seminary will do that to a man. Then you go from the discipline and the rigidity to being all alone in a parish, without structure and company . . . we fall prey to that loneliness."

"Did you steal this from the jeweller?"

"You collected the insurance after he told you it was lost."

"Casper, you have to let go of the past. I have. I'll be leaving Glastonbury soon. I've got word I'm in line for a larger parish in Bath."

"What's that—your fifth transfer? Have you been receiving church-led counselling before each reassignment?"

The Zipper's head snapped back as though he had physically been hit.

"No need to answer. All bishops keep confidential files. The Catholic Church's Code of Canon Law compels every diocese to preserve a secret archive in a locked safe—in your case, a record of your transgressions."

"Only the bishop has the key to the archive."

"And one day you'll be the bishop—the keeper of the files. I do believe your superiors in Rome are fully aware of your proclivities. Rather wonderful, isn't it? A fox in the henhouse. It must give you an invincible feeling. What is a young boy's word against that of an esteemed man of God like yourself?"

"You have become a bitter, twisted man."

"I'm in good company."

"What is it you want?"

"Ten boys."

"For what purpose?"

"I'm a filmmaker and a businessman. Photo sharing peer to peer does very little to generate income. I have other ideas."

Wobbling off on my bicycle, hardly daring to breathe, I made my way home to Dyehouse Lane. I didn't want to hear the Zipper agreeing to Casper's deal, but I knew he would.

After the meeting in the playground, not even the thought of accumulating more cash for Nathan's fine was enough to make me return to the Pint Room. I stopped skipping school, even though my classes felt just as pointless as they ever had. But it was something to do, and being surrounded by my classmates gave me a feeling of normalcy. Once again, I walked home with Arthur most days. He was knee-deep in work for Miss Phillips. If he wondered why I was suddenly hanging around so much again, he was smart enough not to ask.

But it couldn't last. On a Tuesday morning, early, my mum sent me to the co-op to grab some groceries before I left for school. Just as I was past the till and out the door, Casper came up behind me and grabbed my bag, then headed for his green Merc. So as not to make a scene, I followed.

"Get in," he said.

"I've got school."

"You've been AWOL for weeks, Ernie. You have to know there's no turning back for you now. You would go straight to juvenile detention and I could go to prison for a very long time for what we've already done. I'll say it nicely. Please get in the car. I need you to come with me to London."

"Now? This minute? Those are for my mother." I pointed to the bag with the potatoes, the half gallon of milk and two boxes of Weetabix.

"Yes, I realize. I've had a tip about a kid who lives in a foster home in Tower Hamlets in the northeast of the city. All you'll have to do is talk to him, soften him up. The usual. He could be your kid brother. Blue eyes that make you look twice."

Casper handed me the bag and dug a photograph out of his inside pocket to show me. He was the finest-looking boy I had ever seen, but so young. A lamb to the slaughter.

"I think this time I'll pass."

"I don't think you will. My client is willing to pay triple."

"Quimby?"

"No. This one's a BBC telly star. Your take will be five hundred pounds."

I stood there, eyes on the ground, but Casper knew he had me.

"I was certain you'd come around. The distribution for this will be huge. The UK, Germany and the Netherlands, and points east. I've begun to build our base through internet relay chat rooms. CompuServ CB Simulator."

More allurement. I tried to make my mind a blank place where no processing could occur.

"I could use a hand with the photography," Casper said. "Photography and programming are good bedfellows. Imagine manipulation. Image analysis. Instead of dodging, burning and masking, I'm working on becoming totally digital. I'm in contact with two fledgling online communities. Members only, where each person is known by a username. There's lots of money to be had. Computers are the future for us."

"Go on."

"First I'll teach you how to make your own prints from negatives in a darkroom."

"I'm only interested in learning how to take good shots of animals."

"A worthy subject." He gave me a long sideways glance to show that he was paying lip service. We both knew the real substance of Casper's operation was children.

I stared at him a second longer, then said, "Wait a sec."

I crossed the road and gave the bag of groceries to the homeless woman who lined her shoes with newspapers.

"I love you, Nathan," she said, mistaking me for my brother. I slipped her a fiver, and her face creased with joy.

I got inside the green Merc, put on my seat belt after Casper shot a look my way, and we set off for Tower Hamlets. Neither of us spoke. After a while, I palmed a pink Quaalude from my pocket and dry-swallowed it. "What's a username?" I asked.

"It's a means of authenticating people for an online service. Nothing you need to know right now." We went back to an uneasy silence.

Eventually, Casper briefed me on the name of the local school, the name of the foster family, and gave me the photo so I could study the boy's face. When we reached Bethnal Green Road in St. Peter's Ward, the streets were quiet, shabbily forgotten, and a mirror to my own hopeless feelings.

He pulled to the curb in front of a restaurant. "Stay in the car. It's a dangerous neighbourhood. I'm going to grab some breakfast takeaway."

After he returned with packets of food, we drove maybe five more minutes, then parked. We were a half block away from where the boy had been fostered out. We watched the street until we saw our boy coming along the pavement: thick mop of white-blond hair, dirty about the mouth, tiny ankles exposed by socks that didn't have enough elastic to embrace his skinny calves. He was wearing the same Smurf sweatshirt as in the photo. A wisp of a kid, walking with a bit of a limp. But that face.

"There he is, Ernie," Casper said.

I got out of the car, carrying a still-warm bacon sandwich wrapped in brown paper, and caught up with the boy in a few long strides.

"Off to school?

"Yah."

"Have you got your pen licence yet?"

He looked at me for a moment, then got it and laughed.

I said, "So you're still sharpening your pencils."

"Yep, and I also forgot my kit. I'll have to do PE in my underpants." He looked back to the care home, gauging whether he could make a run for the kit and get back to school before the bell rang.

"Don't worry, I've done that in my time. It's uncomfortable, but survivable. Hey, you look a little scrawny for a prince. What did you have for breakfast today? Pancakes with syrup? Scones smothered in clotted cream and blackberry jam?"

He stared up at me for a moment, maybe wondering where the joke was, and then answered. "Dry cereal. Milk is only on Sunday."

"I've got a bacon sandwich here. Want to share?"

He nodded so fast my heart gave a big twinge.

I unwrapped the sandwich and handed him half. When he opened his mouth to take a bite, I saw that he'd lost some of his lower baby teeth. Maybe he was so malnourished at the foster home, the adult teeth wouldn't grow in at all. When he'd polished off his share, licking the grease off his fingers, I handed him mine. For which I received a look of total wonder.

"What happened to your leg?" I said as we started walking towards his school.

"Nothing," he said between bites.

"You've got a bit of a gimp."

"Mrs. Pussett says a big wind pushed me down the stairs."

"What? Like an inside wind?"

"Yup."

"And this Mrs. Pussett. She a friend of yours?"

"No. She hets people."

"She eats people?"

He laughed behind his hand, as though that was an area of his face that needed protecting.

"No. She hets people."

I was about to ask him if he meant Mrs. Pussett hates people, but just then, Casper pulled up beside us and said, "Anyone need a lift?"

"I do," I said. Then I asked the boy, "Do you?" His mouth was too full with the last of the bacon to answer, so I opened the car door and we both climbed in.

He swallowed, then said, "Are you taking me to school? It's over there by the blue gate." He pointed with his chin to a sign that read St. Augustine's Catholic Primary.

"I see it. Hey, there's an arcade over on Diggon Street. Want to come with me?"

"I ain't never been to an arcade."

"What's your name?" I asked.

"Hatley."

"Hatley! That's a grand name for a boy. Do you have a last name too?"

"Nope."

"Are you from Ireland?" I asked, detecting the lilt of Mrs. Mullins, our neighbour.

"Is that a care home?"

"Not really. How old are you anyway? I'm guessing seven and three quarters."

"Nope, I'm ten, just small is all."

He smiled at me then, out of the purest face I'd ever seen. Clear blue eyes, long lashes, smooth skin. I touched my own cheek, where it was scarred from the first gory. How could any parent have fostered this kid out? Why was this wholehearted boy not living in a real home?

Fontaine suggested a quick stop at Toy Temptations to buy Hatley some Lego. Soon enough, we were at the arcade, the boy sitting in the driver's cockpit of a video game, weaving down a virtual road, laughing in sheer joy.

Then we moved on to taking down animated bad guys in *Asteroids* and *Space Invaders*. After an hour or so, Casper whistled for us to come along.

It took me next to no time to persuade Hatley to come on another adventure: a trip down the A303 to the playground behind the Zipper's family home in Glastonbury. The drive passed easily. Hatley was good company, not overly chatty but totally impressed by the back seat strewn with Lego, video games and bags of sweets.

At the park, for a while we competed to see who could swing the highest, and then Hatley moved to the roundabout. I gave it a few good twirls, waved goodbye and headed for the willows along the road.

"Aren't you staying with me?" I heard him cry out.

I turned and he leapt off the whirling merry-go-round, tripped and fell. I walked back, and he scrambled up and threw himself into my arms. I disengaged, then knelt and put my warm hand over the scrape on his knee and gently wiped off the blood.

"Don't go," he said, looking at Casper, who was leaning against the upright post of the swing set, waiting.

"I have to," I said.

"But I need to go home now. Tea is quarter to five. If I'm late, Mrs. Pussett will have another fit. I'll be sent to the grubber."

"What's that?"

"A terrible place down in the sewer. She says there isn't any light at all and it's cold and wet."

"She's only trying to keep you and the other kids in line. There's no such thing as a grubber."

"There is. Matty Helmsforth went there. I ain't seen him since."

"Maybe he was adopted."

"Mrs. Pussett said that if Matty was adopted she would eat her Sunday hat. He cried at night. Every night. No one would want him."

I got on my knees in front of him and took his hands. "I'll come back. I promise."

He stared at me for a long moment, then gave me a weak smile of resignation, as though he'd already been lied to a thousand times. Without looking at me, he limped back to the roundabout, and kneeling on it, gave a great push, his hand trailing over the ground as it twirled.

I crossed the grassy pitch, then ducked through the willows to the Tor, climbed the tiered steps, and lay on the floor of St. Michael's Tower, listening to the howl of the wind.

—

Late that night, I rode my bike over to the pawnshop. Hatley wasn't there, which made me both anxious and relieved.

Casper handed me the five hundred pounds, along with a fifty-pound tip. "You were brilliant."

"Did someone take the boy back?"

He gave me a tight little smile. "I gave him to Father Ziperto. He took him to Birmingham."

I stared at the floor. "That's sick."

"Don't go soft on me now, Castlefrank. I've already told you it's far too late for that. I need you to go to the post office tonight. I've got thirty envelopes that need dropping into the postbox."

Thirty customers with addresses near and far—even as far as Australia and Singapore. He held them out, saying, "Take them, for God's sake, and get out of here. I can't stand your mopey face."

I took the envelopes from him and tucked them inside my rucksack, along with the wad of cash. Then I rode over to the dumpster behind the co-op on Silver Street and disposed of them.

Chapter 16

ARTHUR

On a rare warm Sunday in early May, Ernie showed up at my flat just after tea, and persuaded me to put down the book I was reading and come out with him. Mum smiled at us both, handed Ernie a couple of her warm biscuits, and shooed us out the door. We ended up sharing a joint lying on the grass on the Tor, watching the sheep—harmless hillside grazers standing around waiting to be eaten or shorn. After a long quiet time, Ernie said, "I wonder if they feel sad when they're separated from the flock and sent to slaughter? I wonder if the others notice?" His tone was light, but when I glanced over at him, he had pulled out a knife. A real knife, a switchblade. He'd mastered the one-handed closing technique, softly clicking the blade in and out of the black handle.

"Is it legal to own something like that?" I asked.

"Of course not."

Ernie tucked the knife away and leapt to his feet, then dragged me to my own. He waved for me to follow him down the steep, grassy slope, and through half a dozen fields, slipping over the wooden stiles to the children's playground. Dusk had fallen, and we sat on a bench to catch our breath. In front of us, the iron A-frame swing set with its four rubber U-shaped seats was outlined against the darkening sky. From his pocket he withdrew the knife and walked over to the swings and made several gashes to each of the seats. "Carbon steel," he called. "Sharper than a razor."

"What the hell are you doing?" I asked with a nervous laugh, coming to stand beside him. The knife sliced through the rubber like butter.

"What does it look like?"

I was laughing when I said, "Ernie. Stop. You'll be arrested for vandalism." He closed the knife and set it on a nearby bench, then began to climb up one side of the A-frame. At the top, he ordered me to feed him the chains and the slit rubber seat of the first swing. I swung it high and he caught it and managed to loop it over the top bar. At first, I was laughing too hard to feel any sense of danger on his behalf, but it had to be a fifteen-foot drop to the grass. I fed him the second swing. Around and around the top bar it went. Not even the tallest adult would be able to unfurl it without a ladder. He shimmied back down the frame.

"Stop," I said, putting my hands on his shoulders. He pushed me away, climbed up the other side and demanded I feed him the third and fourth swing. I didn't, but he managed to haul them up himself, his muscles fed by some inner fury.

Raindrops began to fall. He dropped to the ground, then circled the children's roundabout, fruitlessly looking for ways to disable the mechanism. Then he ran to the slide and shook the ladder as if to dislodge it from the earth.

"This isn't worth it," I yelled.

"Yes it is."

In the distance, we heard a police siren.

I hissed, "Ernie, let's go," and I made a run for the trees. He finally stumbled after me, a good fifty feet behind. Halfway up Tiller's Row, I heard a whimpering coming out of Ernie over the rain, which was now falling heavily. To preserve what was left of his dignity, I didn't let on

I'd heard. All I could do was put one foot in front of the other as the rain bounced off the road and the sideways wind battered our cheeks. By the time we reached the fork at Tor View Avenue, I was drenched and Ernie's white T-shirt was clinging to his thin chest like a second skin. He stopped, still crying, and tilted his face to the sky, his collarbones and ribs etched in shadows. He turned left and I watched him disappear into the night. There was no goodbye. My heart pumped with fear, my breathing ragged with it.

After I was sucked into a deal with the Zipper, it meant I was also always half-in with Ernie no matter what he chose to do, or didn't choose to do but it happened anyway.

That week, all students in our year had to take the compulsory field trip to Bath to study the geothermal activity beneath the remains of the Roman spa in the centre of the city. Ernie sat silently beside me on the one-hour bus trip, which wound through Shepton Mallet and Stratton-on-the-Fosse. When we reached our destination, we queued with the others at the ticket booth in the roped-off courtyard.

Nodding at me to hold his spot, Ernie stepped away into the centre of the courtyard. Fishing birdseed from his coat pockets, he held out handfuls on his open palms, and before long wrens and sparrows were hopping along his arms or resting fearlessly on his shoulders, tiny, feathered brothers and sisters that felt he was a human being safe enough to cling to. In those moments his face was luminous, with no hint of the self-loathing that seemed inseparable from our secret life. Spellbound, none of our classmates even thought to tease him.

But then Ernie dropped his arms, scattering the seeds. Catching my eye, he nodded towards a small boy with a tangle of gingery hair who was sitting next to his mother, eating a sandwich, on one of three wooden benches facing the entrance. I put my hand over my eyes to shade them from the sun. Was that a large Lego Batmobile on the ground at his feet?

Ernie waved for me to look more closely as the boy's mother leaned to brush crumbs from her son's crested V-neck grammar-school jumper. I shivered to see the familiar silver crucifix hanging from a chain around his delicate neck. My stomach clenched.

As he rejoined me in the queue, Ernie whispered, "Another special gift from our good friend, the Zipper." We watched the boy kick his legs back and forth as he took bites of his sandwich, his feet dangling above the Batmobile.

"What of it?" I said, trying to sound disinterested. I looked again. The boy's polished black Oxfords were neatly tied, his trousers ironed and tidily hemmed. I turned away, but Ernie couldn't stop staring. Maybe the boy would adjust, I thought, even bounce back. No. He would never bounce back.

Ernie hissed in my ear, "That cross signals to other predators that this is a boy *willing* to do what we've been doing. Believe me, Arthur, *I know*." With his finger on my chin, he turned my face to his to make sure I was listening. That I understood. I twisted away, but Ernie leaned closer to my ear. "Arthur, we can't pretend that we don't know what's happening anymore."

I thought about the wallet I'd left at the till in the bookshop, and the way Ernie had torn the bus ticket into four little pieces in the bus, and about all the weekends he'd been gone, and that for so many months I'd hardly seen him. I had never been approached by anyone except the Zipper—and who else would, really, after I'd grown so tall. I hadn't let myself believe that Ernie might have done sexual favours for people other than the priest. The idea of him or anyone else being shopped around made me feel despicable, dirty, complicit.

"If both of us come forward to accuse the Zipper, it will carry more weight. We'll be believed. And all of this will stop."

Stunned, I stared at him for a second. We'd never spoken out loud about anything that had happened to us. Then I heard myself say, "No."

His hand clenched, and I thought he might slug me. Just then, the line started to move and I turned from him and followed the other students filing into the Great Baths.

Once we were inside Ernie grabbed my arm, but before he could blurt out anything else, I wrenched myself free and turned to find myself face to face with a bronzed actress portraying a Roman matron from two thousand years ago. As I let her take my elbow to lead me towards the shimmering hot springs, Ernie ran back through the entrance.

I couldn't keep my mind on what the actress was telling me and soon excused myself, saying I had to go look for a friend who had taken sick. Outside, I scanned the area beyond the red velvet stanchions where we'd lined up for tickets. The bench was empty and the boy gone. A dejected Ernie appeared beside me. "I was too late, Arthur," he said. It was if the boy was a wounded orange-and-white kitten, a skinny squirrel, a lost canary. He made his way to the bench and sat, staring into space, ignoring the pigeons gathering at his feet hoping for more seed. I left him there and went back to learn what I could about the mechanics of ancient plumbing. The balance of the field trip smeared to a blur in my mind: green water, slabs of stone, disintegrating columns, the bronzed head of Sulis Minerva.

On the bus back to Glastonbury, Ernie refused to sit with me, taking a seat on his own across the aisle. I was the only one who seemed to notice or care that the heat of his righteous anger was fogging the pane where he leaned. The hair on the back of his neck was matted with sweat and his cheeks bloomed pink like he was running a fever.

I should stand by him, and all the younger boys, I knew I should. But I was hoarding the Zipper's gifts of cash for my "university fund" and intended to use the money for exactly that purpose. Money I couldn't return or expose without a degrading explanation. How could I inform on him when, in effect, I'd been paid for my silence. Even more shameful? My complicity in our encounters. There were times when it hurt, or I bled, or I was scared, degraded, embarrassed, guilty, but I'd also felt physical pleasure—which confused and horrified me. Is it still abuse if you enjoy it? On that bus ride back from the Roman baths, I questioned my self-serving mercenary excuses, my tolerance of wrongdoing, and accused myself of being no better than a rent boy. But even more, I questioned my friendship with Ernie and all the terrible things we knew and never talked about. I couldn't bear the thought of the classmates around us, all laughing and horsing around, singing rounds of "Fish and Chips and Vinegar," finding out what had been done to us. Knowing what we had done to ourselves. I wanted nothing more than to be just like them, one of the carefree others, untouched by scandal. From my lonely spot across the aisle, I felt eons away from Ernie, and that wasn't far enough. I too leaned into the window, my cheek heating the pane, and gnawed my lips raw, the way I did each Monday when the lock of the vestry door slid into place.

For several days after the school trip to Bath, I tried to stay out of Ernie's way. Then, in science lab, he came to stand beside me at the sink. He stank of pot and the whites of his eyes were bloodshot rings around giant pupils darkened to black marbles. I turned to leave, and he seized my wrist, whispering fiercely, "I told the warden at St. Nicholas about the Zipper. I told him everything that has happened to me."

My entire body resisted his words. Shivering from my neck to my knees, I looked around to see if anyone was listening.

"It did no good, Arthur." Ernie was almost crying now. "The warden told me I was a dirty little liar. Said he'd heard nothing but bad things about me and my family of criminals. Then he called me a selfish prick and said I should be ashamed for trying to bring down a holy man, so I told him exactly where he could get some really good prick. Up his arsehole. I told him how many times the Zipper had given me five quid for a hand job, knowing I'd give the cash to my mother so she could pay the butcher, or the gas and electricity. What does that say about my mother, Arthur? Why has she never asked me where the cash comes from? I figure my stepfather must have a clue, because now when he hits me, he tells me he's trying to beat the poofter, not the devil, out of me."

I thought I might go deaf from all the blood pumping in my ears. "Did you tell your mum too?"

"Of course I didn't tell her. She'd throw herself off the Clifton Suspension Bridge if she knew the whole of it. She came close when Nathan went to jail."

"Your mum has always been nice to me," I said. Stupidly, it was all I could think of.

"Everyone is always nice to you, Arthur."

In that moment, that felt like the worst of insults.

Ernie wasn't done. "For the last eight months, the Zipper has arranged for the church to pay our rent, but I still hear my mother cry herself to sleep at night."

Numb, I wondered about my own mother. I had no idea whether the church ever helped pay our rent, though I knew the Zipper had lined up the insurance job.

Ernie licked his lips, dry from whatever he'd smoked, or maybe from his anger. "The warden told me not to show my face at St. Nick's again, and said if I did, he'd call the police. Did you know the district police officer is the warden's brother-in-law?"

Ernie was as livid as I'd ever seen him, his hot weedy breath on my left ear, which already burned with our shared shame.

I scanned the room. The teacher, wearing protective goggles, was measuring chemicals. Our classmates, bent over their workstations, seemed oblivious to Ernie's meltdown.

"Guess who was in earshot as I was yelling at the warden. The Zipper's brother. Afterwards, he walked down the hallway to his office whistling 'Be Not Afraid' like he hadn't heard a thing. Arthur, people know what's going on." We both already knew the Ear Whacker had a snarly disdain for every boy who stepped into the vestry.

Ernie turned to the sink and began vigorously washing his hands. "Do you want to know what else I told the warden? Nobody *buys* sex to survive. People *sell* sex to survive."

Ernie turned the knob on the hot tap as far as it would go and washed his hands.

"The warden told me I was the one with no moral compass. 'You'd steal the sterling collection plate if it wasn't needed to bring in more money for your next haul,' he said. 'You're the kid who tried to burn down the church with the choir inside. Blameless choristers,' he shouted. 'I'm amazed you weren't sent to prison with your brother. Have you nothing better to do than spread lies?' I even told him I'd sold the Zipper's photographs of naked altar boys to other perverts—'You know the ones,' I said. 'The Zipper keeps them in those albums under the vestments.' Then I told him I'd been penetrated. That's when he put his hands on my throat and said, 'You Castlefrank boys should be behind bars just for being alive.'"

Ernie lifted his eyes to mine. "There is nobody who will protect us. Nobody. I was foolish to try."

He turned off the tap and fell silent. Both hands were bright red, his ruddy knuckles swollen from the scalding heat.

I leaned on the edge of the sink, feeling both hollow from the unfairness of it all and flooded with relief that Ernie had stopped talking before anyone else heard him.

"Who's to blame, Arthur?" he said then. "I am. You are. We are." For the first time in our friendship, Ernie looked at me with real contempt. "I needed you to come with me."

Unable to meet his eyes, I turned away and saw that the teacher was waving at us to return to our lab benches.

Behind me, Ernie whispered, "Declan Entwhistle was an altar boy at St. Nick's."

I turned back. "Who?"

"The Entwhistles moved away to Bath a while ago now, but that wasn't far enough. Someone told him if he ever spoke up, photos would be shared with his family and friends. Declan took his own life."

"How do you know this?"

"I just do. His suicide note read, 'I hope everything that is wrong with me dies with me.' Just like us, he'd become a part of the abuse and he couldn't live with that." Some unspoken horror flickered in Ernie's eyes.

All I could do was to stare at him, as the teacher's voice faded to a faint muttering in the background. And then, his anger suddenly burned out, Ernie shrugged and went back to his workstation, as though nothing had happened with the warden, as if he hadn't just accused me of betraying him out of cowardice. As if Declan Entwhistle were still alive.

I was overwhelmed with a wretched need to flee the classroom, disappear, and start my life over in a country where no one spoke English or had any idea who I was. Ernie had ripped open the stitches concealing our secret life, hoping to put a stop to the abusers, and had been the one blamed instead.

I trudged to my own place, sat and opened my science textbook, and began to read. In my mind's eye, though, all I could picture was Ernie standing broken in front of the outraged warden, accused of malicious slander. That man was an acquaintance of my mother's. He wore a plaid bow tie to mass on Sunday, and was trailed into church by a wife with a chilly smile and his four children, young girls so well behaved they could sit through the most boring sermon without fooling around.

I could hardly tell myself, let alone the warden, that I had also been penetrated: my body, and so too my mind, with the idea that what had been done to me was beyond questioning. I felt lost, but it seemed like Ernie had been swallowed whole. I'm still sickened that I found myself anxiously hoping against hope that the warden wouldn't say anything about Ernie Castlefrank's accusations to my mother.

—

I found Ernie the next day in the music room. He wouldn't meet my eye. When he made to leave, I blocked the door. At last, he said, "Mrs. Brophy is on maternity leave. Did I ever tell you that she mailed me a card last Valentine's? She signed it 'your secret admirer,' but I knew it was from her. She's the kind of person who worries about people like me, who don't have a hope in hell of receiving a red heart from anyone. I stole a baby swing and left it by her car. I think she thought the staff had passed the hat."

"I didn't even know she was pregnant."

"There are other ways to be a mother," Ernie said, touching some of Mrs. Brophy's sheet music.

I walked home with him after school. We each tried to patch up our differences, but we both knew that something between us had dissolved like sugar in hot tea. A line had been crossed, and there was no way back.

No one was home when we got to Ernie's house, and we holed up in his bedroom and listened to old music by Emerson Lake & Palmer and "Tuesday Afternoon" by the Moody Blues on his Sanyo stereo, smoking weed with the windows open and incense burning, an attempt to buffer our sense that we were damaged and worthless. The dope did little to chase away the thoughts I was trying to erase. I was haunted by the idea that because what the Zipper did sometimes felt good, I must have wanted it, Ernie must have wanted it, and the little boy with the crumbs must have wanted it too. I could have called for help, or run away, or ratted out the priest long ago. I didn't. None of us had, until Ernie tried and failed.

Like all of the boys he'd so carefully chosen, I'm guessing, I hadn't been able to push away his rapt attention and affection, which felt like the funnel tide in the Bristol Channel rushing towards me. That, and then the football tickets, the chemistry set, the fivers and tenners for university, the computer games, were beyond resisting. I was coaxed into believing that he offered me a form of love. Intoxicated by the Zipper's attention and affection, I believed the lie.

Ernie spoke through a haze of smoke. "Stop worrying, Arthur. I never mentioned your name. You're off the hook. It's what you've wanted all along. To be off the hook."

He inhaled again, winced and coughed. "What is the point, really? Life is one steady trudge towards death, through a dark wood, dodging invisible enemies all the while. The evil people look exactly like the good people, and neither give a rat's ass about what happened to us." Spacing out each word, he said very slowly, "When the saints and the tormentors are one and the same, we do not matter." I heard the catch in his voice despite the hardness of his words. After that we were silent, like the old days when we each carried the burden alone.

Not only did I struggle with those same pessimistic thoughts, but after years of shameful silence, I thought it was too late to reveal the truth. I would never tell anyone what I'd done, what I still sometimes did, not for as long as I lived. The Zipper's words remained as alive in my mind as if they had been spoken in the last ten minutes: "If you tell someone, you kill us both."

The next day, I stood lookout in the hall, while Ernie smoked a joint in the cleaner's supply room at lunchtime. The smell was a dead give-away, but he didn't care. He had already taken a pink pill and then a white one, and I was scared for what he might do next. Whatever it was, it took medicating, sedating, erasure. And me, his usual accomplice.

"Come to my flat after school," I pleaded, through the closed door.

"I can't. I have something else I need to do." I heard the brief buzz of the custodian's drill, then Ernie's voice. "You head back to class now, Arthur. Why don't we ride our bikes out to your grandad's orchard on the weekend?"

I knew that trip wouldn't happen, and in hindsight I realized that Ernie had known too.

Chapter 17

ERNIE

I lay on my usual couch in the Pint Room and burned a second hole in my torso with a lit cigarette. Casper had been in the darkroom all night, drinking endless cups of coffee and reproducing images. He worked weird-shit hours, depending on when new stuff came in. When he came out for another refill, he said, "What the hell is that disgusting smell?"

I didn't answer, just covered my stomach with my bare hand, the scent of tobacco and burnt flesh stuck in my throat and nose.

"Time to get busy, Ernie," Casper said. "I need you to stuff envelopes. You know the drill: first-class postage is for local customers, and air mail for Europe and overseas."

After a couple of hours of silent stuffing and stamping, we were done.

Casper lifted his eyes from the last tick mark he'd placed in his little black book, and took a good look at me. "Something's been off with you recently. Are you sick?"

"I've never been better." I knew Casper wouldn't push it.

"I'm glad to hear it," he said. "To survive in this business, you need to be cold-blooded, trusting to reason, not emotion. Something your brother never got the hang of—you could teach him a thing or two about impulse control." He closed his black book, locked it to his belt, and stared idly for a moment at the stacks of envelopes, assorted lists and telephone directories from a dozen towns that sat beside the business phone he'd had installed, with its four separate lines for fielding orders. He turned to ogle the Commodore that sat blinking on another table. I could practically read his mind. Computers are the future.

"Right. Tomorrow we're heading to a new location—somewhere more private."

"Are we using Hatley again?" I asked.

"No. Someone else. Two girls this time. Sisters."

"Sisters?"

He just looked at me for a long second, then picked up our night's work and handed over the thick stack of banded envelopes. "Don't post them all in the same letter box."

I hadn't asked, but he told me anyway. "We'll be headed to the Windsor Arms on Corn Street in Bristol. I've booked a suite for three nights."

When he looked away, I slipped another pill into my mouth. Quimby had two daughters in knee socks and ponytails. I couldn't stop thinking about the beautiful ginger-haired boy outside the Roman baths with the sterling crucifix around his neck. He'd worn the same jumper in the hotel room where I'd first met him. As I'd watched him, his mother had leaned over to brush the breadcrumbs off his jumper. She was a pretty woman, and young herself. The boy's legs had wagged back and forth like a dog's tail. The Batmobile we'd built together was on the ground at his feet. He'd been ecstatic to be given such a coveted toy. When he saw it, his laugh had rung out so loudly, I'd almost put my hand over his mouth the way the Zipper had in the cupboard with the cassocks. In the two hours I'd been with him, we'd only been able to complete the frame, the steering system, and the beginnings of the front bumpers. Before I snuck away, I told him we would finish it together. The pieces had been everywhere on the floor in the hotel.

And there the model was, weeks later, completely built. Who had finished it with him? It would have taken at least eight more hours. Poor kid. Buggered at least five times.

When he'd turned his head and our eyes connected, the boy had dropped the rest of his sandwich. The bread separated and a pigeon seized the moment to steal the pink meat. What was his name? Eddie? Ricky? Rocky? I had wanted to rush over and tell him that it was okay he finished the car with someone else. Buggered. My mind whirled. I would get on my knees and tell him everyone knew it was wrong. Big kids. Little kids. Adults. *This is our secret. Don't tell.* Stop all this. It's disgusting.

It was like Arthur had gored me in the eye with a hot poker when he refused to stand beside me in front of the warden. His betrayal felt worse than all the groping I had endured in the vestry with my eyes closed and my mind doing math equations. On the bus home from Bath, I boiled with resentment over the way his mother loved him, the way he found escape in his books, his ability to move past what had been done to us. I hated his Miss Congeniality act the most. I wanted him to be malicious, to be cruel. I wanted him to be like me, empty and unwanted. Now I had no one left except Nathan. Lick the stamps for the letters for Nathan. Lick the stamps for the letters for Nathan. Lick the stamps.

The minute I'd opened my bloody mouth to tell the truth, I realized that I'd misjudged the warden. I thought he was a true family man, a defender of children, but all I saw on his face was revulsion and disbelief. He seemed to think that it was me who was perverted, otherwise how could these things even be coming out of my mouth. What the Zipper had done to me couldn't be believed. I had performed fellatio on him in a bathroom in Birmingham while another priest praised my beautiful hair and captured the moment on camera and video. In a flash I saw that the Zipper had counted on that—on me never being believed. When I got back from that trip, I took my stepfather's straight razor to my hair.

In science class, I'd run the water so hot I'd burned my hands. I had an out-of-body feeling at the searing pain, the lobster flush of skin up to my wrists. Shock. Numbness. Heaven. Arthur couldn't look at me. Nobody else noticed or cared.

After I posted the Zipper's—no, our—envelopes, I went home, but not to sleep. Around two in the morning, I left the house with a bag of Quaaludes, strips of plywood, and the hammer, screws and drill I'd borrowed from the cleaner's supply room. My feet took me to the Zipper's empty house on Tiller's Row. I broke a window with the hammer and shimmied through, careful not to cut myself. I climbed the stairs to the boys' bedroom and lay down on one of the bunks and recited "The Raven," hugging myself for comfort as I rocked back and forth. Back and forth. Back and forth. Leave my loneliness unbroken. Leave my loneliness unbroken. For evermore.

The hammer and drill were inches from my left hand.

When someone came in through the front door, I lurched upright. I heard stumbling footsteps, and then I thought I heard crying, maybe mumbling, maybe both. I put my hand on my thumping heart. The sounds grew louder. *Stop crying*, I wanted to scream. Never have I had to endure such a desperate sound coming from another human, and I had to fight the urge to join in. I pulled up my knees under the familiar blanket and waited for the Zipper to find me. Downstairs, a door slammed shut. Then came a frantic scurrying. Claws skittering on wood. A cat, a dog, a raccoon? A wild animal inside the house?

When something shattered, I got out of bed and crept down the stairs. His back was to me. Short black hair neatly combed. Baggy wool pants. Brogues. He half turned and threw a cushion, and a squirrel scrabbled away up the curtains, paws clinging to the fabric, swaying in airy nothingness. It wasn't the Zipper, but his twin brother.

My eyes followed him as he reached for a fire iron. With a frantic swipe, he brought the curtains crashing down, along with the squirrel. The Ear Whacker thrashed up and down, pummelling the balled-up layers of fabric until the animal stopped moving and blood seeped through the material, red against the curtain's white. He turned and fell to his knees in front of the large crucifix that hung on the wall and began to recite prayers in Italian. *Padre nostro che sei nei cieli.* Then I heard him hiss in English, "If you tell someone, you kill us both."

I was half-hidden by the staircase and certain he didn't know I was in the house—he couldn't have been speaking to me. I crept back to my bunk and hauled the covers over my head, immobilized by his words. Needing a better hiding space, I moved into the cupboard and closed the door, my fear of being found trumping claustrophobia.

Just before dawn, I heard the Ear Whacker leave the house. I left the cupboard and went down the stairs to the living room and picked up the bloodied curtain to reveal the dead squirrel. I unfastened the clasp of my crucifix, the same cross as the one draped around the neck of that little boy who had walked through the door of the Elm Guest House Hotel, who now, like me, would never be the person he might have become. Then I knelt.

Chapter 18

ARTHUR

I spent the weekend staring at the ceiling, trying not to think about Ernie stealing the custodian's drill, yet hoping for the ping of a pebble on my bedroom window. I made so many trips to the loo, eliminating everything but my swirling thoughts, that my mother couldn't help but notice and offer me ginger ale.

On Monday morning, I was a few minutes late for first period, and arrived to find my classmates reeling from the smell emanating from inside Ernie's desk. But no Ernie. Soon, the school janitor, wearing thick black rubber gloves, removed the whole desk from the classroom, trailing drops of something blackish that glimmered where they fell.

"It's a dead squirrel," someone whispered in a quivery voice, and everyone hissed like Ernie had murdered their pet hamster. As Mr. Henry tried to restore order, I reviewed every hour of the previous week, wondering what I had missed, wondering what I could have done differently. My friend Ernie would never have hurt an animal.

I spent the day craning my neck in every new class, hoping I'd see Ernie sitting in the back row with his nose in a *Byte* magazine as if nothing had happened. Late that afternoon, the headmaster called me down to his office over the intercom. I waited an excruciating forty minutes in his small anteroom, head in hands, with only three empty chairs for company. I don't think I'd ever been more conscious that I was a scholarship boy, same as Ernie, and that maybe they'd find me guilty by association and refuse to cover my fees.

I still couldn't accept the idea that Ernie had killed a squirrel. He relied for solace on the creatures he found in the sky, the trees, and the tall grass on the banks of the railway tracks that ran behind his house, the same kind of reprieve and solace I found in books.

I was so lost in thought, I jumped when the secretary tapped me on the shoulder.

"He's ready for you," she said. "I'm sorry you've had to wait so long. He had some calls to make."

Maybe to the police?

I followed her in and came to attention in front of the headmaster's desk.

"Barnes," he said, folding his hands and looking up at me. I couldn't help but notice his abundant white nose hairs. "I'm just off the phone with Mrs. Castlefrank, who says she hasn't seen her son since early Saturday. She hadn't been worried because he often stays away at the weekends. When he wasn't home this morning, she assumed he left to serve at early Mass. When did you last speak to him?"

"Friday. At school. Last time I saw him was at lunch."

"Any signs of something going on with him?" He waved at the wooden chair beside me, and I sat, head down, nervously clicking the end of a Biro with my thumb, until the headmaster offered, a little impatiently, "The janitor said someone broke into the supply room."

"I don't know anything about that." My first lie. I was alongside Ernie when he broke in: he'd long ago stolen a master key that opened all the doors at school, including the ones for the supply room. The janitor— a drowsy-looking man who already seemed retired—was out swabbing the main hallway and Ernie had said he wanted me to keep a lookout while he smoked a quick joint. When he emerged with the stolen tools and saw the look on my face, he told me to eff off.

"Barnes, it's no secret you and Ernie have both been to youth court. Has he got himself involved in something illegal? For your own sake, now would be a good time to speak up. Have you seen him in the last three days?"

"I haven't." Under his steady gaze, I found myself in full Judas mode. "We haven't been friends for a long time. I don't know why Ernie did what he did. If it was him." It would make no difference here, I thought, to mention Ernie's love of animals.

The headmaster made notes. It flashed across my mind that our carefully hidden secret life was about to break open and I had nothing to offer in my own defence. The Zipper had been giving me money for certain acts—wasn't that illegal? Could I tell this man that I'd once heard Ernie crying in the locked vestry as the priest told him where to put his lips, and I had pounded on the door, then run away as though my life depended on it. That when I realized that I wasn't the only boy to have been given a crucifix, I'd buried mine, but I didn't know how to stop what was happening to me or to any of us. I didn't know how to escape, or where to go, or who to tell. We were prisoners because of what we had agreed to do, over and over again.

No. I had few words for the headmaster, a by-the-book man in an itchy-looking suit who would most likely rather not know any of it. After a few more moments of silence, he closed his manila folder, capped his pen, and sat back as if ready to call it quits. But then he opened a drawer, picked something up and extended a closed fist towards me. He studied my face for a long moment, then opened his hand to reveal a sterling crucifix. "This was wrapped around the dead squirrel's neck. Why would Ernie have done such a thing?"

I inhaled, trying to disguise my shock, only to release my breath with such force I surely gave away how upset I was. As I gripped the arms of the chair trying not to blurt out anything incriminating, the head said, "I also found this most distressing. Hanging a crucifix off the neck of a reeking squirrel is wicked even for a Castlefrank."

He dropped it on the desk, sat back and laced his fingers, his eyes on me. "Perhaps I shouldn't have shared that with you, Arthur," he said. "I most definitely shouldn't have disparaged the family. Forgive my lapse in judgment. In all my years as a headmaster . . ." He cleared his voice and then swallowed some phlegm. "Please accept my apology."

I hunched forward, my elbows on my knees, and pressed my fingertips into the sides of my skull, squeezing my eyes shut. When the headmaster stood up and came around his desk to rest a gentle hand on my shoulder, it entered my mind that I had to speak up. I sat up and our eyes met, and the words formed, but to my everlasting mortification, instead I began to cry, and then to sob in great, shoulder-shuddering gasps. I was weeping for Ernie, for myself and for my lack of courage, completely undone by the headmaster's compassionate touch. I couldn't stop sobbing long enough to explain that the Zipper had fed some essential part of Ernie when he was a small boy, only to suck him into something that defied extrication. I had been that same needy kind of boy.

"Let me get you a glass of water," the headmaster said, and left the office, closing the door behind him. I could hear him speaking to his secretary as I struggled to get a grip. I was fifteen, far too old for crying.

How would I even begin to explain myself to him? Would the head care to know that my mother had never quite recovered after my father's death? That Ernie was constantly stoned, and at fourteen had agreed to drive three hours away to have a bath with a priest, and then tried to act like it was nothing, except he'd shaved off all his curls afterward, leaving trails of dried blood on his scalp. The headmaster knew all about my book reviewing, but I didn't want him to know that Miss Phillips at the bookshop had rescued me from being a lowly thief, by showing me how to find the broken places in literature that made me feel less alone, less of a misbegotten loser. And that even so, I had remained a chronic shoplifter.

He returned with the glass of water, handing it to me, then standing over me until I took a shaky sip. Going back round his desk, he sat with a sigh. "For two years running, Ernie has scored in the top percentile in all of Britain in the International Mathematical Challenge, despite rarely completing his assignments. Cambridge University called to consult with me after he'd requested a reading list from their computer science curriculum in order to teach himself coding. His intellectual gifts are such that I felt I could be lenient about his truancy, although a couple of his teachers did request a suspension, or even expulsion. No doubt he told you all this."

No, Ernie had never told me he'd sat for the math tests, or gone beyond *Byte* magazine and whatever the creepy pawnbroker could teach him when it came to coding. Given how much school he'd been missing, I couldn't believe he hadn't been expelled.

"Was there trouble at home, beyond his brother's situation, I mean? I understand that Ernie has been sent to the nurse once or twice for a split lip and bruising." In a quieter voice, he said, "It sounds like he was being raised in fairly harsh circumstances."

"I don't know." The whole story was on the tip of my tongue, but I couldn't find the courage to defend my friend. The warden hadn't believed Ernie. Why would anyone believe me? Instead, I asked through my tears, "How did the squirrel die?"

The head's eyes were once again full of uncomfortable kindness. "It looks like a blow crushed its skull."

No matter why the animal had ended up in his desk, I knew Ernie hadn't caused its death. My friend wouldn't swat a mosquito, squish a spider or step on an ant. I clung to the idea that the squirrel hadn't suffered, just as I hoped that Ernie, wherever he was, wasn't suffering, or at least not as much as he had been when I let him down.

When I'd calmed down, the headmaster released me from his prim office. As I walked back to my locker, I heard traffic moving along Benedict Street, the air brakes of a bin lorry, the swooping and chirping of birds, and the unmistakable slap of a tennis ball hitting the red brick wall of the school playground. I had the most surreal feeling that for everyone else, it was an ordinary Monday.

It was a relief that most of the students had gone for the day—no one was around to see that I'd been crying. For sure, Ernie had stopped crying a long time ago. That's the thing. When you do something over and over again, it starts to look and sound and feel normal.

The next day, my mother suggested I stay home from school. I didn't. I couldn't. Ernie was gone and I felt like I had to appear unimplicated. She told me that he would turn up like he always did. In my bones I knew this time was different, but I tried to tell myself I didn't care.

I did stay away from the Copperfield and Twist. Some part of me didn't want to lie to Miss Phillips, the one person who had overlooked my worst faults. She knew that Ernie was my best friend, and if she asked me where I thought he had gone, I worried that either more sobs would emerge or, worse, the truth would spill out. After I got home from school each day, I lay on my bed and pined for the part of myself that reviewed books for undamaged children and I waited for someone to come along with instructions on how to move forward. Each night, with no success, I tried to understand the scribbled-over part of Ernie that I had missed or he had hidden.

That Sunday, the warden caught me alone in the churchyard after mass. After expressing some feigned worry about where my friend Ernie might have run off to, he asked if I'd ever observed Father Ziperto being inappropriate with anyone.

I said no, in what felt like the lowest showing of my character. With each denial I dug an even deeper hole for the truth.

The next evening, a week since the dead squirrel had been found and Ernie had vanished, my mother sat listening to the radio while I was washing up the dishes. The sound of the water rushing out of the taps obscured what the announcer was saying, but I noticed when she got up and shut the radio off with a sigh, her face clouded with worry. She went to the junk drawer and fished out a newspaper clipping from that day's *Somerset Gazette*, saying, "Dry your hands, Arthur. I think you should read this."

I did as I was told, then took the clipping and sat at the table. The article reported that on June 14, a week ago Saturday, Constable Deirdre Blackburn had fielded a call from a male who refused to give his name but who reported vandalism at an address on Tiller's Row. A minute or so later, a second call had come in from a woman who reported the sounds of drilling at the same address, a house that was supposed to be vacant. Blackburn had sent two officers to check it out.

They parked their car and walked through an iron gate into the front garden of a two-storey house. Strips of plywood had been roughly screwed into place over the front, back and side doors, a smallish footprint showing in a scattering of fresh sawdust on the ground near the rear entry.

"Why are you showing me this, Mum?"

"It's just so curious, Arthur. Father Ziperto once told me he and his brother grew up on Tiller's Row, and I'm sure it was at this address." She leaned across the table and picked up the newspaper. "If I recall, it was a Sunday evening and he had come for tea. He spoke of a beautiful stone wall in front and a big garden out back. I asked him about his calling to the priesthood. He said his family had moved from Italy to Somerset when he was ten, a dislocation that had shattered his mother, who didn't speak English. Instead, she spoke religion, he said. Countless times she made plans to leave the family for a religious order in Poland that favours silence. Father Ziperto told me he chose the priesthood to keep the family together. Rather selfless."

Then she asked, "What kind of vandal boards up the doors?"

I looked at her as blankly as I could, wondering if those words from the Zipper to my mother were more deceit. Then I turned back to the dishes, though I could feel my mother's eyes on my back.

As I saw it, Ernie's disappearance had sent the Zipper's intricate spider's web to trembling, and he'd been working to reinforce his defences. The Zipper had called my mother two or three times to offer God's solace about my missing best friend. "He recited Psalm Thirty-Four to me, Arthur," she'd confided. "The Lord is close to the broken-hearted and saves those who are crushed in spirit. I think he wants you to reflect on that too."

The hypocrisy, I said to myself. His other favourite recitation was "God is love" from the Book of John.

My mother's Catholic faith had blossomed under his renewed attention. I hadn't the heart to extinguish her certainty that she and the priest's ministry could somehow carry me over the loss of my friend. I also didn't know how long I could avoid my "duties" at St. Nick's. What would the Zipper pay me now that his favoured boy was gone—worse, what would he need me to do?

One thing I couldn't quite reconcile was why, in that first week, then weeks, then the summer months after Ernie vanished, neither my mother nor I reached out to Mrs. Castlefrank. I know my avoidance heightened rather than lessened my anxiety. As far as I knew, my interrogation by the head of school was the only formal investigation into Ernie's disappearance. I was outraged that he was being treated as dispensable, but equally relieved that I had not been held accountable.

Still, if my mother and I couldn't help listening for his step on our stairs, what must Mrs. Castlefrank be feeling? Even if she'd never been the mother Ernie needed, I don't think he'd doubted that she loved him in her own subdued fashion. Married to a creep, one son in jail and the other a runaway . . . maybe in some twisted way my own mum couldn't help but judge her for her inability to keep her family together. No matter how harsh or hypocritical such a judgment was.

For myself? Part of me was desperate to be verbally taken to the ground for my cowardice. Anything was better than the heavy, introspective silence that made the nights yawn forever. Instead of coming clean, I lived in a kind of vacuum.

Although I thought about the pawnbroker incessantly, it was easy to avoid the man who'd once made me feel the weight of a gun. Ernie's friendship with him made next to no sense and I wrestled with the need to know more, mostly subduing it. For certain, Ernie had been up to all sorts of madness with Casper Fontaine, earning cash to pay his brother's fine. But what? Since I was afraid of the answer, it made more sense not to ask the question.

Chapter 19

Summer came to an end, and Ernie was still missing. I'd spent my time carefully honing my disinterest in most things except books, driven by the sickening feeling that my thoughts might leak out of my ears or eyeballs if I wasn't vigilant. I'd put in my days at the bookshop, as if my whole world wasn't teetering on a precipice, and I would catch Miss Phillips watching me hunched over my little desk, the words in front of me at times as indecipherable as sandpiper footprints on dry sand.

At night, I read and wrote my reviews in the corner of the kitchen where the light was the strongest, tapping out tragic endings on the light blue portable Olivetti Miss Phillips had loaned me. When I went to bed, I honoured my friend by reciting "The Raven"—I'd managed to memorize the lengthy poem, though I did not have his dramatic flair—and then slept with the light on.

At the opening assembly of the new fall term, I felt the antennae of all my classmates turn to me as the headmaster spoke of the elephant in the room: Ernie Castlefrank was still missing. People said he'd joined the Jesus Army, a cult that wooed members in with street-based evangelism, or he'd become a drug dealer, like his brother, or he'd ripped off someone dangerous and made a run for it. He was the first student ever to go missing from St. Columba Catholic College, but to many of the privileged students and their parents, the fact that he was a scholarship boy from a family whose name was linked to drugs, alcohol, poverty and incarceration made his disappearance feel somewhat deserved.

The headmaster did his best to burst the juicy rumours. "It's all been terribly upsetting to me, and I'm sure to you all, that Ernest Castlefrank, St. Columba's finest mathematician, has still not returned to Glastonbury. Blessedly, we have not had any reports that something untoward has happened and so I suggest that we continue to assume he is safe and that he *will* come back to us. I've asked Father Ziperto from St. Nicholas here today to lead us in a prayer for his safe return. If any among you is in touch with Ernie, I would consider it dishonourable if you didn't let me know immediately."

My stomach clenched as the priest came striding to the microphone—I'd taken a summer break from my altar boy duties, though I'd often had to put up with his significant looks when my mother invited him for tea. I bowed my head over passages in my textbook about the economic impact of the Industrial Revolution and didn't lift it again until the Zipper had blessed us and was gone.

"Please rise to sing the school anthem," the headmaster then requested, and after the school music teacher had thumped out a short musical introduction on the old piano to the side of the stage, we all stood and sang "And Did Those Feet in Ancient Time."

The last chords were still in the air as we filed out into the corridor, me with my head down, doing my best to be invisible despite my height. But after school that day, I finally mustered up the courage to go ring the Castlefranks' doorbell. Ernie and I would both turn sixteen at the end of October, and sitting in that assembly where the headmaster's well-meaning words made no lasting impression on anyone, and the priest's hypocritical prayers turned my stomach, made me realize that, if nothing else, I needed him to come home in time for my mother to bake us our mutual birthday cake.

On the doorstep, I bolstered my nerve to meet either stony silence or angry accusations, then pressed the doorbell. Ernie had been gone for three months, with not a word. He'd been saving to pay his brother's fine, and surely, he'd come home soon if only to make sure that Nathan was released from jail without a hitch.

Someone was playing the piano—stopping and starting—inside the peeling, two-storey house, a classical air that was a far cry from the punk-folk of the Pogues. I rang the bell again, and heard slippers against wood, the familiar squeak of a loose floorboard. The music carried on as the front door opened. When she laid eyes on me, tiny Mrs. Castlefrank looked momentarily off-kilter, then used the corner of a faded yellow apron to wipe away a gush of tears. "Oh, Arthur," she said, "at last."

The words tumbled out—"I should have come sooner"—and I meant them. She didn't need to know that my anger at her—why hadn't she done more or loved him better—had been such a stumbling block. She beckoned me inside with a bird-like hand, the bones prominent under scarce flesh: she looked twenty years older than the last time I'd seen her. In that instant, I realized I needed to protect my own mother from a pain I hadn't known existed until that very moment. Mrs. Castlefrank was being tortured, yes, but she had also been spared from the knowledge of what had sent Ernie away. I hadn't been able to tell my mother what the Zipper had been doing to me because of my own shame; now I also realized what it would do to a mother to realize she hadn't been able to protect her son.

The hallway, saturated with the trapped odour of boiled onions, was papered with a faded pattern of green Swedish ivy. On one wall was a lineup of photos in homemade frames crafted from branches glued together. Ernie's mother caught me gaping at close-ups of whiskers, fur, paws, claws and the wet snout of a badger. His work, for certain, but he'd never shown me. "I put these up after he left," she said. "Ernest never would have hurt a squirrel the way they said he did. You know the feeling he has for animals, especially the ones who have been injured in some fashion." She waved her hand towards the photographs to prove it.

My bowels swished. I asked if I could go up to Ernie's bedroom. Truth be told, I needed to use the toilet something awful. She was waiting by his door when I came out. "I've gone into his room countless times," she said, "but maybe you'll see something I've missed." As I followed her into Ernie's room, the music stopped, and she looked over her shoulder, then gently closed the door behind us.

Ernie's small bed was covered with the same shiny blue spread, and no clothes seemed to be missing from his battered wooden dresser. He and I had Scotch-taped a poster from David Bowie's Middle Finger series over the cracked ceiling, and the tape had given way along one side to expose the rafters. In a corner of the room, there were still several bags of sunflower seeds and peanuts in the shell, beside a pile of small metal cages, overlooked by a scary raven skeleton that seemed far bigger than I remembered. In another corner was an empty aquarium, and the remnants of a chemistry set that had come with dire warnings about misusing its components. Naturally, we had disregarded the warnings. I rubbed the toe of my trainer over the burn mark on the floor, wondering whether Mrs. Castlefrank knew it was Father Ziperto who had given Ernie the chemistry set.

The Zipper had always been able to identify exactly what each of us wanted. Ernie told me that the priest had once given football-mad Slanty McEwen, the poorest kid in the parish, two tickets to see West Ham defeat Manchester United two goals to one, and afterwards, all the other mothers in the congregation had lined up to invite Father Ziperto for Sunday supper in case such beneficence fell on their boys.

Ernie's mum hovered by the door, her lips holding tight against the release of any emotion. At last, she said, "After Nathan was sent up, Ernest's whole life became animals and photography. Did you know he was installing a darkroom in the cellar?

"And remember the wasp's nest in the bushes, Arthur? Remember when he stepped on that nest, and got at least two dozen stings, and I made a baking soda paste to cover them? You were there. You helped me hold ice packs on his shoulders and neck. I've hardly ever been so frightened. I sat right next to him on this bed, held his hand and watched for wheezing or tightness in his throat. He let me do that for him."

I looked at her without understanding the expression on her face.

"He let me hold his hand," she repeated, and grasped her own hands as if to remind herself what it was like to touch her son.

I, too, found it hard to be touched.

A sombre melody drifted in from the back of the house and broke the spell.

"Did you buy a piano?" I asked.

Mrs. Castlefrank took a moment to think about my question, her reddened fingers with their bitten-down nails fretting with a corner of her apron. "Nathan put Ernie onto someone he knew, and Ernie arranged it." She went to the window to pry it open and invite some air inside. I went to help her.

Ernie had told me about a pool table arriving in the middle of the night, like it was something that happened to every family. But he didn't tell me that he had wrangled a piano from somewhere. Perhaps he did it to spark a truce of sorts with his stepfather. Most of my appreciation for music had come from Ernie, I realized. He heard the difference between a viola and a violin and could hum the melody chiming from an ice cream van weeks after it had meandered through town.

After we'd lifted the sash a few inches, Mrs. Castlefrank said, "My husband plays many instruments. The violin. The saxophone. He used to perform in an orchestra. When his hands don't hurt him too much, he likes to play that piano."

I looked around Ernie's room for objects I might have seen at the pawnshop, fearful I would spot something illegal, like the handgun we'd seen behind glass. In the darkness of my own bedroom each night, I dwelled on half a dozen scenarios of what could have happened to Ernie, each one more dire than the next. Maybe I was looking for proof that none of them had happened.

I stood at the window, looking out to see what Ernie would have seen. More precisely—to see where Ernie might have gone.

Mrs. Castlefrank said, "They're no longer live."

"What is?"

"The tracks. Nathan and Ernie used to play a game they called 'how close is too close.'" I saw her shiver.

Her gaze moved to Ernie's desk, and she pointed to a red binder. "Did you know that Ernie was getting paid for some of his work as a photographer?"

I shook my head.

Her eyes closed for one or two long seconds. "Of course, I love all those images of baby badgers, but my favourite photographs are the three he took of you."

A snake of fear crawled down my back, my mind flashing on the Monday photo sessions in the vestry. She beckoned me to the desk and opened the binder to show me. Ernie had captured me unaware. In one shot, which he must have taken the summer we worked in the orchard, the sun glinted on my crucifix where it nestled into the small cave of my throat. I quickly flipped on through the catalogued pages, half reading the meticulous dates and places. The last sleeve held a carefully cropped black and white photograph, unsigned and undated, that captured the eagle-like nose, the fan of eyelashes, a faint stubble above thick lips. I felt sick to my stomach. *Ernie, where the hell are you?*

"He's taken it with him," Ernie's mum said. In a daze, my mind had travelled beyond Ernie's bedroom—to the vestry, to the dead squirrel, to the cemetery. I sat down on the bed.

"Arthur?"

"Pardon me?" I asked.

Mrs. Castlefrank gave me her first level stare, and I saw that Ernie carried his mother's face in every feature, the small straight teeth, high forehead, the pale hair. "He took his camera. It was one of the few things he took when he disappeared. He kept it right here on the shelf with those rolls of film. Oh, and his Commodore." *Ernie had a Commodore?* I could feel my face burn red. I had a surreal but fleeting feeling that I was at the wrong house.

She picked up the binder and sat down beside me on the bed, hugging it to her chest. I could smell her rank body odour. Mine was worse.

"After he left, I looked to see if he'd taken one of me. When I couldn't find any, I fancied he took them with him." She flipped the book to a page where several photos were missing and let out a joyless laugh. "Where is my boy? Why hasn't he called?"

Ernie had once told me that his mother wasn't built for family, or love—that she couldn't be counted on to step up for her sons. I hadn't expected such devotion to her sons. I had a craving to correct Ernie.

She shrugged then, and said, "Forgive me for all this whinging." She looked out at the tracks, as I had done. We heard more piano music. "Walter and Ernie seemed to be getting along at last. Walter was overjoyed to have a piano in the house. It gave him a sense that all is not lost." She paused to reflect. "One Sunday at supper Ernie had set the table and then brought out a new camera to take a photograph of some strawberries in my best crystal dish. Walter asked him where he'd got the money to buy it, and when Ernie didn't answer, he accused him of being a degenerate—he hit him across the face with a belt." Very quietly she added, "When he gets like that, well, there's nothing I can do."

She wasn't telling me anything I hadn't seen with my own eyes.

"I tried to put my arms around Ernie afterwards. He wouldn't have it." She turned from gazing out the window and met my eyes. "I don't miss their fights. Arthur, my husband isn't a bad man. He isn't able to play his instruments at the performance level, though, and he's too proud to go on the dole. Did Ernie tell you he was a violinist for the BBC Northern Symphony Orchestra? I have a drawer full of his concert programs. He's a graduate of the Royal College of Music."

"No. Ernie didn't tell me."

It washed over me that Mrs. Castlefrank was in the confessional and I was listening to her sins. The raggedy truth of it all was that we both craved to talk about Ernie. Some part of me was desperate for her to go on for hours, even as I wanted to flee the room.

"It's himself Walter loathes, but that was hard for Ernie to see." She took a deep breath, smoothed her apron again. In a near-whisper she said, "Thank you for letting me ramble on. Do you think our Ernie is out there, somewhere, making his way as a photographer?"

"Yes I do, Mrs. Castlefrank. I do." I said those words with utmost conviction, a reassurance to myself as much as to Ernie's pleading mother.

"Arthur, is there something of Ernie's you would like to take as a memento of sorts? I have my doubts that he'll be coming home again soon." Her chin wobbled and her eyes filled with tears. I could tell she had reconciled herself to the worst of news. After hearing that he'd taken his camera and a computer with him, I was a hundred percent certain Ernie was alive. I just didn't have the words to offer reassurance.

"Perhaps a book?"

"Of course," she said. She pointed to several stuffed milk crates in one corner of the room. Inside were plastic trays, metal tongs, jugs of developer and fixer, a few *National Geographic* issues with animals on the cover, and a very old copy of *Alice's Adventures in Wonderland*. At the bottom of one crate was a March 1977 issue of *Penthouse* magazine the Zipper had shown me a handful of times. The cover had tiny headlines about Watergate and Stephen King's short story "Children of the Corn," about a cult of murderous children. The bare-bottomed blond-haired woman on the cover was the perfect decoy. Maybe Mrs. Castlefrank thought Ernie was a normal teenager. If only.

I knew Ernie kept his cash in the carved-out insides of *Gray's Anatomy*, a book I had been more than happy to share. I picked up the *Gray's*, which was tightly tied with string, and gave Mrs. Castlefrank a heartfelt smile. I could tell from the book's lack of heft that wherever Ernie was, at least he had some money.

"Do you know what kind of camera he had?" I asked.

She scanned the invisible air in front of her, then shook her head. "No, Arthur, I don't know anything about photography. It was black. Not like those yellow Instamatics."

I nodded.

We both heard an angry shout from downstairs, then the sound of something heavy falling.

"Stella!"

Mrs. Castlefrank said, "Give me a moment."

After she'd gone to see what had happened, I walked down the hall to Nathan's room. If I had the dates right, he still had months of his sentence to serve. Although the room had been stripped bare except for an old record player and a framed poster of a Royal Enfield Interceptor motorbike, I could still smell cigarette smoke, the unmistakable air of Nathan's presence. The cupboard was open, empty but for four lonely hangers and an old Boy Scout uniform.

I went back to Ernie's room, dropped to the floor, peeked under his bed, and pulled out several books about philosophy and computer science with price stickers from the Copperfield and Twist. "You bastard," I said out loud. When I heard Ernie's mother climbing the stairs, I shoved them back among the dustballs under the bed. I was still on my knees when Mrs. Castlefrank came into the room. From deep in the pocket of her apron she dug out a photograph of Ernie, creased along his exposed collarbones, and handed it to me. I stared at the image. Diffused light gave Ernie's eyes an otherworldly blue glow, like the eyes of the Australian shepherd puppy we'd seen pulling a child's sled near the Tor one winter afternoon.

"Don't you want to keep this?" I said, swallowing hard.

She shook her head and wouldn't meet my eye, hands busy scratching at a crusty stain on her apron.

"Thank you," I said. I put the *Gray's Anatomy* and the photo of Ernie into my rucksack, and I stumbled down the stairs and out the door to the renewed sound of thudding piano chords. Ernie's mum followed me to the front stoop.

"Arthur, please thank your mother for the pies. I really appreciate her kindness." So my mother had been in touch.

When I got home, I put my arms around my mum's waist and swung her off her feet.

She laughed and batted at me until I put her down. "Arthur, whatever has got into you."

I couldn't explain the surge of pure joy I felt at the sight of her, so I just ducked my head and asked what was for tea.

"I don't know yet. I've made a cheddar quick bread, but I need to go out for groceries. What would you like to eat?"

"Maybe some chips and sausages," I said, and she smiled at me. It was my usual answer.

Moments later, behind my bedroom door, I opened Ernie's *Gray's Anatomy*. In the carved-out cavity I found a couple of tightly rolled joints and a single plaster in its paper. I examined both sides and found no clue to Ernie's whereabouts. As I held the bandage up to the light, a small piece of white paper slid out and I realized that one edge had been carefully slit. On the paper was a phone number in Ernie's handwriting, stiffly slanted to the right, each digit as neatly printed as though it had been typed on my Olivetti.

I waited an interminable half-hour for my mother to leave the flat, then stretched the telephone cord into the cupboard under the stairs and rang the number. No answer. I hung up and dialed again. Then I sighed and moved to the kitchen table and called again. I grabbed a piece of paper and began to create herringbone tally marks for each ring, the fifth stroke closing out the group. Seven groups of five. No answer. I rang again. My mother returned with groceries, saw my paper covered in tallies and the dismay scrawled on my face. Pressing her palm to my sweaty forehead, she asked, "Are you coming down with something?"

"I'm fine," I told her, and retreated to my room. That night, after she was in bed, I went back to dialing the number from the cupboard under the stairs.

The following day I came home during the lunch break. The flat was empty; my mother was likely at the office. I called again. I took to ringing at random times, before school, after school, from the bookshop, and every time I woke up in the middle of the night. After one last midnight call, I had to accept that Ernie had left me a dead end. I placed the phone back on the hook, went to my room and slammed the door. A moment later my mother knocked.

From the hall she said, "Arthur, I don't know what you are up to. Are you in some kind of trouble?

"No."

"Is there something you want to talk about?"

"No."

"You aren't calling a drug dealer, are you? People say that Ernie had got himself into hard drugs and that's why he ran away."

I didn't answer.

"I'm sorry about how that sounded. I know you miss Ernie, and I do too. Goodnight, Arthur." My mother went back to bed.

Whoever was supposed to be at the end of that number had vanished like Ernie had. Still, the following day I inked the digits on my hand. When it wore off, I wrote it on my hand again, unbuttoning my shirtsleeves so that they hung to the knuckles during school hours. At supper that night, my mother reached across the table, circled my wrist with her cool fingers, and then pushed up my sleeve, exposing the numbers on my pale skin.

"Arthur, what is this?"

"It's bugger all."

She dropped my wrist. "You spent all last weekend in your bedroom with the door closed. I know it's hard, but maybe you have to let Ernie go and try to make a new friend."

"You're one to talk. If friends are so important, where are yours? The only one I can think of is maybe Alfredo, and he's our landlord. Or Mrs. O'Brien. And she's ninety. You hardly comb your hair. You're wearing the same dress as yesterday." My cruel words made her face crumple, then hung in the air just out of reach, irretrievable.

"You're right. I'm no one to talk." She got up, brought her half-eaten sausages to the sink, touched her pale lips. With her back turned, she said, "I was fired from my job. My manager . . ." She put some biscuits on a plate. Her shoulders were as small as a young girl's. She scraped the sausages into the bin.

"Mum!"

"It was too upsetting to explain, Arthur. My manager decided he wanted something I couldn't give him. When I said no, he fired me. That was two months ago. Alfredo was kind enough to lower the rent until we're sorted again. We'll get by."

"But what have you been doing during the day? I've come home from school at lunch and you're never here. I thought you were at the office. You should have told me."

"I talked with Father Ziperto, and he and I decided that you didn't need to know until I'd sorted myself out. I've been doing a lot of volunteering at St. Nick's. I'm sorry. It was wrong of me not to tell you. But don't worry about money, Arthur. I've just got a job as a waitress at a café on Farm Road in Street."

"A waitress? You're a trained chef."

"Well, I have to keep a roof over our heads for the next while. And I'm thinking of writing a cookbook. I know it's a long shot, but I've written to a publisher in London who is quite interested in my pie recipes." She came back to the table, sat down, and briefly stroked my hand where I had written the number.

I said, "I didn't tell you this either, but I finally went to see Mrs. Castlefrank. I looked everywhere in Ernie's room for some hint of where he'd gone, but all I ended up finding was a phone number he'd hidden. I've called and called but no one answers."

My mother sighed, then disappeared into the bathroom. She returned with a cotton ball doused in nail polish remover and rubbed off the ink.

"Please don't call anymore, Arthur," she said. "I know you miss him, but it's time to focus on your studies. Stay out of trouble. Write book reviews for Miss Phillips. Aim for university."

I reluctantly raised my eyes to hers. Even when I'd been caught stealing, she'd always behaved as though I'd eventually find my way through to my true self and expected the best of me. I'd never assumed that she had any advice worth giving.

I got up from my chair and opened every cupboard in the kitchen, found the flour and the caster sugar, baking paper, the measuring cups, baking powder, nutmeg and cinnamon, vanilla bean, walnuts, the rolling pin.

"What are you doing?"

"What are *we* doing, mum? Let's make biscuits, and pies, and cinnamon buns and you can bring them to the café. If you want to write your cookbook, you'll need critical feedback."

"That's a wonderful idea, Arthur," she said, laughing. "The café could use some decent baked goods."

With a jolt, I realized I hadn't heard her laugh in a very long while.

Getting up, she began to search for where she'd tucked her Wallis Simpson apron. Her back to me, she asked, "Do you think Ernie really left the number for you to find?"

Chapter 20

I was glad that my mother and I had cleared the air to some extent. Still, I slept with the light on to keep the shadows at bay. I hid in the bookshop and wrote even more reviews at my desk in the back corner. I didn't feel so much abandoned as inadequate—like I hadn't been enough of a friend. I hadn't. I couldn't bear to look at what connected us. I'd wanted Ernie to keep the secret, the way I was keeping the secret. I tried to tell myself I should be relieved he was gone, because now he couldn't lead me into any more trouble. Instead, I was afraid of what might be around the corner. And everything reminded me that he was gone.

Ernie had taken up so little space when he was slouched at his desk in class, but ever since he disappeared, he remained the talk of the school. Rumours swirled: he had moved to the darkest corners of London, to Manchester, to Birmingham. Kids swore they saw him get in or out of local cars. My own mother thought she'd spotted him in a green Mercedes in the village of Street not two miles from the High Street in Glastonbury. After a skull was found forty yards down a railway embankment near Castle Cary, our classmate Paula Clooney spread a rumour that Ernie had jumped in front of a train. Given his knowledge and appreciation for the railroad and where its tracks might take him, that wasn't a possibility. Ernie would more likely have hopped a train and ridden it away.

On train trips, Ernie always wanted the window seat. He knew the names of the trees we passed, and the clouds—nacreous, cumulus, nimbus. He was ever vigilant for animal life and appreciative of the tiny patches of humanity along the tracks that exposed the lives of the rail-side dwellers in such intimate detail. "I love sad houses," he'd say, pointing to a chorus line of discoloured laundry waving at us, to an upturned self-propelled lawnmower, straggly gardens, leaky drainpipes, a rain-weathered pram that had been turned into a wheelbarrow. "The porch lights are on to keep the rats in their dens," he said. To be a voyeur of decay at such close range was as much of an enthrallment as it was a validation of the scarcities in his own backyard. I knew exactly which days Ernie's mum had had to choose between heating the house and putting food on the table. My mother had been there too before the Zipper had given her a leg up.

Ernie once told me that living beside the train tracks was for people with fewer choices. I was farther from the tracks, but my own choices also seemed limited.

Each day after school I went to the Copperfield and Twist, where I shelved books, packaged up phone orders, and tracked late shipments. I read and reviewed *The Indian in the Cupboard* and *Empire of the Sun*, relieved to have the chance to bask in Miss Phillips's praise. "Arthur, I'm going to hate to see you go," she said one Saturday afternoon, "even though I know that to fulfill your promise, you really must leave Glastonbury. It would be a terrible disservice to yourself if you stayed."

"Oh, I'm never leaving."

In that moment, I couldn't imagine myself anywhere except in Miss Phillips's restorative presence, submerged in stories great and small, hilarious and dismal.

"You may be content to critique the work of other authors for the moment," she said. "But one day . . ."

Her belief that I'd eventually write my own books was a compliment, yet I heard the catch in her voice and saw her eyebrows lift in an invitation for me to open up about my dreams for the future. In that instant I saw the worry lines around her eyes and hoped I wasn't what had caused them. My mother had those same creases.

We were interrupted by the tinkle of the shop bell.

As Miss Phillips moved to her spot behind the counter, I looked up, and there was Mrs. Castlefrank, wearing oversized plastic sunglasses and carrying a large canvas tote. She'd made an effort to dress up, wearing a rosy-coloured coat over a light brown checked skirt and shiny tights, which, even with a wide ladder up the back of one leg, gave her a sleek look. She hesitantly approached Miss Phillips at the till, and said, "I wish to donate some books." Glancing around the shop, she noticed me sitting on the bench in the wildlife section. "Oh, hello, Arthur," she said, giving me a wisp of a smile as I got up to greet her. Then she reached into her tote and produced the books I'd seen beneath Ernie's bed, piling them on the counter.

Her boy-cropped hair was parted on the side, and her pale lipstick matched her pink coat. For the first time I saw that she was in fact a beautiful woman, a carbon copy of Ernie. But when she removed her sunglasses, she revealed the yellowy leftovers of a large bruise on her cheek that reached up towards her eye. The slight scent of her perfume mingled with something medicinal.

"You look nice," I managed to say, glancing quickly away from her damaged face.

She tightened the belt on her rosy coat and smoothed the front lapels. "Thank you. A little charity shop find."

I wanted to say I hadn't meant her coat, but I couldn't get such a compliment out of my mouth. Instead I just smiled, my eyes now on the wobbly grain of the oak floor at my feet.

She pushed the stack of books a little farther towards the till, as though anxious to be rid of them. At least three were volumes of philosophy. Plato, *The Apology of Socrates*. Aristotle on moral virtue. Nietzsche. *Mathematical Foundations of Computer Science* and *Understanding the Computer Age* were the thickest. Miss Phillips picked up the books one by one, her eyes darting to mine. Her finger scratched the little spot on one book jacket where most of the shop sticker had been rubbed off. She crossed her arms and cupped her chin and glanced my way again. From the look on her face, I knew for certain every one of them had been nicked from her shelves.

I shrugged to show her I had no idea, a lie of the whitest in my view, given I'd seen all of these books under Ernie's bed. Then I introduced them. "Miss Phillips, this is Mrs. Castlefrank."

Miss Phillips came around from behind the till and extended both her hands to Ernie's mum, who took them uncertainly but met her eyes. I recognized the expression on Miss Phillips's face from the day she caught me stealing *The Prophet*—no hint of judgment.

"As you likely know, Mrs. Castlefrank, I've met your son. I'm so sorry he's gone missing."

Rattled, Ernie's mum just said, "Oh, please call me Stella. I don't stand on ceremony."

Turning to lay a hand on top of the pile, Miss Phillips said, "These will be a wonderful addition to our used shelves. Thank you for bringing them in. Would you please wait here for just a quick moment?"

When Mrs. Castlefrank nodded, Miss Phillips went to her office and returned with her personal copy of *Jonathan Livingston Seagull*, pristine, and signed by its author, Richard Bach. I knew it was among her most treasured items, along with an autographed copy of Gabriel García Márquez's *One Hundred Years of Solitude*. Miss Phillips was catholic in her tastes.

Handing the book to Mrs. Castlefrank, she told her that it was about a bird whose determination to live more than an ordinary seagull life results in his expulsion from his flock. "We can all be so much more than we are given to believe, don't you think?" she said, and darted yet another look at me, as though I, too, needed to understand this lesson.

"I'm not much of a reader," Mrs. Castlefrank said. "But please let me buy the book from you." She pulled a tissue from her pocket and wiped her now teary eyes and cheeks, which exposed more of the deep bruising. Ernie had gone from one blow to the next, but it was only in that moment that I realized that Mrs. Castlefrank was also being hit hard enough to break blood vessels in her eye.

"No, no, it's a gift. A token of gratitude for the books you've brought us."

"You're very kind, thank you," Mrs. Castlefrank said. She studied *Jonathan Livingston Seagull* for a moment and then tucked it into her canvas bag, giving a small start as she peered inside. "I almost forgot this last one."

She withdrew *Are You There God? It's Me, Margaret.* "Ernie said it was about sex. I can assure you, it's about so much more." Her hand flew to her lips, and I thought she might faint from embarrassment.

Without missing a beat, Miss Phillips went to Mrs. Castlefrank, gently did up the top button of her pink coat, straightened the strap of her handbag over her shoulder and said, "That one is a classic. We've carried it for more than a decade. Please come back anytime, Stella. I'm sure I have plenty of books that you might find will become some of your best friends. I know lots of people who come to reading later in life." Then she delicately acknowledged the truth hovering between them. "It looks like your son found solace in the ideas of our greatest thinkers. You should be proud of that, and of him. I admire people who seek out the truth. Especially when it's about themselves." This time, Miss Phillips didn't glance my way, but I got her message.

Once more Mrs. Castlefrank's eyes filled to overflowing. She gave a little nod and put on her sunglasses. After giving me a quick, awkward pat on the arm, she left the shop.

After she was gone, Miss Phillips said, "I'll never be able to save the world, but I do try to be more than just a bookseller." In a steadier voice she added, "And here I thought it was the pharmacist who was stealing the books. He comes in once a week, browses the shelves, and rarely buys a thing. Not for a second did I think it was you, Arthur, or Ernie."

I looked at her steadily, until she said, "Well, maybe I did have a moment or two where I worried you had returned to your thieving ways, but then I thought, 'Why would Arthur be stealing books about technology and mathematics?'"

Eager to return to less dangerous territory, I said, "Would you like me to put them back on the shelves? They still look brand new."

She stared down at the stack, lost in thought for a moment, and then extracted one of them. "Arthur, of all the burdens that poor woman has had to bear, was there a member of her family who was mortally ill?" She held up *On Death and Dying* by Elisabeth Kübler-Ross.

"I think it was Ernie who was dying."

She gave me a sharp look. When she saw I was serious, her eyes softened. "I see," she said. After a small hesitation, she asked, "Did Ernie ever talk about ending his own life?"

"You mean suicide? No. Of course not."

"I suppose he wouldn't have. Very few people speak openly about a subject like that." She had a faraway look on her face, as though revisiting a forgotten memory.

After another moment or two, I conceded, "I do know he thought a lot about death. Nothing more."

"Did Ernie have those same kinds of bruises . . .?" Her voice trailed off.

"No." My first instinct, as usual, was to deny. But then I said, "Yes. Sometimes. But mental cruelty hurt him much more." I fell silent, but she found my eyes and waited for me to continue.

When I didn't, she picked up one of the philosophy books. "I read this one at uni. As Socrates said, 'The only true wisdom is knowing you know nothing.'"

But I did know something.

Taking it from her, I carried the lot to the shelves. From a twenty-foot distance, I said, "Ernie tried to explain to me that understanding philosophy can allow a person to overcome the fear of death. It was right after his stepfather gave him a beating with the buckle end of his belt. When he started to heal, he let the subject drop." I left out the part about Ernie once asking me to come up with ways to move a dead body. If anything, Ernie thought about murder, not suicide.

"Come here for a minute, Arthur." Miss Phillips beckoned me back to the front desk. "I wasn't going to mention this, but maybe you've already heard about it from your classmates. The newspaper has just reported that a boy from Bath was found dead in a shower stall at school. He was described as slightly built, and in the photograph they printed alongside the article, he had a sweet little face and a mop of curly hair. He was seventeen, but looked younger. I couldn't sleep after I saw it."

"You thought it was Ernie? In Bath?" I staggered back, plunking myself down on a chair. The torn bus ticket was still in my wallet, taped together like a wound.

"It wasn't Ernie, Arthur," she said, rushing to my side. She leaned close, brushing the long fringe of my hair behind an ear with such concern I bolted out of the chair and ran to the loo at the back of the shop. After a moment, she knocked on the door. "I'm sorry, Arthur. Please come out. I'll show you the newspaper, and you'll see for certain it wasn't Ernie."

I opened the door.

Miss Phillips led the way to the counter. Rummaging behind the till, she found a copy of the *Bath Times* and showed me the two columns at the bottom left corner of the fourth page. It wasn't Ernie. In the article the boy, reported to be a teenager who played the flute and had competed in national cross-country races before he hanged himself, wore a blue racing bib and held up an engraved trophy. The final sentences read that, since his unwitnessed death had occurred at school, an autopsy would be performed to rule out foul play. Substance abuse was suspected. The school principal volunteered that the boy had recently dyed his hair from blond to black and had taken to wearing two extra-large hoodies everywhere he went.

"Two hoodies," I said out loud, hugging myself.

"Changing his appearance does suggest something was going on," Miss Phillips said. "The item ran last weekend in the Bath paper, and it was picked up by the *Somerset Gazette* too, even though the boy died a month ago. Rodger Mistlethorpe told me that soon after the piece was published, an anonymous caller phoned the paper to say he'd been an altar server, the oldest boy still on the rota at his local church."

I must have looked stricken again, because once more Miss Phillips felt she had to apologize. "Arthur, I've been more than thoughtless. You behave so calmly when you're here, and your reviews are all so terribly perceptive and mature, I tend to forget you're barely sixteen, with no idea where your best friend has disappeared to, or even if he's still alive. I'm sorry. If I find myself lying awake worrying about Ernie, what must you be doing?"

That little speech and her kindness towards Mrs. Castlefrank at last gave me the courage to tell her more about my complicated friendship with Ernie, including our partnership in petty crime, our day in youth court, and the stolen pen. I told her about all the random facts he retained, his maths ability and love of animals, and the time he recited Poe's "The Raven" in class, to the astonishment of all. But, even with Mrs. Castlefrank's bruise in my mind's eye, I didn't say that he performed that last feat in the aftermath of one of his stepfather's belt beatings, or that his performance also emanated from some grave awfulness I'd never been able to shake.

I didn't say anything about the Zipper either, of course, or about my cowardice when Ernie tried to blow the whistle. What if I told her that I would never drink Cadbury's chocolate milk again. The taste had stayed on the Zipper's lips and lingered on mine. Or what Ernie might have been doing with a dodgy pawnbroker to earn the money to pay Nathan's fine. My random thoughts had silenced me when *Understanding the Computer Age* slipped from my hands before I could slot in into the shelf. Miss Phillips hurried over to pick it up, laying a gentle hand on my shoulder. I took the book from her, and this time managed to shelve it.

I rushed on with Ernie's other strengths. "Ernie could be very persuasive: he once convinced Alfredo—he's the tailor who lives below us—to hem his hand-me-down trousers for free so they wouldn't drag on the pavement. Another time, he got Alfredo to trim his hair with his pinking shears. I'd never heard Alfredo laugh like that."

"Ernie couldn't afford a haircut?"

"Well, his family is poor, but it wasn't that: Ernie loved the zigzag effect!" I laughed, then caught myself when it threatened to choke me. After a while of staring at the shelves, I said, "It was my job to protect him, and I didn't."

Mrs. Phillips touched the raven on my T-shirt, and said, "I wondered why you wear this so often. Now I know."

"Yes, my mother bought one for each of us. Ernie says there's a proverb about how one raven never pecks out the eye of another." Then the bell tinkled again and several customers came chatting into the shop, and she turned away to help them.

I'd finally bought my own copy of Poe. My mother and I had read and reread the poem Ernie had painstakingly learned by heart, circling stanzas here and there, trying to figure out why he'd stolen a copy from the bookshop when he knew how kind Miss Phillips was, and how important she was to me. My mother suggested he must have been trying to get my attention in some way. A cry for help. I really hated that thought.

In my endless search for answers to an attic full of questions, I later understood that Poe's "The Raven," despite the spookiness, speaks of never being able to get out from underneath grief. That was the undeniable awfulness.

Chapter 21

Despite Miss Phillips's care with me, reading about the suicide of the lost altar boy burned a hole in my gut. Unlike my reckoning with Ernie at the science sink, there was no tap I could turn off to stop my thoughts, which also turned to Declan Entwhistle, another suicide, and the boy on the bench in Bath who had sent Ernie off the deep end. During my own sleepless nights, I'd put a pillow over my head to test out suffocation. I'd wonder if one razor blade was enough to do the job in a bathtub filled with hot water. I'd consider whether the light fixture in the living room would hold my weight after I kicked away the kitchen chair.

I stayed away from the hulking stone walls of St. Nick's, whose bells rang daily at noon, reminding me to recite the Lord's Prayer—"Forgive us our trespasses, as we forgive those who trespass against us, and lead us not into temptation, but deliver us from evil." When I was little, my mother said the ringing of the church bells drove out demons, but I had ample proof that they didn't work. At least my mum didn't bother me about why I'd stopped attending mass, putting it down to me missing Ernie. When she leaned on the sink while doing dishes one night and said to the streaky window, "Where's Ernie? Arthur, you must have an inkling," all I could say was, "I don't know, Mum. I promise you, I don't know. And wherever he went, I thought he'd be back by now."

We both craved answers. I couldn't tell her that Ernie had been pushed out of his own life for speaking the truth. That the naked truth about me was that I was nothing but a rent boy.

Ernie had given the money he earned or stole from the Zipper and the church collection plate to his mother to pay the bills or saved it up to pay his brother's fine. I had tucked the hundreds of pounds the Zipper had given me over the years in a shoebox carefully hidden from sight. While the warden had never come after Ernie and me for thieving from the plate, he had taken measures to stop us. And the Zipper often reminded me that I'd already stood in front of the judge in youth court for stealing, that a second court appearance would be less forgiving and would likely land me behind bars.

Ernie worshipped money because he didn't want to be a charity case. I had no excuse. Some days I longed to carry the box outside and release the pound notes to the wind, but cowardice deterred me there too. I could picture the neighbours calling out, *What did you do to get all that money, Arthur?*

When I was little, the Zipper had told me that nobody looked out for me like he did or cared for me like he would. He said, "I will never hurt you." At eight, and nine, and ten, I lived for those words. After Ernie became the favoured boy, on occasion the Zipper would still profess his devotion to me, which made me want to ride off into the woods on my bicycle and scream until my lungs stopped working and I could die from something other than shame. I was trapped either way: speak up or shut up.

I knew the Zipper had other boys on a string. That he was likely doing worse to them than what he'd done to me, and maybe when they were younger. But I didn't have the guts to blow the whistle, because I'd be blowing the whistle on myself.

—

As more months slid by, I kept waiting for something to happen. Word eventually went around school that Nathan had been released from prison, but that he hadn't moved back to Glastonbury. I wondered how Mrs. Castlefrank felt about that, but I couldn't get myself to go knock on her door and ask. Both sons lost in the darkness.

Then the cardboard box that had contained the stereo Ernie had bought for fifty pounds from the pawnbroker showed up outside the door of our flat. My first and only thought: *Ernie is back!*

In a rush of euphoria, I carried it to the kitchen table and tore it open. Inside, wrapped in newspaper, was the black and white marble chess set, and a note from Ernie's mother written on a serviette: "I hope you're doing well, Arthur. You're the only other person I know who understands how to play the game."

I picked up the queens and held one in each hand. I considered throwing them out the window to hear the crack of marble on concrete. Instead, I found myself setting up the board and replaying one of the many games in which my opponent was the person who always claimed the white pieces, who always made the first move. Greasy sweat soon formed on my palms. I wiped them on my jeans and played on.

When I heard footsteps on the stairs, I threw the pieces back into the box and jammed the newspaper around them. Too soon my mother was at the table.

She picked up and examined a white rook. "What a beautiful chess piece, Arthur. Where did this set come from?"

When I didn't answer, she plugged in the kettle, pulled a bottle of milk from the fridge, warmed the teapot with hot water, then turned around to gauge the look on my face. The sparkle had drained from her expression. "You've stolen it, haven't you?" My mother's lips thinned as she stared me down. "And if you think I can't smell the pot you smoke in your bedroom at night, you're dreaming. It's illegal, Arthur. Do you want to end up in jail like Nathan did?"

"You don't know anything," I shouted.

I grabbed the heavy box and tore down the stairs and out to the road, like I was carrying the weight of every Monday afternoon in the vestry. I lugged that box all the way to the pawnshop in Street. An hour of half running, half walking, full sweat. Twice, cars swerved to avoid hitting me. When one driver honked and gave me the finger, I screamed my own obscenity.

When I got there, the shop was closed. I stood there for a couple minutes, at first even more pissed off, and then relieved. I left the box leaning against the side door and roamed the streets aimlessly, trying the handles of parked cars in a throwback to my nights with Ernie. When the streetlights came on, I slipped into a phone booth, fished ten pence from my pocket and called home.

"I didn't steal the chess set," I said.

"I'm sorry, Arthur. I had no right to make that assumption. Come home, please. Your supper's getting cold."

We ate in silence, then I did the washing-up. Both of us went to bed early. Once again, I hardly slept.

The next morning, I dressed quickly and went back to the pawnshop before school started. The box of chessmen was still resting against the door. In the light of day, my best guess was that Ernie had stolen it from the vestry to prevent another boy from being recruited. In that spirit, I decided I would keep it safe in the shadows under my bed. When I bent down to lift the heavy box from where it sat against the steel door, there, stencilled on the metal kick plate in small black letters, was the phone number I'd dialed for days after I'd found it in Ernie's room. The hair rose on the back of my neck, and I looked about.

A name was written there too, scratched and defaced by weather and time so that only someone already familiar would have been able to make it out: Casper Fontaine. The shop was still locked, barricaded and dark, the street as empty as usual. I slid down the door and sat on the stoop as my mind tumbled with possibilities. Finally I got up again, hoisted the box and headed home, certain that Ernie had left me the number because he'd wanted me to know he was still connected with the pawnbroker. What to make of that, though, I had no clue.

Even though she'd apologized for suspecting me, my mother remained out of sorts for days. I'd told her that the chess set was a gift from Mrs. Castlefrank, but she knew there was more to the story or I wouldn't have reacted with such anger. But she didn't come out and ask. Instead, she baked with the radio on, obsessively tidied the flat, painted an ugly claw-foot hutch a beautiful peacock blue, entertained our neighbour Mrs. O'Brien for tea, and did not raise the subject again.

I lived for my afternoons and weekends working at the bookshop, where I had graduated to tending the till. Every so often I would catch Miss Phillips looking my way. She was quick to remove her glasses and rub her eyes, or straighten a pile of new fiction, or pick lint from her favourite blue and white argyle sweater vest. I stockpiled those furtive but concerned glances as though they were gold bars at the Royal Mint. I hadn't quite realized how much I needed her in my corner. Instead of plying me with questions, she fed me books to fill the holes left behind after a person abandons you: my father, Ernie, and even the Zipper, who had left me with a queasy fear that I was accountable not only to my lost friend, but to all Catholic parishioners, to the mother in Bath, to every boy at St. Nicholas in the flush of innocence who'd been given a silver cross on a serpentine chain.

At school, I found it easier to spend my lunch hour in the library with my face buried in a five-hundred-page book than to face the scrutiny of the other students. As my grades began to skyrocket, my social life went into even deeper oblivion; both made me grateful. And so, I was unprepared when Claire Hughes tacked an invitation to her seventeenth birthday party to the metal door of my locker with a wet piece of chewing gum, and then stood so close to me while she waited for my answer that I could smell her strawberry lip gloss. She'd sung with Ernie in the choir and was one of the few who, to my knowledge, had never judged him for being a Castlefrank.

"I'm inviting you personally, Arthur. Friday night. I live on Overleigh Court."

Her school blouse was freshly pressed and her fingernails were pale and smooth. I noticed these small details because I couldn't look her in the eye. A warm flush rose from my neck to my forehead.

"I have to stay in on Friday night and write a review for the bookshop," I mumbled.

"That's too bad because we've ordered a keg of German beer, and it will be the biggest bash since Oktoberfest. Everyone's coming except my parents. They're on holiday in Cairo."

When I remained mute, she pulled the invitation off my locker, leaving a small residue of gum. "You're missing out," she said, and then, as she turned away, she added, "I used to be shy too. That's nothing to be ashamed of. If you don't come, I'll be missing out too."

I spent the next twenty-four hours plagued with regret. Only in my imagination had I ever talked to a girl, let alone asked one out on a date. Because who was I? A boy, a girl? Gay, straight, bisexual? What was Ernie? The Zipper?

And who would even want me? The Zipper was right. No one would ever love me like he had.

While Miss Phillips understood that I was stagnating in some blackwalled cell, of course she misunderstood my mixed bag of conflicts.

The Saturday after the party I chose to miss, she watched me for a while when no customers were in the shop, and then said, "Arthur, I truly believe Ernie will come back. His roots are here."

"Maybe," I said. "At least they haven't recovered his body."

I longed to tell her that I rode past the pawnshop at the very far end of the High Street every so often, and although the shop was always locked, sometimes there were lights on inside. Ernie was alive, and he and the pawnbroker were working together. Proof was in my wallet: a piece of paper with a neatly printed phone number in Ernie's slanted hand. It lay alongside the torn bus ticket.

"Arthur, you've been awfully quiet recently. The books I'd hoped you would review are piling up on your desk."

She was right. In my funk, I had missed not one, or two, but three deadlines. Forever the optimist, Miss Phillips tried to encourage me. "You're too hard on yourself."

"He left without a goodbye. What does that say about how good a friend I was? Believe me, it was my fault."

"I doubt it, Arthur. Whatever happened between you, remember that sometimes our mistakes push us forward." As always, her words were an invitation to share the weight, one I couldn't accept.

All the same, I had to acknowledge that as time passed, a shift was occurring. Although it felt selfish, the longer Ernie stayed away, the more I found myself hoping he wouldn't return. As long as Ernie was gone, my past could stay right where it was.

I got back to work, first sinking my teeth into the nine-hundred-odd pages of *Trinity*, looking to reawaken my kinship with Leon Uris.

His Conor Larkin, shaped by his childhood, believed the Irish peo-
ple had the right to decide their own destiny and that anything else was a compromise. Selling out to the enemy was unacceptable. In contrast, my own bravery was as non-existent as my father's place at the

table, my destiny seemingly shaped by a Catholic Church unwilling to acknowledge its sins.

There were moments when I desperately longed to trust Miss Phillips, except that if I broke my long silence and spoke the words to describe what the Zipper had begun doing to me, and to Ernie, when we were eight— what he was still doing to other boys—I was certain she would fire me on the spot. Once she knew what I had been paid to do, what I had sometimes even enjoyed doing, she would withdraw her friendship and I'd be lost.

On the outside, I looked like the young man I was becoming. I had hair and teeth and fingers that could type. I ate fish and chips from rolled-up newspaper and read storybooks aloud to the children who came to the shop on Saturday afternoon, revelling as much as they did in the magic sleigh rides, friendly bears, train journeys to the seashore, and smiling parents. To keep myself from fleeing as Ernie had done, I had to act like nothing had happened. I was too myopic to see that coming clean would have been the shorter, less twisted path. Instead, I clung to the idea that I had no safe person to tell.

I read and kept on reading, precociously: science fiction and murder mysteries, Kurt Vonnegut, Agatha Christie, Joseph Heller, Philip Roth, Kazuo Ishiguro's brilliant novel about a thwarted life, *The Remains of the Day*, happy to stay in my room and study or work at the shop. I pretended I was too busy reviewing books to pursue a friendship with the likes of strawberry-scented Claire Hughes.

Ernie had disappeared, but the banishment was also mine.

Chapter 22

In the spring of my final year of secondary school—Ernie had been gone for almost two years—my mother asked me to accompany her to a funeral Mass at St. Nick's for her much older cousin, Cynthia. I hadn't known her very well, but my mother had fond memories of her from their shared childhood, and I could hardly say no. The only time I'd set foot inside the church since Ernie had vanished was to appease my mother for an hour or so on Christmas Eve. The first person I'd seen when we'd walked in was the Ear Whacker, who was up on the altar lighting candles. Even from a distance I could make out the downward slant of his full lips, the black half moons under his pouchy eyes. I shrank into my collar and looked up at the choir loft to avoid eye contact.

The Zipper was spry and slim, seemingly ageless; his brother had several chins, fleshy hands, those pouchy eyes and a slight stoop. Whereas the Zipper strode manfully everywhere he went, the Ear Whacker wore crepe-soled Wallabees that muffled his footsteps as he sloped to and from his little office in one of the back rooms of the musty-smelling rectory. He holed up for hours in that office, with the volume of his radio turned up. I thought he was deaf, but Ernie insisted the loudness of the music had nothing whatsoever to do with his hearing, it only helped him maintain his wilful blindness about his brother.

Once, on a Monday afternoon, the Ear Whacker, who had his own key, had entered the vestry moments after I had pulled on my gray trousers. I was twelve at the time, no longer innocent about what was going on with the priest, and my humiliation ran poker hot. With a flick of his hand, he whacked my ear, then grabbed my arm and rushed me out into the corridor and closed himself in with his brother. Normally he cultivated an air of serene indifference, but he'd clenched his thick lips so hard they'd gone purple with a twisted mixture of anger and revulsion. I didn't wait around to hear what was said between the brothers, even though he'd shoved me out without my shoes. Instead, I walked home in my black cotton socks, feeling as steady as a dandelion fluff in the wind.

Father Ziperto was not the celebrant of the funeral service that Saturday. Just that morning, my mother had learned that he'd been reassigned to St. Brendan's in Bath. I was so flooded with relief, I'd almost hugged my mother until I saw that she was shattered. Her favoured priest's absence weighed heavily on her all through the funeral Mass and the post-service reception, where she'd been the one to arrange for the sandwiches and tea.

Since she had taken over the position of head volunteer, she and the Zipper had been in constant touch about choir schedules, baptisms, marriage classes and the like. She spent hours on Saturday mornings folding the weekly church bulletins and prepared the coffee and the biscuits served to the congregants on Sundays. During the funeral service, tears had slipped down my mother's face. Everyone else was crying for Cynthia, but I was pretty sure she was crying because the priest had deserted us.

As I ate a plateful of cucumber sandwiches in the reception room down in the crypt, she stood beside me trying to hide her distress. "I can't understand why he chose to leave St. Nick's," she finally whispered, "let alone why he didn't say goodbye. I guess his focus has already shifted to his new flock."

Couldn't anybody see the dead lambs lying forsaken on the ground?

She hadn't been this devastated by anything since Ernie had left Glastonbury. Or before that, when I'd faced a judge in youth court. Or going back even further, the day my father had died. Floating on my own cloud of soaring relief, I couldn't find the words to soothe her.

I left my mother to make my way to the bookshop, so exhilarated I almost skipped down the paved path. I stopped dead when I spotted the Ear Whacker sitting in his Vauxhall near the stand of willow trees just beyond the church grounds, unmistakable even though he wore aviator sunglasses and a hat pulled low over his brow. The rest of his pale face hung down in flabby folds, and I could see the sweat on his cheeks from five yards out.

"Barnes," he called out his open car window and waved me over. I scanned my surroundings for an easy exit, but it came over me there wasn't much this man could do to me now and I obeyed his summons. He lifted the sunglasses to stare at me as I approached—the cobalt bags under his eyes made the rest of his face look even more chalky. I took an involuntary step backward as though he was contagious.

Hoarsely he whispered, "Come closer." I did, and he thrust a bundle of large envelopes into my hands. "University applications, Barnes. The tuition is free if you're smart enough to be selected. Get out of here."

He let his sunglasses drop and leaned to turn the key, saying, "We have no doubt you'll be a great success."

I blurted, "It's Ernie Castlefrank who needs help, sir, not me."

"Ernie doesn't live here anymore," the Ear Whacker said. "Get away from Glastonbury and make something of your life." He wound up the window, revved the engine, and put the car in reverse, about to back out of the space.

"Why are you helping me?" I yelled.

He hit the brake and rolled down his window again.

"Father Ziperto would have told you this himself, Barnes, but as you know he's had to take up duties at a new parish. He has always had confidence in your academic ability, and so some years ago he began an endowment to cover your room and board at university. It's enough to cover four years. A generosity he only extends to the special children."

Catching those last two words, I turned my back on the Ear Whacker and began to walk away as though I hadn't heard. I knew the truthful answer to my question, and I was pretty sure the Zipper's twin brother did too. Father Ziperto had been transferred to Bath, and a handful of people had an interest in concealing the truth about what he'd been up to, including, to my everlasting shame, me.

I walked to the bookshop, waved hello to Miss Phillips, and went to sit at my desk. Dumping the bundle of university forms in front of me, I fingered each manila envelope as though it was poisoned. I finally stuffed them all into one of the drawers and got to work on a book review. I ended up staring endlessly at a blank sheet of paper, unable to concentrate on anything other than the Zipper's questionable endowment. When curiosity got the best of me, I retrieved them, one by one, and I opened the envelopes: Warwick, Exeter, Nottingham, Durham, Bristol, Lancaster.

The Ear Whacker had paperclipped a small news story from the *Somerset Gazette* to the application for Durham University. The headline read: LOCAL BUSINESSMAN ARRESTED. I scanned the piece, shocked to think the Zipper's twin knew I'd be interested. I let my head fall onto my folded arms to better gather my thoughts and fit the pieces together. Eventually I felt a tug on my sleeve—Miss Phillips, wondering if I'd fallen asleep or wasn't feeling well. I bolted upright to see her reading the clipping reporting that Casper Fontaine of Glastonbury, Somerset, had been arrested and was awaiting a court date.

"Do you know him, Arthur?"

"Not really. Ernie did. He worked for Fontaine the summer he was fourteen and the man taught him computer coding."

"Is that right?" she said. "I gathered from the books Mrs. Castlefrank returned that Ernie had an interest in computer science. Rodger Mistlethorpe has had Fontaine in his sights for a while."

"Why?"

"Well, pawnbroking can have a dodgy side."

Miss Phillips's eyes were now on the pile of applications. "I'm so glad you've decided to apply to university, Arthur. You'll read English literature, no doubt. Is Durham your first choice? Rather far away, don't you think?"

Just then she realized several customers were lined up at the till holding books, and she hurried off to ring up the sales, saving me from answering.

In the days that followed, Miss Phillips didn't ask me about Casper Fontaine, or raise his connection to Ernie: I must have been a human stop sign. She was, however, endlessly excited about my university prospects, especially Bristol, her own alma mater.

"Best to apply to as many as possible," Miss Phillips advised. "The acceptance rate for applicants is far below fifty percent, especially at the prestige schools."

Dutifully, I filled out all six applications, planning to send them on to the central council on admissions in the United Kingdom. In the end, after standing in a queue at the post office, I posted a single application, to Durham University, as far as I could get from Glastonbury and stay in England.

I got in. And that wasn't the end of the good news for my mother and me. Shortly after I received the acceptance letter, I came home from the bookshop one evening shocked to find her about to carve a glazed duck à l'orange, a glass of bubbly at her elbow. She removed her Wallis Simpson apron, poured a glass for me and announced, "Arthur, I've received a small offer for my cookbook. Your mother is going to be the family's *first* published author."

We clinked glasses, smiling at each other, wrapped in the heavenly scent of roast duck. Years earlier, she had clipped the recipe from the *Sunday Times*, and the newsprint had been taped to the fridge ever since, waiting for our lives to turn around.

The cookbook contract was almost enough to offset the recent news that because of his exemplary record of effective parish leadership, the Zipper had been tapped to become the auxiliary bishop of Somerset-Avon. My mother had read the update in the church bulletin the Sunday before, and then dropped the notice on the kitchen table, where it sat like an uninvited guest. A few days later, it disappeared.

I found it in the rubbish, ripped in several pieces. My mother was holed up in her room, but a caramelized apple tart sat cooling on a baking tray. The torn bulletin gave me such a rush of solidarity with my mother I knocked on her door to tell her I would hoover the flat.

One summer Sunday in the weeks before I left for Durham University's Grey College, Stella Castlefrank came for a visit. It was the one and only time I can recall her coming to our flat. Still, since Ernie had disappeared, she and my mother had become something like friends, mostly over the telephone, a rarity given the state of their social lives.

That day, my mother had washed the dust off her Aynsley dessert plates and poured Pimm's with freshly cut cucumber into champagne flutes instead of our everyday chipped stubby glasses. The flutes were on her best silver tray, which only came out now and then for her sister. Purple asters stood tall in a milk-glass vase. She was even wearing stockings and her good shoes with the higher heels.

Mrs. Castlefrank, whom I'd last seen at the bookshop with a bruised cheek and a bloodshot eye, climbed the stairs, pushed open the door, exclaimed about the delicious smells and sat down without removing her pink coat. I came out of my bedroom in time to see my mother lean down to kiss her on the cheek.

"Hello, Stella," she said, untying her apron and hanging it on a hook near the wall-mounted telephone. "How nice that you're finally here."

Almost breathless with excitement, Mrs. Castlefrank burst out, "Nathan just rang me—a reverse charge from a phone box, but I accepted in a heartbeat. We haven't spoken to each other in thirteen months." She picked up the flute and clinked her Pimm's-filled glass with my mother's.

"That's wonderful, Stella."

"He needs to borrow some money," she said, still sounding delighted. "He wants to buy an enlarger, and he says once he's able to sell bigger prints he'll be able to pay me right back. I think he might be having a showing of his photographs at an art gallery. And he's also got a job, with a film company called Reel Fauna, though it mustn't pay that much as of yet. I even have his address."

"You look ten years younger," my mother said with a laugh.

Mrs. Castlefrank dug in her coat pocket and, as if for evidence, she withdrew a little piece of paper on which she'd written the address. "Nathan says he has buyers already lined up for the prints. This might be the turnaround he's needed ever since he got out."

I sidled close to the kitchen table, but she folded the paper in half and pocketed it before I had time to catch the address. I was once again struck by her resemblance to Ernie, the delicacy of her mouth, the otherworldly blue eyes, the vulnerability.

"Nathan sounded just like his old self. Confident. Charming. Naturally, I said yes to the loan. Through thick and thin, I've hung on to a string of triple A pearls I wore the day I married Nathan's father. I've been meaning to get rid of them for a very long time. Where am I going these days?" She gave a genuine laugh and took a quick sip of her Pimm's. "I've already mailed the money. Fifteen hundred pounds, but I've also got a little gift I'd been saving for his birthday. I thought I might surprise him with a visit. Norma, will you come?" She lowered her voice, now softly pleading. "Please say you'll come with me."

That's when I understood that my mother's company was a condition of the trip, that Ernie's stepdad wasn't in on the plan, and probably not in on the sale of the pearls or the loan. She didn't mention Ernie, though I burned to ask.

Worrying her hands in her lap, Mrs. Castlefrank suddenly asked, "Is this a fool's journey?"

"Not if it's a chance to reconnect with your son," my mother vowed. "Of course, I'll come with you, Stella. We'll turn it into a little holiday. I haven't been to West Yorkshire since my husband . . ."

I went into my bedroom, shut the door, and finished my mother's sentence in my head: *died without a life insurance policy.* I heard her say, "The last time I went anywhere was to Canterbury in eighty-two. I was among the crowd of enthusiastic well-wishers who watched Pope John Paul II arrive by helicopter to meet the Archbishop of Canterbury. A great reconciliation between the Catholic Church and the Church of England, a mending of sorts."

"A mending of sorts . . ." Mrs. Castlefrank echoed.

Many phone calls later, they had settled on dates, decided where to stay—The Wrens on New Briggate—and bought train tickets. On the morning of their departure, Mrs. Castlefrank took a taxi to our flat. The driver hopped out and knocked on the downstairs door.

My mother's last words to me: "Don't forget Alfredo is expecting you for supper tonight."

The taxi then carried them on to the Castle Cary railway station. I imagined them behaving like two schoolgirls on an adventure, laughing over their matching hats, grateful for the perfect weather. I'd watched my mother make them a lunch, something with avocado, poppy seeds and dandelion leaves. And as she left the flat, she'd tucked a bottle of elderberry wine into her picnic bag.

———

When I got home that night, I could see from the street that every light in the flat was switched on. I bolted up the stairs and pushed open the door, relieved to hear my mother call out, "That you, m'love? How was work?"

I found her on her knees in the kitchen, cleaning the range as though she was about to put it up for auction. A moment later she stood, removed her yellow Marigolds, and began to grab items from the far reaches of a cupboard, pulling out silver candlesticks, a salver and a warming tray that hadn't been used since before my father's heart gave up. As she began to muscle the tarnish off the salver with a buffing mitt, she asked a second time, "How was work?"

Without waiting for a reply, she removed the mitt, and redonned the yellow rubber gloves in painful snaps and got back on her knees, sticking her head inside the oven.

I felt the urge to run to my room and slam the door. Instead, I stepped close enough to make sure that it wasn't turned on. "Mum, what's happened? Is everything all right?"

I listened to the sounds of her scrubbing. On most days I welcomed my mother's unobtrusiveness, her mostly unwavering acceptance. Now I wanted to shake a response out of her.

"Did you see Ernie?" I found myself finally able to ask.

"No, I did not." She sat back on her heels, then took an interminable time to peel off the grimy gloves, one black and sticky finger at a time. When she got up and laid them carefully on the edge of the kitchen sink, I picked them up and threw them in the bin. If she put them on again, my head would explode.

Not looking at me, she sat down hard on a kitchen chair and started to speak.

"We knocked, repeatedly. No one answered. It wasn't a flat at all, but an industrial-looking building. We waited outside for maybe half an hour, and I was ready to accept we had gone all that way for nothing. It was Stella who suggested we walk down the laneway and around to the back. It didn't feel safe, given the area, but what were our options? She was sure this was the right address because it was where she'd sent the money.

"There was a fire escape that ran up the back of the building. We could see that the door at the top was propped open with a brick, so up we climbed. Beyond the door was all kinds of equipment. Big metal lights and tripods. I could smell vinegar and ammonia. I felt like a trespasser."

My mother's eyelids fluttered, which only happened when she was anxious.

"We walked down a hall into a large room just as Nathan appeared at the far end, coming out of a door with a red lightbulb over it. He was wearing safety glasses and holding plastic tongs. Arthur, I hardly recognized him. He had long hair and a full beard. It was only when he spoke that I was sure it was Nathan. He was really shaken to see us and tried to hustle us both out to the fire escape. He took my arm and managed to get me to the door, but Stella stood as though her feet had been nailed to the floorboards."

"What didn't he want you to see?" My stomach clenched: I was pretty sure I knew the answer.

"Dozens of photos of children tacked on a makeshift clothesline. I can still smell the chemicals. On the floor was a big basket of children's toys. A Sindy doll, some little Matchbox cars and lorries, crayons. Crayons are for the littlest of people, Arthur." She looked up at me for a moment, but I'm not sure she really saw me.

"Stella got close to the photos, as if she hoped her eyes were deceiving her. I pulled my arm away from Nathan and rushed over to steady her." My mother closed her eyes. "Arthur, he had a gun. It was on the floor by the basket of toys. Right on the floor like it belonged there."

She got up and went back to the bin to dig out the gloves as though that was where they were kept. She sat at the table, put them on and once more picked up the buffer mitt and attacked the silver like it was the only activity that could possibly eradicate what she had seen. "Nathan was as shocked as Stella was. He had no words for his mother, even when she asked, 'What in God's name is going on here? What have you done?'"

"Did you ask him about Ernie?"

My mother continued polishing as if she hadn't heard me. "I've never seen anything like it. Children. Some as young as two or three years old. Exposed in indecent ways. What kind of person wants to look at that? Does Nathan have mental problems?" She shook her head as if to remove the memory. "There were photographs of children . . . with men."

When she started crying, I wondered if she had seen an image of the Zipper clipped to the clothesline. I went to the sideboard and filled her favourite teacup right to the brim with gin. She wasn't much of a drinker, but she downed the alcohol in four or five grateful gulps.

"I told Stella I'd wait for her at the little pub we'd noticed across the street and I left her with Nathan."

I got up and fetched the bottle, pouring a little more gin into her teacup, and sat down across from her again. When she didn't touch it, I swallowed it myself, wincing from the burn.

My mother was now staring at the toe of her shoe as she moved it in a little circle on the floor. "I sat alone at a table in the far corner of the pub feeling guilty just for knowing Nathan. I can't even imagine what he and Stella said to each other. When she turned up, she wanted to go straight to the train station. Her new hat blew off as we walked there, and she didn't even stop. A young woman grabbed it and came dashing after us. When Stella wouldn't take it, I did, and managed to thank the girl too. Carrying Stella's hat was the only ordinary part of the day.

"On the train, she sat mute, staring out the window. I left her to her thoughts. Eventually, she got up and went to the loo. When she came back, I could smell that she had been sick. After that, she let me take her hand. 'Thank you,' she said calmly, and then in a voice of such anguish I could hardly keep myself together, she said that seeing those photos was like being stung by wasps. Hundreds and hundreds of wasps. She never let go of my hand all the way home."

I remembered the day Ernie was stung by wasps. He'd accidently stepped on their nest, and they'd attacked. As his mother had once reminded me, that was one of the rare times he'd allowed her to hold his hand.

In the days that followed my mother's return from Leeds, we distracted ourselves with a dozen details for my departure to university. Those trips to the shops for toothpaste, pillowcases and new socks gave shape and purpose to my final days in Glastonbury. My mother was riddled with anguish, but at no time did I share what I knew. I called in sick to the bookshop, a little flu, I said, and stayed home to make sure my mother did too. Each day I thought to walk to the Copperfield and Twist to at least say goodbye to Miss Phillips, and Arfaana, too, and each day I stayed away.

On the night before I was to leave, my mother kissed me goodnight and went into her room without touching her supper. I did the washing-up. Sometime after midnight, she knocked on my door.

"Arthur, are you still awake?"

I was under my sheets and quilt, with the lamp off and the curtain closed. It was pitch black in my room, but I hadn't been able to sleep.

"I am."

She pushed the door open, and in the angle of light from the hall I saw that she was wrapped in my father's red velvet bathrobe. She closed the door behind her and came and lay down beside me as gingerly as if my mattress was made of the thinnest ice. I had a luminous flash of her lying next to me in that same dressing gown after I'd returned from exile at Auntie Belinda's.

"Shall I put the light on?" I asked after a time.

"No," she whispered. I could smell alcohol on her breath. "I have been trying not to say anything to you, Arthur. But there were two photographs of you, and one of Mrs. Willoughby's son, Timmy. Little Timmy."

I rolled over to face the wall with my heart thumping, grateful that the dark concealed my burning blush.

"I tried to only look at your exquisite little face," she said. She was trembling. "You were so young, Arthur. Why did you never tell me that Nathan was taking such pictures?"

When I searched too long for a response, my mother whispered, "No matter, my darling. I took them off the clothesline and I brought them home and destroyed them. Until I saw you up on the clothesline, I had intended to call the police."

She stayed for a few more minutes, breathing softly into my hair, then got up from the bed, leaned down and kissed my cheek and crept away.

My mind spun in circles as I tried to figure it out. Ernie must have managed to steal the key the priest kept on a chain in his pocket that unlocked a secret drawer in the vestry. Maybe he'd even stolen the reams of negatives in unmarked white envelopes that the Zipper kept hidden under the vestments. It was shocking to think that copies of the photos might be for sale on a clothesline in Leeds. Why had Ernie and Nathan done such a terrible thing? Why would they perpetuate what we had endured? Especially Ernie. Though I had no proof that Ernie was in Leeds helping his brother, he had to have been the conduit for the photos of me and Timmy at least, if not the rest.

It came over me even more strongly that I only knew the half of what had happened to Ernie. An image of his stricken and betrayed face flickered in my mind. Maybe his boiling rage had cut a canyon through his sense of right and wrong, but he, at least, had tried to call the perpetrators to account. With each new horror revealed, my sense of what was true and just had only one place to go. Underground.

I lay awake thinking that all the other mothers who lived in Glastonbury would wake up and go on with their lives the next morning. Not
Ernie's. Not mine. Mine would rise and face the day, wanting to turn back
the hands of the clock, maybe all the way back to the day on the train when
she met my father, or at least to the day I was born. And what of Nathan?
I was now certain that he, too, had paid an awful price for his blue eyes,
his silky blond hair, his slim hips, and the insecurity and poverty that had
made him irresistible to a priest.

My pillowcase was now soggy; I dried my eyes with the edge of the
sheet. I didn't know much about his predecessor, but I knew that the Zipper
had an uncanny knack for finding the weakest boys, separating them from
the pack, and then killing them one by one from the inside out.

I found myself whispering to the ceiling, or maybe to my mother, or
even to my long-dead father, "I won't die."

When at last I fell asleep, I dreamed of standing, ashamed, next to
Auntie Belinda at the clothesline in Crewkerne, and feeding her the laun-
dered sheets from my piss-soaked bed, sheets that snapped their presence
in the wind. As fast as we put them on the clothesline, Nathan took them
down and stuffed them into his car.

I woke to the sound of my mother dragging my luggage along the tiny
hallway, and the scent of bacon and freshly baked sweet rolls. From my
window I could tell that the sun was back after four days of mist, fog and
slashing rain. I had a hasty bath, dressed, and went to the kitchen to face
her torment. Still in her dressing gown, savagely tied at the waist, she
had been a swirl of activity: the baking trays stood rinsed on the drain-
ing board, breakfast was on the table, and a tidy stack of sandwiches was
ready for my journey. Worry emanated from her like an invisible cloud of
sulphur. How can the most awful things hover in the same room as something as benign as a ham and cheese sandwich?

I sat down and ate my breakfast as though it were an ordinary morning. Not another word was spoken of the clothesline, the photos, the dolls and toys, and Nathan's gun. As unsettling as that was, I was overcome with gratitude and relief for my mother's unwillingness to press me further. Leaving so much unspoken freed both of us to pretend all was well until my progress at university provided the antidote to the disgrace she'd witnessed in Leeds.

After breakfast, I went into her room to take a last look at the photo of my father holding out the silver lockets. I studied his face. My mind's eye only ever went to his deathbed, to his jaw hanging sideways. The day his heart gave out, my mother was in her best green dress, and the room smelled of perfume, and the seams of her stockings went straight up past the hem like they were supposed to.

"Dad, please help me," I whispered. "I've never asked for anything, but I need you now."

When the phone rang, I put down the photo, went back to the kitchen and picked up the receiver. "Hello? Yes, it's me." I listened some more, shifting from foot to foot. "Yes, I will, thank you. Goodbye."

My mother said, "Was that Alfredo? He's borrowed a car to drive you to the train station."

"No, it was Mrs. Castlefrank."

"Saying goodbye?" My mother plucked the broom from its cupboard and began to sweep, although the floor was spotless.

"No. Yes. In a way." I put on my sleeveless jean jacket. "She told me that you paid a part of Nathan's fine. Two thousand pounds. She said she wanted me to know that I come from good stock, and that I'm to uphold the family name."

My mother stopped sweeping but wouldn't look at me.

"So, it's true? You helped pay to get Nathan out of prison? Did you go into the safety deposit box and tap your rainy day fund?"

"Yes. I paid part of the fine, and no, I didn't sell your father's wedding ring. I believe Ernie may have paid the rest."

"Ernie paid three thousand pounds? And you paid two?"

"Before he disappeared, he came to me to say he'd managed to put together as much as he could. He said he didn't think he could get the rest before Nathan was due to get out. He made me promise not to tell you, Arthur, and I didn't. I've never seen anyone so grateful for something I'd done. Not in my whole life. I remember a time when I had no one to turn to. I guess I also hoped he would know he had someone he could rely on." In a quiet whisper, she said, "That turned out to be in vain."

I swallowed hard, about to ask if she'd given one minute's thought to where Ernie might have come up with three thousand pounds, but I found I couldn't criticize her. All I said was, "That was a lot of money. For both of you."

"I had been saving for years for you to go to university, but you'd become so ambivalent about whether you wanted to go or not, and I ended up thinking that Ernie and Stella's needs were greater. Of course, when you decided to apply, I was overjoyed. I didn't know how I'd make ends meet, but then I got my advance for the cookbook. Still, it wasn't much, and I was so grateful when St. Nick's came through with your endowment even after Father Ziperto had left us. It felt like God's will."

We heard a car horn. My mother came towards me and took my hands in hers, but I couldn't meet her eyes. "I didn't mean to keep it from you," she said. "I didn't know about the rest of it." Her hands tightened, "About . . . the clothesline."

She put her arms around me then, and I leaned down to her, breathing in the scent of caster sugar, cinnamon and lavender. I brushed the dusting of flour from her hair, then stepped back.

She said, "All those apple recipes. I need to write them down for your grandfather's sake, if not for ours and the cookbook I'm supposed to write." She made sure I was looking into her eyes when she said, "I've made an even bigger mistake in my life, Arthur. When I gave you away it was to the only place that still held a piece of my heart, to the only people who could care for you. I thank God every day for bringing you back to me. I hope you'll be able to forgive me one day. I abandoned myself. Not you. Never you."

For the first time I truly understood that she loved me. That I was wanted.

The car horn sounded again.

"I won't walk you down," she said, attempting a smile. "I don't want to make a scene on the street, blubbering over you. You'll be home to visit soon enough, won't you?"

"Of course I will," I said. "I'm your taste-tester, right?"

Gathering my two suitcases, I shouldered through the door and down the stairs to Alfredo, who stood beside the borrowed car with the boot already open. I stowed my luggage and turned to take in Norbins Road. The window of my bedroom, where I had waited for Ernie in the days after he disappeared, the peeling mustard-yellow door of the tailor shop, the thick waist of the chestnut tree where I locked my bike. I took one last mental photograph to fix it all in my mind.

As I got into the passenger seat beside Alfredo, I had the surest feeling—an out-of-body lightness—that I was leaving home in order to be found.

PART TWO

Glastonbury, 1990

Chapter 23

MARINA

In the two weeks before Arthur Barnes left for Durham University, I fully expected him to come around, if not to say goodbye at least to collect his final pay. My eyes drifted to the door each time the little bell tinkled. Perhaps in the flurry of packing, he simply forgot, or his flu had worsened. The sum I owed him was a pittance, really. But I had also packaged up an assortment of books, a parting gift, and I had wanted more than anything to look him in the eye and wish him well.

At my desk one evening near 10 p.m. the phone rang and broke my concentration on the accounts I was trying to catch up on. "Hello, this is Marina Phillips."

"Good evening, Miss Phillips. It's Norma Barnes."

Startled, I said good evening back.

A few seconds of silence ticked by before she said, "Arthur mentioned that you often work far into the night. I wanted to call to thank you for everything you've done for my son. If not for you, he wouldn't have gone to university."

"You've no need to thank me, Mrs. Barnes. Nonetheless, I do appreciate the call. I miss Arthur, and really look forward to seeing him again. I can't imagine how you must feel with your son so far away."

Silence on the line. "Mrs. Barnes, are you still there?"

She'd hung up.

Somewhat stung, I replaced the dead receiver in its cradle. I was about to call Arfaana, who hardly ever went to sleep before midnight, then thought better of it. She'd heard enough from me already about Arthur. And what more did I have to share? My lurking suspicion that his mother had swallowed a Valium that had thickened her tongue before she'd called me, or that I'd been startled to see Stella Castlefrank's pretty pink coat in the window of the consignment shop—the one she'd worn when she'd returned the stolen books? I'd stood at that consignment shop window for so long staring at the coat that the owner poked her head out, and said, "It's only sixteen quid. Would you like to try it on?"

"Another time," I'd said, and walked away. Ten minutes later I hurried back and purchased the coat, took it back to the shop, wrapped it in plain brown paper and left it on the Castlefranks' front steps on my way home.

Two mothers in crisis. Arfaana would say I was letting my imagination run wild.

Attempting to dismiss Arthur, Ernie and their troubled parents from my mind, I opened the bottom drawer of my desk to retrieve a large bag of Maynards wine gums and sat for a time, picking out and eating the blackberry ones, feeling like a seventeen-year-old misfit again. I still remember how I was already donning the chartreuse dress my father had bought me to wear to the convocation dance, when my date, Charles something or other, called and cancelled. I could have stayed put and felt sorry for myself. Instead, I went on my own, though I admit I did it mostly so my father didn't think his expense had been for nothing.

There I found the boy who had ditched me dancing with Arfaana Haq—new to our school—an olive-eyed beauty whose family had moved to Britain from Lahore, Pakistan. Just then a friend of his danced his own partner past Charles, and called, "Your girl is far nicer looking than Marina Phillips. Well done, Charles." Deflated on the sidelines in my poufy green wonder, who was I to argue?

Then a boy in a long linen tunic—Arfaana's brother—came over to me. "My parents told me my only responsibility tonight was to keep my sister off the dance floor."

"We have both failed miserably at that."

"Badi Haq." He extended his hand, and warmly shook mine.

"Marina Phillips."

The song ended and Arfaana extricated herself from Charles. She came straight over to me and, nodding to her brother, hooked my arm and led me out of the auditorium and around the corner to stand in the shadows of a large laurel tree. She let go of my arm to fish a silver flask out of a handbag embroidered with golden snakes. "I'm so sorry! What a boor that boy is." She sipped and offered the flask to me.

"Are you permitted alcohol?" I asked, looking around for the brother in the long linen tunic.

"Are you?" She took another a sip and handed it over. Vodka, somehow perfectly chilled.

Arfaana wore a chiffon sari the colour of a mandarin orange. Her masses of shiny hair were coiled around her head and the skin of her smooth arms reminded me of a bolt of light brown velvet. Beside her I was an overripe pear. Arfaana said, "I hear you are the smartest girl in the school." She tipped up the flask once more and I watched the alcohol slide down her delicate throat. I demurred, but accepted the flask when she offered it.

After that, we were rarely apart. Both of us had chosen the University of Bristol, with Arfaana opting for commerce and me studying English. When we were in halls, we'd go for nightly walks up Whiteladies Road to Blackboy Hill, and then stomp across the Clifton and Durdham downs. A series of rapes had occurred on the downs, and the culprit was still at large, but together we felt invincible. Afterwards, we would drink half-pints of Exhibition cider at the Cori Tap, talking until last call. Arfaana firmly believed that it was a woman's right to do everything a man would do, including getting a pilot's licence, and I was carried along by her sense of indestructibility—men didn't overthink such risky behaviours, so why should we?

And it was Arfaana who said, over dinner with her brother and me, just after the two of us had graduated, "You need to ask your father to co-sign a bank loan so you can open a bookshop somewhere in England. Nothing will make you happier." She and Badi, now a medical student and still her hapless chaperone, had become my closest friends and allies. Shouting over the live music at the Cori Tap that night, Arfaana revealed herself as just a little jealous, saying, "In Pakistan, a woman who wants to aim higher in education is certainly encouraged to do so. Otherwise? She must marry. Now I've got my degree, I'll need to do everything I can to dodge the suitors my mother has been lining up. You, Marina, have so few restrictions."

It was 1972, and I could have given her chapter and verse on the unspoken expectations British women faced, but when it came to me, she was almost right. My father claimed unless women were free-thinking, enlightened and informed, civilization would remain backward. When I'd told her and Badi about my father's progressive thinking, both had marvelled.

"Come on, Marina, you know your father will support you. As I see it, all you need is enough cash for inventory, rent and pedestrian-friendly signage. The way you moon around bookshops, I bet you already know exactly where you'd like to set up shop."

I gave her a rueful smile—I did know.

Arfaana gave me a gentle poke in the ribs. "Nobody in their right mind would open a bookshop if they want to earn a decent living. But when it comes to reading, and the collection of books you have amassed, you've never been in your right mind. As I see it, selling books is a form of philanthropy, and in that, Marina, you will surely succeed."

—

With a start, I realized I'd consumed every blackberry wine gum in the bag. Dropping the remainder back in its drawer, I collected my coat and locked up. I had half a mind to stop by Norma Barnes's flat. Mostly sure I'd only be intruding, though, I drove home.

It was past 11:30 by the time I stood fumbling in the dark to unlock the door to my tiny flat. Inside, I flipped on the lights and hung up my anorak. On a small pad on the hall table, I scribbled the words "On Children"—a reminder to find Khalil Gibran's poem for Arthur's mum. Perhaps it would be a comfort. My answering machine was blinking. With the press of a button, I listened to a message from Arfaana asking me to call when I got home. I dialed her number.

"You're late again. You'll burn out at this rate."

"Yes, I'm aware of that. I was actually going to call you from the shop earlier. I had a strange conversation with Arthur's mother, who called me to say thank you."

"Well, that is surely the strangest thing I've ever heard. Hardly anyone says thank you anymore." Arfaana's tone was teasing, if a bit testy.

"It's just that she sounded sad, or maybe defeated. Her voice was so flat, as if she had something else she wanted to tell me but didn't know how."

"It sounds to me like you're reading too much into a nice gesture."

"It made me think of Ernie."

"Everything makes you think of either Ernie or Arthur. Ernie is long gone, and Arthur has moved on. Don't you think it's time you moved on too?"

"I can't shake the feeling that something dreadful happened right under my nose and I missed it. Do you think I should drop by to see if Arthur's mother is okay?"

"Oh, for goodness' sakes, Marina. Mind your own business."

"I could call her back and mention I have a book I think she'd like."

"I think you should pay attention to more pressing matters in your life, like finding yourself a bigger place to live. A place with sunlight. I'm surprised your flat doesn't have bats. On that subject, what I phoned to tell you was that an estate agent called the shop today while you were out to confirm your appointment to look at houses. This is your third agent, I think? It's time to let go of Arthur Barnes. You've done enough for that young man."

I didn't think I had, but I knew better than to insist. After a bit of less charged to-and-fro, we said goodnight.

I walked from the front hall to the living room. Where was that book? Right there on the shelf. In my hands, *The Prophet* fell open of its own accord to the right poem. I reread it quickly, then put the book down and took my achy feet to the kitchen, where I plugged in the kettle. It was not lost on me that my friendship with Arthur had begun the day he'd cut a page from this very book. As upsetting as the deed was, it made me curious about a thirteen-year-old who read Gibran.

I assumed his parents would be well read, perhaps academics. I was wrong there. Fatherless. Hungry for something I couldn't define. He signed his note of apology "Arthur W. Barnes," including the middle initial—an affectation that made me smile and also gave me the impression he craved attention. I was wrong again. He was quiet and introspective. Which made me wonder, on numerous occasions, about his friendship with Ernie. I, too, had heard the police sirens the day Ernie's brother was arrested on Magdalene Street. But somehow, Arthur and Ernie had had enough common ground to become best friends.

Giving the book to Mrs. Barnes would be the perfect bookend to a rather extraordinary time in my quiet life—managing, maybe redeeming, a thief.

The day I'd caught him with *The Prophet*, he had worn his clothing like armour—a buttoned-up shirt under a jumper under a jacket—

everything done up tight. His long reddish fringe fell into his eyes, and just the trace of a moustache was etched above his lips. I saw a gentle boy hidden underneath heaps of clothing and long hair, and I'd actually liked him.

Saying to hell with the late hour, I picked up the phone and called Arfaana again.

"What's eating you?" she said instead of hello.

"It's just that I've never had the experience of witnessing a child grow up, let alone leave the nest, so missing Arthur as much as I do has taken me by surprise. I knew he was leaving, and I think it's the best thing that could happen to him, but I was unprepared for how forsaken I'd feel. I can't help but imagine how much more bereft his mother is. And then there's Mrs. Castlefrank. Two sons gone."

I waited, then, for Arfaana to grant me absolution for my obsession with these boys. All I heard was her quiet breathing on the other end of the line, until she said, "Is that everything?"

I said, "Not exactly. I've had an excellent idea. Will you come and work at the shop full-time? You've helped me out on weekends on and off for years. You know the shop as well as I do."

"I was wondering when you would think to ask me. I accept. Goodnight, Marina."

I brushed my teeth, washed my face and went to bed.

The following day, a Sunday, I dutifully called Constance Bradley, the estate agent. "I'm free to look at houses this afternoon at one o'clock if you're still available."

She picked me up at my flat, and over the course of several hours we viewed six listings. Each was either too dark, too expensive or too in need of repair. She dropped me home at four. At five, she called to say that a new listing had just come through for a three-bedroom house on Tiller's Row. "It's officially on the market tomorrow," she said. "Its front garden is mostly laid to lawn with a patio area that gives a lovely view towards the Glastonbury Tor. The rear garden is bordered by tall cedar hedges and leads to a playground where parents take their children on sunny afternoons. Do you want to take a peek?"

Without much in the way of hope, I agreed. She collected me at the bookshop the next day at noon, bearing sandwiches and fizzy drinks.

A crowd of mature trees obscured the front of the house. Opening the padlocked black gate, Mrs. Bradley revealed a terraced stone path bordered by overgrown bushes. "Glorious," I said, following her in. "It's so secluded, I feel like I'm in another country."

"The owner, Sofia Brambillia, died in the late seventies," Mrs. Bradley said. "From what I can gather, the house has been empty since. I'm not sure why it's only gone on the market now."

Once through the front door, I was surprised by how tidy the place was. "The family has kept it up, at least," she said, "though if you decide to make an offer, we'll have a home inspector in to make sure the place is sound." After we looked around the ground floor—the agent opening windows to air the place out—we climbed the staircase. From an upstairs window on the landing, I could see the top bar of a swing set and the expanse of a lovely little playground.

I couldn't help but blurt, "It's ideal. I love the privacy of the back garden and the masses of wisteria clinging to the archway at the far end. I've looked at so many properties over the years, and this is the only one—well, you must have heard how indecisive a client I am."

She smiled. "Sometimes the stars align. And they are motivated sellers: the house is listed at below market value. At that price, there will likely be multiple offers, so we'll have to move quickly."

"I can see myself living here."

She beamed at me. "That's a good sign! Let's head downstairs for a minute and check out the furnishings the seller wishes to include."

I followed her to the ground floor and walked with her from room to room as she consulted a list that included the mahogany dining room table, six Hepplewhite chairs and an upright player piano.

From the ghostly shapes on the pale walls, I could see that several large crucifixes had been removed from different rooms. Mrs. Bradley saw me eyeing the discoloured outlines and said, "Someone in the office told me they were Gorhams. No doubt the family was very devout."

"Gorhams? Is that a form of religion, Mrs. Bradley?"

"Please call me Constance. And no, absolutely not!" She laughed. "Gorham was an American silversmith, a master craftsman from Providence, Rhode Island. He made a sterling tea service that's still in use in the American White House, and his company's crucifixes are quite valuable."

Constance Bradley took out a handkerchief and began wiping the marks on the plaster walls to little effect. "Clearly, you will have to paint," she said, turning around to smile at me again. I took in her electrocuted white hair, glass earrings the size of door handles, and her patchy, beetroot face. I smiled back, wishing I'd known this dishevelled gem all my life.

"Funny that she kept those child-sized bunk beds in the room upstairs. They look pre-war, and mighty uncomfortable."

"My sister and I had bunk beds," I said. "She insisted on sleeping in the top one because she felt too confined in the lower bunk." I put my hand over my mouth, surprised that I'd shared something so personal with a stranger.

"I'd feel that way too. From what I could tell the bunks are built in, but they don't look like they'd be too tricky to remove. It's a bit morbid, but my first thought was maybe one of her children had died and she couldn't bear to redecorate the room. Or like me, she was hoping she'd be a gran. Judging from the collection of old books I found in the drawer underneath the lower bunk yesterday, either explanation could work. Do you have a rare books section in your shop?" She ran a hand through her feral hair, which only made it more disorderly. "My hair will not lie down, does not even take the slightest notice of a brush or a comb." I found myself rooting for any grandchildren.

Asking me to hang on a moment, she climbed the stairs and, after some thumping around, came back to me with what turned out to be a first edition of Edith Nesbit's *The Railway Children*. I opened it to the title page where there was an illustration of three children at a split-rail fence waving large white handkerchiefs; their father, an innocent man, had been falsely imprisoned, leaving them parentless. Closing it, I ran my hand over the maroon and gilt cloth cover. It was in near-perfect condition. I pressed the book to my chest, appalled that tears had gathered in my eyes.

Constance reached into the pocket of her cardigan and handed me her wrinkly linen handkerchief, then realized that it was covered in grime from where she'd tried to clean the wall and stuffed it back into her pocket. Laughing, I wiped my eyes with my fingers.

"I am going soft," I said.

"My favourite kind."

Taking a moment to compose myself, I lifted the lid of the piano bench and found it filled to bursting with sheet music. On top were two brightly coloured books: *Beginner Piano for Children* and *One Piano Four Hands*. Underneath was a vast collection of scores by Chopin, Puccini, Scarlatti, Vivaldi. Constance, now opening and closing kitchen cupboards to see what else the owners might have left behind, called, "When I was a child, we had a player piano. They were quite the rage in the twenties when my father bought it. Sadly, I lacked the discipline to play anything but the most rudimentary tunes. Are you musical?"

I was only half listening. I picked up one of the children's instruction books, opened the cover and scanned the copyright page. Lakeview Music Co., London 1988. I returned it to its place inside the bench and joined her in the kitchen. "Did you say the owner died in the seventies, and the house has been unoccupied ever since?"

"That's what I'm told. You'll definitely want to change the locks, though. While I was here doing a quick look to see if we wanted to take the listing, a gentleman walked into the back garden, came around the house, and then made his way out to the street through the front gate, which was odd because I was sure I had locked it behind me. Perhaps the place sat empty for so long the locals use the property as a shortcut. Though once you've moved in, I doubt anyone will trespass."

"Constance, I do want this house. Apart from the player piano, I don't want the furniture, though, so I hope that won't be a problem."

"I'm sure we will be able to work that out," she said. "And here you told me you were indecisive!"

Four weeks later I moved to the little house on Tiller's Row. The last of the owners' furnishings had been removed, save for the piano, the bunk beds and the trove of children's literature, which in the end I couldn't bear to see go. Most of the books were in English, but there were several well-thumbed ones in Italian, Polish and even Russian, which made me think well of the mother who'd carefully hand-selected these gifts of story and faith for her children. *Le Cronache di Narnia. Le Avventure di Alice nel Paese delle Meraviglie. La Sacra Bibbia.*

I'd had the place freshly painted, but it hadn't needed any other repairs. As I surveyed my new home, I was surprised to find that one item I hadn't asked to keep had been left behind in the former children's bedroom upstairs: a combination Mother Goose lamp and cassette player, sitting on the floor in the corner.

Sighing, I carried it out to the car, and the next day on my way to the bookshop I dropped it off at Mrs. Bradley's office to be returned to the former owners.

Chapter 24

On her first day as my full-time assistant at the Copperfield and Twist, Arfaana breezed through the door at eight o'clock sharp. She wore a green and aqua sari patterned with the image of a girl on a swing whose two thin ropes disappeared up into the branches of a tree in blossom. She called, "I've brought your favourite Karachi halwa," then appeared like a vision and placed the Indian version of Turkish delight and a Thermos of warm masala chai on my desk.

I stared up at her.

"What is it?" she said.

"Your sari."

"What about my sari?"

"It's beautiful." I didn't mention that it reminded me of Arthur and a photo he'd once shared of him and Ernie and a sycamore tree.

"An heirloom passed down from my grandmother."

"I'm glad you wore it to mark your first day."

Arfaana's enthusiasm for the business proved to be a blessing and a curse. Prior to working in the shop, she'd managed Downey's, a small but well-known business offering embossed, debossed and foil-stamped handmade stationery. To the owner's great dismay, when he moved the company to the London borough of Hackney, she took her leave and relocated to Glastonbury.

That first Monday at the Copperfield and Twist, customers were few, as usual, and she spent hours studying the books, reviewing sales, inventory and remainders. By lunchtime she was burbling with ideas. We needed to add maps, bookmarks, journals and notebooks to our shelves, even postcards and birthday cards, so everyone who comes through the door would find something they wanted to buy. When the weather was fine, she proposed, we would set up a couple of tables outside the shop to sell used books, just like the Strand in New York City. And what about offering customers hot tea and biscuits from Fortnum and Mason, so they'd linger and browse?

A little flustered and overcome, I said, "And to think that recently I've been lying awake at night thinking about who might buy the shop."

"You need to widen your perspective, Marina. What is the next generation of readers looking for from a bookshop? If we figure that out, then we'll be successful beyond your most outlandish dreams."

At 6 p.m. I flipped the sign on the door to closed, and we flopped onto the pair of easy chairs in my office.

My mind once more drifted to Arthur, who had so often sat where Arfaana was now, talking to me about the book he was reviewing.

I made us a pot of Darjeeling, and after I took my first sip, I sighed and admitted to Arfaana that the pattern on her sari reminded me of a photo Arthur once showed me of him and Ernie in the apple orchard. "He didn't ever really show emotion, as you know, but he was glum that day, and I just immediately told him, 'Arthur, you and Ernie will be happy like that again.'"

"Whatever made you say that?"

"I don't know. I was worried about him. More than I usually was, I mean. That was the week I found a lost wallet at the till, and I was sure Arthur had had something to do with it, though I was careful not to ask. When I got in touch with the owner—his name was Quimby—I wasn't exactly surprised to learn he had never been a customer. I'd already noted that his home address was a grand street in Bath, and it turned out he was *the* Martin Quimby, the multi-millionaire construction magnate. Sir Martin, I should say, since he'd been knighted."

"That is odd. But hold on, I thought I read recently that a man named Quimby was caught in the toilets at Crewe station with a young boy."

"I rather doubt it, given Sir Martin's standing in business and politics. All the same, the wallet incident has stayed with me. I can even recall the book Arthur was reviewing that week. Shel Silverstein's *The Missing Piece*. You know that one: a circle who is missing a pie-shaped wedge sets out to find it. Arthur's final line was that being perfect isn't all that it's cracked up to be."

"Maybe the stolen wallet was a pie-shaped wedge looking for its circle."

"Too clever. After I read his draft, I did ask him if he had been thinking about someone when he wrote it, assuming he would say himself or even Ernie Castlefrank. Instead, he blurted out that Father Ziperto was looking for something he couldn't find. Ziperto was the Catholic priest over at St. Nick's. I was so startled I didn't have the presence of mind to ask Arthur what he thought the priest was missing. It was such a strange thing for a teenager to say."

"Didn't you tell me he was an altar boy? He and the priest must have been close."

"Yes, he was. He didn't ever speak about those duties, though. And I can't remember him mentioning the priest again."

On her second day, Arfaana was just as punctual. She was already well versed in the basics of being a bookstore clerk from her stints pitching in at the shop, and she proved a quick study when it came to everything else. For the first time in months, I imagined I could be fully happy running the shop without Arthur.

Soon Arfaana was offering contests and giveaways that the customers loved. She busied herself decluttering and beautifying the place. The carved table she set up to display our top sellers, placed so it was the first thing you saw when you came in the front door, was a showstopper, and sales ticked upwards. Maybe knowing how much it would please me, she bought a second table for the children's section on which we displayed "Arthur's Picks": perennial bestsellers from the moment of his first review.

"I have an idea for the window," she said in a quiet moment one afternoon.

"I'm listening."

"Let's reupholster an overstuffed armchair in plushy royal purple velvet and set it in the window underneath the warm glow of a spotlight, and then pile it with so many books they spill onto the floor."

"But so few of the book titles will be legible."

Arfaana waved that concern away. "Just say yes. You won't regret it, I promise."

While the chair was being upholstered, she created a faux wall covered in parchment paper on which she hand wrote, using a large calligraphy nib from her cache, the opening sentence of a book that was for sale in the shop. In a nod to our history, she picked it from a list of fifty sentences Arthur had compiled and left behind in a folder on his desk: "Mr. and Mrs. Brown first met Paddington on a railway platform . . ."

She was ready with two more. "Miss Brooke had that kind of beauty which seems to be thrown into relief by poor dress" and "It was a bright cold day in April, and the clocks were striking thirteen."

To my amazement, the changing window immediately became an enticement to enter the shop, and even more so after Rodger Mistlethorpe mentioned our efforts in the paper. "A screaming comes across the sky" drew in an unprecedented number of passersby, as did "I had the story, bit by bit, from various people, and, as generally happens in such cases, each time it was a different story."

In those first weeks, my personal favourite was from Camus: "Mother died today. Or maybe, yesterday; I can't be sure."

Customers would burst through the door, calling out *Middlemarch* or *Nineteen Eighty-Four* or *Gravity's Rainbow*, and become giddy if they were right. Arfaana, in a swirl of colour inside and out, had made running the shop a whimsical delight.

A month after I'd moved into my new house, Constance Bradley called to say she had a little thank-you present for me for using her services, and wondered if she could take me for a drink. Instead, I invited her to come around one evening after the shop was closed. "Wouldn't you like to see what I've done with the place? It's terribly cozy," I said, and of course she said she would.

When I opened the door to her knock, I found her almost unrecognizable with her wild hair caught under a tight-fitting orange beret, but the sweet smile and ruddy cheeks were the same. She was carrying an open box with the Mother Goose lamp sticking out the top, juggling it and her oversized purse and a mesh shopping bag. I ushered her in as rain began to leak from an overcast wet-towel kind of sky.

Constance set the box and bags down in the hall and removed the beret. Her white springy hair leapt up, restoring my confidence that all was as it should be. "It's hard not to look like a French cartoon in this type of hat," she said, patting her coils.

"I think you look smashing. Let me take your coat."

After we'd settled on two bergères in front of my tiny fireplace, Constance withdrew a mound of rose-coloured tissue paper from her box and handed it to me. Inside was a hand-painted wooden bird feeder. "Perhaps you could hang it at the far end of your garden to entice the cardinals. In the car, I've got a rather tall pole for you too—otherwise, you'll be feeding the squirrels."

"I don't mind squirrels. I wish I had half their energy." I picked up the bird feeder. It had twelve round holes and a copper finial. "Thank you. This is beautiful, and thoughtful, but you really didn't need to do this."

I had set out a plate of Appleby's Cheshire, black olives and foie gras to nibble on. I poured the wine. Constance picked up her glass and drained it. I refilled it. As she started to take another sip, she thought better of it and set the wineglass down. Her usual ebullience seemed undermined somehow, but all I could think to ask was, "Every *i* has been dotted and *t* crossed on the sale, surely?"

"Oh, yes." She nodded emphatically, her cheeks aflame from the alcohol. She picked up her glass and gulped. "It's the lamp," she finally said, pointing to the box. She laughed nervously, found her familiar white handkerchief in a pocket, and dabbed her lips. "The former owners never picked it up from my office, so I gave it to my daughter. She asked me to return it to you."

"But it's not mine. And why didn't she want it?"

Constance pulled Mother Goose from the box, stood it on an end table, leaned over to plug it into the electrical outlet, and switched it on. Golden light shone from underneath the goose's white porcelain chin. From her handbag, she withdrew a cassette. She placed it in the cartridge, hit the play button, and sat back down. "Track one is about three minutes. It's called 'Mordred's Lullaby' and it's haunting. Legend has it that Mordred betrayed King Arthur."

"The singer's voice is lovely," I said as the melody filled the air.

"There are several more songs on Side A. I've listened to them all half a dozen times. None of them are the usual children's lullabies. They're soothing, yes, but also touched with melancholy, as though something precious is lost or just beyond our reach. Have you ever tried to catch a snippet of memory, but as soon as you do, it totally vanishes?

The essence of some sweet nostalgia. That is what these songs all evoke for me."

She folded her hands in her lap and we listened through to the last track, during which the light under the goose's chin dimmed.

"It's quite ingenious, isn't it, that someone retrofitted this antique lamp in such a dear way. A comfort to both mother and child," I said.

She hit the stop button, ejected the cartridge, and flipped it to play Side B.

A male choir sang a Gregorian chant. She said, "It's called the Kyrie eleison. The harmonies are eerie and monastic. I sang in my church choir and used to know the lyrics. All I can remember now is 'Would I have followed down my chosen road or only wished what I could be?'" She took another enormous gulp of wine. "Kyrie eleison means 'God have mercy.'"

"It's mesmerizing."

"Keep listening," she whispered. "It seems to me that the two sides were recorded on different occasions. The sound quality is not quite the same."

The chant ended. Five seconds of silence was followed by a man reciting a list of numbers, enunciating each one carefully: "70 105 110 100," followed by a tiny click, then "69 114 110 105 101," followed by another click, then, "67 97 115 116 108 101 102 114 97 110 107." Hairs rose on my neck.

"The rest of the tape carries on in the same fashion," Constance said. She ejected the cassette and laid it next to the lamp. Mother Goose went back to being a benign piece of porcelain. "I've had a good think about them," she said, "and I believe they might be bank account numbers." For a split second, the shimmery orb of her earring caught a ray of light from a meek sunset dropping behind the cedar hedge. The rain had stopped; the sky was a swim of black clouds streaked with coral.

I said, "They must have had a good many accounts, then. That was a very long recitation."

When Constance didn't laugh, I said, "Mind you, I have no idea what else they could be or why they were recorded on the other side of a tape of children's lullabies."

Soft creases showed around Constance's eyes and mouth, her expression completely serious. "I came to Glastonbury in 1970 because I'd been widowed, and I'd heard it was a sacred place where people hope to find what they're missing. It has such a history of magic and legend. Glastonbury, the Isle of Avalon. The isle of apples. But it's a place of mixed messages—Christian monks and New Age seekers sharing the same steep path up the Glastonbury Tor to enlightenment."

"I, too, came here in the seventies, to open my shop."

"A good decision, I imagine?"

"Yes. For the most part. Bookselling has been my life."

"I don't know you well, Marina, but I feel there's a bond of some kind between us. Human behaviour is so damned unpredictable. Until my husband died, I thought I was the strongest person alive, but it turned out I can come undone if I can't reach a light bulb to change it. The tape has got under my skin somehow. Several times I went to toss it out, and stopped because of those lullabies on Side A. But something strikes me as sinister about the numbers on Side B. It's ridiculous—an old woman like me as spooked as a child. You must think I'm daft."

"That voice and those numbers unsettled me too."

She smiled at me gratefully. "I guess I just need to get it out of my hands. Perhaps the lamp would look charming in the children's section of your shop? Maybe on that little desk at the back where that old typewriter sits now?"

"I think it would be perfect."

And in that instant she beamed her relief and I became the caretaker of Mother Goose and the cassette.

Our wine and cheese party over, Constance got ready to leave, but she had one final question. "Was that the only item the previous owners left behind? Everything else was gone?"

"Yes, it was. Everything else was gone, except for the bunks and the children's books, which, at the last moment, I asked to keep. For some reason, it felt wrong to dismantle the beds." I was about to add that I'd come upon the lamp in the corner of an empty room, and that I hadn't recalled seeing it when I viewed the listing with her, but I decided it would only add to her worries.

"It's all such a mystery," she said, jamming the beret back on her hair. "Maybe you're the one to solve it."

The following day I brought the lamp to the shop.

"And where did you find this lovely old goose?" Arfaana said, taking it from my hands. She agreed that the perfect place for it would be on Arthur's desk in the children's section where it could shed its soft light on storytime.

That night I asked her to stay on for a bit after we closed and played her the B side of the tape as we sat perched on the tiny chairs reserved for children.

"The man speaks English perfectly, but I think I detect a hint of an accent," I said. "Can you hear it? The number six sounds ever so slightly different. More like *seex*?"

Arfaana shook her head. "I don't hear it. Marina, just because your estate agent decided to hand this off to you doesn't mean you have to pay this tape any mind. Didn't you say the previous owner died in the seventies?"

"But what do you think? Are they bank account numbers?"

"Doubtful. Probably a code of some sort, but who cares? It's been a long day, and it's time to go home."

But before I left, I dialed the *Somerset Gazette* and asked for Rodger. I knew he usually stayed at work even longer than I did.

After we said our hellos, I asked, "Would you happen to know the name of a retired police officer with time on their hands, or maybe a computer specialist?"

Rodger sighed. I'd bothered him one too many times for information about Casper Fontaine's arrest, consumed with curiosity as to why a clipping about it was on Arthur's desk.

"I'm sorry to trouble you, but you must know someone I can consult about a cassette recording that was left behind at the house I purchased."

"What is this all about?"

"It might be nothing at all. But on one side of an ordinary cassette is a selection of eerie lullabies, and on the other, a male voice recites a long series of numbers interrupted by clicks."

"Curiosity killed the kitten, Marina."

"Please, Rodger."

He sighed again, but I could hear him spinning the thick Rolodex on his desk.

"The name that comes to mind is Giles Robinson. He's a police officer, but he's out on disability leave waiting for a cornea transplant. His brain is a labyrinth of stored information and he has all manner of connections. He's housebound until after the surgery, and it might affect his career if it doesn't go well—he's on the verge of going blind—so you'll have to go to him."

Rodger fell silent for a moment as he kept on searching, then he sighed. "Looks like I don't have a home number for him, and the police won't give it to you. I'll call you back tomorrow. Oh, and by the way, I finally found out why your friend Fontaine was arrested: they charged him with distributing obscene photographs."

Shocked, I said, "He's scarcely my friend. And why didn't I see anything about that in the paper?"

"Hardly news we like to print, especially as he wasn't convicted. However, my source told me he was selling photographs taken by a Leeds photographer by the name of Nathan Castlefrank, whose works sexualize children but apparently have artistic merit, at least according to the argument Fontaine's barrister made at trial. I don't know why Arthur kept that clipping, but I do know neither of you should dig any further. You're both out of your depth with a man like Fontaine."

"Nathan *Castlefrank?* From Glastonbury?"

"Do you know him?"

"I don't."

"But you know *of* him?"

"Of course. His conviction on drug charges made him notorious around here. Surely you remember, Rodger. Your paper was all over that story. I'm just surprised he's become a photographer at all, let alone one who produces work with any artistic merit, no matter how controversial." My mind was whirling from thoughts of Arthur to the missing Ernie to Nathan to poor Mrs. Castlefrank with a face full of bruises.

"Well, if I were you, I'd stay away from him too."

"I'm investigating a cassette tape, Rodger. Not a drug lord."

After we hung up, I stuck the cassette at the back of my bottom drawer. We'd find different music for Mother Goose to play.

And that's where the tape stayed. It turned out that Robinson's eye surgery did not go well, and I simply was not going to bother a man who was now blind. A man with a young daughter to care for.

Chapter 25

At the end of a long, late November Thursday, the light gone by four-thirty in the afternoon, I found myself unable to ignore the bleak fact that Arthur had not only left without saying goodbye, but he hadn't responded to any of my letters. I still hoped he'd come home for the Christmas break, but would he pick up where he left off at the shop? I doubted it. It was time to face the fact that my days of being able to glance at him hunched over his typewriter, or gangling around the shop recommending books to our customers, young and old, were likely over.

"You're looking awfully melancholy," Arfaana said. I looked up to see her standing in my office doorway with cups of tea for us both. She'd just locked the front door, so she added a dribble of whisky to our cups before she sat across from me.

"I was just thinking it's time we packed up Arthur's desk. Even if he drops by, he's not likely to work here again."

Without missing a beat or rolling her eyes, she said, "Would you like me to do it?"

And that is why I love Arfaana.

When I nodded gratefully, she said, "Should I throw it all away?"

"No, box it up and carry it in here, if you don't mind. I'll have a quick look through to see what he or his mother might like to hang on to." I sighed. "I'm fine, but I do miss Arthur."

The next morning, during a lull, Arfaana tackled the clear-out. Arthur's desk was so overstuffed she needed to slide a ruler in through the crack at the top edge of each drawer to push down the contents enough so she could pull it open. She dumped everything into a large cardboard box, deposited it on the floor of my office and then went to cover the till.

I closed my door and started to sort. I found dozens of half-written book reviews, random passages transcribed from Edgar Allan Poe and old homework assignments, some in duplicate. I read two versions of a short essay covered in what looked like cigarette burns about the history of the zipper: one on its promotion of self-reliance in young children and the other about how the zipper allowed for fewer opportunities for unintentional exposure than a button front. I put both versions in the keeper pile, feeling rather bewildered by the sense of humour of teenage boys. Or at least of Arthur.

Arfaana knocked. She opened the door a crack, and said, "I did a last check through all the drawers and found this, wedged into the back. It must have fallen between the drawers." With a questioning look, she handed me a gold-plated Parker pen.

"You found it! This was the pen Arthur used to write a first draft of his reviews before he lost it a couple of years ago. It's the same pen that landed him and Ernie in court for shoplifting."

I looked up to see that Arfaana was confused. "Surely, it was confiscated?"

"No doubt. After they'd been caught, Ernie went back on his own and pinched another one, then gifted it to Arthur. It did cross my mind to suggest Arthur return it. But I just couldn't bring myself to do it. It was such a daring declaration of friendship."

I didn't say more to Arfaana, but I thought the pen had also repre-sented something much more fragile and ethereal—his future. Arthur had been upset when the pen went missing, or rather, devastated. In hindsight, I should have bought him another one.

"Shall I send it to him by post?" Arfaana asked.

"Yes, please," I said. "No—hold on, maybe he'll stop by over the Christmas holidays and we can give it to him then."

"Have you heard from him?"

I shook my head.

She gave me an uncomfortably understanding look, then went back to the till, where she began tallying the day's receipts. I returned to the box. Under several more layers of unfinished drafts, I found a few rather bent photographs of Arthur from when he was younger. And one of Ernie. At fourteen, Arthur had been freckly, lanky and awkward, all arms and legs, broken-out skin and straggly ginger hair to his shoulders. He'd since morphed into the most handsome man. A sharp jawline. Slim without being muscular. Beautiful eyes, if a bit sad. Of course, I had no idea what Ernie looked like now, but as a boy he was perfect symmetry, his features androgynous verging on pretty, with full lips and almond-shaped blue eyes. Opposites, yet both boys' faces were deeply arresting. These photos, too, were keepers.

At the very bottom of the box, I came upon a red jewellery case, two inches square, and made of the softest hand-stitched leather. Inside was a dirt-coated sterling silver cross, nestled in stained creamy satin. At the util-ity sink in the staff room, I ran it under water to remove what looked like tiny clumps of earth. The chain was broken in two places, but the unusual three-dimensional crucifix was lifelike in its perfection. As tiny as it was, I felt as though I could reach underneath Jesus's arched back and lift him off the cross. I went looking for Arfaana.

She held the cross in her palm as she studied it. "Jesus looks so real. I can practically see his agony. It's a shame the chain is broken."

I took back the necklace and used a tissue to shine the crucifix. "The Cross is a great contradiction. An upright post with a transverse bar used to inflict a violent death, yet now it represents love *and* hate, the accused and the forgiven, mortal sin and purity, defeat, victory, redemption. And, not to be forgotten, coming back to life on the third day."

"All that in one tiny crucifix?" Arfaana teased. "We believe that Allah has no offspring, no gender, no body, and is unaffected by the features of human life."

"Perhaps suffering is more relatable when we see it in the human form." I brought the crucifix closer to my eyes, so I could examine the fine human details of muscle and hair, the nails through the hands and the suffering expression, so finely wrought.

Arfaana looked at me with sudden concern. "It looks valuable. Do you think it was stolen?"

"I can't see Arthur stealing something like this," I said.

"Perhaps you should take it to that jeweller down the Gauntlet and ask him to repair the chain and I could send it to him by post—along with the pen?"

Arfaana was making it clear that she thought my relationship with Arthur W. Barnes was at an end.

Still, I took a piece of her advice and called Simon Fouracre, the crinkly-faced and elderly watch and jewellery expert she'd mentioned, to ask if he would repair and evaluate the necklace. We'd became friends over our years of long working days and similar worries about making ends meet.

"Drop it off anytime," Simon said. "I'll have a look and call you when it's ready."

Instead of asking me to come by the shop, a week or so later he invited me to the George and Pilgrims hotel for a pint in their lobby bar. "There's no charge for the repair," my old friend said, "and the drinks are on me. I'll see you at six in our regular spot in Jack Horner's Corner." He hung up before I could ask a single question.

The one blot on an otherwise seamless friendship was that Simon could be counted on to be late and I'm always punctual. I arrived early, of course, and stopped for a moment to appreciate the imposing three-storeyed edifice that has stood on the High Street since 1439, with its mullioned windows and front facing of yellow stone. Above the arched entrance are three carved panels bearing the coats of arms of the Glastonbury Abbey and of King Edward IV. As fat as he was, Henry VIII was rumoured to have stayed overnight on the second floor, squeezing up the narrow stairs and through the tight passage to sleep on a carved and gilded bed before issuing his edict dissolving Glastonbury Abbey.

I had chosen a table that allowed me to study a familiar hand-drawn quote on the wall: *The place which is now Glaston was in ancient times called the Isle of Avalon . . . and Morgan a noble matron and ruler of these parts, and kin by blood to King Arthur, carried him away to the island . . . that she might heal his wounds . . .*

Eventually, Simon came trudging under the archway in his signature waxed Barbour, over a white shirt with his usual bow tie, this one a gaudy green. He claimed a proper necktie would dangle in the broken clasps, knotted chains and stubborn, tickless watches he repaired. "What are you thinking about?" he asked as he sat down.

"A question I should have considered long before this. Was King Arthur a real person or simply a hero of Celtic mythology?"

"Historians have never been able to confirm his existence. But don't tell the tourists." As he leaned over to peck my cheek, I breathed in the familiar slight scent of machine oil. After we ordered two beers, and plates of bangers and mash, he withdrew the red box from the pocket of his coat.

"Wherever did you get this? The leather case itself is quite valuable. And an artist named Gorham made the cross. A master silversmith. A hundred years ago the company began a system of year-marks to denote when a piece was made." He turned it over. "The geometric cartouche indicates the decade," he said pointing to it. "This one is 1982."

The surprise of hearing the Gorham name a second time in a matter of months made me sit back in my chair.

Simon noticed. His crinkly eyes widened as he waited for me to explain. When I didn't elaborate, he said, "Don't tell me. I don't need to know. When you have worked in the jewellery business for as long as I have, you shouldn't ask questions. It's just that for a time, there were a number of priests who brought me necklaces just like this one asking me to adjust the chain length. Catholics are a rather secretive bunch, so I never did ask any of them about it, but I came to fancy them as a marker of a cult of sorts. If I were you, I would invest in a thicker chain—these tiny serpentines don't live up to the beauty and heft of the crucifix. But I will ask this: You have always been my favourite atheist. Have you converted back to Christianity?"

"I'm a book-peddling humanist, Simon, not an atheist. I believe there is a divine value of some sort in human life."

"Still finding your way, are you? Did you lose your Christian faith somewhere along the line?"

That got my back up a little. "Faith isn't like a wallet that can be mislaid. I'm not one of those believers who think that God can be called upon to find it."

"Faith or the wallet? I admit I rarely find myself in a Catholic pew anymore. I'm mostly parked around the corner and my foot is an inch or two from pushing the gas pedal to the floor and peeling out of town." He took a bite of sausage, chewed for a time in contemplation, then said, "Last time we met I believe we debated the Last Supper. You said that the fact that Jesus did not celebrate Passover with family members was a break with Jewish tradition."

"There were no women at the table, nor even any cooking the meal. There wasn't a child in sight. The preparation was in the hands of the twelve disciples."

"You got me thinking. Perhaps that was no ordinary Seder dinner— Jesus was founding the priesthood."

"And nobody dares to correct the Son of God? I suppose it's the only plausible explanation to justify the absence of females."

"How is it that we always end up talking about religion? Why don't you tell me about the bookshop instead. The whole town is jabbering on about your window display. And is that young man still helping you out?"

I shook my head. "Arthur's gone off to university, as he should." I smoothed my cloth napkin across my lap a number of times before saying, "One last thing about the cross. I had to scrape the dirt off to see that it was made of sterling, which made me think it might have been buried at one point. Is that significant?"

"Hmm. Curious. A ritual of some sort, you suppose? Burying a crucifix? I've never heard of such a thing. However, you linger long enough in this town of mystics and pagans and anything seems possible. At the market last Tuesday, someone was selling dragon's eggs, a fairy door and a witch's bell. It seems everyone is looking for another dimension, spiritual or supernatural."

We both laughed, ordered another round, and turned our attention to the piano music.

Out on the street at closing time, Simon volunteered to walk me to my door. I waved him off and strolled home alone, awakened to something unsettling despite what had been a pleasant evening. Arthur, always Arthur. To be certain, a door had opened in my quiet life when I caught him defacing *The Prophet* and it had closed when he left for Durham.

The boy had breached the walls of my quiet life, and even as cautionary voices—my own and others'—urged me to scurry back to safety, I gladly gave him more and more of my time and thoughts. With an ache, I realized that, even with the bright presence of my best friend in the shop every day, I was lonelier than I could stand.

When I walked through the door of my new house, I felt the silence of a home with one occupant, its rooms populated with inanimate objects: wardrobes, crockery, beds under soft linen, my mother's mink coat wrapped and stored in the cedar-lined cupboard. Without human voices, a house is just an address.

On a scrap of paper, I scribbled a line for the window: "Once there were four children whose names were Peter, Susan, Edmund and Lucy." I wandered up the stairs and into the room with the bunk beds. I found the book where I'd left it. Aslan died to save Edmund's life.

Chapter 26

ARTHUR

My objective, once I'd landed at Durham University, was to be as inconspicuous as possible. On my sixth day in halls, there was an insistent knocking on my door. Though it was past noon, I was still lying on my bunk in tracksuit bottoms, rereading a Fabulous Furry Freak Brothers comic as rain beat against the window. I opened up to find a woman with long blond hair holding a wet list of room numbers, who told me it was an absolute obligation for new students to join the campus tour even in a squally downpour. Like a nursery school teacher, she stood and supervised as I put on a shirt, an overcoat and some green wellies.

"Don't you read your notices? It's induction week. You were supposed to respond to the invitation days ago, not wait for me to round you up."

"I'm sorry," I mumbled.

"Have you got a brolly?"

"No, I don't."

As we left the residence to join her group of bright umbrellas, a heavier rain began to slap our heads and shoulders. The warm sun of Glastonbury seemed unimaginably distant.

The limp paper disappeared into her pocket, and she unfurled her own brolly. "You'll have to share mine."

"I don't mind the rain."

Paying no heed to my standoffishness, she looped her arm through mine and pulled me close.

And for a time, I found tramping across the soggy campus a pleasant distraction—these were grounds, after all, that had been stepped upon by thousands of students since 1832. As Durham's sights and history rolled off the tongue of my umbrella-mate, my mind wandered to where my own steps would take me. Though little nuggets did stick. For instance, "A certain local woman named Mrs. Clements had the avant-garde notion to grind up her mustard seeds in the hope that they'd produce more tang. English mustard was invented right here in Durham." I had a pang for my mother and her apron.

Pulling me to a stop in front of the cathedral, my guide then boasted that the university ranked in the top ten worldwide for theology, divinity and religious studies.

I extracted myself from her grip.

"Would you like to go inside?" she asked. "It's magnificent. Roman-esque, Gothic and Norman architecture. This is the seat of the Bishop of Durham."

"No," I said more bluntly than I intended.

The others did wish to go, though, and so I waited outside, alone. It welled up in me that I should tell her my own sense of Christianity had been damaged by the likes of Mrs. O'Brien, our neighbour on Norbins Road, who believed that acts performed by the priests were divine, which meant that when I was ten, I'd had the sickliest feeling that I was being assaulted by God. I pulled the sleeves of my wet jumper down to cover my knuckles, and let the sideways rain seep into my bones.

After my guide and the other trudging freshies re-emerged, I feigned interest in a marble carving in order to evade an eager theology student who regaled me with the necessity of women assuming roles in the Church of England. I resisted telling her that I had rejected religion ever since the day the Zipper had me recite a dozen Hail Marys while I was being sodomized.

At last, the tour was over, and I slipped away and into the library. Solitude would be my salvation.

Miss Phillips had coached me on how to apply to university, but not on how to succeed once I was there.

From day one, I was sustained by two things. First was the packet of books that Miss Phillips had dropped off at our flat before I left—a gift that went unthanked. It was no surprise that the woman who had been guiding my reading since I was thirteen had picked titles that opened my mind, including a 1978 Booker-nominated novel by Bernice Rubens, *A Five Year Sentence,* with an unusual premise. Its opening lines: "Miss Hawkins looked at her watch. It was 2:30. If everything went to plan, she would be dead by six o'clock."

The flap copy read, "On the morning of her retirement from her dreary job in a candy factory, Miss Hawkins has decided to end her life, but by day's end she is sentenced to live."

I didn't read the novel so much as surrender—like I'd swallowed one of Ernie's Quaaludes—to its characters' woolly world of desire, deprivation and reinvention. I had the urge to call Miss Phillips and ask her why she'd picked this one, but I didn't.

Disappearing into those books meant that I could keep my social life devoid of complications at the same time as encounter fascinating people safely on the page—and think about their misalignments, neuroses and failings rather than my own.

Second, my courses in English literature more than met my expectations, as the professors zealously pushed me to more advanced reading and critical analysis that went far beyond the level of my contributions for the bookshop.

Soon enough, a letter arrived from my mother. I tore it up and tossed it in the bin, had terrible regrets, and went back to the mailroom to retrieve the bits only to find that the rubbish had already been carted away. I could not deal with the fact that my mother had seen the naked photographs on the clothesline in Leeds that were responsible for sending Ernie into the shadows. Easy enough for me to avoid the subject altogether now that I couldn't hear her crying in the bedroom next to mine.

When Miss Phillips wrote, I didn't open her letter, but at least I didn't rip it up or throw it out.

After I finished the Rubens, I went back to her gift stack. I didn't sleep for days, lost in the pages of *Peter the Great: His Life and World,* spell-bound that a ten-year-old who had been crowned co-tsar would ultimately change the balance of power in Europe. It made me wonder what happens to other children who find themselves in impossible situations. Pushed by Miss Phillips to excel at writing, I had grown, but I had not grown up. Too many unsaid horrors lurked in places that I refused to confront.

In late October when the grassy football pitch had become too cold to sit on, the students decamped to the Palace Green library. A mildewy mob of dank, lanolin-scented woollen jumpers filled every seat of my refuge. From the beginning of term, I'd favoured the same stiff chair at an ancient banquet table with a view out a towering cathedral window. Next to me now, on most days, sat the umbrella girl from the tour, usu-ally wrapped in pink and blue Fair Isle and faded denim that matched her pale blue eyes, brown clogs on her socked feet, which set her apart from the other girls in the library, with pink streaks in their hair, platform shoes and T-shirts that exposed their midriffs.

One afternoon she finally introduced herself. "Hello, I'm Lisetta Holmqvist." She spoke with the slight Scandinavian accent I'd noticed on the tour.

In return, I gave her a wan smile to let her know she was unwelcome in my invisible bubble.

I lost track of the number of days that went by before she leaned over and whispered, "Do you speak English? You're so quiet. Even when you turn the pages of your book, you make no sound."

"You mean, do I speak?"

She nodded.

"No," I mumbled, glancing briefly at the exit, my escape route, and then I went back to my fat Russian biography.

From my years working at the Copperfield and Twist, I was an expert at reading book spines. From inside a giant canvas satchel hand-stitched with purple wildflowers, Lisetta pulled out texts on geomorphology, sedimentology, geological engineering, mineralogy, paleobiology and tectonics. In contrast, the monumental 928 pages of *Peter the Great* had never looked so inviting. At the bottom of her great pile of drudgery was *Mere Christianity*, by C. S. Lewis. Perhaps she wasn't as unidimensional as Mr. Fernsby, my old maths teacher.

She kept making overtures. "I'm undecided about the best way to move forward in my life," she whispered next, her elbows resting on a book called *Fossil Echinoids*. For a moment I looked at her with interest. She said, "I'm trying to care about the age of rocks. From your unwavering focus, I guess you don't share my ambivalence."

From my brief study of her carefree face and wide-eyed gaze, I could tell that no one had hurt her. Instead of cracking the geology text, she now stared dreamily at the other students traipsing in and out of the library as though she was collecting research for a sociology experiment. I returned to my book.

"Are you a fan of Simon and Garfunkel?" she asked next, scooting her chair a few inches closer.

"No," I said with as little warmth as possible.

"What about 'I Am a Rock' from *Sounds of Silence*. It's my favourite song. I can't help but think of you now when I listen."

I wanted to groan and roll my eyes. I had nothing to offer such a frivolous girl

"It's about a man who deals with emotional detachment," she went on. She sounded matter of fact, rather than critical, as though the songwriter's intentions had nothing whatsoever to do with me. "It's just that you are so quiet. Apparently, we all speak an average of forty thousand words a day. I'm afraid you haven't even begun to use your portion."

I couldn't hide a smile.

I went back to my book.

She didn't. "I'm quite good at predicting personality types," she said. "That woman over there. Look at what she has piled in front of her. Jane Austen, Fanny Burney. Sylvia Plath. Steinbeck. Ernest Hemingway. Obviously, she would rather get to know a single person deeply than skim the surface of a dozen. And that one, beside us . . ." she lowered her voice, and nodded to the left. "*The Lord of the Rings*. Fantasy. A dreamer. Probably sleeps through his first class."

I said, "People who read crime stories. Are they criminals? Or just learning?"

"That's eleven."

"What's eleven?"

"Eleven words." She pointed a finger at me. "You? You're reading to become an escape artist. Be careful. Harry Houdini took one too many blows to the stomach before he died. And who was it that said, all work and no play . . .?"

"I have an essay to finish."

She pointedly noticed my lack of paper and pen. "Best of luck."

The next day, I moved to a different seat in the library, at a small table in a dreary corner with poor light. She found me again, early one afternoon, and dropped a piece of paper in my lap. I picked it up and read, "'Destiny may ride with us today, but there is no reason for it to interfere with lunch.' Peter the Great."

"I've just eaten," I lied, but I couldn't help but smile to think she had sought out the nearly thousand-page book I was reading and spotted that specific quote.

She placed her needlepoint bag on the table with such a loud thump it made me think of the car handles Ernie rattled during a theft and sat down beside me. Then she set a paper-wrapped tuna sandwich on the table, opened it and took half. After a while, I picked up the other half.

Later, after the lights flickered to signal the library was closing, she followed me to my residence, caught my wrist, slid her smooth, soft hand into mine, and kissed me on the mouth. "I think you should tell me your name." I felt as if I'd been stung by a jellyfish. I had never been kissed. I knew the shape of a man's fingernail better than the curve of a woman's lips. She stepped back and peered up at my face. "Do you fancy men?"

She caught me so off guard I was legitimately struck dumb.

"Because you don't seem to be attracted to women." She was blunt, yes, but so non-judgmental I felt not only disarmed, but strangely alive— definitely attracted—yet all I could muster was a quick shake of my head as I bolted for my residence. Rattled, I dropped my keys, and had to stoop to pick them up before I could get the door open.

"I'm not interested in you either," she called out, "as smart and as bloody handsome as you are."

I jogged along the hallway to my room without looking back and climbed into bed without turning on the light or taking off my clothes.

My mind grew crowded with images of the Zipper making me recite the Lord's Prayer while his hands were busy in my underpants. Most Mondays he also made me go straight to the confessional booth after we were done and atone for committing the sin of masturbation—physical pleasure to be washed away with Hail Marys. As I grew older, he would sometimes grab a copy of the newspaper from a shelf in the vestry and praise my book reviews, leaving no superlative unspoken as I was pulling on my clothes.

I could still picture every detail of a biblical illustration the Zipper had shown me when I was ten—men and women falling headfirst, arms flailing, from a blackened angry sky into the leaping orange flames of hell. With the book on his lap, he had instructed me that I should consider it a blessing to walk in fear of the Lord. "Such fear perfects our hope of staying in God's grace and someday being with Him in the happiness of heaven." His finger tapped the flames, then appeared to rest in them, impervious to the fire. "You mustn't ever tell anyone what we are doing. Revealing our little secret would kill us both."

I wouldn't, and I didn't.

When I was older, maybe fourteen, the Zipper told me after we'd had our Monday encounter, "Monastic silence is a way to avoid sin. The epistle of St. James dictates that silence is the only way of suppressing the sins of the tongue. We must live by God's rules." He'd been honing me for silence since I was eight. I took him at his word.

My mother, too, had honed me from childhood. She was rigid in her stance that the priests were morally superior and lived a humble celibate existence at a distance from the sinful parishioners they had been assigned to minister. She thought that both Jesus and the Zipper walked on water. It was only the altar boys who drowned.

Over the next few days, I found myself scanning the tables in the library for Lisetta. Without success. Then I ran into her one evening as I was heading back to halls.

"Why don't we meet off campus," she said. "Do you know the Pisky House coffee shop on Back Silver Street in Fowler's Yard?"

I didn't but I would find it.

Before we went our separate ways, I blurted, "Did you have a bet with someone that you could make me talk?"

"No. Did you?"

I got there before she did the next afternoon and ordered two coffees. When she appeared and came to sit next to me, crammed into a tight corner table in the crowded and noisy room, I might as well have been in the elevator at Dearborn's I felt such a sense of claustrophobic doom. I added another teaspoon of sugar to my mug, and then another, unable to counteract my trembling. I grabbed the hot mug with both hands, then winced at the heat and set it down. She was so close that electrified strands of her clove-scented hair clung to my woollen jumper. I was so overcome with fear of doing the wrong thing with my body, I began to sweat, unable to take a deep breath.

She leaned closer and placed a gentle hand on my arm. "Tell me what you will read next?"

My hands were under the table, leaving moist pawprints on the thighs of my trousers. My breathing was so shallow, I thought I might faint. I couldn't do this.

"I must be getting back," I said. "I have a paper due tomorrow." I got up, shrugged into my coat, burying my fists deep in the pockets to hide my sweaty hands, and headed for the door. Lisetta put some coins on the table and hurried after me.

We walked abreast along the canopied path of the woodland near Hollingside Lane. After a few minutes of silence, she pointed to a rowan tree growing entwined with a honeysuckle, then touched my bare wrist with her fingers, so I would stand still—a touch that reverberated up into my armpit.

"Isn't that a marvel of nature? The winding grip of the honeysuckle has twisted the rowan into a corkscrew. Each species is still alive, somehow, but dependent on the other." She gazed up at me until I nodded. "They look married," Lisetta said and laughed, stepping closer to touch the distorted trunk that looked so out of place among a forest of smooth trees rising straight to touch the sky with their foliage. Her fingers traced the deep grooves of the long spiral. "The natural world is full of strange anomalies and symbiotic relationships. The leafhopper and the meat ant. They need one another to exist. The crocodile and the plover. Who could imagine that a little bird would sit inside the mouth of a crocodile cleaning its teeth in order to feed itself?"

I wanted to remind her of the deepest flaws of human nature, of all the situations where there was a clear winner and an exhausted loser, not symbiosis. But I stayed silent.

"I wonder how long it took for the trunk of the rowan to become so distorted? Years and years, at least, but more likely decades and decades."

Then she put an arm around my waist in that leafy wood, and I began to shake and pushed her away.

"I'm sorry, Arthur. I've overstepped again." She backed up so she could regard the whole of me. "Were you anxious and afraid when you were a child?" In her question I heard only kindness.

Though I was flooded with relief that she hadn't taken my rejection personally, I still hurried away from her along the path. Lisetta gave me twenty yards, and then followed. I had a flash of chasing Ernie through town after the news that Nathan had been arrested spread around at school. I wanted to tell Lisetta to leave me alone—to get away from me before I revealed my horrible secrets, before I confessed that I was too damaged to be any kind of man. At the same time, I wanted her to hold my hand and never let it go, to tell her that the smell of her hair was something I tried to conjure when she wasn't near, to confess that I now lay on my bed every night and thought about touching her. But how could I do any of that? I didn't know how. I never got to discover sex on my own terms and was thwarted by a vow of monastic silence.

Behind us, the twisted embrace of the rowan and the opportunistic honeysuckle was lost in the darkness of the embankment.

Lisetta had caught up to me. "It must be awful to feel anxious," she offered.

I nodded to acknowledge the sweetness of her statement, and walked faster, unable to cope with her empathy. Or worse, her freedom to say whatever thoughts came into her head. But I finally answered. "Yes, it is. My father died when I was six. I saw his dead body go bumping down the stairs." It was a fat lie to blame my father, instead of telling her that the Zipper had robbed me of my childhood. I rushed on, "And I don't have any brothers or sisters." As though being an only child was the reason for an anxiety attack in a cozy café beside a beautiful girl with smooth pink lips and kind but probing eyes. She looped her arm through mine and I hoped she couldn't feel the wild thumping of my heart.

We walked on for a time in silence, my panicked heart rate eventually slowing.

Lisetta wasn't done with me. She said, "I look at you, and on the outside, I see a dashing man with thick, wavy hair and such beautiful skin your freckles seem painted on. You're graceful too, with no hint of masculine swagger. In my next life, I'll come back as your sister. Everyone needs a sister."

One seemingly guileless sentence after another, ripping away my armour as if it was only sticking plaster.

She went on. "Another wonderful thing about you? The amount you read. You could set a Guinness world record. Or maybe you've learned to fall asleep with your eyes open. Is that how you do it?" She paused for breath, then asked, "And what about your mother? Is she dead too?"

"She's alive." I was surprised to find myself offering up my mother's story to Lisetta. It was more understandable than mine.

"She was young when she had me. A teenager. Catholic. Already pregnant on her wedding day. Because of her condition, no priest would marry my parents. In the eyes of the church she is devoted to, she was never my father's lawful wife. Her best sacrament is Confession."

"Punishment for her sins?"

"That, and guilt. It's a Catholic speciality."

"So you're illegitimate? You'd fit right in at home—half of all Swedish children are born out of wedlock."

I wasn't used to barefaced questions that required answers, but her easy laugh was reassuring. I said, "They ended up marrying in an apple orchard in full bloom, a display, my mother has always said, that was infinitely better than a row of invited guests."

"It sounds like a dream wedding."

"She walked down the aisle amidst a thousand pink and white blossoms. Her mother boycotted the whole affair, but her father, my grandfather, acted as the officiant. It was in his orchard in the West Country, near a postage stamp of a little village where everyone knows everyone's business. Still, as a Catholic, she's an unwed mother."

"She sounds like a woman who wrote her own rule book. And now?"

"She's a baker." There didn't seem to be any reason to mention the long years when she was a flop as an insurance broker. "Her speciality is apple pies. She once told me it was her way of thanking the apple trees for blessing her marriage."

Lisetta withdrew the copy of *Mere Christianity* I'd noticed from her wildflower bookbag and waved it at me. "C. S. Lewis writes that a ban against premarital sex is so difficult to maintain and so contrary to our instincts that it begs the question: Is Christianity wrong or are our instincts wrong?"

As flustered as I was to be talking about sex, I said, "My teenage mother had a few sips of whisky on a train and her best instincts went flying out the window. She said my father's baritone voice was as seductive as a musical instrument. Think of the Pied Piper who played a magic flute and lured the unsuspecting rats to the river. My mother's better judgment didn't have a chance."

"The human voice is the oldest instrument, the most natural, the most valuable. Lewis also compared our instincts to piano keys, and human ethics to the pianist."

"What do you mean?"

"I think he wrote that no piano key is a right or a wrong note, just right or wrong at a given moment in the musical score. From that idea, he argued, too, that there are no good or bad impulses. Lewis also wrote that the doors of hell are locked from the inside—that hell is a place of our own choosing."

I felt comfortable enough to offer her the most benign version of the Zipper. "The parish priest back home used to say that every saint has a past, and every sinner a future. Impulses, if you like. All bad choices are forgiven with the proper amount of contrition. It helps to blur the lines between right and wrong."

"That's convenient, isn't it? There'd be no one in the pews if sinners remained unforgiven. But is sin even relevant anymore?" she asked.

"It's the thing that separates humans and God. God is perfect and we are not. Jesus took the punishment."

I could feel her eyes on the side of my face. She said, "Do you really think that an almighty being knows when you have crossed the line and spends time deliberating on when and how you will be punished for it?"

I shrugged.

We walked the path in silence, Lisetta only inches from my side. When her hand brushed mine, my thoughts turned from sin to the memory of her kiss. If she knew what my lips had done, she would stop speaking to me, let alone kiss me again. As though she was reading my thoughts, she stroked the inside of my wrist, startling me.

"Where did you go there? I lost you for a moment. At least your mother's parents didn't ship her off to the nuns to give birth in shame, the way they dump some of those Irish girls in the Magdalene Laundries."

"Our parish priest did tell me I was lucky I wasn't fostered out."

"What a horrible thing to say to a little boy. Clearly, your mother wanted you and loved your father. In a tight-knit village the effects of gossip and disapproval would have been magnified. The way I see it she had steel for bones."

I didn't view my mother as having had a teaspoon of defiance, but suddenly, her decisions at eighteen seemed unexpectedly brave. Braver than my own.

When I dropped Lisetta at the gates of her residence, I wasn't sure if I was threatened by her directness or smitten.

On our second walk, we stopped to watch two men playing chess on a stone board outside the Pisky House. One of them had most of the pieces off to the side. I could see the checkmate trap.

"Do you play?" Lisetta asked.

"No," I said.

"Liar."

"I'm not lying."

"Yes, you are. You were moving the pieces with your eyes."

"Okay, maybe I've played once or twice."

On the nearby green, two boys wearing baseball mitts were tossing a hardball back and forth. Nodding at them, Lisetta said, "An American pastime. Everyone loves a game. Have you ever held a baseball? My logic professor brought one to class."

"No, I haven't. I'm the farthest thing from an athlete."

"We were discussing the number 108—a number that connects the sun, the moon, and the earth. Galileo claimed that the universe is written in a mathematical language, with 108 being the most revered of all numbers, sacred in mathematics, geometry, astronomy. It turns out that a baseball has 108 stitches, which is just a random fact, and yet we crave a reason. Logic is the process of scrutiny that allows us to understand our convictions, uncover our strengths and flaws. Are you logical?" she asked with a laugh.

"I don't have a head for numbers."

"Well, 108 is the number for the wholeness of existence. *The Game of Logic* by Lewis Carroll is on the curriculum. Of course, he is most famous for writing *Alice's Adventures in Wonderland*, but he was also a mathematician, a photographer, an inventor and an Anglican deacon."

"Why, sometimes I've believed as many as six impossible things before breakfast."

"You know him! Well, of course, a bookish man such as you would know Lewis Carroll. Still, he's rather controversial now. We had a heated discussion in class about whether his relationship with children included an erotic component."

"Lewis Carroll?" The Zipper was a great fan, and he had given Ernie a copy of *Alice in Wonderland*.

"His real name was Charles Dodgson, and he took photographs of naked girls and was intensely fascinated by childhood. The discussion in our class got pretty intense—we are a culture that sexualizes youth, even as we are repulsed by pedophilia."

"Was Carroll really a pedophile?"

"That's never been proven. His reputation needs little burnishing, but he remains mostly beloved."

Feeling like I was forever a magnet for ideas that swam unspoken in my head, I changed the subject as we continued our walk on the lane that ran along the back of the Botanic Garden.

"And what about your family, Lisetta?"

"My father is Swedish and my mother is British," she said. "I'm trying to live up to my father's standards. He's a hiking enthusiast whose day job is as a mining engineer. I'm an only child as well, smothered by too much parental attention. I counted the minutes until I could escape."

"I did the same, except it was seconds I counted."

I stopped at the next cross street, which would lead me back to my room, and watched her walk home along Hollingside Lane to Van Mildert College. She didn't turn around, just lifted her hand and waved to let me know she knew I was watching her.

The following week I spotted Lisetta arm in arm with a muscled type in a purple Engineering jersey who leaned down to kiss her in public. Her delighted laugh rang out across the quadrangle. How could I blame her? We'd been together twice, excluding all the times we'd sat together in the library with me refusing to talk. I watched them break apart, then chase one another like exuberant puppies only to fall into each other's arms again. Such a public display of physical attraction. Instead of jealousy, I was flooded with relief.

Chapter 27

Shortly after I saw Lisetta kissing her engineer, a parcel arrived for me. Although the penmanship on the packaging was unfamiliar, the postmark was Glastonbury. I tore open the paper to find a copy of *The Stranger Beside Me: The Shocking Inside Story of Serial Killer Ted Bundy*. I stayed in bed, skipping all my classes, and read the book from cover to cover. It wasn't her handwriting on the package, but no one else sent me books, and I worried that Miss Phillips had picked this one for me because she'd found out about the Zipper. It didn't really make sense, but that's all I could think of, given that her book choices had always been intentional.

The author, Ann Rule, knew Ted Bundy before and after he was arrested for a series of rapes and murders that occurred from 1974 to 1978. I underlined. I circled passages. Rule wrote, "Looking back, we see it is often casual choices which chart a path to tragedy." I imagined Ann Rule being manipulated and fooled by Ted Bundy. I imagined a mother on the sidelines of a cross-country race, whooping for joy to see her son cross another finish line. I wondered if Bundy could have been stopped.

When I managed to fall asleep, I had sweaty dreams. Otherwise, I stared up at the corners of the ceiling where the darkness was deepest as my thoughts spun out of control. The Zipper was about to become a bishop in Bath, where he would have influence over dozens of parishes, hundreds of new boys. I saw the bruises on Ernie's arse. I saw the child with the crumbs on the bench in Bath. Before he disappeared, Ernie told me that Declan Entwhistle had gone to the police and complained about a priest. His story must have died when he did.

After a frantic week of nothing but obsessive reading and thinking, Lisetta came to the door. At first, she knocked softly, whispering my name. How would a person like me ever manage a genuine friendship with such an unblemished girl? If beautiful, unharmed Lisetta had continued contact with me, she too would rot from the inside out. The knocking stopped. She went away, only to return a half-dozen times more. Finally, in my most disrespectful voice, I shouted, "Can't you get it through your head? You mean nothing to me! Leave me alone."

"I don't believe you." She banged on the door with her fist.

"Go away!"

In that moment I hated her. Lisetta wanted intimacy, transparency and vulnerability. She wanted to lie next to me. I responded to her smell, the soft shadow cast by her eyelashes, the tender skin on the underside of her wrists where silver bracelets jangled when she waved an arm, but I couldn't possibly be a part of such intimacy.

What if I became like the Zipper?

I began to rip the pages out of Ted Bundy's life. Then I tore each one in half, and half again, and scrunched the pieces in my fists until the muscles in my hands went into spasms. I dropped the balled-up paper on the floor, so many mutilated pages that they made a mound beside my bed. I thought about setting them on fire. But I couldn't get off my mattress in order to find a match, repeatedly paralyzed by reliving the moment when I refused to help Ernie blow the whistle.

At last, Lisetta persuaded the supervisor from the student well-being office to unlock my door. He waded through the torn papers to open the window, letting in some fresh air, then came to sit beside me. Though I was unwashed and unhinged, I tolerated the firm arm he placed around my shoulders. Anything was better than being alone and prey to my tortured thoughts.

He and Lisetta took me to the mental health facility at County Hospital. On a gurney in the emergency department, I turned away from them both to face a septic-looking green wall and tried to shut off the tap of my thoughts.

The university's chaplain soon arrived. After asking Lisetta who she was to me, and not being satisfied with her answer, he shooed her out the door. He soon found that I had less desire to talk to him than to the two who brought me there. I spent forty-eight hours in the hospital on an IV drip before I was designated an adult at risk and assigned a psychologist and a social worker. The social worker kept asking me whether I should call my mother and let her know what had happened. I was an adult, I pointed out, and insisted there was no need to distress her.

I'd got myself into such a state of dehydration, I'd nearly died, so it took time to persuade the hospital staff and the university officials that I was not suicidal, just a homesick fresher going through a bad patch. On my fourth day in hospital, Lisetta returned, after persuading the nursing staff that she was my half-sister. I don't know how, given her noticeable Swedish accent.

"I've had to tell a lot of lies to be in this room. I hope you're worth it," she said. "Why is it that when you have a mental crack-up, they leave you to while away the hours all by yourself, when it's the last thing that will help? Not only did I claim to be your half-sister, I had to say I was in training as a psychotherapist so that they'd let me stay past visiting hours."

Despite her jaunty tone, Lisetta's red eyes were full of tears and her nose was dripping. Catching me staring, she wiped the excess fluids on her sleeve. "Too gross?"

"No," I said. "I know things are really difficult for you right now."

"Ha, ha," she said. "Very funny." But then she did start to laugh.

When I smiled back, she reached for my hand. "If not for me, you might have starved to death. Or worse." Her blue eyes were unwavering.

I looked away, and instead of thanking her, I told her I'd had a few sessions with a nice-looking social worker from Ireland.

"How nice?"

"Why are you here, Lisetta?" What I really wanted to say was, *Please don't leave me.*

"I'm attracted to academic brilliance. I've decided that high levels of intelligence are correlated with social anxiety. Ignorance is bliss. That's why I'm here."

"You need to switch out of geology."

"I'm an earth scientist, not a geologist. Arthur, I think you have the mistaken idea that a person who is born into difficult circumstances, or endures hardship and deprivation, is doomed to be punished in perpetuity. Or fate has had a hand. As I see it, the older, wiser souls choose the most difficult lives because they can handle the burden."

"I thought you were interested in fossils. When did you become so New Age?"

"I can't help but believe we live an assortment of lives."

"I'm not sure I want even one."

"Imagine if someone you admired rang your doorbell and said, 'Hey Arthur, I don't have anybody to take on this lifetime born into the third generation of extreme poverty in Calcutta. You'll be a slumdweller sleeping in the gutter next to the rats, with no access to education or running water, and you're going to contract cholera at age eight and die. However. You will teach profound lessons of love and resilience to your parents, siblings, aunts, uncles, the Red Cross nurses, and so on. Your little face will end up on a postage stamp.' Are you up for it?"

"I think I'd say no, what else have you got?"

"The point I'm making is that you have choices. We all do."

So far, I'd made nothing but terrible choices.

"In the library when I was stalking you"—she paused to smile at me—"one of the books you were reading was *A Farewell to Arms*. Hemingway says that life breaks all of us and we need to find our power in the broken places. Nobody gets to remain the starry-eyed child they once were, because the world eventually shows all of us that life is cruel."

It was hard for me to imagine that Lisetta had been subjected to cruelty.

"Stop allowing the circumstances of your birth and your father's early death to define you. You're not the only one to suffer. I'm about to lose a parent too."

I looked at her in shock.

"My mother has Lou Gehrig's disease. She's got two years at most. Somehow, she sees her condition as the unexpected gift of a trauma that has opened her up to the wonder of life itself. You've been given the same gift, and now you have to figure out how to use it." She bent down and grazed my cheek with a kiss, walked to the door and waved goodnight.

When I thought she out of earshot, I said to my pillow, "Lisetta, when I'm released, I will try to confess why I ended up in here."

Like a shot, she was back in the room, eyes on mine.

"Arthur, you have no need to confess anything. Sure, I don't understand why you wince when I touch you, but right now I don't need to know."

She was wasted on rocks.

After I was released from hospital, Lisetta and I never spoke of my breakdown. But some undeclared border between us had been navigated, and we were together much of every day. I picked up where I had left off with my essays and reading, and finished the term without a single failing grade. My marks were nothing to write home about, although I did receive a note from one professor inviting me to his office to discuss my essay, "The Literary Imaginings of Child Democracy." Somewhat unburdened, I was finally able to open and read letters from my mother and Miss Phillips, though I still wasn't ready to write back. I learned that the bank had foreclosed on the Castlefranks' house on Dyehouse Lane and Ernie's mother and stepfather had been evicted. I imagined Mrs. Castlefrank's shame. Another public loss. And then I wondered if Ernie even knew he had no home to return to. On second thought, he likely figured that out a long time ago.

I decided that I couldn't face Glastonbury for the Christmas holidays, and finally called my mother to tell her that I would remain on campus. I think she knew what it was I really couldn't face. Though I could tell she was distressed and missing me, she only said, "All right, Arthur. I'll have more time to work on my cookbook. I'll pull a Christmas cracker and watch the Queen's speech with Mrs. O'Brien instead. Merry Christmas, my darling boy." My mother wasn't one for endearments and for a few moments I considered purchasing a train ticket.

Lisetta went home briefly to see her family, but she was back a couple days before the new term started. I surprised myself by the depth of my longing for her. We took to walking beyond the outskirts of Durham to the ruins of Barnard Castle in Teesdale. On our first visit, she said, "Charles Dickens stayed in this very castle while he was researching Nicholas Nickleby. The harsh realities of the poor and the powerless. Can you imagine what this place has witnessed? Centuries of murders, rebellion and conquests, and yet some of the defensive walls are still standing."

Lisetta, like Ernie, was a mine of information. In that instant, staring at the ruins, my life seemed small and irrelevant. Somehow her words liberated me to say Ernie's name out loud to her for the first time. Soon I was telling her about what I had gotten up to with my best and only friend before her: the tactics involved in stealing sunglasses from parked cars, our close call in youth court—even Ernie's stepfather's "first gory" belt

and what he did with it. I was about to talk about the beating that preceded Ernie's performance of "The Raven" when I stopped short. She didn't press me. Instead, she said, "So you were a hooligan? That's hard for me to imagine, given how quiet you are now."

She stopped walking to stroke the smooth suede-like bark of an aspen. "Is Ernie at university?"

"No. He was brilliant at maths, but he dropped out of school to become an animal photographer. His brother works for a company called Reel Fauna Films."

"They work together making animal movies?"

I nodded. I so wanted it to be true. "Ernie has an uncanny way of gaining their trust, especially the birds, but even rodents and snakes. I've seen him feed a baby puff adder from the palm of his hand. Small animals feel safe with Ernie. He always had guts."

"And now?" She pulled at my sleeve.

"What do you mean?"

"You said he *had* guts." She hung onto my coat as if to prevent me from dashing off before I answered.

"It's only that I haven't seen him in ages. We don't keep in touch." I hoped I wasn't sounding defensive.

She let me off the hook by asking me to tell her about Glastonbury.

I told Lisetta that Glastonbury was a small place burdened with the outsized mythology of King Arthur, and that it was once called Avalon, the Isle of Apples.

"There was a time when every cottage had an apple tree or two," I said.

"We've got a bank holiday coming up in a couple of weeks. Shall we visit your hometown?"

When I didn't respond, she switched gears. "Tell me more about your friend, the snake charmer."

That made me smile.

"One night Ernie and I snuck out to climb the Tor and smoke dope inside St. Michael's Tower. It's the lone turret of a church built in the fourteenth century. It was stormy, and the tower is roofless. The wind was howling and whipping our hair, spooking us out of our minds. I was freaked partly because Ernie had just told me that in Glastonbury the veil between this world and all the other worlds is razor thin. That night, it seemed true."

"Is he spiritual?"

"Oh my God, no. At least not in any organized Christian sense. When we were kids, we tried to burn down the church . . ."

"What?"

I was now regretting how free I had become. "Another time. Anyway, when he and I were in the Tower that night, we heard the most unnerving sound I'd ever encountered. Ernie said it was a nightjar. I thought it was a bat, but Ernie was pretty sure he was right. They have uncanny big eyes, he told me, and their cry is a harrowing, rattling sound. They hunt at night, and are notoriously elusive and difficult to see. Ernie knew a lot about birds, and especially ravens."

"Why was he so interested in ravens?"

"I don't really know. He said they connect the living and the dead, and that when a soul dies, the raven goes looking for it. For a mathematician he was strangely spiritual."

"Ernie seems to loom large in your life for a person you've lost touch with. Arthur, why don't you reach out again?"

I avoided the question, launching into more stories of Ernie's brilliance. I told her that he was the only person I knew who stole a science textbook because the ones at school were below his level. "He tried, once, to teach me about MS-DOS. All I remember is that it's some kind of operating system for personal computers. He had a book called *Computer Vision*. It made fossils look interesting."

Lisetta put a light hand on my shoulder, turning me to face her. Her eyes were soft. "For the first time since I've met you, you're talking with real animation. Let's take the train to wherever he lives so I can meet your old friend. When I was home, I told my father you come from Glastonbury, and he told me that along with all the Arthurian stuff, legend suggests that Joseph of Arimathea may have travelled there after the Crucifixion to found the first Christian church in England. Such rich history in your hometown."

"You told your father about me?" I wiped my nose with the back of my hand.

"Arthur, what is it?"

"Nothing at all," I said. I bid her a curt goodbye and rushed off, leaving her standing at the rim of the Barnard Castle ruins.

"You are not normal," she called.

"Ernie left home. I don't know where he is," I yelled back.

"So what you are saying is that *Ernie left you.*"

"I left him first."

"And then what?"

I stopped and turned to face her. "He never came back." I put my back to her, and started to run.

I crawled into bed cradling my fears, narrowly averting a second panic attack and possibly another breakdown. It took maybe an hour for my heart rate to resume its regular beat.

It had been on the tip of my tongue to tell Lisetta about the sterling crucifixes and Ernie's trips to Bath. That he'd bunked off school to get there, came home angry and reckless, with his pockets full of money. *Loose lips sink ships.* I said it over and over, as I lay under the covers in my darkened room.

When a puffy-eyed Lisetta took her seat at our table in the library the next day, I passed her an apple pie I'd bought at the Dusted Knuckle. She reached across the table to push it away, changed her mind, and lifted the edge of the waxed paper. It was hard to tell if the look she gave me was for the pie or for me. Her red eyelids, blue eyes and splotchy face unexpectedly reminded me of the way Ernie looked after the orange and white kitten had died. I picked up and cradled the pie in both palms and tilted my head to the exit. She was right behind me. We ate every crumb, sheltering from the pelting rain under the portico. With her mouth full she said, "You went out and bought me an apple pie to say you're sorry?"

"Yes. And I *am* sorry, Lisetta. I told you my mother is a baker whose speciality is apple pies. It was the first thing that came to mind."

"An intrepid unwed mother who's become a baker, a friend who believes that ravens carry the spirits of the dead to and from the afterlife. Is there more I should know about you?" She fell silent for a moment, then said, "I'm thinking about accepting your apology."

"What does a rock eat?" I asked her.

She shrugged.

"Poma-granites."

We both laughed until the hiccup stage, and then she wiped her buttery lips on the tail of my shirt. As intimate as that was, I didn't panic.

"Do you believe in the power of ravens?"

"Yes," I finally said.

"Then one day you'll find Ernie again."

Chapter 28

MARINA

At noon Arthur came through the door of the bookshop and shrugged off his overcoat, dropping it and a large shopping bag on his old desk. He'd had a recent haircut, and his face was clean-shaven, endless freckles over blooming skin, set off by the collar of the white shirt he was wearing under a brown leather vest.

The sight of him, here at long last, froze me in place. During his first year at university, he hadn't come home for Christmas or for Easter break. And then when the long summer holiday came, his mother had dropped by the shop to tell me he'd had to take two summer courses to bring his marks up in classes where he'd fallen behind—he'd been ill during his first term and had missed several weeks of school. He'd only been home once since he'd started university, spending one bank holiday at his grandfather's orchard doing a hundred-odd repairs for the old man.

Still, I hadn't stopped writing, and posting parcels of books, and finally Arthur began to write back as if there hadn't been a long silence between us. Witty letters, full of opinions about literature, mostly, and especially the books I'd picked out for him. In one of them, he asked, rather diffidently, why I thought he'd be interested in a book on Ted Bundy, and

I think he was relieved when I told him I had talked to Arfaana and realized she had mixed up my slips and had sent that one to him by mistake. When I extended an invitation for him to come and work at the shop this Christmas—if he was coming home for the holidays, that is—he'd telephoned to accept. I think I kept my voice steady, but it had been so wonderful to hear him agree, to hear his voice at all, it might have shaken just a little bit.

But then he hadn't shown up when the shop opened this morning, and I'd almost given up hope that I'd ever lay eyes on him again.

Now here he was.

Arfaana saw me standing speechless behind the counter and went to shake his hand. "Better late than never," my always direct friend said.

"Hello, Arfaana. I just got to Glastonbury. The train was delayed by freezing rain, and then when it passed, we had to stop for an hour at a time as branches that fell on the tracks were removed. I'm sorry I'm late, but I'm here now." Arthur beamed as he scanned the familiar shelves and took in all of my friend's innovations. "I see you've made your mark."

When he saw me, he came towards me in a rush. Then he stopped himself and went back to his old desk to pull gifts from the shopping bag: a pie from his mother, some Swedish chocolates from a girl he'd met at school, and several copies of an essay he had written that had been published in *Palatinate*, the Durham University newspaper.

I thanked him profusely, forcing myself not to ask about the girl who provided the chocolates, and grateful he'd given me a way to recover from the shock of seeing him at last. I was now smiling so hard my cheeks were beginning to ache. Since the shop was busy with Christmas shoppers, we took to our stations. It was as if Arthur had never been gone. It was a thrill to have him back in the shop shelving books and welcoming customers. Even more thrilling, or perhaps reassuring is the best word, was to see that the hooded look he'd worn for months on end after Ernie's disappearance was gone.

One day of the seasonal rush blended into another. I hardly left before 11 p.m. The liveliness, pace and camaraderie helped us cope with the long lines at the till, the ghastly wet nappy someone left in the children's section, and above all, the pressure to make appropriate gift recommendations or guess what a customer was looking for from the faintest of clues. I tried not to be frazzled by the customer who said, "I'm looking for that bestseller about a dog." Luckily, in that particular case, Arthur knew the title.

The day before Christmas Eve, Mrs. Barnes came into the shop to drop off several mince pies for the holiday crowd. "I won't keep you long," she said to me as she set them down on the little round table. "I can see how busy you are. I just wanted to thank you, once more, for all you've done to help Arthur. He is as happy as I've ever seen him." She gave my hand a little squeeze, waved at her son, and then hurried out of the shop, leaving me to chastise myself for the many months I'd spent imagining her in a state of Valium-swaddled heartbreak. Clearly, I had been projecting my own heartache.

Soon after she left, a customer brought his book purchase to the till, and as I rang it in, he said, "Did you know that mince pies were originally made to celebrate Jesus? They were rectangular in shape to imitate the manger. And then the baker would roll out and cut a pastry baby Jesus to lay on top of the mince. Some people think the traditional shape was meant to be a coffin, but it was the farthest thing from that." The man was thin, with a terrible pallor that suggested an illness, an impression reinforced by the way his overcoat hung loosely off his shoulders. He was shabby and unkempt, his straggly grey hair in need of a decent cut, but still vaguely handsome.

"I don't think I'll ever look at a mince pie in quite the same way," I said as I handed him his purchase and his change. He wished me a quiet Merry Christmas, and slipped away, quickly replaced by the next customer in the queue. I heard the tinkle of the door as he left, and glanced out the mullioned window with long leaded panes to see the street had turned over from day to evening, and the lamppost, festooned with trailing garlands, was spilling a glistening light.

I considered the half-dozen pies from Mrs. Burnes, each with a pattern of pastry stars, and not the baby Jesus, spread across the dark mince. Then I glanced out the window again to see that the man had stopped to study our newest window display: "Ships at a distance have every man's wish onboard." I wondered if he knew it was from Hurston's *Their Eyes Were Watching God*.

I dragged my own eyes back to the customers, then excused myself. "I'll only be gone a moment," I said. "Please help yourself to a complimentary chocolate while you wait." I picked up one of the pies, and hurried out the door just as the man crossed the street towards the King William Inn. I had to run to catch up. When he heard my footsteps, he turned. Coming to a breathless stop in front of him, I held out the mince pie. At first, he didn't understand it was a gift.

"For me?" I had the distinct impression it had been a while since anyone had given him something homemade, or anything at all, and I ached for his loneliness. Finally, he slipped the handle of his book bag up his wrist and accepted the proffered pie with both hands.

"Yes. For you. I really must run. I've abandoned my customers."

He called after me as I headed back across the road, "My mother always made *chiacchiere* at Christmas. Sweet fried dough."

I looked over my shoulder to see him standing there gazing down at the mince pie I'd given him. I turned around. He met my eye and told me, ever so quietly, "If the twisted pastry ribbons didn't break while they were frying, she called them angel wings. My brother and I could never quite master making angel wings that wouldn't break." He took a few tentative steps closer. I could barely make out what he said next. "Sometimes, I heard crying. In the vestry . . ."

Perhaps he hadn't wanted me to hear, because he nodded at me then, and trudged away down the street. "Merry Christmas," I called after him.

Arthur was behind the counter dealing with customers when I came back through the door, and for just one moment, he wore that old haunted look.

On Christmas Eve, we locked the front door after the church bell pealed for the seventh time. I hit stop on the Mother Goose lamp, ejecting the Christmas cassette—a concession to our customers not yet sick of carols and "Frosty the Snowman"—and tucked it into a drawer of Arthur's old desk. Dog-tired but happy, we three roamed the shop gathering stray books that had been perused and then abandoned willy-nilly, and reshelved them. The last slice of mince pie was gone, as were all the Swedish chocolates and several tins of toffees I'd also set out for the customers.

At half past seven, with the shop more or less back in order, Arthur came over to me at the counter. Arfaana had just ducked into my office with her calligraphy set, calling out, "I'm going to get a jump on next week and write out our new window quotation."

Arthur was regarding me so earnestly I wasn't sure what was about to come out of his mouth, but what he said was, "Is it all right if I go now? My auntie and Grandad have come in from Crewkerne, and my mother is making a feast for us before they head off for midnight Mass."

"Of course. Please go home. And thank your mother again for the pies. Such a kindness."

Arthur cocked his head at that, a curious expression spreading across his features.

"Arthur?"

He sighed. "It's nothing. Only that my mother used to bake a mince pie at Christmas for Mrs. Castlefrank. I had planned to visit Ernie's mother when I came home, but she and her husband moved away soon after I left for Durham. My mother just told me that she's passed away from cervical cancer, or perhaps a complication from a transmitted disease." Arthur's eyes dropped to the floor as if he wished he hadn't said that last part.

"I knew she'd moved away, but I hadn't heard that she died. That's such sad news, Arthur."

Neither of us mentioned Ernie, though it felt like his presence was hovering in the air between us. One more opportunity lost.

Then Arthur did something that was very un-Arthur like. He stepped forward and gave me a brief hug, then let go as though he'd been scalded. "Miss Phillips . . ." he said, "I just wanted to thank you for everything you've done for me. Your letters mean a lot, and I'm sorry that I took so long to write back. Along with your generous gifts of books. I promise I'll start writing more reviews."

"I'd love that, Arthur," I said. "Get off with you now, and I'll see you in three days. Have a wonderful Christmas."

His eyes dropped to the floor again. "I'm sorry," he said, "but I won't be in again. My mother and I are heading into London the day after Boxing Day to meet with her editor. Her manuscript is done, and they want to discuss edits and a publication schedule."

I worked hard to not look as disappointed as I felt. "Arthur, please give her my congratulations. A first cookery book! I'm sure we'll sell many copies right here in the shop."

It was a relief to see Arfaana emerge from my office. As she came over to us, Arthur turned to her. "I've never seen the shop so hectic at the holidays. The window display has made all the difference."

"I'm just about to put up another one of your suggestions. Marina said you used to roam the shop on quiet days opening random books and finding the best sentences." She laid the new calligraphy on the counter, and read it aloud. "Generally, by the time you are Real, most of your hair has been loved off, and your eyes drop out and you get loose in the joints and very shabby. But these things don't matter at all, because once you are Real you can't be ugly, except to people who don't understand."

"When I was six, I went to live in Crewkerne for a couple of years," Arthur said. "That was the only book I had with me."

Arfaana went back to the children's section and returned with a copy of *The Velveteen Rabbit*, which she gave to him. "This book belongs to Arthur W. Barnes," she announced. "It's definitely a favourite, though I'm not sure I believe that one line, 'When you are Real you don't mind being hurt.'"

"Thank you, Arfaana. I'll treasure this. My old copy . . . well, let's just say it completely fell apart."

"For Marina's sake, don't be a stranger. This week you've shown me why she thinks you are worth all her fuss. Let me get your coat."

While Arfaana went off to the coat cupboard, I hurried to my office. I came back with Arthur's pen, which I'd wrapped, and an envelope containing his wages for the days he'd just worked, along with a cheque for the money he had forsaken when he headed off to university. I handed them both to him after he'd shrugged on his coat, and he stuffed the pen and the envelope into the pocket, telling me I shouldn't have.

And then it was time for him to go. We'd been so busy, we'd barely talked. I'd found out next to nothing of his time at school, or the company he kept, or the thoughts he guarded. I consoled myself with the idea that he was thriving, that he might even be happy, that a woman had given him the chocolates.

"When will you return?" I asked, attempting to hide my distress over his leaving so soon.

"Maybe next summer. My course load keeps me busy, but I'll do my best to write some book reviews for you and put them in the post. My plan is to stay in Durham and get a doctoral degree."

"How wonderful," I said. By now I had walked him to the door, where we stopped, both of us awkward.

Arthur looked towards the back of the shop. "I do like the musical Mother Goose lamp that you put on my old desk. Ernie used to sing nursery rhymes." There it was at last, Ernie's name. Arthur didn't stop. "Ernie was always singing and whistling—Annie Lennox, Grace Slick, the Pogues, the Moody Blues. He would stand on top of the Tor and pretend he was Justin Hayward and belt out, 'I'm looking for a miracle in my life.' He did the best birdcalls, too."

We stood there looking at each other for a moment, and then he said, "Well, my mother is waiting. Thanks, Miss Phillips, and bye, Arfaana. Merry Christmas to both of you, and Happy New Year too."

And he was gone.

A few minutes later I noticed that he'd left his denim jacket, the one with the arms cut off, draped over a stool at the till. I carried it to my office and hung it on a hanger on the back of my office door, and sat down at my desk with a sigh.

Then I heard loud knocking, and Arfaana called out, "Hold on, let me unlock the door."

The bell tingled, and Arthur rushed into my office, his colour high. First, he showed me the lost and found pen with a dazzled look of wonder, and then the cheque, which he waved. "Miss Phillips, you've given me the wrong amount of money. This is a hundred times what I am owed at least."

"No, Arthur. It's all rightfully yours."

Startled, he met my eyes and then immediately dropped his again.

"Rodger Mistlethorpe paid me on your behalf for every book review you wrote for the *Somerset Gazette*. Years and years of reviews. And Leon Uris left you a cash gift as well. I invested every single penny of those earnings on your behalf—I wanted to make sure you had enough money to attend university. But then, somehow, your mother managed to take care of that."

I watched him processing the information.

"It was terribly wrong of me not to tell you, and I should have sent it to you sooner, Arthur. But selfishly, I wanted to put the cheque in your hand. Please do something outrageous with the money. Go see the world. Canada. Australia. Wherever you've always wanted to go."

"Miss Phillips."

I felt a shiver up my back at the shakiness in his voice.

He finally looked up at me. "There was a time when I couldn't imagine that my life would get better. I wanted it to end. But it did get better. You're the person who gave me a chance at that better life, and I will never forget it."

Speechless, I got up and retrieved his denim jacket from behind my office door and handed it to him, and managed to give him a nod and a brief pat on his arm.

Maybe he could see that my throat had closed and another hug from him would be my undoing. In any case, he smiled at me, tucked the cheque and the pen back in his pocket, and walked back out the front door without another look back. Walking tall, his shoulders squared, whistling a tune I knew. What was that song?

From the mullioned window, I watched Arthur stuff the jacket into the rubbish bin, a few yards from the door, and then he was off.

Arfaana found me standing at the window and put a light hand on my shoulder. "Marina, you were right about Arthur's influence with our customers," she said. "We sold twenty-seven copies of *A Christmas Carol* thanks to his review. Why do people never seem to tire of reading about Tiny Tim?"

When Arthur had disappeared from view, I turned to my friend and said, "I think it's all those qualities he wrote about. There's the nostalgia surrounding Christmas with its expectations of family reunions and all past grievances forgotten. The unexpected benefits of gift-giving. Though we can never be sure we have made a difference with our actions, sometimes it turns out we have."

"Marina?" Arfaana touched my sleeve. "Did you give him back his little silver necklace? The one you had repaired."

"No, I didn't. It's still buried somewhere in my office. I thought he would be here next week . . ."

"Next time," she said, even though in my own ears my excuse sounded vague and somewhat self-serving. "Also, speaking of the benefits of gift-giving—I haven't had a moment to ask you if you knew the man who spoke to you about the mince pies? Handsome in a defeated sort of way. Badly in need of grooming."

"I knew of him. His brother—they might have been twins—was the priest at St. Nicholas who left without telling the parishioners. Arthur's mother was especially devoted to him, and I remember Arthur mentioning the priest taught him how to play chess when he was an altar boy."

"Why in heaven's name did you chase after him with a pie in your hand?"

"I heard real yearning in his tone. Maybe Norma's mince reminded him of his childhood, or his own mother—after I gave to him, he told me about some angel wings she used to make when he was a boy. He just seemed terribly lonely, that's all."

"All right, my friend. Interrogation over. Get your things. If I don't drag you out now, you'll be here until New Year's Eve."

Just as I was about to obey her order—benevolent dictator that she was—I saw headlights approaching along the mostly deserted street: all the shops were closed, and most people in town were at home already feasting or wrapping gifts. I watched as the car slid past, and there in the passenger seat of an old Mercedes was a young man with delicate features and long dark curls who turned his head away the moment he saw me. Except for the deep brown hair, I could have sworn it was Ernie. Had my silence and Arthur's fond memory conjured him?

No, it couldn't be him. Ernie was long gone, his mother dead and what little family he had was shattered. Why would he ever come back to Glastonbury?

Arfaana appeared at my shoulder with my coat and my purse. "Come on, you," she said. "You're coming to my flat to drink some wine and eat whatever I can find in the cupboard. Then we'll put our feet up and watch *It's a Wonderful Life*. I much prefer it to *A Christmas Carol*."

Chapter 29

ERNIE

Casper and I sat facing our collection of computers in the Pint Room below the pawnshop. We were supposed to be hard at work, but Casper couldn't stop yawning—he was just back from the fourteenth National Computer Security Conference at the Omni Shoreham Hotel in Washington, DC, where he'd successfully impersonated a Dr. Karl Prosanto from Carnegie Mellon University. Casper had gathered over thirty research papers and had attended, all the while discreetly taping, sixteen panel discussions without running into anyone Prosanto might know. Now we were putting in long hours applying what he'd learned. Soon, all of our mail-order business—the retailing of photographs, CDs, DVDs and magazines to a carefully cultivated customer base—would be moving online and we were uploading accordingly.

"Jet lag?" I asked.

"I don't feel the time change, but I hardly slept the whole conference. I was in stellar company. The US Department of Defense, the Air Force Academy, several banks, the Mitre Corporation. To this point, users have wanted their technology to be easy to use and protecting their data was an afterthought. That's all changing, which is why it's finally time to make this move. Once we're done here, we'll have the largest database in the world, and it'll have both data integrity—secure against unauthorized uuuuuu and user confidentiality."

"Was there a session dedicated to encryption?" I asked.

"Phil Zimmermann was there pushing his end-to-end encryption. He said his freeware has the potential to be the most widely used email encryption software in the world. It's early days, but it's coming. I wish it would get here even sooner. Physically copying our wares and sending them to our customers by Royal Mail now feels like delivering the goods by donkey cart."

I got up to retrieve a stack of new photos. I'd recently realized I'd become a mortician of sorts. I no longer saw the dead eyes of the children. It was all just an assembly line. A laborious process of copying, wrapping, addressing and stamping. Casper and I each had our own porcelain envelope moistener.

"These ones need to be cropped," I said. "Palm trees on the wallpaper. Where is this? Beechwood?" I'd lost track. "It could be recognizable."

Casper pointed to a second set. "And those need to be doctored to make the participants more anonymous. I may need to do them all over again." He got up and disappeared into the darkroom. Hs newest fascination was for the technique of morphing using Gryphon software. The best faces in our trove could be transposed onto the faces of other children doing extreme acts. It meant that we could serve up more variety of poses to Sir Martin using his favoured boys.

I was itching to create a database of clients right now. Casper insisted we wait until encryption was reliable. But we were long past him being able to keep track of customers in one tiny notebook he chained to his belt. He'd filled a dozen or more and had bought a small safe to lock them inside.

I was wearing him down with every major mailing, though. Searching through all those little notebooks to find the exact clients who would most appreciate a new find was more time-consuming than copying the photos, stuffing the envelopes and doing the post box run.

The other reason I wanted to get everything we did online, frankly, was so I never had to come back to Glastonbury. Nathan was still in jail when I'd left Dyehouse Lane, and I'd had no choice but to stay with Casper. He let me put a mattress on the floor of a storage room beside the Pint Room. I'd gone home twice since, and only to retrieve a few things I'd forgotten. Each time I snuck into the house, I lay on my bed for hours, listening as my stepfather watched the telly, likely with my mother in a chair beside him, her hands busy with sewing or darning. Once, I found myself dialing our home number. When my mother answered, I hung up without a word.

Nathan got out that September. He didn't come back to Glastonbury, but I guess he'd called our mother from time to time until her surprise visit to Leeds. Then, somehow, he found out she'd lost the house and moved away. She was dead now. Cancer. She'd already been dead to me, so I wasn't sure how to feel about that.

Casper came out of the darkroom, looking satisfied—despite what he said about uploading all our wares, he was addicted to developing images—and went over to our ancient enlarger.

"Gotta take a pee," I announced, and headed for the lavatory. I didn't want to be in the room when he noticed that I'd buggered up the machine somehow.

While washing my hands I looked into the mirror, and there I was, brown-haired and brown-eyed. When Casper told me we had to be in Glastonbury for several days, we'd both changed our appearance. He'd done one of his radical facial hair and head shavings. For me, he'd advised women's hair dye and cosmetic contact lenses. Even Nathan hadn't recognized me until I raised my shirt and flashed the circular burn scars. Still, on Christmas Eve, when Casper drove us past the bookshop on the way to get some takeaway and I'd spotted the proprietor in the window, I'd turned my head. Better to be safe than sorry. And I decided I wasn't going to go out again until it was time to head back to the Reel Fauna studio in Leeds.

I got back to work, while Casper fiddled with the enlarger. When he sent a questioning glance my way, I said, "It was working fine earlier."

He and I were both tired of our shoestring existence. The sooner we could move online the better. Then we would be able to tap a gold mine, serving a global market of customers who would pay us handsome money to access digital channels categorized by age, gender and fetish.

For now, we ploughed our occasional lavish paydays from delivering special goods to our handful of wealthy clients back into the business. Our overheads were high. The security systems. Rent. The photo equipment. Computers. Covering the costs of hotel rooms for the likes of Sir Martin.

Every now and then, Nathan half-heartedly offered to sell drugs to bring in some cash to float us, but the fear of going back to prison for even longer if he was caught kept him from dealing amounts large enough to be worth it.

Nothing stopped him from using, though. It was painful to see my brother so bloody wasted, so painful it prompted me to lay off drugs and alcohol myself, which had not been easy. Nathan drank without any joy, straight from a half-gallon vodka bottle like it was Gatorade. When I saw the state he got himself into after he got out of jail, I cried about how little he cared about himself. Less than I cared about myself. Not anymore.

Maybe because of all that numbing, Nathan had more of a stomach than I did for the recruitment of unwitting children. He and Casper had been to Thailand on several occasions, where they found boys in the bus stations or wandering the streets haggling for baht or American nickels in the most forsaken parts of Bangkok. "The mothers are always on board if it means they can eat," Nathan told me, one glassy-eyed night. But our best videos were obtained when he and Casper could remain in situ for extended periods, developing a strong enough relationship with a child and the mother that they could manipulate them into compliance with the broadest range of sexual acts. The slums of Manila were a favoured hunting ground—Casper would be the benefactor who fed their families while Nathan charmed the children in Tagalog.

For the first year or so after I left Dyehouse Lane, I spent most of my time in Casper's basement, only venturing out in the dark to drive to post boxes within a fifty-mile radius. I spent my days learning everything I needed to know about coding. Sometimes, I was hit with a wave of nostalgia that made me forget my anger, and I'd walk by Arthur's flat late at night and stand there a while in the shadows, staring up at his lighted window. I was never tempted to knock. I was beyond anything he would understand now. Correction: he'd understand, of course, but he would tell himself he didn't.

Then Casper got arrested. He was soon released on bail, and the charges were eventually dropped. But the pawnshop became a hot spot. We were lucky no officers ever searched the premises. Still, Casper got spooked and rented us a truck to move everything to the studio in Leeds. In the loft, we built a sliding wall to hide the unlawful material, and I threw my mattress on the floor in yet another storage space.

Then, out of the blue, my mother showed up with Mrs. Barnes. Nathan must have been high when he'd asked her for a loan and then, when she'd agreed, given her the address so she could send the cheque.

He tried to hustle them both out, and Arthur's mum, whose normally pink cheeks had gone dead white, left without being asked twice. But our mother stayed put. She was freaked out by the clothesline of images, by the baskets of kids' toys, and most especially by the gun, a Maxim 9 with a built-in silencer. When Nathan gingerly picked it up in order to check that the safety was on, I wonder if it crossed her mind that he might shoot her. Instead, he threatened her with the spectre of not just him, but her younger son, going to jail if she blew the whistle on what was going on. She might have preferred to be shot.

That was the last time I saw my mother. I'd watched the whole disaster unfold from the door to my storage room, which I'd opened barely a crack. I could have killed Nathan myself when he mentioned me, though from the look on her face, my mother wasn't that surprised. I hadn't turned up dead, so where else would I have run to?

She was wearing a pink coat I'd never seen before, and lipstick, and she looked so young, even pretty, that for a moment I felt sorry for her.

Nathan took off after he got rid of her and was gone for three days. Some kind of crack binge.

Casper broke into my thoughts. "I got the enlarger working again. You deal with making the copies, and try not to screw it up again."

Nodding, I took the photograph from him and started the process of making fifty prints. It was the one of Declan Entwhistle, by far the most requested image of all the photos we'd accumulated. In it, he was still the perfect man-boy at the focal point of a gruesome contortion of bodies and faces. His suicide had put an end to his humiliation. At least he'd never know that soon images of him would be digital and live on the web in perpetuity, moving from one computer to the next. He'd died back when Nathan was awaiting trial and sparked one of my brother's binges. I'd barely known Declan, but when Nathan saw me with my head buried in an issue of *Byte* magazine, all cavalier despite the news, he'd lashed out, accusing me of being a machine instead of a human being.

Then, it wasn't quite true, but I took it as a compliment.

Chapter 30

MARINA

Christmas of 1991 was the last time Arthur worked at the shop. He came in once or twice during his next summer hiatus, but he chose to work at his grandfather's apple orchard. I could hardly blame him for picking fresh air over the dim interior of my wood-panelled store. Then we held a little launch for Norma Barnes's cookbook on a Friday evening in September, and he'd given the speech, turning his mother's cheeks hot pink and having his usual effect on sales. Then, when the next summer came around, he was hired as a sessional instructor at uni, and he'd spent this last summer that way too.

It had been long and soggy and wonderful for book sales, but as soon as school began, it turned quiet. Arfaana had taken advantage of the lull to attend a family reunion in Lahore. When she got back, she was mildly disapproving of my choice of a quote from Carson McCullers's *The Heart Is a Lonely Hunter* for the window: "In the town there were two mutes, and they were always together." I shrugged. I didn't want to tell her that it suited my mood as I surveyed the fallen leaves hustling along the High Street, but of course she knew. I was happy to have her back.

It was a Saturday afternoon in early November—Guy Fawkes day in fact—and the Copperfield and Twist was at last crowded once more. Arfaana appeared at my side, put her finger to her lips to shush my greeting, and said, "Listen."

I pressed the till closed, handed a customer her book and the receipt, and cocked an ear. In the children's section in the back, Mother Goose was singing a lullaby. The whole shop fell quiet, as the customers stood still to appreciate the plaintive, somehow familiar, song.

"Did you have a change of heart while I was in Pakistan?" Arfaana asked.

"How do you mean?"

"I mean, I thought you'd forgotten all about that old cassette?"

Shocked, I hurried over to the lamp where it sat on Arthur's old desk, pressed stop and pulled out the tape. Arfaana was right behind me.

"It wasn't me who inserted this," I said. "And unless you're playing a bad joke, it wasn't you either." I surveyed the nearest customers, but I saw no one I thought capable of sneaking into my office and retrieving the tape from my locked bottom drawer.

I whispered, "It's been in my desk ever since shortly after I bought my house on Tiller's Row."

"Perhaps it's a copy?" Arfaana said. "There must be other lamps just like it that play nursery rhymes?"

"Rather far-fetched." As far-fetched to both of us as the notion that someone had rifled through my desk and we hadn't noticed. I held up the tape. "This is definitely the cassette that came with the lamp. I recognize the tiny tear in the label on Side B."

We shared a look of alarm, and then Arfaana went back to the till and I ducked into my office wondering if I should take two paracetamol or three. On my desk was the elastic band I'd used to attach the little slip of paper with Giles Robinson's contact information to the tape. Someone had flattened the paper on my desk, as though it was a note I was meant to read.

I thought I'd better take the hint. I closed the door, sat down behind my desk and at long last dialed Robinson's home phone number.

Mr. Robinson—not a detective anymore, since his failed eye operation—lived on Priorygate Court in Castle Cary, a fifteen-mile drive southeast of Glastonbury. He said he would leave the door open, and I was to knock and come inside at precisely the hour we had agreed upon. I remembered to ask if he owned a cassette player. He did.

I knocked at the appointed time, turned the handle, pushed open the door, and walked through a small entryway into a large living room. On a wooden dining table, I saw noughts and crosses on a black lacquered base, a jigsaw puzzle, a Perkins Brailler, and an elaborate tape recorder with rows of black and red buttons, currently playing Elgar's "Pomp and Circumstance Marches." The room was lush with houseplants: fiddle-leaf figs, parlour palms, peace lilies and philodendrons. The place felt very alive.

I heard a kettle begin to whistle.

"Hello, Mr. Robinson, it's Marina Phillips."

"I'm blind, not stupid. Of course it's you."

I couldn't see him for the plants, but then he stood up from the end of a brown chesterfield whose back was deep and buttoned. He was tanned and whippet lean, in baggy clothing and dark glasses. When he held out his hands, I put down my bag and stepped forward to grasp both of his.

"I can tell a lot about a person from their hands. You don't get enough sunlight."

"Thank you for agreeing to meet me, Mr. Robinson." In his presence, I felt more like a teenager than a woman in her mid-forties. He was vigorous in a way I hadn't expected in a man who couldn't see.

"You've brought some kind of cake with almonds." He wasn't smiling but his face had softened.

"Yes," I said, and knelt to reach inside my string bag. I handed the cake to him.

"Darjeeling?" He tilted his head towards the kitchen, where the kettle was now screaming to be rescued. He had timed my arrival to the moment of full boil.

"That would be lovely," I said. He went to answer the call of the kettle with no hint of limitation. Somehow, I knew I shouldn't offer my help.

While I waited, I stared at the floor. As though knowing where my eyes had strayed, he called out, "I've set up my living room as a game of Snakes and Ladders."

And, indeed, the floor was tiled in twelve-inch tile squares, a checker-board of black and white. Each tile bore a sticker with a number, and someone had drawn the snakes and ladders with a felt-tipped marker. "The game originated in India, did you know? I bet your friend, Arfaana Haq, has the board version. It was designed as moral instruction for children, and adults too, meant to teach us the effects of good deeds versus bad. A good deed takes you up the ladder, and a bad deed slides you down a snake, where the evildoer is reborn as one of the lower forms of life. As you can see, there are far fewer ladders than snakes."

"How do you know Arfaana?"

"I don't know her. Before I decided to help you, I did a little home-work."

Robinson strode from the kitchen carrying a tray holding an old-fashioned tea set with a pattern of pink and white peonies, and a plate with slices of the almond cake. He set it on the dining table, which stood in front of a window with lace curtains that were parted down the middle and held off to the sides like a schoolgirl's ponytails. I remembered that Rodger had told me that Robinson had been widowed with a daughter to raise, which must have been more of a challenge after his eyesight went.

"How old is your daughter?" I asked.

"Fiona? She's fifteen now." He finally smiled. "Her favourite game was Snakes and Ladders. She drew our board when I still had a bit of vision left to appreciate it. I haven't been able to see her face since she was eleven." He pointed to his eyes.

"I'm sorry."

"No need to be. Both of us have adapted. She plans to enter the police service after she gets an undergrad degree, and has her mind set on study-ing at Georgetown University in Washington, DC. We're both hoping for a scholarship."

"I wish her luck."

"It's not luck that will do it, but determination and a lot of hard work. Now pass me your cassette with Side A facing up."

"Side B is the peculiar recording."

"Yes, I remember. Please sit down."

I took the chair at his elbow.

He pulled out the Elgar and set it to one side, and I placed the cas-sette in his palm. We sipped tea as we listened to the lullabies. He cocked his head as though to better discern any added sounds. When he'd had enough, he ejected the tape, turned it over to Side B, and slid it back into the machine. He listened. Stopped. Rewound the tape, tapped on the Braille typewriter, listened, rewound the cassette, typed. A little bell indi-cated the end of the line.

"Very clever," he said, almost to himself.

I didn't dare look at my watch, afraid he'd notice the movement and it would break his intense concentration. My tea went cold, as most of what had to be an hour ticked by. At last, he pressed the stop button and turned to me.

He said, "It's ASCII. The American Standard Code for Information Interchange. It's a seven-bit encoding scheme that represents two hundred fifty-six different numbers and letters. A standard data-transmission code that was used in the eighties by smaller and less powerful computers."

Mr. Robinson withdrew a piece of paper from the Brailler and ran his fingers over it. "What you have on the cassette is a list of ten names and addresses. Maybe ages as well. I believe at least two of the addresses are for churches, or they could be schools. I wasn't able to decipher the last few groupings of numbers, which seem to be a code within a code. I do believe it's solvable, though."

"Do you have any idea why someone would have coded the names?" I asked.

"Not yet, no. Listen, this is your cassette. I could return it to you and you could go away and we would both forget about it. Or you could let me investigate these names."

"That would be the best thing, wouldn't it, Mr. Robinson?"

"Do you have any gut instinct about what these numbers represent?"

"Nothing I'm willing to share with a former detective inspector at this point. My guesses feel too far-fetched."

"People generally seek out a man like me when they sense wrong-doing, Miss Phillips. While I can't follow a trail out in the world that well anymore, I do hear things that others don't. Things that might blend into the background, like the hum of a car engine or the sounds of a railway station. I will try my best to break the entire code and then figure out what it all means."

He ejected the cassette and pushed it in my direction. "I have all I need," he said, pointing to his Brailler.

I tucked the tape into my bag and stood up, ready to leave.

His dark glasses were turned towards the window, the light coming through the pane emphasizing the lines on his face. Maybe he was older than me, not younger. He ran his fingers over the list and said, "Miss Phillips, I've just had a thought."

"Yes?"

"This seems to indicate that two of the ten persons named are deceased." He ran his fingers lightly over his sheet of Braille again. "Those final eight numbers, the code with a code—I believe the last encrypted name is *The Raven*."

He must have heard my sharp intake of breath, but he didn't push me, just stood, and extended a hand, which I shook.

"Please, come back on November twenty-eighth at seven. By then, I will have figured out all I can, and I can give you a fuller account. And thank you for the cake. My daughter will be delighted to have a slice or two for tea."

I couldn't help that my breathing had gone ragged, but I was relieved Giles Robinson hadn't been able see my face. The Raven? Two words that dropped me into Arthur's despair after Ernie went missing.

I was so distracted on the drive back that I missed the exit for Glastonbury. A sky full of mist and fog robbed me of all sense of direction, so I pulled into the next petrol station, filled up, checked my bearings, and realized I was near the Preston Road roundabout in Yeovil, thirty miles off course. I was amazed and alarmed that some autonomous part of my brain had allowed me to drive my car without being mentally present. I turned around, attempting to remain more mindful.

Once home, I put the cassette inside a vintage decoupage hat box from Harrods, an extravagance encouraged by Arfaana that I both loved and was so embarrassed by that I kept it in an upstairs cupboard next to my mother's fur coat.

I put the hat box back on its shelf, drove to the shop, nodded to Arfaana as I headed to my office, and shut the door. I still had the box of Arthur's belongings, and I hauled it out now. I found the photocopied pages I'd remembered, from *The Complete Poetry of Edgar Allan Poe*, on which passages from "The Raven" were circled and the words *nevermore* and *unmerciful disaster* were underlined. Robinson had told me that two of the people on the coded list were dead. I stared at the pages, wondering how in God's name Arthur was implicated. And I didn't even believe in God.

An hour later, Arfaana opened the door to find me on my knees on the floor, with my shoes off and my hair coming unpinned. "Whatever are you doing?" She stared at the dozen small piles around me.

"I was searching for something."

"Are you all right? Your hair is a bird's nest. Can I help you search?"

"I'm fine," I lied. "I found what I was looking for."

I got to my feet, smoothing my skirt. "I've just realized I need a bit of holiday. I'll take the middle two weeks of November, and plan to be back just before the holiday rush. You warned me a while ago that if I didn't take some time off, I would run out of steam. And I have."

Arfaana poured two glasses of water from the jug on my credenza. She stood there smiling at me as I drank both down.

"At last. Where will you go? How about somewhere in the south of Spain. Perhaps the Costa del Sol? Or maybe the Algarve in Portugal? Two young girls have applied for the part-time position we need to fill before Christmas. The timing is perfect."

I sat down at my desk, "I've only just decided to take a holiday, and have no idea where I'll go. I'll trust you with the interviews."

"Really? Is your name still Marina Phillips?" Arfaana plunked herself down in an armchair. "So how was the meeting with Giles Robinson? Not so good, I suspect, since you look like you've run over a dog and suddenly want to go on holiday."

I spun the Mercator globe on my desk, letting my finger troll the equator. "I didn't tell him that my impetus for calling him was that someone had taken the cassette out of my office, and I also didn't say it had been left behind when I purchased my house. I had every intention of doing so, and then at the last minute, I changed my mind. I think he will get to the bottom of all that intrigue, whatever it is, on his own. He told me the numbers are a code. The 'a-ski' code. Or 'ass key.' Something that sounded like that, anyway. The B side of the tape is a list of names and addresses."

"Why would they be coded? Who uses that kind of code?"

I shrugged. "I had those same questions, but I don't have answers yet. There were ten names and addresses. Two of them are dead, he thinks. He's going to investigate."

"Did he imply some kind of illegality? Murder? Did he mention dates?"

"Not overtly."

"It's not like you to come away with so little information," Arfaana said, crossing her arms. "The former owner of your house—did you say her name was Sofia? She died more than fifteen years ago. Or maybe it was longer. Those coded names could be from the war, or who knows when or where. Perhaps it's best if you let her rest in peace before you become even more undone. Please tell me you plan to relax on a beach or sightsee in Rome? I could help you book a flight."

"As I said, I'm undecided." It was the first time in a very long while that I had excluded Arfaana from my thoughts, but I felt an irrational need to protect Arthur, even from her. "I think I'll work from home for the rest of this week as well."

"You've never done that before."

"I've never done a lot of things I seem to need to do right now."

Chapter 31

I took to driving through town after sunset, my car a small, safe cave, gathering the dark. I was unsure what I was looking for, convinced I would recognize it when it came crawling out from its hiding place. I couldn't put my finger on the source of my distress.

I trolled Somerset, from Beckery and south to Street, looping around and back to Norbins Road, where Arthur's mother still lived. I tried to remember exactly when he'd become captivated by Edgar Allan Poe and started wearing that raven T-shirt like it was the only clothing item he owned. Definitely after Ernie was gone. I thought at the time it was his way of staying close to his friend. And then, after I'd showed him the picture of the boy who'd committed suicide, he'd asked me if it was true that ravens carry the connotation of death. Arthur had stared at the photo in the newspaper with dread, even terror. When I pressed him to explain why he was so upset when the boy clearly wasn't Ernie, he'd just mumbled that Father Ziperto had officiated at the boy's funeral service. And why did I keep thinking about how a wallet belonging to a prominent man who had never visited the shop turned up on my counter. That very man had arrived in a white Rolls-Royce, his driver at the wheel.

At some point, one dark night after I'd come home from my wandering, my mind swerved to Constance Bradley's visit and the return of the lamp. I had a sudden pang of guilt that I'd never put up her thoughtful housewarming gift and found myself heading to the bookshop in search of a volume on the construction and upkeep of bird feeders I knew was in the gardening section.

It was well past midnight, closer to dawn. I didn't turn on the lights, just hurried to the right shelf and used my pocket flashlight to search it out. I got back home, damp-chilled and totally exhausted, and fell into a deep sleep. I didn't wake until the middle of the next afternoon. Another first. Seventy-two hours since my meeting with Giles Robinson, and nothing new had been revealed, except the certainty I would make a terrible night prowler.

I was still in my nightgown when Arfaana telephoned to say that an upstairs tenant in a building across the street had come in to tell us she'd seen someone enter the shop at 1:17 a.m. "I rang the police. They've just left. Nothing is amiss."

"Nothing would be. That was me in the shop. I was looking for a book about bird feeders."

There was a long pause. "In the middle of the night? Marina, are you having some kind of breakdown?"

"Goodness no," I lied. Couch-prone and immobile, or driving recklessly, I wasn't sure what was happening to me other than being swarmed by worry for Arthur.

"All right then. Call if you need me, though. The shop's not busy. I could close up and be on your doorstep in under ten minutes."

"No need." After we hung up, I went back to bed.

I woke early. Right after she gave it to me, I had stashed Constance's bird feeder and the long metal pole at the end of the garden under a nylon tarp, where it was now covered in another year's fallen leaves. I got dressed and made myself a cup of tea, which I drank while I read the manual. It recommended that I put the feeder up close enough to trees, hedges and shrubs to give birds a safe, fast retreat whenever a predator came near, but far enough away that squirrels would not be able to make the jump. Ten feet, they said. I'd also need gravel, a spade, rubber boots, gardening gloves and plenty of elbow grease, and a bag of sunflower seeds. The job took all morning. By the end of it, I was filthy, but the feeder was upright and filled.

A small girl in a raincoat, striped yellow tights and wellies had watched the end of the operation through the arch to the playground. She clapped when a single greenfinch swooped low and made off with the first sunflower seed. I clapped too and waved at her, smiling. Hopping and dancing in circles, she ran back to her mother. In that moment I found myself delighted by the sky, the grass, the wind that lifted her hair, the greenfinch—small excitements I'd long since stopped noticing.

I followed the wet imprints of her tiny boots to where she had climbed aboard the red and blue roundabout, which was flush with the ground and easily accessed by little feet. She lay on her back, her knees bent, as a team of children took turns either spinning or being spun. There was no pecking order. Off one came, on went another—the joys shared equally.

My gaze turned to the one man in the playground. He was seated on a wrought-iron bench, perhaps reading the magazine in his lap, the brim of his hat obscuring his face. The *Economist*. Not a recent edition. Maybe retired, maybe a grandfather, though he didn't seem to be attached to any of the little ones. I took my own seat beside a mother with a pram, and watched the children slide, swing and run, charmed by their shrieking merriment. And then, as though a bell had rung, all the children and their mothers or nannies gathered up their things and went home for lunch. Not the man and his months-old magazine. He had closed his eyes, and might have been asleep, his chin deep into his neck.

After my morning's efforts I was starving, and so I deserted my own bench and went back home to put away my tools, wash up and make myself an omelette.

The next day I rose late, made coffee and wandered out with my mug to watch the action at the bird feeder. Before too long, I'd need more birdseed. As I did a circuit of the garden, I glanced out at the little park and to my surprise the man with the magazine was seated on the same bench, as though he'd spent the night there.

After my breakfast I came back to the foot of the garden to look out at the playground again, now alive with small children. The man was still there, tearing bits from his sandwich and dropping crumbs at his feet for the birds.

Each time I came out to tend my garden for the next couple of days, I'd look up from my furious weeding—I was determined to make up for my neglect—to see him still on the bench, either with his head bent over the same issue of the *Economist* or up and tracking the children, alert to the arrival or departure of each and every one.

He never moved from the bench, which meant I had no real reason to confront him. Still, I had the creeping feeling that something was amiss. At the same time, I had the feeling that something was being averted. Half a dozen times from my second-floor window, I saw a car come down the dirt road from Tiller's Row, stop for a moment by the playground gate, and then reverse back out to the main street. As my imagination ran wild, I picked up the phone to call Arfaana, then put the phone down again. How could I share such unsettled thoughts about the coded names, the wallet at the till, and the beautiful cross-country racer who took his own life.

Late one afternoon, the temperature falling along with the sun, I climbed to the second floor to close the window that overlooked the garden. I could just see the top of the man's hat over my hedge. As I pulled the window shut, he rose to his feet and came towards my garden. He walked through the brambly opening and stopped near my bird feeder, where he looked up to where I was standing at the window, removed his hat, and waved.

I waved back. How had I not recognized him? I guess because he had lost even more weight since he'd told me about bakers decorating the tops of their mince pies with a baby Jesus made of pastry. I ran downstairs, intending to invite him in, but he was gone. I rushed to the playground, hoping to catch him, but no luck. He was nowhere to be found. With a pang, I went back inside. I'd see him again tomorrow. Invite him for a meal.

I climbed the stairs to the bedroom with the blue bunk beds and lay down on the lower one. He and his brother grew up here. I imagined them as small boys, falling asleep listening to the melancholy lullabies playing on the Mother Goose lamp until the tape came to an end and the light gently went out. Then realized with a start that cassette tapes didn't exist when Father Ziperto was a boy.

The next day I scanned the playground at all hours, but he didn't turn up. He wasn't there the following day either, and I realized at that point that he was not likely to be back. I had the overwhelming feeling that Father Ziperto's brother had tried to make me understand something he couldn't tell me directly, that he'd passed me a torch of some kind. Now he was gone and I wasn't sure I'd understood his meaning. What was I to watch out for? The children playing in the park? His brother? As far as I knew, the priest had never come back to Glastonbury after he'd climbed higher in the church hierarchy. I was at a loss, but more uneasy than ever.

I went to bed that night thinking about my own younger sister, with whom I used to share a set of bunk beds.

I was sixteen months older than Evelyn, and when she started school, it became my job to hold her hand and make sure she got there and back safely. For a whole year we walked to St. Christopher's on our own. "Don't forget to turn right at the white fence," my mother would say every morning, as she tucked a biscuit each inside the pockets of our matching dresses to be eaten at school break. I felt very grown-up.

But then Evelyn went away, and I spent many days walking to school on my own before I worked up the nerve to ask my mother when my sister would come home and sleep in the other bunk bed again. "Soon," my mother said.

Evelyn was like the little girl in the striped yellow tights at the round-about. She loved to turn non-stop roly-poly somersaults and play hop-scotch, her glossy braids swinging with every jump. She struggled to read, unable to sit still. She'd much rather slide down the banister or climb over the fence to pick daisies in the neighbour's garden or run in circles around the living room than sit on a chair and sound out words. I loved to read, pushing my oversized glasses up my nose, and did all I could to please my mother. Most breakfasts, Evelyn spilled her milk, more interested in talking to the blue rabbit dancing on her mug than drinking the contents.

Despite our different temperaments, she was my best friend.

Then came the day it was my turn to sharpen all the pencils before class started, an honour awarded by my teacher, Mrs. Gleason. My sister and I left early, and I tried to tug her along, but Evelyn refused to hold my hand. I couldn't be late for Mrs. Gleason, so I gave up and ran ahead. Not once did I look back.

At the end of the day, Mrs. Gleason walked me home, holding my hand tightly in her own. I told her we had to turn at the white fence. We did and I saw daisies strewn on the ground. I picked up one to take to Evelyn. The house was empty, though, which thoroughly confused me. Where had my sister and my mother gone?

Mrs. Gleason stayed with me until my mother came home. She thanked my teacher for bringing me back and staying with me, and she told her to please inform the headmistress that Evelyn would be away for a few days. I noticed that my mother's coat was misbuttoned and that she hadn't combed her hair, but Mrs. Gleason didn't seem to mind.

Later that same week, in October of 1957, I came home from school to find a newspaper spread out on the low table in the living room. On its front page was a photograph of a plane hovering over plumes of black smoke. My mother was sitting on the couch, looking dazed. She said something had happened at the nuclear power station at Calder Hall, but that I wasn't to worry. A year earlier my father had gone to the nuclear site at Windscale, Cumbria, a remote and isolated location, to oversee the opening of an atomic weapons program. He was rarely home, but when he was, he always told us that he was doing something important, that the job wouldn't last too much longer and then he'd be back. Now the Cumbria sky was filled with fire and black smoke and Evelyn wasn't in her bed.

Two terrible events in the same week. Somehow, I conflated the two, and whatever happened at Calder Hall also became the explanation for my missing sister. All I could think of was how much I missed Evelyn and me singing nursery rhymes in rounds, swinging our arms as we marched around the house.

> *London's burning, London's burning.*
> *Fetch the engines, fetch the engines.*
> *Fire fire, fire fire!*
> *Pour on water, pour on water.*

Thinking I would cheer my mother, I sang it for her. She slapped me, then got on her knees and hugged me tight.

"You were supposed to hold her hand," she whispered.

"But she's coming home in a few days, you said."

"God might take her home."

"Home where?" I looked around me.

It was another month, I think, before I'd pieced together that Evelyn had run into the middle of the road, or a car had come up onto the pavement, or she'd chased a squirrel thinking it was the smiling blue rabbit on her mug. Nothing was certain except my mother's inability to keep going and my father still stuck in the place where the sky had turned black with smoke. If I asked about Evelyn, my mother's face would collapse.

In that month, I developed so many fears I couldn't sleep unless my door was open and the hall light was on. At school, always well lit, I found something tragic and thrilling about telling my school friends that Evelyn had hit her head and God might take her. It made me the centre of attention, which I'd never been with my lively sister around.

Each day my mother made me sit beside her while she prayed her rosary and begged God to save my sister. All those entreaties, too, to St. Jude, the patron saint of lost causes, and nothing happened except that my mother turned into a stranger who sometimes wore her nightgown long into the middle of the afternoon.

And then Evelyn died.

Two days later, my mother told me to put on the dress I wore to Sunday Mass. She brushed her hair and pinned it up, and then, as a taxi pulled up outside, she put on her belted blue coat and helped me into mine. On the stiff back seat my mother held her handbag with both gloved hands, but twice she reached out to briefly encircle one of my tight fists.

When the taxi stopped outside a grand stone house I'd never seen before, she told the driver to wait. We got out, and my mother led me up a paved path and then down a dim hallway, her slippery gloved hand over mine, and then lifted me up to look inside a long white box where my rosy-cheeked sister lay with her eyes closed. She was wearing her favourite pink dress. I had the same dress in coral. We got back in the taxi and drove home in silence.

Evelyn was six and had done nothing wrong except preferring to pick daisies, weaving and looping them into necklaces, instead of learning to read and write.

After the taxi dropped us, we found a gift for me leaning against our front door, with a note taped to it. I unwrapped it to reveal a copy of *Charlotte's Web*, and then I read the note.

Dear Marina,
     It is not often that someone comes along who is a true friend and
a good writer. Charlotte was both. And so are you.
Mrs. Gleason.

Forever after, I would think that a good book was the antidote to everything. As if a book could fill up the emptiness left by a person. If not a single book, then a shopful.

That night my mother fell into a rage that saw her drop a dinner plate on the floor on purpose, not by accident, unlike all the crockery Evelyn had broken by being her unruly self. After that, I came to understand that my mother found it preferable to have no feelings at all. She stopped taking care of the house, or me, or herself, her hair growing as long and wispy as a horse's tail. In the weeks that followed my last sight of my sister in her coffin, I woke in joy-filled anticipation, thinking she had whispered my name in the dark or caressed my cheek, only to see nothing but the blackness of my bedroom and the dark outline of the top bunk.

Finally, my father came home, not a scratch or a burn on his physical body. He didn't know enough to simply gather my mother in his arms or how to offer sympathy instead of solutions. I never saw him grieve for my sister, either. He'd tried to hide that she was his favourite when she was alive, but now it was like she'd never been born at all. Shortly after he came home, he disassembled the bunk beds and donated them to the charity shop.

My mother started to lose her memory in her forties. Her mind came in and out like fog. When she became too much for my father to care for, she went into an institution, and I went off to board at Godolphin School in Salisbury. In a rare later conversation with my father, he told me he thought she had emptied her mind on purpose.

For years, my dreams were filled with kisses and laughter from Evelyn; we rode toy trains and hugged rag dolls and otherwise remained little girls together. During my waking hours, I saw portents in any unusual moment—a sudden sun shower, daisies bursting into bloom in a place they'd never been—messages from the afterworld that I hungered to interpret and that tormented me with their joy. Sisterly love. Sibling responsibility. Evelyn had left me long ago, yet still I felt the deepest connection.

I went back to the shop the next evening, a Sunday, unlocked the front door and tidied my office. I opened my desk drawer and lifted out the folder in which I kept everything Arthur had written for me and reread the letter of apology he wrote after he stole *The Prophet*. Then I read his review of the book about a little girl named Anna, displaced by the Holocaust, who left her rabbit behind. Somehow, even so young, Arthur had known that the rabbit was a metaphor for the loss of her home, her innocence and her childhood memories. That single essay had awakened an untended part of my own childhood. No wonder I'd grown to love him.

I called Arfaana in the morning and told her I would leave shortly for Dover. I planned to take the ferry from the coast of England to Calais in France, where I would drive through Normandy to Honfleur.

"Have you booked a hotel?"

"No. It's the off-season, so I think it's safe to take my chances."

I walked. I drove. I went to the salt barns, the forge. Mostly I stood in the wind that scraped the white chalk cliffs of Étretat, overlooking the Atlantic Ocean, my mind a tumble of Evelyn, Arthur, Norma Barnes and my own mother. I puzzled over the Gorham crucifix, the codes, Snakes and Ladders, and the suicide that had caused Arthur to unravel in front of my eyes. I saw him thrust the denim jacket into the rubbish bin, just after he'd thanked me so earnestly for my care of him that it had brought tears to my eyes. For the first time in decades, I prayed to all the angels and saints I could remember to ask for clarity.

I thought back to when I had turned my back on God, and an image of Evelyn's white coffin on the day we buried her rose in my mind. It was so smothered in daisies and calla lilies, freesia and hydrangeas, so alive with blooms, it was hard to imagine her dead inside. But none of our prayers had been able to save her or resurrect her. My mother gave up after Evelyn died, leaving me to think not only that was I to blame, but that I wasn't enough to live for. She found no answers, no solace, in her religion, and neither did I. Alone in my single bed each night, I cried into my pillow, careful not to let anyone hear. My sister and I had many happy moments with my mother, but I couldn't remember any of them.

When Father Ziperto's brother had gazed upon my face, his own a scrawl of grief and pain, my childish responsibilities had risen from their hiding place like a mole crawling out of a burrow. I could see that his burdens—whatever they were—had become too heavy for him to bear. I'd never had the chance to tell my mother that while I had badly needed Mrs. Gleason's approval, I needed a sister even more, and that I didn't want, ever again, the responsibility of holding the life of a child by the hand.

Having paid his respects to me, Arthur had tossed the remnants of his boyhood in the rubbish, saying goodbye to Ernie, and to me too. As I left the cliffs and drove back to Somerset, I felt rested, clear-minded and firm in the decision I'd reached. I would let Arthur live his life, no matter what he had done. More than anything, he deserved a second chance, one that Evelyn was never given.

As soon as I got home, I would write a letter to Mr. Robinson asking him to end the investigation.

Chapter 32

ARTHUR

On July 1, 1996, I graduated with distinction from Durham University with a master's of education and all but my thesis defence complete for a PhD in English literature. Some of the faculty believed that I was a bit of a throwback to an earlier academic era, given that I had dedicated so much effort to exploring the life and work of Lord Byron, one of the leading Romantic poets. He'd had hundreds of lovers, whereas I was still bedazzled by Lisetta alone, and the infamy of his sexual exploits had occasionally outweighed the beauty and calibre of his poetry. Thank heavens my thesis adviser was almost as fascinated as I with the contradiction between Byron's personal mess and the refinement of his work.

Much as a life of books suited me, I was an outlier in academia in another way too, in that I was one of the few Durham students to write reviews and essays for non-academic media while still at university. To me it was as natural as breathing, in that I'd been reviewing literature since I was thirteen. I raised eyebrows, especially, with a provocative essay on the pop cultural significance of JonBenét Ramsey, the little American girl who was murdered in her home, a crime still unsolved. She was six when she died, already a veteran of beauty pageants where she paraded in white go-go boots in front of a jury who scrutinized every aspect of her hair-sprayed, mascara-lashed, besequinned baby body; the line between abu-sive exploitation and showbiz entertainment is as fine as a kitten's eyelash. I perversely aligned myself with JonBenét's talent and precocity, her silver baton flashing through the air as she was gaped at by hundreds of older admirers, in honour of (but never mentioning) my own early success as a writer while I was being buggered by a priest. I found it unbearably signi-ficant that her murderer had covered her small body with her favourite satin-edged pink blanket, as though to keep her warm on death's doorstep. To me, young and blameless JonBenét was so much more than a blue-eyed pageant girl from a wealthy family. Her sexuality in a multi-million-dollar industry was not only encouraged, it was a means to an end.

I did my best to view graduation as the culmination of a contorted journey, one that, like JonBenét Ramsey, I had not chosen.

The post-convocation reception was held on a ship moored near the Royal Festival Hall. Miss Phillips and my mother had taken the train together from Somerset to attend, and both had been delighted at last to meet Lisetta, as Lisetta was delighted to meet them. For all the years we'd been together, I'd managed to dance away from her strong desire to accompany me to Glastonbury, fortuitously, I had to admit, because her mother's illness had drawn her home to Sweden every summer.

The following morning, I was to meet Miss Phillips and my mother for an early breakfast at their hotel, but my mother was late coming down. As we sat waiting for her to take her place, chatting over tea, Miss Phillips produced a book from her handbag—I immediately recognized the copy of *The Prophet* I'd mutilated—and leaned over to tuck it into my ruck-sack, which I'd hung on the back of the empty chair beside her.

"I can't believe you still have this old thing," she said, rezipping the bag. "I should have bought you a proper briefcase for your graduation."

"No need," I said. "I have a sentimental attachment to it." I had a vivid flash of the day Ernie and I had stolen the expensive nylon carry-all. It had been protected by a white plastic anti-theft tag, which Ernie had removed using scissors, a screwdriver, a high-powered magnet, a knife, and a pair of pliers. He'd cut his hand in the process, but was triumphant nonetheless.

"I was wondering," Miss Phillips said. "Did your mother ever know the reason you started writing reviews for the bookshop was to repay me for my silence about . . ." She pointed to the rucksack that now contained *The Prophet*.

"No, I never told her."

We grinned at each other then, both delighted, it seemed, as to what our bargain had produced.

I pulled the book out to examine it and immediately noticed that while Miss Phillips had meticulously glued the missing page back into its proper place, she had dog-eared the upper corner—as if I'd ever forget. She'd also inscribed the title page with a quote from Dostoevsky's *Crime and Punishment*, written in her bookish longhand. *"The man who has a conscience suffers whilst acknowledging his sin. That is his punishment." For Arthur W. Barnes on his graduation, with fondness, Marina V. Phillips.*

"*V*?" I asked.

"Veraminta." She rolled her eyes. "My great aunt. And what about that *W*?"

"Wyclef. A champion racehorse."

She nodded in sympathy.

And then my mother burst into the dining room, full of apologies. "Arthur, I don't know how I slept in. I guess yesterday was just too exciting. I can't ever remember sleeping so well."

A couple of hours later, I put them both on the train, standing on the platform and waving until they were out of sight. That night, in my rented rooms, I tucked Miss Phillips's little volume on a bookshelf beside another literary lodestar, the copy she'd given me of Uris's *Exodus*. Miss Phillips likely would never have guessed how much I cherished the photocopy of *The Prophet* she'd made for me after I'd transgressed in 1986.

I'd carted *those* raggedy pages from place to place, stowing them in a blue hanging file labelled personal in whatever desk I was using—an unexpected lifeline, a gesture of benevolence so unfamiliar at the time that it had taken me years to feel I'd earned it.

Lisetta had graduated alongside me with an MA in education, after staying the course to gain her undergraduate degree in geology. Even before our convocation, she had begun the long process of writing to Canadian schools seeking young, keen and inexpensive first-year teachers. Lisetta's mother had died earlier in the spring, and my own mum was making a life for herself as a cookbook author. Insensitive as it might seem, we both wanted to put an ocean between us and our childhoods.

In mid-July, we got the news that Lisetta had been hired by the Trafalgar School for Girls in Montreal, and I was granted an interim teaching position at Trinity College, a co-ed secondary school in Port Hope, Ontario, the two schools separated by 270 miles and a four-hour train ride. We would be fine, we thought, as long as we could be together on weekends. I phoned my mother, who professed herself delighted that we'd found jobs, even as her voice quivered. "I'll miss you, Arthur."

"I won't be gone forever," I said. "I'll write. I'll come home on holidays. You'll visit."

"This time I know you mean it," she said, and hung up before she broke down.

As I packed before our flight, I was only a little haunted.

A few years into our relationship, I began to tell Lisetta more details of my story—not all, never all—and she had whispered in my ear, "I won't let this define you. It doesn't have to." Slowly I had learned to live outside the bonds I thought I'd never shed. I still wondered, every now and then, about Ernie—where he was and what had become of him. As I zipped my suitcase, the thought went through my head that maybe he was dead like his mother. I sat down abruptly on the bed, my fingers on the stolen rucksack.

No. No way was he dead. He'd looked after himself for as long as I'd known him and he was nothing if not resourceful. Still, every time I imagined the road he was travelling, he seemed woefully alone.

PART THREE

Leeds, 2008

Chapter 33

ERNIE

Locked and secure, the underground editing suite of Reel Fauna was accessed by a lift that descended three floors into the earth. Nathan was sleeping something off in the big armchair in the back corner, undisturbed by the fact that Casper and I were arguing.

"My gut says no," I said. "You shouldn't meet this kid."

"I'm going to be only an hour's drive away. Two birds. One stone. An in-person rendezvous is irresistible. When will I get another chance?"

He was talking about Norman, the boy he'd been carefully cultivating in a chat room for the past year and a bit. He assured me that he had never given the kid even a hint of where he lived; all he'd known about Norman's circumstances was that he was about to turn twelve and his home was somewhere in the United States. Then, in one of their recent chats, when Casper mentioned that he would be attending an encryption conference in Washington, Norman let it slip that he lived in Virginia, a bus ride away from the conference hotel, the Key Bridge Marriott in Arlington, an easy walk over a small causeway to Georgetown, DC, and the assembly rooms.

Norman was into PlayStation and Xbox 360, *Dead Space* and *Grand Theft Auto*. He was talkative. Forthcoming, even. What Norman didn't know was that the photos he'd sent to his friend Casper were now available on 147 websites. Norman had bought Casper's line: once an amateur wrestler, Casper was simply interested in assessing Norman's physique to see if he had athletic potential. One thing had led to another, and another, as it always did with Casper.

"I just don't think you know enough about him. Why take the risk of meeting him in person?" I usually didn't care enough to argue for caution, but something in my bones was telling me that this was a bad idea.

"Ernie, I live for these moments." Casper jangled the loose change in his pocket in time to the jumping of his knee.

I shrugged and gave up. "What you do is up to you."

He changed the subject. "Did you find out why we crashed yesterday? Every goddamn website went down."

"I have System Restore enabled, and we're almost all the way back up. Everything's fine. We didn't lose any uploads."

"Personal information?"

"It survived. I need to reinstall some programs."

"Nobody can write programs like you, but maintaining security is our biggest concern right now. You're the one who told me that malware can crack weak passwords, then bore into systems. I'm still jittery from the ILoveYou virus back in 2000. Fifty million infections worldwide. Jesus. That worm replaced every single one of our JPEGs and we never did recover those files. And MyDoom in 2004. The fastest-spreading virus so far." He was speaking so quickly, I wondered if he was on something. Usually all I had to worry about with him was too much recreational Viagra. He ate those little blue pills for breakfast.

"I know you've catalogued and stored every photo, VHS and DVD I've collected since 1985, and we can re-digitize if necessary. It's our client information I worry about. We need to ramp up security."

He didn't need to tell me about our weaknesses. I spent sixteen hours a day every day maintaining our network and creating new customized online offerings. To my mind, it was Casper who was now our biggest security risk. I tried one more time. "Skip Virginia. Stay in DC. I'm just not sure whether there was any kind of breach when our websites went down."

"I'll attend the conference before I do the meet-up."

"C'mon, Casper. Norman can wait."

"Fine. Just the conference." He cracked his knuckles to show his distaste for being pushed around. If things went sideways for Casper, we'd all be on the ground.

Our success had changed Casper. In the early years, he'd calculated the risk and benefit of every step before we took it. But once we'd started to make real money, it was like he'd been blinded by the vast sums coming our way from the likes of Martin Quimby and a dozen other wealthy European politicians and businessmen. The thrill of sharing illicit material globally to an audience of people lusting after our offerings erased the rest of his caution. Controlling, feeding, and growing an online community gave him a feeling of godlike supremacy.

I still remember the champagne toast when we finally had our own web presence. At the time, we could only afford two bottles.

Casper had lifted his glass and said, "To Martin Quimby, our financier."

It was Quimby who had paid for the hardware. He'd also paid for us to learn the necessary data encryption algorithms. Publicly, he underwrote Reel Fauna's animal documentaries, so that the two sides of our business model twisted together like a red-and-white candy cane. He was listed as the executive producer of seven of our award-winning documentaries, each of which brought in legitimate money. The current project was a film about the migration of Arctic terns—44,100 miles from Greenland to the Weddell Sea. Before that, we'd produced two films about animal

matriarchs: mother love and the sacrifices of African cats and the matri-
archal wisdom that guided elephant herds.

I obsessively watched those films.

I can't lie and say I wasn't pissed when Casper told me, back in 1990,
that I was never going to be a filmmaker. He'd seduced me with visions
of the animal documentaries we'd make. Then, after I'd thrown my lot in
with him, with a twist of the knife, he'd said, "Just because you love cats
doesn't mean you can write a compelling script or direct a documentary
about lions. Your gifts, lad, are mathematical. You're going to be our computer genius."

And that's what I became. A master coder. It wasn't difficult, really,
but it took dedication. Though Casper helped where he could, soon
enough I'd surpassed him. During long, solitary days and nights, I figured out many things for myself. I took courses in Leeds and London
and read everything I could get my hands on, eventually making my
way through Casper's whole collection of *Byte* magazines. The ideas for
linked information systems came from a UK computer scientist named
Tim Berners-Lee, the man who wrote the source code for automated
sharing. Berners-Lee's radical ideas included the ability to modify pages
from directly inside a browser—the first Web editing capability. In the
beginning, around 1992, only a few of us had access, but when Berners-
Lee launched a plea for other developers to join in, Casper signed on and
I went to my first conference. It was a wild meeting of like-minded people
sharing tech information.

The feeling of being on the crest of a wave is so exhilarating it wipes
away all thought of consequences. Ask Steve Jobs. Ask Bill Gates. At a
time when most people were still using a typewriter, Gates created computer software programs for the world's first microcomputers.

Casper soon recruited a German accountant named Zeus, a man
who spoke several languages and had been to prison in a country I'd
never heard of: Palau, which was somewhere near the Philippines. He'd

managed to leap over the wall of the Koror Jail, make his way home briefly to Münster, and then to England. A man on the run, willing to do anything in exchange for employment. We all felt a kinship. Zeus was the one who married the two sides of the business to make it all look legit—creating our candy cane.

We started our push online via a service called BIX—Byte Information eXchange. We used it to build up our own dedicated private network that users could link to through dial-up connections. It wasn't overly secure.

When *Byte* magazine began to host internet discussion boards on which it posted selected editorial content, Casper found another way to serve the clientele. People could hold conversations by way of these forums, posting messages that needed to be approved by a moderator before they went up.

Casper made me the moderator of a set of discussion boards flying under one name: fittingly, the Pint Room. To accommodate the fact that "people are into all kinds of crazy shit," as Casper attested, the Pint Room had a tree-like structure with a main discussion forum and subforums on different topics. Boys. Girls. Babies. Sadism. Within the forum, each new post could be replied to by as many people who were interested in that topic, forming a thread. Front Teeth is our forum about six-year-old boys. Four Wheels is the thread code for a child who rides a bicycle with training wheels.

The more we posted, the more subscribers came rushing forward, which led to the creation of a forum we called, "Must be viewed at least once." We posted enticements in special chat rooms, and the paid subscriptions ticked upward.

Along with steady requests for more of his favourite blond-haired, blue-eyed boys, Quimby provided a list of sadistic suggestions, which Casper once had rhymed off for me: "A dartboard, a hammer, a saw, a wheelchair, crutches, high-pressure hoses." I myself never saw the man in the flesh, but from photos I knew that Quimby was jowly, with a thick

black unibrow above silver-rimmed glasses that obscured his eyes—
the farthest thing from the innocent, unblemished faces of the victims.
Nathan, in his cups, said Quimby was frozen inside and out, and watching
real-life horrors was the only thing that could warm up his dead feelings.
My dead feelings.

I kept track of every detail in my own leather-bound book.

Next, we secured £250,000 to buy a second film production studio in
Walton-on-Thames, Surrey, once again with Martin Quimby as the eager
financier—the "model citizen" for whom Margaret Thatcher lobbied for a
knighthood, because he was such a loyal friend, excellent business partner,
and respected member of his church and community.

Even as we grew through the 1990s, Casper had been the brakes of
the operation. But, ever so slowly and then with a rush, like a boat swept
over a waterfall, he'd become intoxicated by the lure of the forbidden,
by his clients' anticipation for the new never-been-seen footage he would
upload. By their gratitude, adoration and endless appetite that only he
could fulfill. The expressions of polite appreciation and affirmation in
the daily comments he received in every chat room was the elixir that
fuelled his compulsion.

"These are normal people, Ernie," he'd tell me. "Bankers. Teachers.
Landscapers. Dentists. They are educated. Respectful." I was all too
familiar with what he meant, given that I was the moderator. The customers could have been sharing information about needlepoint.

He wasn't wrong, but he wasn't seeing straight either. So now, if
anyone was hitting the brakes, it was me.

Casper broke into my thoughts.

"Ernie, since I'll be in Washington, you'll need to take the trip I was
going to make to Albania. It's a footage pick-up, and should be pretty
straightforward. You'll be meeting Donny Bradgate, a Scot from Orkney,
who runs a string of orphanages for children in Tirana. He arranged for

one of the boys to be gagged and tied to train tracks near Stacioni Kashar station and raped as a train is approaching. He says he paid a local kid to hold the camera and he captured the screams of the boy and the train simultaneously. The meeting to buy the film is at the Diell CaféBar." Casper sniffed a few times, wiped his nose with the back of his hand. "Bradgate will be furious it's not me. I haven't told him you're coming instead, in case he gets spooked and doesn't deliver. You'll have to do your thing."

"Why doesn't he just upload to our site?"

"Slow infrastructure in Albania. They've only just introduced broadband internet. Too unreliable."

In a matter of minutes Zeus had booked the three flights: Washington for Casper, Leeds to Gatwick, and then on to Tirana for me.

The last content run I'd done was to Manila. I found the boys on the street, or outside the cheapest hotels, hungry, dishevelled, shoeless kids who would do anything for food, and a bit of money to give to their mothers, who pushed them forward like livestock. Those women—I saw my own mother's expression everywhere I went, the swollen eyes, the fingers grasping for the coins and bills that spilled to the ground. It made me sick for a system so broken that starving women would offer up their own children to stay alive. Yet I hated them too, and that hate made me vicious. I wanted to spit at them, kick their skinny legs under their polyester miniskirts, hurl sharp stones that would scar. Those mothers would sign up their children for sex with a white man in front of a camera in a cheap hotel with filthy linen and stained floors. Urine, blood, mucus and semen. So they could stand it, or at least not resist, we loaded the boys up with alcohol and sedatives.

Then I carried the "product" back to the UK, disguised in Disney-type packaging, and I uploaded the videos to our new features page, to be viewed by thousands of paying international customers.

—

Before I left my flat in Leeds to catch the hopper flight to Gatwick, I did my usual checklist. Inside my carry-on I had a couple of spare shirts and clean underwear, my laptop and USB cord, a camera with audio-visual output, an ion adapter, cables, twenty decoy children's DVDs, one blank non-rewritable DVD, a toiletry bag, a book of poems. Three burner phones. My passport was high quality. Expensive as counterfeits go, but worth every pound.

The flight to Tirana left on schedule and was uneventful. Each time I passed easily through flight gates and international borders was like an endorsement of the life I was leading, further eroding what remained of my moral compass. Long ago, I'd given a church warden the chance to stand up for what is right, and he'd failed. His reaction, and that of Arthur, who I'd always thought had more virtue than me, had undone me then. I was the one who dug myself in even deeper. The one thing I'll give Arthur is that he'd never felt sorry for himself. Weak-minded people are the ones who feel sorry for themselves after they have been tricked, hoodwinked, betrayed and let down. Arthur wasn't weak-minded—he was a survivor who had walled off what was done to him. And what he'd done to me.

I checked into my hotel in the early evening and spent the next twenty-four hours acting like a tourist as I got my bearings. I scouted Bradgate's orphanage, which looked clean and orderly—good camouflage. Took a green bus to the city centre.

Soviet-era architecture. Pink pastel buildings surrounding Skanderbeg Square and the National History Museum, covering Communist rule and the anti-Communist uprisings of the 1990s. The Albanians I encountered were courteous, helpful and humble.

The café was located in Blloku, a fifteen-minute walk southwest of the city centre. It was a leafy neighbourhood that, during the Communist years, had been closed off to all but the party elite. When I got there, I took a corner seat on the terrace and watched Bradgate at the bar sipping a bosa. He was fleshy and pink, his thick fingers dusted with white hair, his beard silvery and neatly clipped. No sign of any edginess.

I heard him address the waiter. "*Më sill një tjetë.*"

Another malted beverage slid across the counter. When he smiled, his eyes crinkled and I could imagine the Christian children at his orphanage calling him Santa Claus. Make-believe. Children can be made to believe.

He protested when I took the stool beside him.

"Who the Christ are you? You've been eyeballing me all night."

"I'm the courier. Nothing more."

"And I'm the Queen of England."

I ordered a coffee. I flipped open a burner phone and called him. Bradgate's hand went to the vibration in his pocket and he withdrew a BlackBerry. I showed him a text from Casper that read "Ask for the code."

Bradgate looked me in the eye.

"Raven," I said.

We did the exchange in the men's toilet—the camcorder tapes for a stack of American cash—and then Bradgate left the bar. As was my custom, I lingered long after he was gone, drinking cup after cup of espresso and finally ordering some food, which I barely touched. When the busboy started to stack the chairs on the tables, I left a sizable tip and slipped out, vigilant.

It was 2 a.m. A clear night. Warm, humid. The trees were rustling. Green-necked wood pigeons were gathered on the pavement, and I regretted not sticking some bread in my pocket. "Sorry, fellas. The cupboard is bare."

A little farther along the street, a young girl, maybe ten or eleven, was sitting on the sidewalk, hugging her knees, her long black hair grazing the pavement. I crossed the street to get away from her. Calmly, she rose and began to follow me. I took a side street. She closed the distance until she was on my heels.

I jogged. She was faster. I stopped. She circled my waist with her arms, pressing her face into my back, breathing "Please, please, please."

I turned and she pulled me down to sit with her on the narrow road. Such an old face for someone so young. She held my hand. I smiled at her. She smiled right through me like she knew who I was, or what I was, or where I'd been.

From the pocket of her dress, she pulled out a photo of a boy and held it up so that the streetlight illuminated the image. A beautiful boy with almond-shaped eyes that were a golden topaz. "*Vellai im*. Brother," she said softly.

With gestures and passable English, she conveyed that she'd found him near the tracks and taken him straight to the police, inciting a raid of the orphanage.

Had Bradgate just left the boy where he lay?

"Bradgate," she said. If I understood her right, she was telling me that after Bradgate had left the bar, he had been arrested. Three other staff members at the orphanage were also under arrest. TV reporters were on the street in front of the orphanage, filming.

She fell silent and put her hand out. I gave her eight thousand lek, about fifty pounds, and then I let her lead me back to Mother Teresa Square. She was dry-eyed—I couldn't be sure if the boy who was raped on the tracks was her brother or if I had been conned. Tingling, burning hives began to cluster on my neck.

We stopped in front of an older woman, who was seated on a grand expanse of floodlit yellow steps in front of the museum. Same topaz cat eyes. Long black hair. The mother had her hand out. I took out my wallet. "No," she said. "No money." She had me follow her to a row of brick houses on Dervish Hekali in the old quarter. She pulled me inside a far more impoverished orphanage where young children, even babies, were asleep on mats on all the floors. I gave the mother and her daughter all the money I had in my wallet. American dollars. British pounds. The mother spat in my face, sweeping her arm around the place. "Bradgate," she roared. "*Paratë e gjakut. Hesht paratë.*" Blood money. Shut-up money.

Several children woke to the anger in her voice.

Then she stepped outside and threw the money to the winds. The orphans ran to rescue the bills.

The daughter wiped her mother's saliva from my cheek and disappeared into the shadows.

On my circuitous way back to my hotel, I smashed the burner phone and disposed of it, piece by piece. Up in my room, I turned on the television to catch an early newscast on Radio Televizioni Shqiptar. They were already broadcasting footage of Bradgate's orphanage and of him handcuffed in the back of a police car. Then the coverage shifted to the brick house on Dervish Hekali, with close-ups of the girl and a dozen Albanian children.

The girl had seen me at the bar with Bradgate, but she didn't know my name or where I was staying, and neither did he.

I locked the videotape in the small safe under the minibar, stripped and stepped into the shower. When I got out, I tried to sleep. After a few hours, I gave up and turned on the lights, then watched the tape from the train tracks. It wasn't as unnerving as I'd expected. I'd steeled myself against the boy's topaz eyes, but he was blindfolded. The whistle of the train was musical rather than deafening, and the boy didn't scream, too drugged to react.

I transferred the video from the camcorder onto my laptop and burned a single DVD, then destroyed the tape. I inserted a thumb drive into the laptop, followed the prompts and waited while it wiped the hard drive. When all was securely deleted, I reinstalled a pristine version of the operating system.

The taxi back to the airport that evening was hot and stuffy. In a toilet stall, I removed my sweat-soaked shirt, donned a clean one, combed my hair, added a pair of horn-rimmed glasses and went to check in.

At security, I removed my shoes, placed them and my cabin luggage on the conveyor belt, and asked if my DVDs would be vulnerable to the X-ray scanner—nineteen copies of Animated Christian Stories and one DVD, inside an identical sleeve, destined for the Pint Room.

"No sir, they will be fine. Do you have exposed film?" The guard's deft hands had already unzipped my bag. "How was your vacation? Did you visit Sarandë? The most beautiful mosaics can be found in the remains of the fifth-century synagogue there. You saw them?" He looked up with steely eyes.

"Yes I did. The highlight of my stay, in fact."

"And your name is?"

"Warren Faulkner." He studied my passport. "Your line of work?"

"I'm a Christian Bible studies teacher." I tapped the plastic case with the DVDs. "Scripture lessons for children."

He withdrew one DVD. On the cardboard sleeve was an illustration of Noah's Ark under a multi-hued rainbow. Without looking up he said, "Eventually the rain stopped, and all the animals were saved. Thank you, Mr. Faulkner." He handed me the DVD. "Have a safe flight."

I gathered my things, slipped into my shoes and walked to the gate.

No police officers waited for me there. To deal with the flood of adrenalin, I settled in the first-class lounge on the second floor and read poetry: William Blake's "Cradle Song" from his *Songs of Innocence*.

Out the windows I could see that the British Airways plane had arrived, and passengers were disembarking. Casper texted on burner phone number two. "All okay? 100 new memberships. Anticipation is building." I tossed the phone in the trash.

Onboard, from my first-class window seat, I looked out into the darkness. Topaz eyes. I fogged the pane with my breath.

A flurry of text messages were waiting for me when I landed. All from Casper.

"We'll install the new operating system when u get here."

"Then the open-source Tor browser."

"Where are u?"

I didn't answer.

Several unmarked vans had taken to parking near our studios in Leeds, so, as pre-arranged, I was supposed to drive straight from the Gatwick airport to a suite Casper had rented under an assumed name at the Pennyhill Park Hotel in Surrey. Nathan was already there, with several of our computers.

A five-minute bus ride took me from the terminal to the long-stay north car park and my silver Ford Fiesta, a nondescript supermini. When I was in the driver's seat, I texted back.

"Bradgate was *arrestato*."

"And you?"

"All good."

"What happened?"

"Raided. After we did the trade in a café bar at rush hour before it all caved. No witnesses," I lied.

Just over one hour of driving would get me to Pennyhill. One more hour to flush the topaz eyes from my system.

I turned on navigation and followed its prompts to the hotel.

The ivy-walled Pennyhill was on London Road, Bagshot, 120 acres of posh Surrey parkland. Pristine, manicured, perfumed. The antithesis of a sex act in a fleabag hotel room with peeling wallpaper and no hot water.

I took the stairs two at a time to the suite. Three knocks in quick succession, and then five more. Nathan opened the door, drew me in and pounded my back, a brother's already drunken welcome. Spread across every flat surface was our computer equipment. Nathan was almost unrecognizable; a tweed flat cap was pulled low over his eyes and a shabby beard streaked with grey covered the lower half of his face, yet failed to disguise the angry, crusted fissures at the corners of his mouth.

His light-blue double-breasted suit and white trainers couldn't hide how thin he'd become. Cocaine was an appetite suppressant. So was heroin.

"I'm gutted," I said, and flopped into a velvet chair.

"Our kid had a close call in Tirana," Nathan said to Casper, who was sitting in the room's largest, plushiest armchair.

"Bradgate will be charged, for sure," I said. I wanted to close my eyes and sleep.

"Have you seen the footage?" Casper asked.

"It's not quite as advertised, but it's solid."

"Good. Fresh meat for our clients. While you were gone, I secured another million and a quarter from Quimby for film production in Walton-on-Thames. We're shutting down Leeds. We need better post-production editing suites."

"What does he want in exchange?"

Casper gave me a fixed look.

"Wouldn't Downing Street like to know his other hobby?" I prodded.

"Who says they don't?" Nathan said, as he was plugging in the home server. "He's a philanthropist who has supported public housing to the tune of ten million pounds. Gives him the keys to the kingdom. Our kingdom. Erases his sense of wrongdoing. Must be okay if millions of like-minded men all the world over are begging for what we're selling."

Nathan went to the bar fridge and removed half a dozen mini-bottles of vodka, gin, scotch and rum. He twisted off the caps and drained four of them, then gave each of us one tiny bottle. "I can order more from room service."

"Unwise," I said.

Casper said, "Ernie, once the Tor network is up and running, we'll have a web server that can host our entire operation. We will finally be encrypted, anonymous, untraceable. In the clear."

"You think I don't know that?" I'd spent years learning the ins and outs of encryption programming and explaining it to them both.

"Tor's slower than Firefox and Explorer, but it will protect our identity online—namely our IP addresses—by encrypting our traffic in at least three layers and bouncing it through a chain of three volunteer computers randomly chosen among thousands around the world. It's genius. Perfect anonymity."

"Why did Tor finally go public?" Nathan asked.

"No clue, though I guess if navy intelligence officers are the only people using it to share classified information, they wouldn't be too hard to find." I closed my eyes and took a sip from my tiny bottle of Russian vodka.

Casper said, "We'll be able to give Quimby what he's wanted for a very long time."

"Nothing is ever enough for Sir Martin," I said.

"Is Tor really foolproof?" Nathan asked, poking his fingers in the moth holes of his blue blazer.

"Is any system that illegally procures victims foolproof? It's not designed to completely erase tracking on the web, just to make it bloody hard to trace actions back to their origin."

I watched Casper. The risk of being caught was its own intoxication. He'd become an expert at meeting children online, cultivating a relationship, then going in for the kill.

"How was Washington?" I asked.

"Worthwhile."

"Norman?"

"I told you—I decided not to meet him this time. I'm going back."

"When?"

"I haven't decided. Maybe Friday."

I lay down on the duvet, finished the vodka and hoped it would lull me to sleep.

"The timing of the Tor browser going public couldn't be better." Casper was up now, and moving from device to device, checking the percentages of the download.

As useful as Tor would be for our clients, the next breakthrough
was months away. From a private online chat room, we'd learned that
unknown cryptography experts using the alias "Satoshi Nakamoto" would
be implementing an unregulated form of online payment called Bitcoin.
Payments to the Pint Room would soon be anonymous.

With his back to me, he said, "You asked what's in it for Quimby.
He's requested a one-of-a-kind film in exchange for underwriting the next
documentary and the new studio. A snuff film. Something that has never
been attempted before. Since you've always wanted to make movies, you
get to make this one. You know the kid already. Hughie Digby. He's that
eight-year-old in Tower Flats foster care who you took to the London Zoo
and the aquarium. Quimby will pay more if we deprive the boy of food for
a week. On the day of the filming, he will have the look Quimby is after."

"What look is that? Already dead?"

"Groom him carefully. Quimby doesn't want a victim, he wants a
hungry participant desperate to please."

I made for the lavatory and locked myself in.

"You gotta wonder how a man like Martin Quimby feels entitled to
order that a boy be killed for his pleasure. Why aren't the rapes he watches
on his mobile phone, over and over, enough? Something terrible must
have happened to that man as a kid," said Nathan from the other side of
the door.

I raked my scalp with my fingernails.

Casper weighed in with the money at stake, as usual. "To date, seven
hundred people have already paid three thousand pounds each to live-
stream Hughie's demise—clients in Italy, Germany, the US and the UK,
and elsewhere, all habitués of the most exclusive level of the Pint Room."

I stripped and got into the shower and let the hot water pour over my
itchy hives. The heat made them spread. I turned up the temperature.
Quimby and his kind . . . so many of them out there. Buying. Selling.

Uploading. Downloading. Chatting. Sharing. Streaming. And now killing. The dirt-encrusted surface of rock bottom was looming closer.

Casper had established user rules, and we were respected for that. Each elite viewer was required to upload and share their own photos and films depicting ever-escalating abuse before they could access deeper levels of our site, which meant that our own loyal customer base kept the supply chain flowing.

Wouldn't the Zipper be proud?

Rock bottom.

Chapter 34

MARINA

In the many years since my fateful trip to Normandy, I'd been overtaken by a lingering malaise that came and went in waves of self-attacking thoughts.

Recently I had given Arfaana much to fret about; my mutterings about finding a buyer for the Copperfield and Twist and moving to a European coastal town like Sintra or Cinque Terre had become more frequent. I had also taken to brooding at home, several days a week, comforted by books, gardening and feeding the grateful birds and squirrels, so that she had to do most of the work of managing the shop, and our friendship.

Constance Bradley had been right. I had taken to gardening. The squirrels had names. The goldfinches were eating white millet out of my hand. I'd long since stopped looking for Mr. Ziperto to reappear on the playground bench with his back issue of the *Economist*. The greatest of my recriminations came from knowing that he had challenged me to right a wrong, and I had ducked. His battle, not mine. My battle, not his. Our battle. Everyone's battle.

On a Sunday in June, my home phone rang. I didn't pick up. Midway through the afternoon, Arfaana banged on my door, looking as cross as I'd ever seen her. She was carrying sweets—I could smell the gulab jamun, milk and sugar and cashews. After she put them down on my kitchen table, she reached to pull several leaves and twigs from my hair.

"You are becoming the bird lady of Tiller's Row. And you're avoiding me. Is that a nest in your hair?"

"I was in the garden."

"You've become the garden. And you can't survive on cups of tea alone. I've seen more fat on a bobby pin, Marina. What have you eaten today?"

When I demurred, she blew up. "I had to fight with my father to let me attend university. I have had to endure a thousand conversations with my mother about my status as a Pakistani spinster. She bemoans the fact that my green eyes have been wasted, that I've lived without a spouse, without children. But I actively chose this path, including running the bookshop with you, Marina. I continue to fight for my choices. But you have given up. You should be ashamed. Do you need to see a doctor? Are you fighting an incurable illness you haven't bothered to tell me about?"

I hated to see her so angry with me. It was the last thing I wanted. I said, "It's true I may have become a little complacent. It's just that I've realized that my passion for books has not been enough."

"Complacent? Is that what you call living like a hermit crab on an empty beach? You are the most admired woman in this town, yet you act like you have no reason to go on!"

Arfaana brushed past me and roamed the house, checking to see how much of my life was in disarray. I had books on the kitchen counter instead of bread and bananas. The flowers she sent for my birthday a month earlier were stagnating in brackish water in their glass vase. She fingered the wilted petals, which caused them to drop and scatter on the coffee table.

"Any objects, flowers or otherwise, that remind us of death and decay reduce the vitality of a home. Feng shui 101." She carried the stinking flowers over to the bin and dumped them in. After she had rinsed the vase, she sat on one of the kitchen stools and fished her own linen hand-kerchief out of her handbag to wipe her fingers, unsure about the cleanliness of my tea towels.

"I picked up the reins at the bookshop happily, Marina, and the business is thriving. I want your depression to be a success, for you to have the time to work through whatever is troubling you. But you show no signs of doing that. You won't even talk to me about what's eating you alive.

"And so, I'm giving you two choices. Sell the shop, and I will move on, from here and from you, or make a plan with me to reinvent ourselves together. What can I do to bring you back to the land of the living? Where have you gone?"

"I'm not sure. I've been hiding, as you know. And I've been thinking of my sister, Evelyn. In Hebrew, her name means life. Yet she's the one who died."

"It does seem ironic."

"I confess my hope is gone, Arfaana, along with most of my courage."

"I will help you find them. We are strong women. Why don't we give ourselves the rest of this decade to execute a vision on behalf of all women. The men have had the last two thousand years, and we shall have the next. The quote in the window this week is from Mary Wollstonecraft: 'Taught from infancy that beauty is a woman's sceptre, the mind shapes itself to the body, and roaming round its gilt cage, only seeks to adorn its prison.' If I remember right, you wrote a thesis on Wollstonecraft's bold and brazen life." Arfaana filled the kitchen sink with hot water and Fairy liquid and began washing up the dishes, muttering over her shoulder, "I can see that you are less than convinced."

"I'm ready to sell and move on."

"Oh, for God's sake." Arfaana spun around. "You've been saying that for a decade. So what are you waiting for? The sky to fall? World War

Seven? Marina, selling the shop would kill you, and you know it. That's just not in the cards."

I went over to the player piano, lifted the lid of the bench and retrieved the piano books for children. *One Piano Four Hands. Teaching Little Fingers.* I kept my back turned to my friend.

"Marina, why are you hugging those music books when I'm talking to you." And then more softly, "Why, for heaven's sakes, are you crying?"

"I have been the worst kind of bystander."

She came to me, turned my shaking body around and drew me into a hug. "Talk to me, Marina."

"I closed my eyes for such a long time. I thought I could walk away. Wait right here."

I put the piano books down on the bench and climbed the stairs, where I fetched a letter from my Harrods hat box. Back in the kitchen, I placed it on the counter and plugged in the kettle to buy a little more time. I selected two newly washed mugs. "Before we reinvent ourselves, there is something I must do. I will need your help."

Arfaana's face softened, and she came to sit on a stool. "Anything, Marina. I'm sorry I was so cross. But it's been awful to have been so excluded from your mind."

I stared down at the letter. "When I saw the postmark, I resisted opening it. In fact, I waited several days."

"We're all entitled to our secrets, Marina. I'm not insisting you tell me yours."

"This secret is making me sick inside."

After I'd read it the first time, I'd carefully resealed the envelope with PVA glue and tucked it in the hat box. With a dinner knife, I now slit it open again. "May I read it to you?"

Arfaana nodded. First, I pulled Arthur's silver crucifix out of my pocket and placed it in a little porcelain dish. Her eyes widened. I cleared my throat.

January 1, 1995
Giles Robinson
27, Priorygate Court
Castle Cary, BA7 7HT

Dear Miss Phillips,

I received your note asking me to desist from pursuing any information recorded on the cassette using the ASCII Codes. I respect your
decision. However, I had already discerned the bare facts and have
decided to send them to you and trust that you will either dispose of
this letter or contact me with further instructions.

I was able to successfully unscramble the code within the code.
On page two you will find a list of the names of ten boys. The addresses
associated with each name are all churches in the counties of Somerset
and Avon; the schoolboys seem to be between the ages of nine and
seventeen, although two of those boys, as you know, are deceased,
one to an unfortunate suicide, and the other because of a drug overdose.
The names were grouped under one acronym: GBH. Following
the ten names were two more acronyms—CPR, CBBS—and four
additional bits of encrypted information. Decoded, they are the
Pint Room, Reel Fauna Films, the Raven and Tiller's Row.

If any of this information is personally relevant, or if I can be
of further assistance, you know where to reach me.

Thank you, once again, for the almond cake. It was a feast.
Giles Robinson

"CPR? Cardiopulmonary resuscitation?" Arfaana asked.

"No. I believe those initials stand for 'child pornography ring.'"

Arfaana stared at me. "And GBH?"

"Grievous bodily harm. I think CBBS stands for 'computerized bulletin board system.'"

"You think? These are only guesses?"

"I suppose so. When I first read the letter, I researched the acronyms, and what I found shook me to my boots. And so instead of digging

deeper, I glued the envelope shut and put it away. I'm sorry I didn't share it with you."

"Marina, the letter is more than a decade old. You told me at the time that the detective had found nothing of consequence."

"I betrayed your trust, and for that I have no excuse."

"Is Arthur one of the ten boys?"

"No. It's much worse, I'm afraid."

I beckoned her to follow me into the garden. We walked to the far end where the wisteria was so overgrown, I could no longer pass through the opening to the playground unless I crawled on my knees. The sounds of children laughing and shrieking were as present as ever. A woodpecker began a drum roll, drilling a hole in the large willow.

"I have another confession to make."

"Whatever do you mean?"

"I don't expect you to remember. It was so long ago even I sometimes imagine it didn't happen. There was a man who came to the shop during the Christmas rush that last year Arthur worked at the bookshop. Remember, I left the till with one of Mrs. Barnes's mince pies?"

"I don't, but go on."

"Maybe three years later—that November when I suddenly decided I needed a holiday? —I saw that same man sitting on a bench in the playground here. At first, I didn't recognize him, he was so changed. He looked as though he was close to death."

"Why did you never mention this?"

"I've hidden a lot from you, Arfaana, and I have suffered because of it. For most of one week he sat in the same spot, day after day. Of course, until then, I had never been home during a workday, so he may have been sitting there much longer. From the moment I noticed him, I kept an eye on him, but I let him be—there was nothing salacious about his behaviour, and believe me, I searched for it. Finally, it came over me that he was guarding the children. It was the way he scanned the horizon, alert for God knows what. For the life of me I couldn't determine another reason for him to be there, though it was puzzling that he stayed on long after the young mothers and their children had gone home."

"You should have called the police. It all sounds predatory."

"That thought crossed my mind, but I hesitated. And then I recognized him. He was the man I'd given the mince pie to: Father Ziperto's brother. And I realized something more. Remember the cassette tape with the old lullabies that came in the Mother Goose lamp? It was his voice on Side B, intoning those numbers. Mr. Ziperto had deliberately left the cassette in the house for me to find."

"How could he have known it would be you who bought the house?"

"My estate agent told me it had been empty for a long time and had just gone on the market, with the family eager to sell. As a son of the owner, he would have seen my name on the offer. And he knew I was a mentor to Arthur. But I chose wilful ignorance rather than accept that the tape was left for me to act upon. Terrible deeds were perpetrated in this house. Of all the houses I looked at with estate agents, this was the house I purchased. Is that random? Was there some kind of divine plan?"

"Why are you so sure that something awful happened here? It's so unlike you to jump to conclusions."

"Because I was handed so many little pieces of the puzzle. There was a teen suicide in Bath in 1988. I don't think we ever talked about that. Rodger Mistlethorpe told me the boy who died left a note accusing an unnamed priest of inappropriate touching, which his newspaper didn't report. Someone had got to Rodger and he agreed to hush it up. In the best interpretation, maybe he thought he was protecting the boy's memory. He told me in confidence—clearly it troubled him—and I'm betraying his trust by telling you."

"Who got to Rodger?"

"Whoever insisted the details of the suicide note needed to be kept a secret."

"Who has that kind of power?"

"I don't know. Anyway, after my visitation from Mr. Ziperto, I took that holiday to Honfleur in Normandy to examine my conscience. I came back thinking I needed to let it go, in order that Arthur could live his life."

"Surely you don't think Arthur had anything to do with this?"

"No, I don't. But then Robinson's letter arrived, and I remembered how obsessed Arthur had been with Edgar Allan Poe's 'The Raven.'" He wasn't on the list, and I was certain he wasn't a perpetrator, but he had to be implicated somehow. He and Ernie both. It's easy to be sucked into a life of crime. As a boy, he was certainly susceptible. Remember, I met him when I caught him stealing from me. And he was arrested once and went to youth court, where he was convicted and sentenced to community service. And then when he began to work at that little desk in the bookshop, a stray wallet showed up at the till, and Arthur couldn't look me in the eye for an entire week. The wallet belonged Sir Martin Quimby, the philanthropist. He and his driver arrived in a white Rolls-Royce to retrieve the wallet. How in heaven's name did Arthur manage to steal something from such an esteemed public figure? A man who lives in Bath."

"I remember you told me that the wallet contained close to five hundred pounds, which hadn't been touched. If Arthur was truly a thief, why were the wallet's contents intact?"

"I have no idea. Another time Arthur showed up at the shop with a new Sony Walkman. I found it in the trash later that day, along with the packaging. Never used. What boy does that? Clearly, it was stolen property. Also, he wore suede Nike running shoes, which even I knew cost a fortune, though his mother had lost her job and was working as a breakfast waitress. And then, after all I'd done for him, he left town without as much as a goodbye. I didn't know what to think. I did continue writing to him, and sending books, always our mutual language. Eventually he settled in at university and began to write back, and as you know, he came to work with us that one Christmas and he was once again the brilliant boy I'd loved. And before he left, he thanked me wholeheartedly. When he walked away that time, I was able to let him go."

"You're not his mother, Marina. As much as you wish you were."

"Believe me, I know that. The other thing that troubled me was that as a teenager, Arthur's only friend was Ernie Castlefrank, from a family so tainted by scandal I could never understand why they connected. As awful as it sounds, it was as if they had something on one another. Some part of me was filled with relief when I learned that Arthur had a girlfriend and real traction at university. It was like I'd been given a gift of sorts for my silence. After Arthur graduated, I remained on high alert for something untoward to befall him, but the only thing that happened was that he and Lisetta eventually broke up."

"Children?"

"Not that I know of. I don't think they ever married. Arthur has become thoroughly respectable. He's published dozens of influential articles about boys' education. He's been a keynote speaker at Stanford University's Faculty of Education. All these years since he left for Canada, I've been able to close my eyes and be happy for the Barnes family. Except that, as you have witnessed, I have been preyed on by sadness and anxiety. Would my life have been different if I'd had a child of my own? I didn't have a strong urge to be a mother, and yet when I turned fifty, I mourned that lost opportunity like a death. Something vital had passed me by. Not motherhood, but love. So what have I accomplished with the life I've had? A gift denied my sister. Have I made a difference? That the *New York Times* listed my shop as a UK destination of note is not enough, when I may have failed to secure the safety of ten boys."

"Eight," Arfaana said very quietly. "Only eight are alive. At least they were when Mr. Robinson sent you that letter. So let's find out what has become of them—it's never too late to right a wrong. The library will have old telephone books and civic directories. You may have let it drop for all these years, but I'm sure Giles Robinson will still be willing to help us."

"Oh, Arfaana, I had the mistaken belief that if Arthur left town, all would be well. I was so wrong, and that message has just been driven home in the most distressing way."

I beckoned Arfaana to follow me across the garden, into the house, and up to the spare bedroom on the upper floor. I used a stepstool to retrieve the Harrods decoupage hat box from its shelf in the cupboard. I lifted the lid, reached in and handed Arfaana a silver USB key with a tiny cardboard hangtag that said "The Pint Room."

"Recently, I received several pieces of correspondence, in a large envelope addressed to both me and Arthur. The thumb drive was inside."

"Right, that package came to the bookshop. I was the one who dropped it at your house."

I now led her to my tiny office and sat at my desk. Arfaana pulled a second chair close. We plugged the USB key into my computer and waited for it to load. I selected the first file. "Shall I read it out loud?"

Arfaana nodded.

I clicked and the screen filled with a newspaper article.

At the close of Casper Fontaine's trial in Richmond, Virginia, the federal prosecutor told the jury and a roomful of journalists and spectators that the defendant's abusive, exploitative actions towards pre-pubescent boys were those of a truly depraved individual who had shown no remorse. The staging and filming of live sex acts perpetrated on innocent children during the 216 separate incidents covered by the charges meant that if convicted Fontaine would face several lifetime sentences, with no possibility of parole. The prosecutor stressed that society must value the safety of every child, and that the defendant's actions demonstrated, beyond any doubt, that he was an ongoing threat to that security. The jury convicted Fontaine on all counts and his sentence will be declared in the coming days.

Fontaine's enterprise, Reel Fauna Films, produced nature documentaries, one of which won an Academy Award. But its main purpose was to provide cover for computer-savvy predators to produce, share and spread deplorable depictions of child sexual abuse. With this prosecution, the justice system has shredded several layers of anonymity on the dark web and held the perpetrators of exploitative child pornography accountable.

Arfaana leaned in. "Marina, who is Casper Fontaine?"

"He's apparently gone by many names, but he was born and raised here in Glastonbury. You might remember his old business—the pawnshop on the High Street beside the Uptown petrol station. His company, Reel Fauna, used to have its main studio in Leeds."

"And the code Robinson cracked implicates Fontaine in what happened to those boys? We must track the survivors down now and persuade them to initiate criminal charges, or perhaps a lawsuit."

"What if asking them to reveal what happened to them is as wounding as the original abuse? Will anyone be left standing?"

"You tell me."

I got up and walked over to look out the window so Arfaana wouldn't be able to read my face.

"I've spoken to Ernie Castlefrank."

"How did you find him?"

"He was the one who found me."

Chapter 35

ARTHUR

The first shoe was dropped long ago. Finally, the other one hit the floor with a phone call from Miss Phillips.

"I'm glad I found you," she said. "How is your new position in Montreal?" Her tone was jaunty, and she displayed her usual goodwill towards me as we chatted a little, catching up.

Then, after clearing a sudden frog in her throat, she said, "Arthur, I've sent you a package that, for once, doesn't contain any books. Inside, among other things, you'll find the sterling crucifix you abandoned in your little desk when you left for university so long ago."

It was as if a bell had rung, and I was about to face the hand of judgment.

"I guess I was hoping you would find it one day," I said. "Or that someone would and then be able to make sense of what it signifies."

I heard a faint sigh.

In a voice so gentle it made me tear up, she asked, "Are you able to come home for a while? It might be best."

The silence between us stretched, as I thought of all the ways she had looked out for me when I was most vulnerable.

She cleared her throat. "Come home, Arthur. Someone is waiting for you."

And, of course, I knew who she meant. I had a sudden irrational desire to defend my university thesis, my teaching life, my hedonistic existence frequenting art galleries and museums, classical concerts and blues clubs. To justify my silence. My unmarried status. The woman I'd let slip away, the love of my life, telling myself I was moving on because of another academic opportunity too golden to resist.

In truth, a part of me never left Father Ziperto's vestry. With Lisetta's help, I had pardoned the Zipper and thought I'd moved on. But perhaps only certain things that are undone can be retied—a pair of shoes or a bow tie, fly buttons or zippers that hide a nakedness that needn't be examined. In all our years together, I'd only given Lisetta the watered-down version of the vestry, the chess lessons, the chocolate milk on the lips of the priest. She knew I still shrank from the most innocent of human touches, but I hadn't shared my fears of becoming an abuser of children myself, or the impetus for the criminality of my youth. And when, inevitably, and in the fullest flush of anger, she finally pushed me for more, I'd said goodbye. She'd called me a coward, but she'd left me.

"Arthur, are you still there?"

Miss Phillips had been speaking, and I'd missed her words.

"Yes. Yes. I'm sorry."

"I asked whether you've heard of the Tor browser." She spelled out the name.

"No," I said. "The only Tor I know is the grassy slope in Glastonbury that leads up to St. Michael's Tower. Because the tower was roofless, Ernie thought it was a gateway for the souls of the dead."

She laughed dryly. "Perhaps there truly are no coincidences."

"Miss Phillips?"

"I believe the Tor browser can lead to a different kind of death. Tor offers anonymity to the people who search its contents. Though it was developed by US Naval Research to protect online intelligence, it's now the gateway to a fully functional marketplace where hidden customers can buy from hidden sellers. The dark web."

A few seconds ticked by. What had any of that to do with me? The navy. Intelligence. The dark web.

"Until soon, my dear Arthur. The parcel should arrive by Friday morning."

"I'll look out for it," I said.

We exchanged a sweet goodbye, with Miss Phillips telling me just before she rang off, "Arthur, you're the finest boy I've ever known. It's been a great gift to know I was a small part of your life."

Was I about to be indicted?

I sat in my office thinking about the only person, other than my mother, who had treated me with unconditional love, and in that moment my body was flooded with the knowledge that Miss Phillips knew. *Maybe she'd always known.*

The mailroom was deserted. My ominous package, sent priority post from Glastonbury, lay on the counter. I scribbled my signature on the slip, walked up three flights of stairs to my office, locked it in my bottom drawer, and went to class. There, I nodded to everyone assembled and turned to face the interactive whiteboard. I erased the keynote I'd intended for discussion today—*Hamlet is disputably the most persuasive tragedy in English literature*—and replaced it with, *It is extremely important to know what you don't want to find.—Leon Uris.*

Then I walked out.

My feet took me to Victoria Bridge, overlooking the roiling waters of the St. Lawrence River. Conflicted, and responsible, four hours later I returned to McGill University, no wiser than I'd been before I'd fled. Outside my office door, I moved the slider under my name to read: *Arthur W. Barnes is out.* A quick scan of the hallway assured me it was empty of students. Inside, I turned off the overhead lights and the table lamp, and sat at my desk. I lifted the lid of my laptop and typed TOR, then clicked enter.

THIS CONNECTION IS NOT SAFE. DO YOU WISH TO PROCEED?

I clicked yes, and a screen opened:

Tor Project. Anonymity Online. We believe that everyone should be able to explore the internet with privacy. Tor Browser prevents someone from watching your connections or knowing which websites you visit. Tor directs internet traffic through a free, worldwide, volunteer overlay network consisting of more than six thousand relays. The browser's location and usage are concealed. The Tor Browser uses a random path of encrypted servers known as "nodes." The bouncing from node to node masks the user's identity. This allows our users to connect to the dark web without fear of their actions being tracked or their browser history being exposed.

The darknet.

I closed my computer and sat in a different kind of darkness.

Out the window I kept watch as students left the university for the day. By 10 p.m. the quadrangle was empty. I assumed those young people were now all safe at home, or somewhere with friends, but what was safety? What was security? The change in my life's trajectory had begun with a petty crime—one that Miss Phillips managed to turn into an opportunity that in the end had offered me psychological safety. I knew a good part of what Ernie had endured before he disappeared, but what about after? Had anyone ever done for him what Miss Phillips did for me?

I went to my door to check that no one was working late in any of the offices down the hall, then locked myself inside my own. I opened my bottom drawer and retrieved the package. With shaky hands, I cut through the protective layers with my green Stanley knife, lifted the flap, and withdrew several numbered envelopes. Even after so many years, I recognized Ernie's penmanship and found myself making a small animal sound—a mix of relief and love. Given how badly I'd let him down, until that moment, I'd been certain I had been excised from his memory.

I drained my water tumbler to deal with the sudden dryness of my mouth, then gingerly sliced through the thick tape of the first envelope. It contained a sheaf of boarding passes from Manila, Bangkok, Singapore, Moscow, Jaipur, Harare, Johannesburg, Tirana, paperclipped in order of date, from 1996 to 2008. Each flight had been taken by Warren Faulkner who, it seemed, was always assigned seat 2A in first class.

I set them to one side and opened the second lumpy envelope. In it were two USB flash drives, numbered 1 and 2.

I plugged the first one into my laptop's port. A menu popped up. I opened the link.

October 13, 2009

Dear Arthur, at last we are reunited. More than twenty years. It is a pleasure to greet you on the page—always your preferred meeting ground. I have murdered hours, weeks, months, thinking of you. Of me. Of him. Scraps of this letter have lined my pockets from the day our mothers went to find Nathan in Leeds. You might have guessed this, but now I will confirm—I watched it all from a back room.

Despite how our lives have turned out, I have always valued our friendship, and admired your talent for writing, your wholesome ideas.

You deserve to be where you are. A professor. Tenured. Safe.

My talent is that I understand the internet. The world regards me as a cybercriminal. Elusive. Unsafe.

My crimes expose the darkest side of humanity. I live-stream sex acts to a community of subscribers. The very ones that you and I were paid to perform. Maybe you will understand why I need to create situations of extreme risk so I can feel alive. Remember when we lay in the arms of a sycamore tree and everything good seemed to be ahead of us? I could cry, but my eyes don't make tears anymore. They don't even shut, as far as I can tell. I sleep with them wide open so my dreams won't haunt me.

What happened to us as boys? It can't be written over by what we are doing right now. It's still there, glowing like a flashlight under your mother's blanket.

For the longest time I blunted my pain with the sweetest of pleasures—revenge. But once I had my fill of retaliation, pain turned to bitter regret. I need to forgive you. I also need you to forgive yourself.

To the casual observer I may look like my heart still beats. But I died a very long time ago, as only you will understand. I have marvelled that you've been able to seal away the damage, whereas I carry it around everywhere I go, like a cancer. I am a cancer. I'm so tired. I know I just mentioned forgiveness, but, Arthur, how did you make peace with all the people who let us down? Why did you? I remember you once quoting at me something about how the only thing necessary for the triumph of evil is for a good man to do nothing.

The perpetrator and the bystander.

Given what I've done, I often think I was born evil. But was I? Do little children understand right from wrong? Do they actively choose the wrong, or are they pushed into it?

After I set the church pew on fire, the Zipper took me to his boyhood house on Tiller's Row, and there he kissed me. That kiss erased all my terrible fears of being caught, of being found out, of being unloved, and so I let him kiss me again and again. You and I were of the age that we gobbled up all that we were fed. The Zipper told me I had a golden heart that matched my golden hair. He told me I was beautiful, smart, funny and brave. He said I was so special that he couldn't live without me. I knew it was a lie, but it made me strong. The Zipper's love also made you stronger, Arthur. At first.

He knew my family had fallen apart, and he knew that you, too, were a wounded boy, whose father had died and whose mother had given him away. The predator always knows who is unprotected. Children are so gullible, and impressionable, and easily manipulated. I learned from the best of the best, but me wanting to hurt others? That came much, much later. The day I spoke to the warden was the last hour of my childhood. Maybe even my personhood. I'm sorry if it was yours too.

Did you know that the headmaster never once informed my mother that I was bunking off school? Whether I was there or not was of no concern to him, which made me feel as unwanted as the shit I spread to repulse the Zipper. I've met dozens of boys who believe they are worthless. We have 300,000 subscribers in 60 countries who clamour for pictures of those worthless, defenceless children.

I'm dead on the inside, Arthur, but as Warren Faulkner I travel first class. I drive a black Mercedes. I own a Rolex, a Piaget, and a Patek Philippe. I draw the line at Cartier, because even the sight of one of those still burns my insides like overproof vodka. Oh yes, I have been to Moscow and tasted the best. The children do not need to speak English when you have a Russian contact to facilitate the filming.

We are an international success. Reel Fauna's film about aquatic extinction was nominated for an Academy Award for feature-length documentary. It played on the big screen in the US, the UK, Austria and the Netherlands. Martin Quimby has been to the Academy Awards representing Reel Fauna. So little is as it appears. Behind that veil of respectability, we've amassed thousands of tiny films, some so debauched they defy logic. The commodity we peddle is children, a commodity with no voice. Disposable. A thing. Like me. And you.

Casper Fontaine taught me that lawlessness is in the eye of the beholder. When so many people clamour for your product, you cannot help but shift your position in favour of decadence. What is it called when an institution with a billion members urges its leaders to cover up rampant debauchery? Corruption? Hypocrisy? Marketing? Protecting a larger good? I guess some people believe that last idea.

What set Casper Fontaine apart from so many others with similar inclinations was that he was able to create a social group of like-minded

men and teach them how to lure children, how to abuse them, and how
to make sure those children wouldn't tell anyone. And bring it all online,
reinforced by a search engine loaded with millions of depraved images
that proved to his subscribers many others have the same urges. Casper
promoted child abuse as a soothing sexual orientation, claiming there
was nothing wrong with a man and a boy having sex if both consented
to it, and then he monetized that aberration. What guarantees consent
when you are nine? Tickets to a football match?

My own motives were equally selfish. I was willing to transform
myself into a master software engineer using the means at my disposal.
To pursue a life of revenge on myself as much as others.

That is all gone. My motives, and my selfishness. I should thank our
national treasure, Sir Martin Quimby. In the beginning we coagulated
around Quimby because he was wealthy and had the approval of our
prime minister.

On the outside, he is the softest piece of suede. Inside? As dead as
I am. Neither of us has the luxury of feelings. The clues to his depravity
have always been in plain sight, but his deep pockets are blinding. Our
ordinary clients were content with downloading the photos and videos
that we created, uploaded and indexed in specific categories on our
website with barely a tremble of their moral code. We knew, better than
they did, that they were on the hunt for never-before-seen footage.
When an eager crowd is cheering you on, the incentive to misbehave
is irresistible.

I became the caretaker of that insatiable clientele. The Zipper's
photographs have travelled far and wide, Arthur. Along with so many
others. An image on the web is passed from person to person, website
to website, server to server, maybe forever. There are people who live
with that anguish. There are people who couldn't live with it.

Martin Quimby is not the ordinary client. In his way he is extraordinary. My dead heart would start to pound when I heard his requests.
It seems I needed my heart to pound for something.

He was the first client to request a child in nappies. A dewy two-
year-old with sloping shoulders and dimpled thighs. He felt entitled to
abuse such perfection. Since our first encounter in Bath back in 1987,

he has continued to be relentlessly well-connected, wealthy and invincible. Year after year, he financed our film business in exchange for our servicing his ever-escalating appetites.

Now Quimby has requested a snuff film in exchange for underwriting a documentary about the threatened migration of the Chatham albatross. His name will go on that documentary as executive producer, to show that he is the epitome of a concerned environmentalist. His name won't go on the work I've dubbed *Necros Pedo*.

He has already paid me £100,000 to produce this film, for which I have agreed to groom, film, rape and kill an eight-year-old British orphan named Hughie Digby. A snuff film. For nine months, Hughie has been under my wing. He loves to read. I have taught him the harmonica. To heighten spectacle and generate anticipation, Quimby wants the film to have three acts. Rape. Torture. Death.

Don't despair, Arthur. If I squeeze my eyes tight, I can see your face. We are riding the bus, and you're about to collapse so I keep my arm around you.

People have spent a long time looking for the Raven. It's no surprise that Miss Phillips eventually tracked me down. You must know she didn't do that for my sake. Maybe you might be surprised to know that when I realized she was close, I picked up the phone and called her. I advised her to contact Scotland Yard before she reached out to you, and she did that some months ago.

The walls are closing in. Very soon the world will learn that Casper Fontaine and Nathan have been arrested. It was a police sting in Virginia. Fiona Robinson, a young policewoman born in Glastonbury but working in Washington, DC, posed online as an 11-year-old boy and made contact with Casper. Eventually the "boy" agreed to meet Casper in real life at the Hilton Garden Inn in Fredericksburg to play a game of chess where the loser had agreed to perform an extreme sex act on the winner. Nathan was to be the cameraman. But after Casper and Nathan set up in the hotel room, they were interrupted by twelve police officers. How rich that Casper, such a clever man, was lured to meet the boy in Virginia, a US state with the harshest of sentencing for such crimes.

In their hotel suite, the police found his three laptops, with thousands of photos and hundreds of films of naked children all carefully indexed, along with several compact discs.

I can hear you thinking, "What happened to Nathan?" My brother has struggled with addiction. Authority. Loss of family. He has spent his whole life in a state of danger. With this arrest, he merely embraced the familiar.

Soon it will be over. We have been infiltrated. Our servers are being tracked by police officers in Brisbane and Oslo, as well as the US, Canada and the UK. In chat rooms, I watch them impersonating our real clients. It took me hundreds of hours to build a custom responsive website from scratch—user-friendly, mobile-friendly, a work of extreme ingenuity. The Pint Room, we called it. My code names are on this USB key, though you're the one person I don't need to tell that I am the Raven. It goes without saying that my enormous talent will be underappreciated. I am the master. I am also the monster.

I have two requests, Arthur. The first is an appeal to you as a writer. You have a story to tell. Our story. You know only a small piece of it. I will provide the rest. Please call Rodger Mistlethorpe and show him how the decades-long cover-up of clerical abuse—the wilful blindness of the church, and the collusion of local powerbrokers in maintaining that cover-up—has contributed to the proliferation of child abuse on the dark web.

On the second USB key you will find the complete timeline of our dark web and internet activities from 1992 up to the present, as well as the usernames and passwords of our five largest databases.

It's important to go after the buyers, and to keep going after them. It's the simplest of microeconomics. If there is a demand, supply will follow. When one encrypted website is taken down, three more spring up. You need to stop the buyers.

I have explained everything to you in my files, as if we were still in the arms of the sycamore trees in Crewkerne. I think we can both agree that if we were to start our lives over, we would include that one perfect summer. When I lie awake that is where I go. And also to your mother's face, looking up at us from the ground, camera ready to capture our brief happiness. Her arms were wide enough for both of us, though you and I had a hard time believing that. Maybe she did too.

I have magical thoughts that Miss Phillips will help you write this story. If I know one thing for sure, she has always had your back.

Begin by telling the world that the creation of the Tor browser was a gift like no other for those intent on finding a community of offenders eager for outlawed services. The Garden of Eden. Because of one apple, innocence and bliss become sin, misery and death. The anonymity offered by Tor gives its users the most powerful notion of being invincible and above the law.

I have also mapped out my trajectory since we lost contact. If you trawl slowly through the years documented on the thumb drive, you can piece together most of my charred life.

I was given such a small heart for love. Room for Nathan, and room for you. And just enough space for your mother. Your heart was always bigger than mine, Arthur, and so when you get to my second request, please know that I am counting on you to do what is in the realm of the possible. We had impossible lives. I've seen too late that we don't have to wear the chains those lives forged for us. Don't think I'm not aware of the length of your own chains, even if you cannot see or feel them anymore. How many times did the rooster crow when Peter turned his back on Jesus for the third time? Twice, you denounced me.

I think you are ready to open the last envelope.

My fingers were shaking as I opened it. Inside I found a deed indicating that Ernie had purchased my grandfather's apple orchard in Crewkerne in the name of Norma Ella Barnes. Separate bank statements and invoices indicated that the mortgage had been fully paid, repairs had been financed, and staff had been hired.

A pink sticky tab flagged the second-last page.

Arthur, Hughie Digby lives at the St. Augustine's foster home in Tower Hamlets. I have paid the operator, Charles Wentworth, a large sum of money to release Hughie into your custody as his guardian. Please know I broke ranks. I didn't let anyone touch him. I groomed him instead to see that everything is possible. He came too late, but he's the son I never had and never was. I have fatherly feelings for him, a gift that I am not entitled to receive.

I have been starving for something I couldn't find or even name. It came in the form of Hughie.

I have to trust that there is another world waiting for me, but my doubts prevent me from believing that any door will open to me.
Your friend,
Ernie

I flipped to the last page, where under the signatures, Ernie had written, *I need help bad, man.—Jimi Hendrix.*

I put down the deed, hung my head, and closed my eyes. The dead-filled twenty-seven club. In that instant, I could no longer wall off my childhood. Gripping the deed with the slanty signature woke me from a long slumber, just as Sleeping Beauty was awakened by the kiss from a prince. I thought of Ernie, walking through life and pretending to be alive. I reread the conditions he had sent me, and with my most cherished possession—a stolen Parker pen—signed my name underneath.

Arthur W. Barnes.

Without Miss Phillips's and Ernie's summons to examine my conscience, I would have been a forever-boy doomed to remain an infantile adult.

In the waking I found myself.

Chapter 36

Dear Mr. Mistlethorpe,

Ernest J. Castlefrank, formerly of Dyehouse Lane, Glastonbury, ate several cannabis edibles, swallowed forty ounces of vodka, and staggered through a dense wood full of exposed roots to the giant wooden cross behind the Benedictine monastery at Ampleforth Abbey. On a tool belt he'd hung a rope, a switchblade and a hammer, and in one pocket, he carried a handful of three-inch spikes. It must have been with difficulty, but he managed to climb the iron ladder affixed to the rear of the fifty-foot cross. It was late on Good Friday, hours past the 3 p.m. service. Ernie was crying as he climbed, crying on behalf of all of Somerset. It may be wishful thinking on my part that he was crying for the rest of us. Ernie had plenty of reasons to cry for himself.

In the woods nature has a thousand ears, but it was the church custodian who heard the hammering and the weeping. When he saw a bearded man affixed to the cross with one arm outstretched, hands and feet bleeding and with a slash across his throat, he thought it was Jesus Christ himself, risen from the dead two days early to repeat the lesson of the Crucifixion.

After the custodian came to his senses, he called the police. Seven minutes later three officers arrived, with a laddered truck. Seeing that

Ernie was still alive, they called an ambulance. While they waited, they climbed the ladder, carefully removed the nail, and carried him down from the cross. On the ground, they bandaged him as best they could and wrapped him in a silver thermal blanket. Ernie was in hemorrhagic shock. After the ambulance carried him away, the police strung yellow caution tape around the thick waists of several white oaks to cordon off the area. An officer who had been with special forces found the note. *I need help bad, man.—Jimi Hendrix.*

Miss Marina Phillips, whom you know well, stayed with Ernie in the ER. After the doctors had done what they could, she was allowed to follow him to intensive care, where she sat, listening to Ernie's ventilator go up and down. Then the night nurse told her to go away and get some rest. She could come back in the morning.

Ernie's heart stopped in the middle of the night. To know that he died before I could find him makes me homesick—not for Glastonbury, but for the person I used to be before I was called upon to keep a secret. Some might consider what Ernie did to be a desecration, but I see dignity in his death of despair.

So, Mr. Mistlethorpe, my request to you: let me tell this story, about a boy who was fearless enough, or who wished so hard for atonement, that he once told a church warden that Father Durante Ziperto had taken the souls of many a boy. The warden denied him, as did I, and that grieving boy became the Raven. With Ernie's terrible, selfless plea, we can fulfill the poem's cry. "Nevermore."

Author's Note

Some stories follow us around for a long time. This is one that has been following me. In 1990, a seven-year-old boy bit a chunk out of a classmate's cheek large enough to require stitches. The psychiatric report cited emotional, physical and sexual abuse. In 2002, a colleague was arrested after using his credit card to buy child pornography in Singapore. In 2008, a Montreal elementary schoolteacher was sentenced to twenty-eight years in a Virginia prison for having an online relationship with an eleven-year-old.

I set out to determine if sexual attraction to children is a mental illness, an orientation, an abuse of power, or a result of access to minors. Researchers have established that there is a distinction between pedophilia and child molestation: attraction itself and the crime of acting out the urges.

Paul Gillespie, then a detective sergeant in the Toronto Police and head of the sex crimes unit, the epicentre of the force's efforts against child pornography, was my first interview. Twenty years ago, in a café on Front Street in Toronto, he said, "We need ways to infiltrate the internet to go after the kingpins, the ones who are producing the greatest content."

I remember wondering about the demand side of pornography. When one porn site is shut down, another three pop up. Years later, Gillespie lamented that the anonymity of the darknet makes it near-impossible to find the perpetrators, meaning the sellers *and* the buyers.

My second interview was with the auxiliary bishop of Montreal, Thomas Dowd. Catholic bishops are still under intense scrutiny as child abuse perpetrated by priests continues to come to light. At his offices on rue de la Cathédrale, I was disarmed to hear him say, "Whatever turns up, write the truth, and do not spare the Catholic Church. They don't deserve it. They had no plan." As a faith-based person, I found those words gave me more courage to plough ahead and write about child sex crimes.

The shame is so deeply entrenched, it took me several more years to find perpetrators and victims who were willing to share their stories. A subset of men were not only willing to talk, but were desperate to share their journey of addiction, divorce and self-harm in the wake of abuse. What emerged from the cobbling together of many fragments is the fictional story of two teenagers, Arthur Barnes and Ernie Castlefrank, who are both targeted by a priest from boyhood, abuse that ends just as child porn is about to go viral on the internet. They travel the same road but to vastly different destinations. How is one boy engulfed, whereas the other is able to find a path out the other side of profound childhood trauma?

Much has been written about the failures of the Catholic Church, and with the story of Arthur and Ernie, I add one more layer. The disgrace of protecting the priesthood, "the oldest boys' club in the world," instead of the children they targeted and abused, continues to be front and centre, as cardinals, bishops, deacons, priests and lay people face ongoing public scrutiny. How could any innocent child hope to pass credible judgement on an organization that claims to represent God yet conveniently divides good and evil? Children's vulnerability was exploited, again and again. Too often the tragic details emerge in adulthood, when precious ground is already lost. Voicing the shock and profound pain of the abused is compulsory, especially as more and more survivors step into the spotlight and share their horrendous realities. It needs to be safe enough for everyone to come forward.

Less known is that such unaddressed child sexual abuse has had a huge role to play in the current crisis of child pornography on the internet, as well as on the even more insidious darknet, a Pandora's box where new web browsers—Tor, i2P, and FreeNet—and untraceable cryptocurrencies provide near-perfect anonymity for people seeking depraved acts of sexual violence. A staggering number of videos and photographs will remain in perpetuity on the darknet. The children in those photos live not only with the fear of being recognized, but with the shame of the act itself. Both invite suicide, addiction and crime. The number of sex offenders on sites like Tor who share banned material is now in the millions.

All of this raises parallel issues. What happened to these perpetrators, rendering them seemingly without a conscience—men who lost sight of right and wrong, good and evil, love and hate? One such individual was Jimmy Savile. Born in Leeds, where part of this novel is set, and buried in a North Yorkshire cemetery in a gold-coloured coffin with a £4,000 headstone, Savile was an eclectic and beloved UK entertainer. The full extent of his secret life was revealed only after his death in 2011. He abused upwards of a thousand children over the course of fifty years. What societal mindset was in place to allow such rampant behaviour to go unchecked for half a century? Knighted by Queen Elizabeth for his charitable work, Sir Jimmy was given carte blanche to offend and reoffend. People knew.

Despite the trade in these images on the darknet, any organization that places protecting its interests ahead of the interests of its vulnerable members—the Boy Scouts, private schools, religious orders of all denominations, the entertainment industry and the like—is facing tremendous fallout.

One final thought: imagine if an influential institution like the Catholic Church—with more than 1.3 billion members—had put a stop to child sex crimes in the years and decades before the internet. Might the current crisis of online predation and pornography of minors have been mitigated?

Acknowledgements

Thank you to Father Fred Dolan and Bishop Thomas Dowd, who encouraged me to write truthfully about abuses in the Catholic Church. Thank you to every person who shared their story, especially George, Will, Estefan, Lorenzo, Elliott and Melissa. You all taught me that honest conversation about what happened in the past is the ticket to tomorrow.

Thank you to my writers' group: Josée Lafrenière, Connie Guzzo-McParland, Gina Roitman and Liz Ulin, who read parts of the mystifying first draft and never stopped believing that a comprehensible finished product would emerge.

In the earliest days, Kathleen Watkins, Monika Quinn, Dianne Gregg, Christina Budweth Mingay, Caroline Dillon, Val Marier, Bill Hemens and Philip Nickels gave me such affirmation about the value of this story, it offset the plague of dark thoughts that invaded my mind in the middle of many a night.

Peter Beverley, Sarah Redington and Vivien Godfrey were endlessly willing to help me translate the novel from English to British. Keith Greig and Sybella Kirkbride generously shared their school experiences, especially university life.

Thank you to Jean-Michel Ares, Einar Otto Stangvik and Leona Kretzu, who helped me understand the Tor browser, VPNs, encryption and IT security, all of which is still a little murky to me despite a multitude of diagrams and personal tutorials. (Remaining mistakes are my own.) Heartfelt gratitude to Kingsley Gallup, editor of *Tourist & Town*, for allowing me to write and edit in the old Kennebunk train station on Depot Street.

Thank you to Ann-Marie MacDonald and James Fitzgerald. Say no more. I will be forever paddling upstream, trying to keep up.

Five people read the entire first draft: my ever-supportive inner circle of Hal Hannaford, Alisse Hannaford, Reid Hannaford, my friend Ann Wilson and my most treasured bookshop owner, Vivien Godfrey. Their detailed input was worthy of a job in publishing. However, I reserve my highest praise for Anne Collins, my editor at Random House Canada, and a woman who dives headfirst into stories of our darkest deeds. I am deeply grateful to RHC's publisher, Sue Kuruvilla, its managing editor, Deirdre Molina, and to Penguin Random House Canada's vice-president of subsidiary rights, Adrienne Tang, who were early supporters too, and were willing to publish *Monday Rent Boy* despite the crushing subject matter. Thanks, also, to my brilliant copy editor, Tilman Lewis. Anyone lucky enough to have Anne Collins as an editor will also be gifted with a confidante, a friend and a person of such substance that I believe her legacy will ripple forever.

I have an extremely supportive family: my husband, my children, their partners. At all times there is someone to help me climb over the next hurdle. With a sister and four brothers, friends, cousins, nieces and nephews, and a wonderful mother, I have access to fond memories, support in times of need and unconditional love. When I was near death, on August 6, 2015, my deceased father swam into my vision, grief scrawled across his face, to let me know it wasn't my time. *Go back and fight.*

This is what I am fighting for.